David Madsen is the pseudonym of a theologian and philosopher. His baroque talent is best seen in his novels: *Memoirs of a Gnostic Dwarf, Confessions of a Flesh-Eater* and *A Box of Dreams* and the cult cookbook *Orlando Crispe's Flesh-Eater's Cookbook*. His work has so far been translated into twelve languages.

From its first publication in 1995 *Memoirs of a Gnostic Dwarf* has been acclaimed as a baroque masterpiece.

Here are a few comments:

"not your conventional art-historical view of the Renaissance Pope Leo X, usually perceived as supercultivated, if worldly, patron of Raphael and Michelangelo. Here, he's kin to Robert Nye's earthy, lusty personae of Falstaff and Faust, with Rabelasian verve, both scatological and venereal. Strangely shards of gnostic thought emerge from the dwarf's swampish mind. In any case, the narrative of this novel blisters along with a Blackadderish cunning."
    The Observer

"There are books which, arriving at precisely the right moment, are like life-belts thrown to one when one is in danger of drowning. Such a book for me was *Memoirs of a Gnostic Dwarf.*"
    Francis King

". . . its main attraction is the vivid tour it offers of Renaissance Italy. From the gutters of Trastevere, via a circus freak-show, all the way to the majestic halls of the Vatican, it always looks like the real thing. Every character, real or fictional, is pungently drawn, the crowds are as anarchic as a Bruegel painting and the author effortlessly cannons from heartbreaking tragedy to sharp wit, most of it of a bawdy or scatological nature. The whole thing mixes up its sex, violence, religion and art in a very pleasing, wholly credible manner."
    Eugene Byrne in Venue

David Madsen

Memoirs of a Gnostic Dwarf

Dedalus

Published in the UK by Dedalus Ltd, Langford Lodge,
St Judith's Lane, Sawtry, Cambs, PE28 5XE
email: info@dedalusbooks.com
www: dedalusbooks.com

ISBN 1 873982 71 2

Dedalus is distributed in the United States by SCB Distributors,
15608 South New Century Drive, Gardena, California 90248
email :info @scbdistributors.com web site:www.scbdistributors.com

Dedalus is distributed in Australia & New Zealand by Peribo Pty Ltd,
58 Beaumont Road, Mount Kuring- gai N.S.W. 2080
email: peribo@ bigpond.com

Dedalus is distributed in Canada by Marginal Distribution,
695, Westney Road South, Suite 14 Ajax, Ontario, LI6 6M9
email: marginal @ marginalbook.com web site : www. marginalbook .com

First published by Dedalus in 1995, reprinted 1996, 1997, 2000
New edition 2004

Printed in Finland by WS Bookwell
Typeset by RefineCatch Limited, Bungay, Suffolk

A Michele, Cuor' Addorato Mio

Spirto ben nato, in cui si specchia e vede
Nelle tue membra oneste e care
Quante natura e'l ciel tra no' può fare,
Quand' a null' altra suo bell'opra cede:
Spirto leggiadro, in cui si spera e crede
Dentro, come di fuor nel viso appare,
Amor, pietà, mercè cose sì rare. . . . .
Che ma'furn' in beltà con tanta fede:
L'Amor mi prende, e la beltà mi lega;
la pietà, la mercè con dolci sguardi
Ferma speranz' al cor par che ne doni.
Qual uso o qual governo al mondo niega
Qual crudeltà per tempo, o qual più tardi,
Cà sì bel viso morte non perdoni?

(*Michelangelo: Sonetto XXIV*)

FOREWORD

It is not necessary for me to relate precisely how these memoirs fell into my hands; suffice it to say that in addition to a sound academic reputation, I also have a private income.

What it most certainly *is* necessary to say however, is that the task of translation presented its own peculiar difficulties. I have tried to overcome these difficulties by maintaining throughout the text a fairly contemporary — and therefore accessible — idiom; many of the expressions which Peppe uses in his fifteenth and sixteenth century Italian for example are virtually untranslatable, and I have taken the liberty of replacing them with modern equivalents. This is particularly so in the case of vulgar expletives. When he uses puns or *double entendres*, I have applied the same rule of thumb: where it is translatable I have kept to the original, and where it is not I have substituted. It is in this way that I have attempted to preserve the *esprit* of the memoirs, which is, by and large, somewhat salacious.

There are several portions of the text (mainly songs, poems or quotations) which I have left untranslated — Peppe's own song for example, Ulrich von Hutten's bilious little political ditty, and snippets of private letters — because I considered it would be a great pity to lose the unique flavour of the original; even to one who does not speak Italian, the radiant beauty of *Nel Mio Cuore* will be obvious. In any case, as our little friend himself points out — all translations are to some degree or other *interpretations*.

The fragments of Gnostic liturgies were written down by Peppe in the Original Greek, but it seemed to me that they should be given in English in this edition of the memoirs, and this has been done; the reader need not be unduly concerned however, since they are for the most part incomprehensible in either (or any) language. There can be little doubt that Peppe's adherence to Gnostic teaching was total and unreserved, yet even he admits in his *apologia pro philosophia sua* that much of its written expression (especially the invention of fantastic titles and grotesque honorifics) is but a prolix attempt to identify the Unidentifiable. To anyone who might be interested in learning more about the historical development of Gnostic rites and liturgies, I would wholeheartedly recommend Professor Tomasz Vinkary's epoch-making tome, *A Study of the Valentinian Sacramentary in the Light of Gnostic Creation Myths*, which has recently been reissued by Verlag Otto Schneider of Berlin in co-operation with Schneider-Hakim Publications, London.

There are many individuals to whom I owe a debt of gratitude for their invaluable help in the preparation of these memoirs, but I feel I must make particular mention of the following:

Herr Heinrich Arvé, who supplied me with much invaluable information on the incidence of sexual perversion in Renaissance Italy; Monsignore Marcello Ciapplino, for his elucidation of those parts of the original text which deal with military and political history; and Dottoressa Patrizia Cezanno, who painted a portrait of Peppe using the description he himself gives in the memoirs, which now hangs in my private library.

The reader may care to know that Giuseppe Amadonelli died on 6th August 1523, the Feast of the Transfiguration, whilst attending Solemn Vespers in the church of Santa Maria in Trastevere, Rome. The precise cause of death remains unknown.

David Madsen
London, Copenhagen, Rome

INCIPIT PRIMA PARS

Clementissime Domine, cuius inenarrabilis est virtus
This morning His Holiness summoned me to read to him
from St Augustine, while the physician applied unguents
and salves to his suppurating arse; one in particular, which
was apparently concocted from virgin's piss (where did
they find a virgin in Rome?) and a rare herb from the
private *hortus siccus* of Bonet de Lattes, the pope's Jewish
physician-in-chief, stank abominably. Still, it was no worse
than the nauseating stench of the festering pustules and
weeping ulcers adorning His Holiness's cilicious posterior.
(Everybody refers to these repulsive afflictions as a 'fistula,'
but I am not constrained by the self-interest of tact.) With
his alb pulled up over his hips, and his underdrawers down
around his ankles, the most powerful man in the world lay
sprawled on his bed like a catamite waiting to be well and
truly buggered.

He *has* been buggered, plenty of times – hence the state
of his arse. His Holiness prefers to play the womanly role,
thrashing and squealing beneath some musclebound youth
like a bride being penetrated for the first time. Not that
I've any personal objection to such behaviour – Leo is the
pope after all, and short of publicly declaring that God is a
Mohammedan, he can do exactly as he pleases. Besides, I
like to think of myself as a tolerant man. I find it easy to
overlook weakness and vice in a field of human activity
which holds no interest for me whatsoever. Even if it did, I
imagine it would take someone with a very peculiar vice
indeed to find anything sexually attractive about a crook-
back dwarf. Which is what I am.

Hence the title of these reminiscences of mine: *Memoirs
of a Gnostic Dwarf.* I think this is an excellent title, since it
is utterly honest: I *am* a Gnostic dwarf, and these *are* my

memoirs. It occurs to me that there are a great number of books and manuscripts offered for sale these days whose claims are entirely meretricious, such as *Being a True Account of a Monk's Secret Pleasure,* or *A Full and Satisfactory Explanation of the Practice of Greek Love* - both of which I have seen in His Holiness's personal library, and neither of which are in any way true, full or satisfactory; you shall not be likewise misled in these pages. It is painfully evident to everyone that I am a dwarf, but my Gnostic proclivities remain my little secret . . . and that of a certain private fraternity. Yes, there are more of us – Gnostics I mean, not dwarves. Later, I shall speak of the fraternity in detail.

His Holiness Leo X, Roman Pontiff, Vicar of Christ on Earth, Patriarch of the West, Successor to the Prince of the Apostles, Holder of the Keys of Peter and Servant of the Servants of God, does not usually call me to read to him while he is having his rump anointed with virgin's piss and rare herbs; on the contrary, he likes to be alone with his physician, and one can well understand why. I was therefore a little surprised to receive the summons. However, reflection on the matter suggests that he is disquieted by the latest news from Germany, where a choleric friar called Luther has been stirring up trouble, ranting and raving about the corruption of the papal court, and it may be that he finds the misanthropic rhapsodies of the holy bishop of Carthage distract him. To speak personally, I find them tedious in the extreme. The papal court *is* corrupt, but what of that? Everyone expects it to be. It's been corrupt for so long, no-one can remember a time when it wasn't, nor conceive of it ever not being so. To speculate on the whys and wherefores, as this Luther seems to be doing, is like asking why the sun is hot or why water is wet, and trying to make them otherwise. Futile. *Vanitas vanitatum.* The trouble with people like our fractious friar is that they think they're a cut above everyone else, and thus ideally qualified to put the world to rights; but the world never can and never will be put to rights, because it is hell. (Now

12

there's a snippet of Gnostic wisdom for you.) That doesn't make me a misanthrope like our holy father St Augustine – on the contrary, if this world is hell, one can only have compassion for those who are obliged to live in it and breathe its poisonous air. And – above all! – to teach them that there is a way out.

"I think this may call for a papal bull, Peppe," His Holiness said to me (for Peppe is my name).

"Lie still, Holiness," admonished the physician, inserting a gnarled forefinger into the petrine rectum with mathematical care. He moved it around a bit, withdrew it, brought it up to his nose and sniffed cautiously.

"Not yet," I answered, disgusted by the antics of this overpaid, underworked scryer of excreta, "let our scripture-happy friend stew a while in his own juice. Besides, he may mean no harm."

"No harm?" Leo squeaked. "*No harm?* Have you heard what he's calling me?"

"Well, one tries not to listen to the latest court *chronique scandaleuse,* Holiness . . ."

"This isn't gossip, Peppe, it's common knowledge. He makes no bones about it. He calls me a usurer, a nepotist, Sodom's favourite catamite –"

"Well . . ."

"God's blood and the Virgin's milk, he'll be attacking the Mass next!"

"Perhaps you ought to make him a cardinal, Holiness."

"Are you trying to be funny?"

"Of course. That's partly what you pay me for."

Leo screamed just then – a long, wailing scream of genuine agony.

"Haven't you finished yet, you witless whore's cunny!" he roared to the unperturbed Bonet de Lattes; Leo's colourful language was well known and hence no-one took any offence at it except the pious – of whom, fortunately, there are but few at court.

"Very nearly, Holiness."

He seemed to be examining a minute piece of shit that

was adhering to a fingertip. Examining it for what, I could not imagine.

"You think I ought to wait a little, do you, Peppe?"

"Precisely, Holiness. Let him walk on thorns a little longer, then let him have it. A real broadside."

"*Exsurge Domine*. How does that sound?"

"An excellent title, Holiness. But save it for later."

"Your Holiness may re-attire," the physician said pompously (in my experience, physicians are invariably pompous), rinsing his hands in the bowl of rosewater that stood on Leo's reading table.

"Well, what's the verdict?"

"The affliction is improved, naturally –" (Note: read *thanks to my skilful and therefore necessarily costly ministrations*) "– but the medication will have to continue. And perhaps an increase in bleedings. I will call again next calendar month."

"I will *summon* you to call," Leo said snappishly. "Your fee is there. Now get out."

"Thank you, Holiness. And – if I may suggest – you might for some period of time refrain from –"

Refrain from accommodating half the young stallions of Rome, I thought.

"– from all highly seasoned food. It would help. The blood must not become overheated."

"Alright, alright. Now go."

De Lattes walked backwards towards the door, bowing and fawning, clutching his little bag of money and his Asklepian caduceus tightly to his fur-draped chest.

Leo hauled himself into a sitting position and glanced around the room with rheumy, vengeful eyes, as if searching for something or someone to strike.

"If my blood is not to become overheated," he said, "I must hear no more of this German friar."

"Does Your Holiness wish me to continue reading from the saintly bishop of Carthage?"

"Luther's an Augustinian, isn't he?"

"So I believe, Holiness."

14

"Then let Augustine go sodomize himself. I feel peckish after all that probing."

Leo is a fairly tall, fattish (some, unkindly, might say bloated), swarthy man; he walks with a rapid waddle and rides side-saddle on account of his ulcerated arse; his face is full-fleshed, his eyes – always watchful and smouldering with suspicion – are heavily lidded, the caruncles thickly veined, and his lips sensuously ripe. Incongruously his speaking voice, although elegantly modulated, is somewhat high-pitched except when he is roused to anger (which is quite often, since he is of an irascible temperament), when it becomes a truly terrifying roar. I have already told you that he has a tendency to use somewhat flamboyant language. He is shortsighted, and when his vanity allows him to he makes use of a small magnifying glass whilst reading. And as you now know, he is a devotee of Ganymede. He likes to be taken from behind by young men. I do not think he is interested in women in the slightest. Oddly enough, there is no public scandal attached to this predilection; either people take it for granted, or they just don't care. In any case, compared to the athletic antics of Leo's unillustrious predecessor but one (well, one and a bit really, since Pius III only reigned for twenty-six days), the pox-riddled and impious Alexander VI Borgia, Leo is a temperate man. Indeed, he is genuinely pious, and always hears Mass before going off to the hunt. He loves hunting.

His Holiness is not at all an unamiable man; in fact, when the occasion calls for it, he is capable of exercising a pungent sense of humour. Once, when I was helping him to unvest after a solemn High Mass, he turned and looked at me with curious eyes, and out of the earshot of the deacons and acolytes who were mincing and prancing all over the place, he said to me:

"Tell me, Peppe ... is it true what they say about dwarves?"

"Is what true, Holiness?" I said, pretending not to understand.

15

He put a pudgy, jewel-laden hand on my arm and drew me a little closer to the pontifical person.

"You know exactly what I'm talking about. Well, is it true or not?"

"See for yourself," I said, and unfastening my hose and pulling down the linen-stuffed leather codpiece, I drew out my prick. All three inches of it.

Leo smiled and sighed.

"What a pity," he said. Then he removed a ring from one of his fingers – a huge chrysoberyl bearing an Egyptian glyptic, encircled by tiny pearls and set in an intricate oval of gold filigree – and pressed it into the palm of my hand.

"Here," he said. "With a cock as small as the rest of you, you deserve *some* consolation."

A gesture, I may say, that moved me profoundly. It was only later, during an audience with the unctuous and gasconading Venetian ambassador, wondering why I had suddenly become the cynosure of surprised and outraged glances as I stood beside the papal throne, that I realised I'd left my cock hanging out. Leo must have noticed, but decided to say nothing. Much to my chagrin, the ambassador had enough self-righteousness to complain about this incident, but he got his come-uppance at the banquet held in his honour that same evening: one of the delightful specialities served up by His Holiness's Neapolitan cook, consisted of larks' tongues basted in wild honey and cassia, each wrapped in a folio of gold-leaf and served on a bed of baby pine-cones with crushed emeralds; not having enough common sense to realise that the cones and emeralds weren't meant to be eaten, he shoved a great spoonful into his mouth and swallowed, before anyone could stop him. He spent the rest of the evening in one of the papal privies, retching up blood.

Leo almost laughed himself into a coma.

I have been His Holiness's chamberlain for five years now, having come with him to Rome from Florence, upon his elevation to the Chair of Peter; before that, I had been retained in his household on rather ambiguous terms, as a sort of superior personal servant. I only came to be known as His Holiness's chamberlain when I joined the papal court; the term 'chamberlain' is somewhat degrading, and certainly inadequate to describe properly the extent of my duties, since I am also his confidant, general factotum, spy, scribe, and constant companion. He has a confessor, naturally – a glacially pious young Benedictine, chosen by Leo because of his excessive handsomeness – but into my hairy little ear are poured all his fears, hopes, dreams and aspirations. I am there, in a sort of way, and insofar as a middle-aged dwarf can be described as 'motherly,' to mother and cosset and console His Holiness when the burdens of his high office afflict his soul with melancholy. I am also on occasions his pimp, although this rather distasteful duty has become less frequent since the trouble with his arse began.

"I think I may have a rather private and personal mission for you," he would say.

"When, Holiness?"

"This evening."

"Any particular preference?"

"Well-built, naturally."

"Well-built, or well-*endowed?*"

"Both, of course."

And off I'd go, loping about the stinking, tenebrous alleyways of the city. Once or twice the young men I approached formed the erroneous conclusion that I was soliciting on my own behalf. A particularly juicy-looking specimen with broad shoulders and sinewy (I nearly wrote 'simian') arms that suggested years of heavy daily labour, looked me up and down with contemptuous dark eyes and said:

"You've got to be joking, of course."

"You'll be well-paid."

"I dare say, but I'm not that hard up. Holy Peter's bones, the monster between my legs would tear your innards out, little runt that you are."

"It isn't for me, you idiot."

"Oh? Who for, then?"

"As I said, you'll be well-paid. Just follow me."

"How well paid, exactly?"

"What about a plenary indulgence?" I said. "You look as though you could do with one."

"Piss off, short-arse."

"Is that the reply I am to give to the Successor to the Prince of the Apostles and Holder of the Keys of Peter? He'll have that monster of yours sliced off at the root and stuffed down your impertinent throat. Well, are you coming or not?"

He came.

I am sure – indeed, I *know* - that Leo is genuinely fond of me; thanks to his generosity, I have managed to accumulate, to console me in my old age, a substantial nest-egg which is lodged with bankers in Florence. I also have quite a collection of rings, all of them consisting of precious stones set in gold or silver, but these are hidden in a private place in my chamber, which I will not describe here. I never wear them. It's not that I don't *want* to, but it has been my experience that for some reason people dislike seeing beautiful things adorning an ugly, misshapen body such as mine. I find this attitude incomprehensible, since no-one objects when a plain-looking woman directs attention away from her plainness by means of expensive clothes and exquisite jewellery – indeed, they seem to *expect* it; but glittering, glamorous dwarves are offensive, apparently.

I may say that it is precisely these multifarious duties of mine, and this comfortable intimacy I have with His Holiness, which prevent my life at the papal court from becoming nauseatingly tedious; I assure you – all you who dream of such things in your secret dreams – that endless banquets, interminable High Masses (*especially* the High Masses), innumerable audiences, receptions, and day after day every conceivable kind of glittering pomp, soon become unutterably wearisome. High Masses apart, I know you will object: "How easy that is for *you* to say, you who have enjoyed all such extravagances!" Well, let me tell you now that I would be happy to exchange my lot for yours, however lowly your calling may be, however revolting the hovel you are obliged to dwell in; but then, if we were to trade the beings we are, one for another, you and I, you'd have to reconcile yourself to living in the twisted, cumbersome body of a dwarf. Would you want that? And I – I would know, by an ontological miracle, the cleanness and purity of straight limbs, the dignity of a head that's a reasonable distance from the feet, the sheer *relief* of being able to stand upright – oh yes, how I used to weep with longing for that. Not anymore. Later, you will learn how and why the weeping and the longing ceased, and in what manner I learned to accept myself as I am.

Speaking of High Masses, I might say that these were always somewhat problematic for poor Leo, since some of them dragged on endlessly (and still do, alas), and His Holiness would invariably be overcome by the need to relieve his aching bladder. It was painful to watch him wriggling and squirming on the papal throne, swathed in his heavy pontifical vestments, his face a mask of agony as the choir screeched on and on with some twaddlesome litany. I don't think he ever actually pissed in his underdrawers, but he must have come pretty close to it. Happily, I was able to come up with a little device of my own invention, which solved the problem: I stitched together two pieces of soft leather lined with otter's fur to make a kind of casing or sheath, which fitted snugly over His Holiness's fat penis; from the tip of the sheath I ran a tube, also of leather, which was attached to a lined bag that I bound with silk to his right calf. The entire apparatus was worn beneath the underdrawers, and enabled Leo to pee freely, standing or sitting, in the middle of solemn High Mass (or indeed, in the middle of any protracted ceremony) without anyone knowing what he was up to. Only the blissful expression of sweet relief on his face would have given the game away, and then only to the acutely observant. His Holiness was absolutely delighted, and suggested that in the interests of east-west *rapprochement,* I might care to send one to the Patriarch of Constantinople, who was apparently obliged to endure even longer liturgies than our own; I did this, but received no reply. I didn't get the apparatus back either. Sometimes I like to think of the curmudgeonly old renegade happily peeing his way through the most prolix and tedious of ceremonial marathons, thanks to my ingenuity; they say that the eastern schismatics are full of piss and wind, anyway. Actually, I later discovered that it wasn't my own invention at all, and that such devices were quite common; I read that even the physicians of the ancient kingdoms of Egypt used them to ease the sufferings of those who were unable to urinate. Needless to say, I didn't tell Leo this, and as a reward he gave me another ring – a truly stunning emerald set in scalloped gold, said to have once belonged to the holy Apostle John himself. However, I don't believe that for a moment. Not unless it popped out of the ganoid belly of a gutted fish.

Leo's cousin Giulio – a cardinal, needless to say – is continually creeping about the place, sucking up to Leo in the hopes of further benefices and endowments; secretly, he despises him. Ah, but if this contumely is secret, I hear you ask, how do *I* know of it? Well, it isn't exactly the deepest and darkest of secrets (except to His Holiness himself) and furthermore, I overheard Giulio one night in a corridor in the papal apartments, discussing with Lorenzo, His Holiness's nephew, how much it was going to cost to assure himself of the papacy when Leo went to meet his Lord with a lot of explaining to do, and how it was to be managed. I listened to them unseen – one of the advantages of being a dwarf is that you're less obvious, especially in the dark; in the dark people tend to look straight ahead, not down. Their conversation left no doubt that Giulio and Lorenzo regarded Leo merely as a temporary source of income. They were quite explicit in articulating their disgust at his sexual inclinations and habits, and I shall not repeat their comments here, out of respect for His Holiness. Besides which, Giulio's hypocrisy is quite breathtaking when one considers that His Eminence has been humping his way through the ladies of Rome's patrician families for years *and* finding time to fit in (literally, as well as chronologically, if you catch my drift) the occasional good-looking young lad. The following morning there he was, sneaking into the papal bedroom again, even before Leo was up and about, oozing charm and dripping flattery. I despise him. His Holiness deserves better. However, I shall write at greater length of this manipulative creature a little later.

Please do not think that Leo is a gullible man simply because his cousin deceives him with false devotion – he is far from it; however, it is an obvious truth that the heart is more willing to be duped than the head. His Holiness is in all other respects an individual of profound acumen. I recall, for example, the affair of the miraculous icon. This was a religious painting, executed in tempera on wood and inlaid with gold, such as is very popular among the schismatics of the east, and it was brought to Leo by a Venetian merchant of apparently impeccable credentials who informed the papal court that he had acquired it for a fabulous sum from an Ottoman dealer, who had himself purchased it from a close relative of a certain Caliph, who . . . and so on. He told us that its history was long and thrilling, hallmarked by mysterious disappearances and reappearances, miraculous healings, clandestine bargaining, and even robbery and murder. He said that the icon, which was of the Theotokos *orans*, the Mother of God at prayer, was reputed to have been painted by blessed Luke the Evangelist himself. After all this preliminary salesman's waffle, it did not take him long to get to the point: his asking price was three hundred ducats. Some of the assembled court gasped at this, even though (while nobody believed the rubbish about St Luke for a moment) it could not be denied that the icon was truly exquisite.

Leo sat back on his gilt chair, his feet *almost* touching the crimson velvet footstall, one plump hand under his several chins. He smiled a slow, secretive, contented smile.

"No," he said.

The court gasped again, and the pale, supercilious-looking merchant frowned.

"Your Holiness is refusing such an ancient artifact? A representation of the Holy Mother of God, with such a lustrous pedigree that it is not beyond probability that the blessed Luke himself executed the work?"

"No," Leo said again. "I am not refusing such a marvel. I am refusing what you offer me."

"But Holiness – surely for the greater glory of the Holy Roman Church –"

"Take him away. Let him cool his enthusiasm for his wares in a cell. I don't mean the monastic kind, either. Away!"

The merchant was led off, still protesting. I never saw him again; I doubt very much if anyone else did either, and the icon still reposes on Leo's bedside table.

Later, when we were alone, I asked him:

"But why? It was a wonderful thing, surely?"

"Indeed it was," the pope answered, "but worth no more than thirty ducats. It was probably done less than fifty years ago. Even if it *is* older, it's certainly not the antique that avaricious little bastard made it out to be."

"But Holiness, how do you *know*?"

Leo sighed, and placed a fat hand on my knotty shoulder; I hate anyone touching me anywhere near my hump, except him.

"Have you ever seen the Holy Shroud of the Lord?" he asked.

"The linen sheet in which the body of Jesus was wrapped, and which is impressed with his image?"

"Yes."

"I've never seen it."

"There is a bloodstain – a trickle – that seeps down from his hair, in the centre of his forehead. Blood, we suppose, from the thorns that pressed so deeply into his poor head.

That miraculous image of the trickle of blood was mistaken by the icon painters of the east for a lock of hair, and you will see it in all the later representations of the Lord. The *later* representations in the eastern style. Did you see such a lock in the icon we were shown, and which we were asked to believe was so ancient?"

"Yes I did, Holiness."

"Therefore?"

"Therefore it is *not* ancient –"

"At least not as ancient as our thieving friend would have had us believe. It is indeed a beautiful work, but many of the same kind are to be found all over the east."

"Your Holiness astounds me!"

"My dear Peppe, I am perhaps not so much of an ox as I look."

As a matter of fact, we were frequently plagued by all sorts of shifty, seedy-looking characters hawking relics of every kind: a phial of the Virgin's milk, wood-shavings from the workshop of St Joseph, one of St Agatha's breasts (in colour and texture this resembled a prune –"She must have been rather a small person," His Holiness remarked, amused), an arrow that had pierced the flesh of St Sebastian, and most grotesque of all in my opinion, a pubic hair from the groin of the saintly English Cistercian, Aelred of Rievaulx – presumably plucked out by one of the many *special* friends he made during his life in the cloister. This latter intrigued Leo no end, for he was very fond of Aelred altogether, and had read *De Spirituali Amicitia* with intense pleasure, so he gave quite a sum for it. I do not know what became of it, but being so small and light-weight, it was presumably difficult to keep track of. Even Leo did not go so far as to have a pubic hair mounted on satin, encased in a gold reliquary, and hung on the wall of his chapel, where all the other pious flotsam and jetsam reposed.

"For purely *private* devotion I think," he remarked coyly to me.

Some came with no wares to sell other than their alleged

personal talents: "I shall transmute lead into gold, Holiness . . ." or: "I am accompanied at all times and in all places by an angel, Holiness, and for a small financial consideration, shall attempt to materialize him for you . . ." and even: "The futures of men are as an open book to me, my lord pope!"

To this last, Leo said:

"Can you read your *own* future, then?"

"Indeed I can."

"And what do you read, pray?"

"Travel, Holiness; journeys across the sea, consultations with powerful men –"

"You're wrong, I'm afraid."

"Holiness?"

"Your future is in a damp, dark place somewhere in one of my prisons."

I've told you already that Leo demonstrates a fine sense of humour when the occasion demands.

He wasn't in the mood for humour, however, when a summary of Martin Luther's attack on indulgences arrived for His Holiness's perusal several days after the humiliating examination of his arse.

"What? How, by the scourging of sweet Jesus, does this idiot imagine I am to finance the reconstruction of St Peter's? The work is already going too slowly for my liking. The preaching of indulgences is an absolute necessity."

"The war with France hit the papal coffers hard, Holiness."

"Don't remind me of that poxy Mechelen League; thanks to that arrogant little tit-sucker Francis, I barely have enough funds to pay my cook. Peppe, this is too much. I think – what did I say I'd call it? –"

"*Exsurge Domine,* Holiness."

"Exactly. It's time for a papal pronouncement."

"I would counsel patience, Your Holiness," I said.

"Christ's blood, I've been patient for too long already!"

"They say that Frederick of Saxony protects this German heretic . . ."

"I know, I know."

"And Maximillian cannot last forever . . ."

"I know that too."

Leo heaved a pitifully deep sigh.

"Besides which," I said, suddenly and fortuitously inspired, "Master Rafael arrives this afternoon to work on your portrait. You need to be in a relaxed frame of mind for that. Forget the mad monk for a while."

At the mention of Rafael's name, the anger melted from Leo's eyes, and they became dreamy, full of poignant yearning.

"Yes, Master Rafael," he murmured.

As I am sure you must immediately have guessed, Rafael is a handsome fellow, thirty-five years old but looking twenty-five, slim and willowy of figure, all poise and grace and sweet sadness, bulging sumptuously between the legs – with either nature or artifice; rumour has it that it's so long, he has to roll it up inside his codpiece. I don't believe this; after all, would the God who was cruel enough to give me this twisted, stunted body, have the generosity to bless a man with the face of an angel *and* a ten inch cock? They say that women finger their private parts and swoon when Master Rafael passes; Leo almost does the same at the mere mention of his name.

"Rafael," he repeated. And the mad monk was quite forgot.

Four years ago, against what I consider to be sound advice, Leo appointed Master Rafael as chief architect of the new St Peter's, in succession to Bramante; I am sure that this was only because Leo had been so impressed by the *stanze* Rafael decorated (exquisitely, I admit) for Pope Julius. Yet why should we assume that a talented painter must also be a talented architect, any more than we would expect a skilled physician to be a skilled singer too? These days I doubt that anyone expects a physician to be skilled *at all*; in case you haven't already guessed, I've got a raw nerve about physicians.

Rafael not only looks like an angel, he paints like one too. His elegant, effortless strokes are a joy to watch. He had Leo sitting dressed in simple morning attire at his reading table, a pious book of some kind open in front of him, his little crimson fur-edged *camauro* pushed down onto his rather ungainly head. On the damask-covered surface of the table there was also a beautifully chased bell, and in his pudgy left hand Leo held his magnifying glass. I think he was supposed to be examining the illuminations in the book. Giulio had somehow managed to worm his way into the picture, and his supercilious, badly-shaven face was beginning to emerge on the canvas; he was depicted with one hand resting ominously on Leo's chair, the upper half of his body bent in a fawning, unctuous gesture. For some reason I could not quite fathom, Cardinal Luigi de Rossi, who had happened to walk into the room during a previous sitting, was now a permanent fixture in the portrait. I did ask if I could be in it too – an idea Leo approved of – but Master Rafael, casting his lovely doe's eyes up and down my ugly little body, said quietly:

"Alas, it would be beyond my skill. I am able to paint only what is beautiful."

There was clearly no malice whatsoever in this remark – it was merely a statement of fact – and so I did not take offence.

"Can't you *make* me beautiful?" I asked. It was only a tiny glimmer of hope.

Rafael shook his head, and his gorgeous pennanular tresses moved like ripples of water in a caressing zephyr.

"I cannot undo nature," he said sadly. "I can only imitate it."

And with that, I had to be content.

"Are *you* beautiful then, Holiness?" I asked Leo later.

"No," he said, "but my money is." Then he farted, uttering a little squeal of pain as he did so.

In fact, His Holiness was a prodigious farter; he was

famous for his farts. They came, with surprising frequency, in various degrees of duration and odour; sometimes it happened on the most inappropriate of occasions, such as an elevation to the cardinalate, or at dinner with an ambassador, and even during Solemn High Mass. That was one thing I *couldn't* invent a device for. He once let rip with an absolute stinker whilst granting an audience to some curial prelate; writhing with embarrassment, and anxious to preserve His Holiness's dignity at all costs, the silly little sycophant muttered:

"I beg Your Holiness's pardon."

"Why?" Leo said, all wide-eyed with innocence. "What have you done?"

The prelate knew that *Leo* knew that *he* knew who had been responsible for the fart, and found himself on the horns of an impossible dilemma. You could almost hear the fucus stirring in the stagnant pond of his mind. Red-faced with shame and confusion, he said:

"I think – quite possibly, I mean – that I may have involuntarily passed wind."

From that moment until the day he died (which was soon afterwards, and of humiliation, I always insisted), the wretched idiot was known to the entire papal court as 'the man who possibly farted'.

A papal toady once suggested that the expelled air should be bottled, or sealed in jars, and sold as objects of devotion. Leo was furious.

"Do you suggest that I go around with a jar strapped to my arse? Or am I to inform the entire household whenever I feel a fart coming on, that they may come running from the kitchens armed with phials and bottles?"

Short of money though he always was, even Leo wouldn't stoop to hawking his own bottled farts.

Quite simply, Leo was continually out of funds because he was continually spending: rare manuscripts, exquisitely illuminated books, fabulous jewels, ancient artifacts from far-flung parts – whatever spoke to him of human skill and ingenuity, of the workings of the human mind and the march of human history, he bought. This is hardly surprising when one remembers that Marsilio Ficino and the enigmatic, esoterically-inclined Pico della Mirandola were his boyhood tutors. Leo's father, Lorenzo the Magnificent, certainly knew what a sound education was all about. Mind you, they do say that it was none other than Giovanni Pico della Mirandola who first introduced Leo to the tender art of buggery at the equally tender age of eight, which was when – predestined for high ecclesiastical office by his shrewd, arrogant, overbearing, self-indulgent and, yes, truly *magnificent* father Lorenzo – he received the tonsure. Pico della Mirandola had his head stuffed with all this occult hermetic nonsense and tried to stuff Leo's head with it as well, but did not succeed; he also tried to stuff his arse, and was only *too* successful, I gather. An inordinate fondness for books and buggery were Pico's most enduring bequest to His Holiness; it's the books that really damage the papal coffers.

Leonine Rome has been a lucrative haven for every peddler of verses, penner of plays both decent and indecent, artist, philosopher and *littérateur;* scholars and classicists, librarians, *colporteurs* and antiquaries thronged the court. Indeed, at the time of his election, it had been widely assumed that Leo would introduce a golden age for scholars, poets and artists, and the city was adorned with inscriptions which declared the arrival of the epoch of Pallas Athene. If Julius II had paid homage to the art of war, everyone looked to Leo to pay homage to the Muses; and indeed he did, rather profligately. Such devotion was not cheap.

Master Rafael dined with us in the evening. Much to my annoyance, the pope put him in *my* chair, close by himself, and I was consigned to the end of the table. I saw Leo glance at me with doleful eyes, as if to say: *I know, I know, but I'm utterly smitten with him, so forgive me for once!* Well for once I wasn't in the mood to forgive, so halfway through the breast of chicken served with spiced colchicum sauce, I shamelessly introduced the subject of the mad monk, knowing only too well what an effect this would have on Leo.

"Did you say something?" he hissed at me, his eyes no longer doleful but smouldering.

"Yes. I asked Master Rafael what he thought of this German heretic, Luther."

Rafael smiled, and with that smile, the cherubim and seraphim must surely have fallen into rapture. It was the kind of smile that shouldn't be permitted on a human face. Zeus would have given Olympus for it; as it is, quite a few titled ladies have given their virtue for it, I gather.

"I'm afraid," he said sweetly, "I am not a theologically-minded man."

"It's nothing to do with theology," I replied. "It's a political matter."

"Oh?" Leo managed to say. "And what do *you* know about it, you pint-sized cunt?"

"As much as your Holiness does, I think. The German princes are disaffected because they resent the flow of cash making its way to Rome from the sale of indulgences –"

"The *preaching* of indulgences, you mean."

"It's all the same, as Your Holiness well knows. Ever since you came to that arrangement with Jacob Fucker –"

"Fugger! Jacob Fugger!" Leo shrieked, thumping his fist on the table and splattering colchicum sauce all over the place. Fugger was the banker who advanced the new Archbishop of Mayence's installation and dispensation tax to Leo, and saw to it that half the proceeds from the sale of indulgences in his diocese went into the papal funds; with consummate Hebraic cunning, he persuaded Albert that ten percent of the other half properly belonged to himself, and took it.

"God knows what Albert of Brandenburg wanted with the archbishopric of Mayence anyway. Actually, on reflection, I think the whole thing is economic rather than political."

Leo threw a half-eaten piece of chicken at me, just missing my right eye with a sharp bone.

"That wasn't very polite," I remarked. "You're embarrassing Master Rafael."

Merde! I'd been on the winning side, until I forgot myself and spoke that adored name.

"Rafael," Leo said, moon-struck again. And again, Rafael smiled. He smiled directly at Leo this time, and I might as well have suggested that Luther be the next pope, for all the effect it would have had.

Later, in an expansive mood because Rafael had accepted the invitation to stay the night in the papal apartments, Leo chided me.

"You were very naughty, Peppe. I've a good mind to spank you."

To my horror, I saw a curious speculation dawn in Leo's eyes, as if he were privately weighing up the pros and cons of actually carrying out this threat.

"Don't even dare to *think* of it," I said.

This morning, I saw Rafael coming out of Leo's study with a faraway, pondering look on his lovely face, and I thought: *I wonder?* Exactly *what* I wondered, was whether or not His Holiness had at last managed to pluck the forbidden fruit. I followed Rafael as he floated dreamily down the corridor like a living canephorus, trying to see if I could detect any tell-tale spots of blood on his hose; this was not too difficult for me, since his small, muscular buttocks were only a foot or so beneath the level of my eyes. After a moment or two however, he sensed my presence behind him, and turned to confront me.

"What do you think you're doing?" he said.

"Ah. You have such an elegant way of walking, Master Rafael. I was just – well – I thought I might improve my own deportment by imitation."

He said nothing, but he laid a pale, willowy hand upon my head for a brief moment, then he was gone.

I didn't see any blood. I'm not surprised really, since everyone knows he keeps a very beautiful mistress. Leo must have slept alone with his futile yearnings.

★

The vignettes I have offered you so far have of course amounted to a portrait of His Holiness Leo X, Giovanni de' Medici, Successor to the Prince of the Apostles and Holder of the Keys of Peter. I have tried to describe a man who is both a complicated and a simple individual: in his sexual exploits, his political machinations, his humanistic love of art, music and books, and in his mercurial disposition, he is complicated; in his piety, he is refreshingly simple. Somehow he manages to keep these two sides of himself separate, in watertight compartments. For example, he can (and does) spend hours poring over some desiccated old tome dedicated to the propagation of a hermetic doctrine whose heterodoxy makes Mohammed sound like a Dominican by comparison, then trot off happily to Mass; he can rise from his bed in the morning, sore with repeated penetrations by some young lad imported from a miasmal alleyway, then kneel at his prie-dieu in front of an image of the Mother of God, with genuine tears of devotion in his protuberant eyes. I've long ago given up trying to make too much sense of it; it's the *whole* man, with all his contradictions and paradoxes, that I love. There: I've surprised myself by admitting it so explicitly. Yes, poor old Leo, I love him.

Not everyone feels as I do, however; in fact there are (perhaps I should say *were*, since most of them have been dealt with in typical Medici fashion) quite a few who hate him with a virulent hatred. Last year there was an attempt on his life by several disaffected cardinals, which – fortune be praised! – Leo survived. Actually, it was a rather clumsy effort at poisoning – the old-fashioned method of pest-control popularised by Alexander VI Borgia (now roasting in hell, we all fervently hope) and his murderous brood; you can always find some old hag in a shit-stinking hovel ready to mix a deadly brew for a price. The whole of Rome, they say, is a poisoner's den, and I for one believe it. His Eminence Cardinal Alfonso Petrucci paid with his life for this abortive attempt to rid the world of Leo; he died, by all acounts, screaming and struggling, blue in the face, all control of his bowels lost, and everyone knew then that the heart which ceased to beat was not only treacherous, but also pusillanimous. His Eminence Cardinal Francesco Soderini (or 'God's Sod' as we all knew him) was fined and imprisoned but later fled, along with Cardinal Adriano Castellesi. A chastened man, Leo introduced a bunch of his own cronies into the sacred College of Cardinals, and everything has been as sweet as roses ever since; of course, this *may* be due to the perfumed enemas which most of them are in the habit of taking. Cardinal Ridolfi apparently has his scented with lime-flowers.

However, I am mindful that these scribblings of mine do bear the title *Memoirs of a Gnostic Dwarf*, and hence should primarily be about me; it is therefore my intention to proceed with the story of *my* life, rather than Leo's, even though he will inevitably figure prominently in this story. It would not be exaggerating the case to say that I owe everything to him – and I do mean *everything*. I owe him my daily bread, a roof over my head (and a palatial one at that), money in the bank, status and position, and – above all else – I owe him my dignity. It moves me deeply to write these words.

I will begin with an account of my childhood, and of the chthonic world in which I was obliged to survive; I will relate the adventures that I stumbled into in my older years, my initiation into the Gnostic Brotherhood, and my early life with Pope Leo X – then Giovanni, Cardinal de' Medici. It never ceases to amaze me how, in such wondrous fashion, the threads of our two lives were drawn together by some invisible and fathomlessly benevolent Will; Leo was made a cardinal when he was a boy of thirteen; at the same age, I was earning a living (if you can call it that) by helping my mother to peddle cheap wine to the scum of Rome. Christ's blood, how *incongruous* a marriage of fates can you get?

But I do not wish to anticipate my story; let us begin, as the holy Evangelist John does, in the beginning.

Deus, qui neminem in te sperantem nimium affligi permittis
In the beginning was not, for me, the Word, but the pain. In the beginning was the pain, and the pain was with me, and the pain *was* me. It constituted the entirety of my burgeoning consciousness. I knew almost nothing else but this. They told me that as a babe in arms I cried not for my mother's milk, but for release from pain. This suffering was, I am inclined to think, twofold: at its heart it was both an experience of actual physical pain and also of psychic protest that my soul had been enclosed in such a twisted, malformed, recalcitrant body. My mother and the physician (whose quality of service was proportionate to her capacity to pay, and therefore indifferent), assumed that my suffering resided solely in the agony of crooked bones; they had no idea (and why should they?) that my *spirit* cried out also, in violent objection. Many years later, after I had been initiated into the Gnostic Brotherhood, I composed some verses to reflect my experience; I would like to share them with you now.

In the beginning was the pain:
the pain was with us, and the pain was in us –
the structure, the frame, the shape of the sound
that spilled from our mouths like blood from a wound,
the only way we knew we were.

In the beginning was vulnerability:
a reason for hiding, crawling away
back to the womb and the uninscribed stone,
to the deep-interred peace, before flesh and bone
knitted together in mute, blind form.

In the beginning was the hurt:
precisely etched on the warp of the heart,
a laid-bare sign, a tell-tale mark
signifying how we had abandoned the dark
and shuffled inexorably into the light.

In the beginning was the motion:
the perpetual rape by shape and form
of wayward spirit, wandering far,
to where the integuments of error are
insistently whispering of sibilant death.

In the beginning shall be a return
to a place where beginnings couple with fire
and, burnt-out, conceive the point
when socket by socket and joint by joint,
the knot of our birthing shall be undone.

Hardly a masterpiece, I know, but it did (and still does) express a little of the philosophy I have made my own, and which has faithfully succoured me as I cross this bridge of sighs we call earthly life. I am proud to say that the Master of our little fraternity has incorporated several of these verses, set to a canorous chant of his own composition, into our liturgy.

My mother once said to me (I suppose she had saved up this little gem of venom, nurturing it like a viper in her bosom, until I was old enough to understand what it meant) when I tried to climb up into her lap:

"God knows, I should have suffocated you at birth."

There was a time when I would have wholeheartedly agreed with this; now, however, I am rather glad that she did not suffocate me at birth. Strange, isn't it, how one can always learn to love oneself, however ghastly one is?

I was born in the year of Our Lord 1478, the sixth of the inglorious pontificate of the Franciscan pope, Sixtus IV – by all accounts a man most unlike the gentle founder of his Order, and a successor of Peter whose nepotism makes Leo's shameless dishing out of favours to members of his family look like casual acts of dispassionate kindness. The house in which I was born was little more than a hovel, in the Trastevere area of Rome; they say that the Trasteverini are the devil's own, and it's a view I'm inclined to share: they're pig-headed, coarse, fiercely independent, and they're all jackals and rogues to a man. The shit that I leave behind every morning in the papal privy is cleaner and sweeter than some of the scum you come across in Trastevere's stinking gutters. Certainly, they have no time for anything as sentimental as pity for a deformed child; at least that was my experience. Oh, believe me, I'm not excessively bitter about it – after all, surviving Trastevere life endowed me with the will and instinct to survive almost anything. I was kicked and pelted with rubbish, and abused and beaten up by every bully of a *gamin* and *lazzarone* daily. You might claim that this could well have happened anywhere, and you would be right; all I know however, is that it happened to me in Trastevere, and I'll never forgive it for that. For years now I've been pestering Leo to have the whole area flattened and re-built, but he keeps telling me he doesn't have the money. This is quite true, but it doesn't stop me pestering him.

My mother had been widowed after just two weeks of marriage to a neighbour's son, in the most grotesque of circumstances: the man who did not live long enough to become my father was sleeping in the hot afternoon sun outside Santa Maria in Trastevere, after a drunken binge with his cronies; he must have turned carelessly and grazed his ear or his cheek – at any rate, there was blood some-where – and a pack of crazy stray dogs ate half his face away before someone managed to drive them off. He died of shock a day later. My mother said to everybody:

"He was gobbled up by his own kind."

My mother sold wine, tramping the streets with a wooden cart loaded with demijohns of sour, vinegary gut-rot which she occasionally managed to mix with a little Frascati. God only knows who my biological father was. I later learned that I was conceived as the result of a brutal act of rape, so I suppose he could have been anyone who goes in for that sort of thing.

"I couldn't fight him off," my mother said, when she finally got round to telling me the unedifying story of my genesis.

"Why? If you'd beaten him off, I wouldn't have been born."

"He was too strong for me. Besides, I was pissed at the time."

"Who was he? Would you know him again if you saw him?"

"Know him? I'd know him in the darkness of hell itself, which is where I hope he is now, the cockless bastard."

If this description was in any way accurate, my unknown progenitor must have suffered his de-cocking subsequent to my conception, I presume; however, I suspect it was just wishful thinking on my mother's part. She was much given to that sort of imaginative rhetoric. In fact, coming across a particularly belligerent or tight-fisted customer, she would often set her colourful little predications to song:

> *Don't your balls hang low?*
> *Did your cock never grow?*
> *Oh, if all the ladies knew*
> *Just what I know of you!*

"Who was my father?" I persisted. "Who was he?"
"Mind your own sodding business."
And that was that.

As soon as I was old enough – I was never *really* able, but I managed somehow – I accompanied my mother on her rounds, and relieved her by pushing the cart, which was wondrously heavy. I did it by placing my hump against the back of it, between the handles, and walking backwards. Sometimes my twisted, stunted legs buckled under me and I fell, and inevitably one of the demijohns (usually a full one) came sliding down onto my head. With equal inevitability, my mother would shriek: "Thank Christ it was only your sodding head!" and burst into peals of laughter which were all the more cruel because they were absolutely genuine. Once, when an empty demijohn actually shattered against my skull, she laughed so much she wet herself. There she stood in the middle of the street, her beefy hands on her hips, her legs apart, a stream of hot, steaming piss running down her shins onto the cobbles, her head thrown back as she shook with guffaws; and I thought: *This is not my mother.* It was as simple as that – an instant, conscious, sober decision, and from that moment until this (she may be dead, for all I know) she has been as alien to me as a straight spine. If I refer to her as my mother in the pages which follow, it is only for the sake of literary convenience, and to save myself the trouble of inventing an epithet more accurate, if less charitable.

Only once did she ever demonstrate affection, and it was in the most inappropriate of circumstances, with the most grotesque of intentions. She was drunk, of course. I was curled up on my mattress, feeling slightly sick from the chitterlings I'd had for supper, naked because the night was hot and sticky, wide-awake and dreaming futile dreams of some far-distant homeland way beyond the stars, where I belonged, where I would be beautiful instead of ugly, where my heart would burst with the ecstasy of being loved, not despised. I can't help it if that sounds sentimental, it's just the way it was. You must remember that these were the dreams of a child. Childish, yet bearing their own truth however, for years later I came to learn that such a homeland really and truly exists, but this is something you shall hear about in due course. It is as far removed from the heaven which the priests tell us about – whose more elevated circles are apparently already filled with popes and prelates and kings (they seem to get the best of both worlds) – as fire is from ice.

Anyway, my mother staggered into my room, her bodice half open and soiled with unpleasant-looking, indefinite stains.

"Well now," she crooned in a horrible parody of affection, "will you just look at the little naked thing! Isn't he just like a cherub, all pink and plump and hairless?"

It was true that my body hair had not yet begun to grow, but then, I was only twelve at the time.

She threw herself on the bed, almost on top of me, her face pressed close to mine, her hot breath stinking of wine and vomit.

"Gimme a kiss, sweetheart," she said, putting her thick arms around my body.

"Don't – you're drunk – *please* – "

I had given up calling her 'mother' since that demijohn had shattered on my head.

"Drunk? You cheeky little bastard! Don't you love your old mother, then?"

I did not have the courage to say no; at least I had the integrity not to say yes.

To my horror, she put one hand down between my legs and grasped my penis. I wriggled and writhed, but could not escape, since the weight of her body pinned me to the mattress.

"God knows, I could do with a big one of those inside me," she said. Parody was being replaced by mawkish self-pity.

"Come on, sweetikins, let mother see it get a bit longer, a bit thicker."

And self-pity gave way to the most excruciatingly abhorrent amorous advance.

"No. No, no, no, no –"

"You'll like it, I promise, I promise. See what lovely feelings mother can give you."

I knew what those feelings were from my own rather timid and anxiety-ridden bouts of self-stimulation, but the idea of my mother arousing them in me was repulsive. She began to rub and massage my penis with slow, lascivious strokes, all the time crooning and burbling into my ear.

"When it's good and stiff, you can stick it in me," she said with unnerving frankness.

"I won't. Get off me!"

With her free hand she started to pull up her skirts. I caught a glimpse of some great dark, damp, hairy mound, and I smelt a sudden sharp-sweet odour; but there was another odour in the room too, and it wasn't coming from my mother's private parts.

"The lamp, look at the lamp!" I cried, for a slight breeze from the open window had brushed the length of sacking that hung across it against the flame of the little oil-lamp, and it was already beginning to smoulder.

"We'll be burnt alive!" my mother screamed, instantly sober. She leapt up with surprising agility in one so heavily built, snatched down the sacking and threw it on the floor. She stamped up and down on it repeatedly. When it had finally ceased to smoke and fizzle, she stood there breathless, panting, her hands on her hips.

"Is it out?" I said.

"Of course it's out, no thanks to you, you little pig. I've told you before not to have the lamp burning all night. Christ, what am I that I should have money to go up in flames? A cardinal's whore?"

Then she looked at me with fierce, vengeful eyes.

"You!" she hissed, and I knew that she was suddenly aware of the enormity of what she had tried to do, the shameful absurdity of it.

"I hate you," she said. "I've always hated you. You were begotten in hate and you were born in hate. Look at you, you twisted, ugly, wretched mess of a half-man. The mark of hate is stamped all over your vile little shape. You're not a person, you're a – a *thing*. Go to sleep. You've got to push the cart early tomorrow. Why in the name of all the saints and angels did God have to make a creature like you?"

That was precisely the question I asked myself every time I awoke in the early morning light to find myself, disappointingly, still alive.

★

39

It was a strange, subterranean world that I moved in, its horror and its darkness sometimes taking on the aspect of unreality; I knew that essentially I did not belong to it, any more than I belonged to my mother, yet I accepted it for what it was. I had to, in order to survive. My mother had brought in one or two physicians to look at me in the early months, but then she decided that since nothing could be done about my pitiable deformity, it wasn't worth spending any more money on the impossible. In accepting my lot, I also came to understand that suffering was universal, and that there wasn't anyone who was without pain of some kind; the difference between other people's suffering and mine was merely one of degree. Obviously I couldn't formulate it in those words then, but that was how I understood it.

Providing you with an explanation of how I am able to formulate it in those words *now*, brings me to the story of Laura.

Laura! The very name is like the sound of the first drop of rain as it falls, breaks, and releases its sweet coolness on a parched wasteland; it is like spring air in the countryside after the foetid miasma of a privy; it is like the light of resurrection following the tenebrous disintegration of death. It is all this and so much more. And if this be but the name, I leave it to your imagination to guess at the reality signified. I say 'reality' because the lady Laura became, for me, the only real human being other than myself in a savage nightmare of shadows and chimeras. The lady Laura Francesa Beatrice de' Collini. My hand trembles as I write.

I will tell you how I first met my archangel.

I had made it my habit in the cool of the evenings, while my mother was doubtlessly accommodating some sozzled lecher up against a wall in a dark alley somewhere, to go into the church of Santa Maria in Trastevere. I did not go to pray, since I had inherited not a jot of piety from my mother, and felt no inclination to develop any of my own; I went simply to sit and look at what was beautiful. A private communion with everything that had passed me by: serenity, silence, loveliness. I gazed up at the mosaic of the apse, and felt for a brief while that my soul was lifted and made one with it; what it depicted was of no interest to me — it was simply its perfection that enthralled, captivated and set me for a period free.

I always drew unabashedly curious looks, since people were not sure whether I was a deformed child or a poor, crippled old man, in the enchanted crepuscular depths of the church; so it was that when I felt a gentle touch on my gnarled shoulder, I assumed that someone had plucked up enough nerve to actually ask me *what* I was. I turned, ready to snap, but instead of impertinently inquisitive eyes or a lascivious mouth, I saw the most ravishingly beautiful girl I had ever beheld in my young life. She was the unselfconscious, exquisitely tender loveliness of the mosaic come to life. The pale, tranquil features of a young madonna were framed in an oval of hair that had all the fineness of spun gold. The distilled light slanting in from the open doors of the church shone in a gold-green nimbus around her head. She was an utterly dazzling and disconcerting vision.

"What is your name?"

"Giuseppe," I murmured. "Peppe for short."

"My name is Laura. How old are you, Peppe?"

"Almost thirteen. I've kept count."

She smiled.

"That's good. I would very much like to talk to you, Peppe. May I?"

"What about?"

"Perhaps after your devotions —"

"I don't have any devotions. I just like the dark and the silence."

"So do I; and it may be that we have more things in common than that. Will you come with me?"

I could no more have refused her request than a starving man could refuse bread and meat. What a strange pair we must have made, she and I, as we walked out of the church

41

into the humid, stale air of the early evening! One day, someone will write a story about a shining beauty and a dark, deformed beast; perhaps they already have.

"Where are we going?" I asked, for she had taken my hand in hers, and was leading me with quick, light steps that I found difficult to match.

"Not far. To my house. It is very near here."

"Who are you? Are you a queen?"

"I'm grateful for the compliment Peppe, but no, I'm not a queen. I am the lady Laura Francesca Beatrice de' Collini. My father is Andrea de' Collini, a patrician of Rome. There –" she pointed with a slim finger that bore a silver ring inscribed with a curious symbol – an equal-armed cross set within a circle, "– there is my house."

Her 'house' was a small palazzo on the corner of an intersection between a narrow, foul-smelling *vicolo* and a broad street lined with shops specializing in ecclesiastical accoutrements worked in precious metal: chalices, patens, lavabo bowls, cruets for water and wine, thuribles, episcopal rings and croziers. I was certain that I had been down this street on several occasions, but I had never before noticed the almost square-shaped building of pock-marked grey travertine marble.

"Is it very old?" I asked.

"Less than a hundred years. It has an interesting history; Baldassare Cossa once spent a night within its walls. You must remind me to tell you all about it some time, Peppe."

Baldassare Cossa was for five uproarious years the Antipope John XXIII, sharing his claim to Peter's throne with Gregory XII and Benedict XIII, but I understood nothing of that at the time. God knows, I understand little of it now, except that it demonstrates in the most garish and hilarious way how far the Holy Roman Church is from the truth of Jesus the Nazarene, upon whose blessed Person it claims to be founded.

"We live on the top floor," the lady Laura explained. "The other apartments are rented out."

We passed through the great carven oak doors, inlaid

with bronze studs which had turned green with age, and entered a spacious, cool courtyard in which a fountain splashed discreetly, and where there were many varieties of plants and ferns in terracotta pots. The feeling was one of privacy, shade and quiet refreshment.

I climbed the stairs only with great difficulty, but the lady Laura was patient and kind, pausing every few moments to give me time to regain my breath. This in itself was a complete novelty for me, since hitherto my experience had told me that any stumbling or clumsiness is followed by a blow, as surely as day is followed by night; I suppose I had somehow concluded that it was normal for people to hit cripples. Indeed, it *was* normal where I came from.

"You poor sweet," she said in an unutterably tender voice. "Be brave! They're only stairs."

At the top of the staircase, beyond another set of doors, these small and rather plain, I found myself in a charming anteroom; there were beautiful frescos of strange-looking trees and birds, the colours faded to soft, crumbly blues and pinks and pale ochres. There was a small carved table of some intricate and puzzling design, and on it stood a silver pitcher; I later learned that this table had been brought at great cost from the Languedoc region of France, near Toulouse, and that it had once stood in the house of a Cathar *parfait*. I had never heard the word '*parfait*' before; I don't even think I could have pronounced it.

A man entered the room from a door in the wall opposite us, dressed in the plain dowlas smock of a domestic servant.

"You were not expected back so soon, my lady," he said quietly, respectfully.

"No matter. We have a guest for dinner."

Then, turning to me, she said:

"You *will* stay to dinner Peppe, won't you? We have so much to talk about."

And my bewildered silence betokened an affirmation whose eloquence entirely transcended the use of words.

*

The dining room was magnificent. A series of paintings on the ceiling depicted (so the lady Laura informed me) the descent of Sophia from the highest heavenly realm into the chaos of material form.

"Who is Sophia?" I asked.

"She is an active principle of wisdom, my sweet."

"I don't understand."

"No, not yet you don't. Through her error, Yaldabaoth came into being; there! – you see him? The creature with the lion's face in the corner, he whom the Jews adore. Yet Sophia repented of what she had done, and came down to illuminate the darkened minds and hearts of those whom Yaldabaoth had imprisoned and obliged to worship him alone."

Then, sensing that incomprehension had given way to disinterest, she paused.

"You like the room, Peppe?"

I was quite overwhelmed by it. There were luxuriously thick rugs on the marble floor, strange and wonderful tapestries adorning the walls; the dark, heavy furniture and the crimson gold-fringed drapes at the balcony windows indicated unselfconscious wealth. The long table at which we sat was covered with a rich damask cloth, and the silver platters and bowls glittered in the candleglow. Everywhere there were candles! Candles casting a mellow, holy light that enveloped us like a benediction. We cut up the food with our knives and I brought it to my mouth with my fingers, but the lady Laura used a little device with two prongs, the like of which I had never seen before.

"It's called a *forchetta*," she said, laughing gently. "Here – you try."

I tried, and I managed, but it felt uncomfortable to me. I had never eaten off a platter before; I had never drunk wine from a glass goblet; I had never patted my lips as she did, so charmingly and unobtrusively, with a square of stiff, snowy white linen. I suddenly felt like weeping.

"Do not be disturbed," she said softly, with a little sadness in her voice.

"But I am. I can't help it."

44

"I know. All this –" she waved a long, slender arm in the air, "– this means nothing. It amounts to no more than circumstance. You feel that we have but little in common, Peppe? You and I?"

"I feel," I said, stumbling over my words, "I feel I – I don't belong here."

"But you *do* belong!" she cried, and her sudden earnestness surprised me. "We have everything in common, believe me."

"I don't understand. I don't know why you made me come. You're so beautiful, and me – I'm so –"

"So ugly?"

"Yes. Ugly."

"But you're not frightened, are you, Peppe?"

"No. I'm not frightened."

Then she did an extraordinary thing. She rose from her chair and began to unfasten the furbelow of her bodice.

"What are you doing?"

"I want to show you something."

The brocaded silk cascaded about her waist, and with unhurried, expert fingers, she unfastened the plain white genappe undervest beneath.

"Look at me, Peppe. Look."

One breast was perfect: smooth, full, young, firm, the little pink nipple standing out against its darker, goose-fleshed aureole; the other however, was hideously malformed, a small, shrivelled prune of a thing that was hardly a breast at all, more of an unsightly excrescence. The skin all around it was wrinkled and puckered, mottled with a fuliginous nevus that spread down the side of her body to her waist.

"Am I beautiful now, Peppe?"

I could not speak.

"You see?" she said, smiling, "I told you we would have more in common than our love of darkness and silence."

Then she covered herself.

"Come, it is time for us to talk."

*

It would take an eternity to tell you of the unheard-of, undreamed and fantastic things she spoke to me about, nearly all of which were entirely beyond my understanding. She used the word 'heresy' frequently, and this I knew was a deliberate and wicked denial of the holy truth revealed by God through his Church, for which men must be severely punished if their souls are to be saved. She told me incredible stories, the weaving of myths and legends, of a fraternity of men and women who had survived torture and persecution across the centuries to disseminate the real truth about the living God. She uttered sounds that belonged to a foreign tongue. Her lovely face grew sad at some moments, then angry, then patient, and finally joyful. She related tales of cruelty and love, she spun dream-pictures with the brightly-coloured threads of exotic and incomprehensible words, telling me of some deep, enduring mystery of which she and I were a vital part, to which we belonged, which our destiny would never allow us to escape. When at last she folded her hands in her lap to indicate that she had finished, my mind was whirling, my eyes wide with the wonder of being confronted with a dazzlingly alien reality, exquisitely, hypnotically tantalizing because totally ungraspable, yet aglow with the lustre of absolute meaning. I was filled with the sweet melancholy which only a song without words can perfectly convey.

"You will come here every week," she said. "I will meet with you in the church, as I did this evening. We must lose no time in having you educated, on both a spiritual and a practical level. It begins with the practical, my sweet."

"What's that?"

"We must teach you to speak, to read and write."

"I know how to talk already," I said, a little chagrined.

"Everybody knows how to *talk*, but how many truly know how to speak? Talking is a physical ability; speaking is an art. You must learn to *know* what you want to say, and how best to say it. This will require polish, *finesse, patina.*"

"I don't know what you mean."

"*Exactly*. You must find out for yourself. With help, of course. Then, later, there are other people I want you to meet. People like us, Peppe. People who know. People of truth."

She stood up and extended a hand.

"And now it is time to leave," she said. "Luca will take you to the courtyard."

"I know the way."

"He will need to unbolt the door. It is always locked after I have come home in the evening."

She bent and kissed me lightly on the forehead.

"Until next week, Peppe. Be faithful. Be strong!"

Of course, I was physically incapable of skipping for joy as I made my way home, but my heart did it for me, leaping and bounding, crashing wildly against its encaging musculature.

My mother was eating cheese and drinking her own gut-rot when I got back. She paused long enough to let out an enormous, ripe belch, and ask me threateningly:

"Where have you been?"

"In church."

"You sodding little liar! Since when were you last in church?"

"It's true. I met a beautiful lady, and she lives in a palazzo like a princess. She's going to teach me everything. *Everything*."

"Are you pissed? What beautiful lady?"

"The lady Laura Francesca Beatrice de' Collini."

My mother looked at me for a brief moment with dull, unfocussed eyes, as if weighing up the possibility that her *thing* of a son might actually have been able to arouse pity in someone at last – and a rich, titled someone at that – and what opportunities such an unlikely event might promise.

"Did she give you money?" she asked guardedly.

"No."

Her shoulders slumped.

"Piss off, then."

"The trouble with you," I said, "is you've got no *finesse.*"

"No what?"

"Finesse."

I was sure I had pronounced it correctly.

"If you can't eat it or drink it or fuck with it or sell it, I've got no sodding need of it," she said, going back to her supper.

Then she looked up at me and grinned horribly. There were slivers of half-dissolved cheese in the crevices of her teeth.

"A beautiful lady!" she hissed. "What beautiful lady would have anything to do with you, you little runt, unless it was to hire you as her arse-wiper? Ha! Go on, piss off and leave me in peace."

That night, I slept the sleep of the blessed.

And so began my education. For two hours, one evening a week, I sat with the lady Laura in the library of her palazzo while she patiently drummed into me the essentials of grammar, pronunciation, the written word, of rhetoric and style, of the development of language. She spoke to me of great and marvellous books, of poetry, of music and painting, of drama, and the story of human history. She uncovered a little of the secrets of the heavenly bodies, of how the movements of the stars above us affect the fortunes of our lives here below. She told me stories of faraway lands which bake and broil under the violent heat of a relentless sun, where strange and fabulous beasts stalk their prey – some with horns on their heads, some whose skin consists of beaten metal, others who require human flesh to survive. She spoke of one beautiful creature in particular – a horse-like animal which bears a single, carven horn in the centre of its forehead, and which can be tamed only by resting in the lap of a virgin. I learned the names and titles of those who rule the kingdoms of this world. I used first my fingers, then my brain, to perform complicated calculations.

I began to understand how to reason logically, what syllo-gisms are, why some arguments are valid and others not, and I studied the long, tortuous history of human thinking, which is called *philosophy*.

The teaching she gave was heuristic, and in me she perceived that the intellect was quick and eager, and that while the stunted and deformed body struggled helplessly earthbound, the mind was able to take wing and soar unfettered.

"When does it come to an end?" I once asked.

"When does what come to an end, my sweet?"

"Knowing. When do we know *everything?*"

"Never! Oh, Peppe, never! Not on this earth."

And so we continued. We sometimes sang songs to-gether, and she was delighted (I was totally taken by surprise) to discover that I possessed a light, high singing voice, whose quality was enhanced when accompanied on the gittern. I have long since come to believe that music offers the perfect analogy of ideal human relationships; I mean that if we could conduct ourselves as the vocal parts of – say – a madrigal do, then a little bit of heaven would be brought down to this hellish earth. For each note is as worthy and as beautiful as all the others, making its own unique contribution to the whole, and without which the whole would be diminished, incomplete. Sometimes one voice rises to prominence, soars in its melody, then sinks back into harmonic mutedness or even rest; then another takes its place, rising and falling, and then another, so that of this free-flowing rhythm a warp and woof is constructed in which each single vocal thread is conjoined to its fellows effortlessly, seamlessly, and it is a great, single living and breathing organism. Notes lower on the scale do not resent those higher up, for they complement and balance each other perfectly; even those which slip into chromaticism do so because they are directed to by the will of the composer – the flattened or the sharpened tone adds poign-ancy, surprise, exaltation or pain. Without them, the lis-tener would soon become bored. There is never any competition between the parts, for the requirements of melody and harmony govern their movement, which is not capricious, and each tends inexorably towards the same end – that ultimate chord which signals the completion of the piece, and in which there is silence in sound, poise in oscillation.

If human beings could live their lives like that! If every man knew the value of the other, recognized the contribution of each to all, believed in the high and the low, the flat and the sharp, put his faith in the hidden harmony of the final chord of resolution! But then – but then, if pigs could dance an *allemande* . . .

One song in particular suited me, and it became a special favourite of mine:

> *My love is sweet as honey wild,*
> *that gilds my tongue so I may speak*
> *with words of gold that ever seek*
> *to laud her beauty, chaste and mild.*
> *My love with fervent sighing pray'd*
> *That of my heart, love's psalm be made.*

It was a profound joy for me to sing this as she sat motionless, bathed in candlelight, her face a vision of contemplative serenity, her eyes lightly closed; then, her chair became a goddess' throne, her golden hair a galaxy of night stars, and the painted, gilded room our own private corner of heaven.

I began to lead a double life, for exigency obliged me to; with the lady Laura I was free to demonstrate and be proud of what I had absorbed, but with my mother I had to feign the old ignorance. Although this excited me and made me feel that despite the obvious evidence of my deformity, on display to the entire world, there was something undeformed, something fresh and clean and bright and rich within, which the world could never know of, it also caused indifference and dislike of my mother to turn to hate, and it made that hate fester and grow with every day that passed. The more I learned of the beauty of language, the more I loathed her coarse obscenities; the more I acquired in the way of good manners, gentleness of spirit and courtesy, the more I resented her habitual squalor; the more knowledge I came to possess, the more I harboured a barely-suppressed contumely for her fathomless ignorance. But suppressed it was, for my own safety's sake; God knows, a wine-bibbing slut was a common enough thing where I lived, but a wine-bibbing slut with an educated, articulate dwarf for a son – that would have provoked adverse, even dangerous, comment. For I had begun to suspect that the world to which the lady Laura had introduced me was not without its perils, and the group which met at her house not without enemies. I did not know the precise nature of these perils, nor who the enemies might be, but I sensed their presence. Tragically, this suspicion of mine was to prove only too horribly well-founded, as you shall soon hear.

Yes, I had met the 'other people' of whom the lady Laura had spoken, and there was forged between us a bond so deep, so powerful, that it bespoke a mystery in which we participated without being fully able to grasp. Our conversations together were those of strangers in an alien land; the silences we shared were eloquent; the loyalty we felt, each for the others, approached the dispassionate fervour of love. We did not call it love, for the abuse which promiscuous usage has heaped upon that word would have tainted the reality it signified; however, we knew it for what it was. Furthermore, we sensed that there was yet to come a further link in the fast-forged chain of our friendship, but we could not guess at its nature. I myself believed that it would be some profound and hitherto unrevealed teaching given by the lady Laura herself, but until she chose the moment to give it, we were content to wait in patience.

At least, on the surface of things (for our comradeship struck roots far below the surface), one common denominator among us was evident: there was Pietro, a handsome young man in his twenties whose finely sculpted features were marred by a hideously purple nevus that covered most of his face; there was little Barbara, who had no arms to speak of, and whose pudgy hands seemed to sprout from her shoulders; there was Angelo, who with his elongated ears and hairy jowls looked like a sad, patient wolf; and there was Giacomo, who hardly possessed a face at all – at birth a caul was discovered to have welded itself to his head – his tiny black eyes glittered and blinked in a mess of twisted, webby flesh. These, who had known suffering such as I had known – who, until the miracle of our coming together, had taken suffering for granted – these were my kith and kin.

So the years passed, and the lady Laura's house became *my* house, her world offered itself to *me*, and I was caught up in its plenitude of light and knowledge; slowly I was being transformed both in her eyes and mine, but clandestinely in the cruel and rheumy eyes of the world. Yes, the years passed, but the words of the Hebrew psalmist were fulfilled, and a thousand ages were as but a single day come and gone for us.

Gone, like a watch in the night . . .

One evening, I arrived at the lady Laura's house to find her alone.

"Where are the others?" I asked, surprised and disconcerted. "Has something terrible happened?"

"No. Come, sit by me, Peppe."

Our hands joined, spontaneously and unselfconsciously.

"How old are you now, Peppe?" she said.

"This is the year 1496," I answered. "I am eighteen years old."

"So you are."

"It is the fifth anniversary of our first meeting, that evening in the church. Do you recall it?"

"How could I not, my sweet? I recall it with tenderness. Besides, I have every reason to recall it: it was perfectly planned."

"Planned?" I echoed.

52

"Of course!"

"You mean I was – well – that I was *chosen* in some way?"

This had never occurred to me.

"Yes. In every way."

"You knew of me before we met?"

"Certainly. I used to see you pushing that cart through the streets, bruising your poor back. I was there, watching, when your mother lost control of her bladder. It was cruel, hateful laughter that brought her to it."

I bowed my head.

"Don't do that," she said, lifting my chin with the palm of her hand. "The shame is hers, not yours."

We were silent for a moment, then she said softly:

"You are eighteen, Peppe. Even in such a wretched body as yours, you must have noticed certain changes. Have you? Feelings, too – longings, vague stirrings of desire –"

"Of course."

The night my mother had tried to seduce me came suddenly into my mind, like the unexpected and unwelcome pain of a recurrent sickness after a period of health. Then I had been pale and hairless and smooth, but now my armpits and my chest sprouted a thick, dark growth, and there was a great cloud of stiff, bushy hair between my legs. I frequently experienced wet dreams, and I very occasionally masturbated; strange as it may seem, these acts of furtive onanism did not centre around some garish fantasy of a sexual act that was unattainable for me in reality, but rather on vague but intensely satisfying feelings of comfort, warmth, safety and happiness. They were in any case entirely private; they could not be shared because people think that the idea of sexual pleasure for the physically deformed is revolting and immoral. The more I reflect upon the inward deformity of men's souls, the stranger and sadder this phenomenon seems to me.

"You know then," the lady Laura went on, "what I am referring to."

53

"Yes."

"And yet, my dearest Peppe, it is an experience which you *must* appropriate, if you are finally and irrevocably to reject it. It is a piece of knowledge – amounting to no more than a scrap, a tatter, I grant you – that should be yours, if you are to ascend to higher, more subtle and refined spheres of *gnosis*."

"My heart is beating faster," I said.

"Yes, I know. But do you understand the significance of what I say?"

"Certainly. You are telling me that I must possess carnal knowledge in order to leave it behind forever."

"Oh, yes, Peppe, yes! Exactly!"

"I think I – that is, all of us – have felt for some time, that our education was to take a qualitative leap. That it was to come from you."

"You are right. That leap is towards *spiritual* knowledge, as distinct from factual knowledge, linguistic ability and social refinement. Everything else here has been a preparation for it. But because of the nature of this gross world in which we are obliged to live and breathe – truly, it is hell! – and because the divine *scintilla* within us is imprisoned by the coarseness of flesh, with its own pitiful urges and demands, we must have the deepest experience of it before we can once and for all turn against it. For be sure of this: ascent to *gnosis* cannot be half-hearted; you cannot crane your neck upwards to catch a glimpse of heaven at one moment, then look down regretfully and longingly to the mud and mire the next. The break must be complete. The divine realms know nothing of the flesh, and they require that any aspirant to the glories they contain, with the promise of ultimate release, should know nothing of it either. Now, since we have been born into this carnal pit we call earthly life, knowing nothing of the flesh for us cannot mean ignorance of it; therefore, our path is that of knowing it, then subsequently rejecting and despising it. You cannot reject or despise what you do not know. However, once known, the rejection and the despisal must be absolute, total, forever. Do you understand this?"

"Yes," I said, hardly managing to get the word out.

"More importantly, do you believe it?"

"I am ready to believe it," I answered. I was trembling uncontrollably, as though suffering from an ague.

"Good. It is I myself who will pass onto you the knowledge which, once assimilated, must be rejected."

Then she seemed to read my mind.

"Do not be anxious about the others – they have already acquired their knowledge."

"But when? How? I mean –"

"In the same way as you are about to acquire it, my sweet. For each of them it was arranged."

"You yourself? That is, were *you* their teacher?"

She shook her head slowly.

"No. Barbara and Giacomo taught each other."

"Together, the two of them?"

"Certainly, my sweet. There are many well-appointed rooms in this place. I made one over to them for a brief time, for their own private use."

This idea seemed to amuse her, and she laughed gently.

"And Angelo? Pietro?"

"They also taught each other."

"But they're both men!"

"That hardly matters, does it, when the object of gaining this knowledge is solely that it may be rejected and de-spised? Two men are just as good at acquiring it together as two women, or a man and a woman. The hypocritical sexual morality of this world has nothing to do with us. Be patient, Peppe, you will learn. Each one of them has taken the irreversible decision to join me in ascent to the higher spheres. They are committed. They fully understand the intense pleasure that carnal love can bring, and they have fully and freely abandoned it. And you, Peppe, my dearest sweet, will you do the same?"

In a voice hushed, like the breath of a guttering candle flame, I looked up at the lady Laura and said:

"I will."

★

The great bed with its viridian velvet canopy enshadowed us, and the rich, amber glow from the silver cresset bathed us in its golden radiance, so that we seemed to be no longer wounded, crippled things but gods, dripping nectar and honey from fingertips, thighs, toes, lips. The silence cradled us as we lay naked, wrapped in each other's arms. Her hair fell about my gnarled, knotty shoulders, and absorbed me into the ambit of her tenderness, like an anemone drawing in and enfolding some minute sea creature. I was caressed by her shallow breathing, her one beautiful breast pressed close to the hairy brambles on my shrunken chest, now beaded with the perspiration not of apprehension but acute anticipation. With infinite and courageous understanding, she had reached behind me and placed one cool hand on the bony contour of my hump, and I, in an exquisite moment of reciprocity, bent to kiss the dark place – hid in the pulsatile shadows of her body's landscape – where no breast grew.

Her other hand held my cock; she pulled back the foreskin with her fingers, moving them with a languorous but persistent rhythm, and I felt myself begin to quiver with tentative life, becoming stiffer, harder, nodding and bobbing into an erection. In response, I pressed my knee into the oleaginous calix of her humid sex. We kissed a little, then drew apart, then kissed again. Her lips tasted of something sweet, something apple-scented and fresh. Her hot, pink tongue came out and touched mine, and I sucked on it hungrily, like a luscious little sweetmeat.

"Oh, I feel it coming!" she said. "I am almost ready."

She pulled herself away from me and rolled onto her back. The nimbus of hair on her pubic mound was like a little bush of flame in the enchanted light; her skin, the smoothest marble overlaid with translucent gold.

I gently placed myself on top of her, holding myself up by leaning on the palms of my hands. The tight, blood-gorged tip of my cock was touching the plump lips of her sex.

"Now," she whispered, "now!"

56

I pushed myself in, and sank onto her. Our lips met. Her legs wrapped themselves around my buttocks, and she moved them with me as I began the first slow, tentative thrusting which no-one had taught me, but which came as naturally and as easily as breathing. It is the ageless wisdom of the body – even a body as grotesque as mine – that is the only true instructor in the techniques of love, and whose autonomous confidence now transcended the hesitation and shyness of inexperience.

It started as a fire somewhere in the small of my back: a searing, liquid fire that was as unstoppable as a flood-tide, pouring down underneath my scrotum, down through my cock and into the sucking depths of her body, where I was buried deep, held fast by the relentless embrace of powerful muscles; the fire became a molten conflagration, circumfusing my innards, and something of immense and terrifying purpose rent a gash in the fabric of my psyche, through which my liquescent heart seeped out. It was so excruciating I did not think I could bear it a moment longer without dying, yet it was so intensely sweet I did not wish it to stop for even the shadow of a moment.

"Laura! Laura! Laura!" I cried, and my groans were her epithalamium, the repeated spasms that shook me as I released my seed in her body, her bridal dance.

We fell asleep holding each other in that green and gold alembic of a bed, the cresset spluttering a sibilant threnody for the passion which had consumed us, now itself consumed. Before I closed my eyes I looked into hers, and saw that a tear, like a tiny jewel, glittered on her dark lashes.

Day is followed by night, sleep by waking, hubris by nemesis, laughter is followed by tears, life by death, summer by autumn. This is the way of things. Perhaps, then, it was inevitable that the ecstasy of my initiation into sexual love was followed by the agony of separation and loss. But I did not foresee it – neither the horror itself, nor the form which it took.

Before I left the lady Laura's house that night, I took with her the Oath of Renunciation, in which I swore to her (and she to me) and to 'the one true God' that I would henceforward live a life which scorned, despised and rejected all carnal pleasure. The form this renunciation was to take was clear and precise: I would abstain from all sexual acts, either with myself or another, or I would engage in them only to abuse their meaning and purpose. I was not entirely sure exactly how the latter would work out in practice, but I understood its import, and I was still too inebriated with the heady brew of my lovemaking with the lady Laura, to really care.

When I returned home, I heard my mother moving about in the grubby little cubicle that served as a kitchen, but I did not wish to see her or speak with her; it would have been like mouthing blasphemies after deep prayer. I went straight to sleep, curled up on my mattress on the floor, and dreamed of paradise.

It was while I was doing the rounds with my mother the following morning, grunting and gasping as I heaved the cart over the tortuous cobbles, that I heard an urgent, frightened voice hiss in my ear:

"Go to the house! They have taken her!"

I turned at once, but saw no-one, neither did I recognize the voice. I thought for a moment it might have been Pietro, but could not be sure. There were hurried footsteps echoing somewhere in a nearby alley, but nothing more. My mother was haggling in a flirty manner with a grizzled old man in a doorway. I set the cart down on its supporting struts and began to run. Or at any rate, what *I* thought of as running.

"Hey! Where the devil do you think you're going?" I heard my mother's voice call behind me, angry and confused. Then I was aware of nothing more, nothing but the blood pounding in my ears as I forced my twisted little legs to move faster.

The doors of the palazzo courtyard were gaping open; so too were the doors to the apartment, as I discovered when I arrived breathless and trembling at the top of the stairs. There was a tall man dressed in some kind of clerical uniform in the little anteroom.

"Where is she? Where is the lady Laura?"

He turned to look at me. His face, gaunt and sallow under a tight cap of close-cropped black hair, assumed an expression of supreme *hauteur* mingled with vague annoyance.

"Name?" he said.

"The lady Laura Francesca Beatrice de' Collini."

"Not hers, idiot. Yours." He spat out the words, harshly staccato.

"Giuseppe Amadonelli. Where have you taken her?"

"If you value your freedom, little cripple, you would do well to demonstrate less eagerness to know the whereabouts of the lady. Are you a friend of hers?"

Somehow, the instinct in me that counselled caution overcame my fury and distress.

"No, not a friend. She's one of my mother's customers – my mother sells wine. The lady Laura owes us money."

"She wouldn't owe anyone anything. You're lying."

"No."

His deep-set eyes smouldered with a ruthlessness, the intensity of which frightened me. He smiled crookedly.

"You can come with me," he said.

"But I can't – I've got to get back to my mother –"

"You should never have left her."

"She needs me to help her sell the wine," I said.

"Then it's her unlucky day. You will come with me."

I turned to see two men in habergeons standing to attention in the doorway behind me. They each carried a cruel falchion. My heart began to thump in my chest, and its every wild beat punched out the rhythm of the name Laura Francesca Beatrice de' Collini.

I was taken to the sombre, smoke-grimed building standing in the shadow of the old basilica of St Peter; this was where those suspected or accused of heresy were taken, to be examined and to be given a chance to defend themselves. That I was now in the hands of the papal inquisitors was clear, and that the lady Laura was also being held somewhere in the same place, was indubitable. But why? What was her crime? Who had accused her of it? Whatever its nature, unless I conducted myself with consummate circumspection, it would become evident that it was also mine by adoption. I decided, therefore, that the only safe course was for me to become, once again, the ignorant little cripple from the Trastevere gutters.

I was put into a small, gloomy room with nothing in it save a single chair, and was told to wait – an unnecessary order, since I had no opportunity to do anything else. Or perhaps I am mistaken; for there was, indeed, only too much of an opportunity (which I involuntarily made the best of) to work myself into a pitiable mental and emotional state, speculating on the lady Laura's fate. This was the horror of it: whatever her fate, it could only be but singular, whereas I was able to create in my feverish imagination a wellnigh endless series of eventualities, each more ghastly than the one it succeeded. It is the same, I suppose, with a man who is facing death; in the tortuous fantasies of the night, as the slow hours crawl inexorably towards morning, he puts himself to death a thousand times over, with more agony and pain and humiliation than reality could ever inflict.

The man who had forced me here under armed escort now entered the room where I sat. He had changed into the habit of a Dominican friar.

"Well, well. Our friend the crook-back."

"Why am I here?"

"You will tell me the nature of your relationship with Laura de' Collini."

"But I told you already. She buys her wine from my mother."

"Don't take me for an idiot. People of her kind don't

60

buy anything from street vendors – least of all that donkey's piss you sell. How long have you known her?"

"I don't know her at all. It's true. We just want the money she owes."

He came and stood close by where I was sitting, and squatted down on his haunches, so that his yellowy, cruel face was level with mine.

"My name is Fra Tomaso della Croce," he said in an unctuous, infinitely threatening tone of voice, "and I have disputed with the greatest minds which heresy has been able to vomit up in the face of Our Holy Mother the Church. I have defeated them all with the sword of truth, bequeathed to us by Jesus Christ himself. Do you imagine for one moment that I have either the time or the inclination to listen to the pathetic lies of gutter-scum like you? I could have you thrown into prison here and now, at once, and the world would never hear of you again, which I dare say would be of considerable benefit to it. So, you will kindly tell me the precise nature of your relationship with Laura de' Collini, or I will cause you to regret the day your whore of a mother ever gave birth to you. Do I make myself clear?"

"It's true that my mother is a whore –"

He stood up.

"I have a better idea," he said. "Maybe a little face-to-face encounter with the noble lady will serve to refresh your memory. Come!"

They were holding her far below street level, in a crypt-like room that had obviously once been a dungeon; she was strapped to a large chair, her hair falling down over her shoulders, her eyes lowered, and I saw that her right cheek bore the marks of a blow – a long, scarlet stain that looked almost like blood against the creamy paleness of her skin. They had removed her shoes. Sitting at a table placed against the wall opposite her was some kind of monk; the cowl of his habit was pulled up over his head, making every feature save the tip of his nose invisible – a face

61

composed of darkness and shadows. In front of him were sheets of parchment, some loose, others rolled up and tied with black ribbon. There were writing materials.

"I've brought a friend to see you," the man called Fra Tomaso said softly.

The lady Laura raised her head fractionally and looked at me with eyes that were absolutely expressionless.

"I do not know him," she said. "You must have made a mistake."

"He claims to know *you*, however."

My heart was in my mouth.

"Yes. I think we buy wine from him. I do not take notice of every cripple who comes hawking to our door."

For a single moment – even less than a moment! – I thought, indeed I *knew*, that those lovely eyes glanced at me with an infinitely tender, depthlessly melancholy apology. I tried, by meeting that glance and holding it, before it vanished like a particle of ice plunged into fire, to tell her that I understood.

"He tells me that you owe him money for wine."

"Does he? How fascinating. I would not know. My father arranges the household accounts together with Luca, our head steward."

"Your father is not in Rome," the Dominican said. "Indeed, he seems to have abandoned it altogether, these past six years."

"Which is the only reason why you have dared to bring me here!" the lady Laura said, suddenly contemptuously angry. "If my father had been here –"

"But he *isn't* here, is he? And you would do well not to play the offended patrician's daughter with me. A heretic has no rights. A heretic cannot afford the luxury of outraged dignity."

"Who calls me a heretic?"

"That is not pertinent to our investigation. It is you yourself who are under interrogation, no other. Except perhaps your deformed little friend here."

He turned to the monk at the desk.

"Read the charge," he said.

The cowled head nodded, and the monk's voice, thin and harsh with the self-righteous malice of fanaticism, began to read the anonymous charge aloud.

"That on the seventh day of the calendar month of June in the year of Our Lord fourteen hundred and ninety-six, you, Laura Francesca Beatrice de' Collini, and on every seventh day for an unspecified period of time both before and after the stated seventh day of the calendar month of June, did, in the house of Andrea de' Collini, patrician of Rome, wilfully and maliciously teach a doctrine contrary to the truth revealed by Our Lord and Saviour Jesus Christ and entrusted to Our Holy Mother the Church through the Roman Pontiff, Vicar of Christ on Earth and Successor to the Prince of the Apostles, viz., that God the Father of mankind did not create this world, that it was fashioned by a demon, that what the stated demon has fashioned is, of its nature, evil in the sight of God the Father of mankind. Further, that on the stated occasions, in the company of other unidentified persons, you did deny the doctrine of the Incarnation of Our Lord and Saviour Jesus Christ, that you likened his earthly body to a phantasm of incorporeal form, and that together with the stated unidentified persons, you did wilfully and maliciously deny the temporal and spiritual power given to our lord pope, the Roman Pontiff, and his successors in perpetuity, by Our Lord and Saviour Jesus Christ, through the person of the Blessed Apostle Peter."

"The charge is extremely grave," Fra Tomaso said.

"It is certainly long-winded."

"Do not clown with me, *donna*. It ill becomes you. Do you deny the charge?"

"Of course."

"What are the names of these other unidentified people? You would do well to tell me, since they will not remain long unidentified."

"If they will not remain long unidentified, you hardly need me to tell you their names."

"You admit they exist, then?"

"No. But I am polite enough to converse with you on

your own assumptions, however much in error they may be."

"The devil's rhetoric!" cried Fra Tomaso, incensed, and he struck the lady Laura on the side of her head, so hard that it snapped back, as if some marionette's string had been suddenly and viciously plucked by an unseen hand.

I wanted to scream out *Leave her! Don't touch her!* I wanted to throw myself onto him, pound at his body with my bare fists, beat the life out of him; instead, I heard my small, ineffectual voice pleading:

"Don't hurt her anymore – please don't hurt her –"

He turned, grabbed a handful of my hair, and lifted me off my feet. The pain was excruciating. Then he let me drop.

"Speak once more," he hissed, "and you'll never see the sun again."

I lay sprawled and twisted where I had fallen, sobs of fury at my impotence, my uselessness, my helpless, stunted, ugly body, wracking me. There and then, my face buried in the crook of my arm, I silently cursed – with every curse that the Trastevere gutters had taught me! – the nameless and malefic being who had imprisoned me in a cage of flesh and bone and mucus. I cursed him, his minions and agents, his principalities and powers; I cursed the pope, the pope's cardinals and catamites and painted whores; I cursed kings and emperors and bishops; I cursed everything and everyone I could think of. And I cursed the suppurating, filthy womb which had propelled me, reluctant and screaming, into this abysmal world.

"You will name your accomplices," Fra Tomaso repeated quietly.

"I have none."

"You are a liar. Admit the charge and they will be unharmed."

"Those who do not exist are immune to harm already, with or without your dubious guarantees."

I heard the sound of another blow, followed by a low cry of pain.

64

"Admit the charges. You cannot hide your guilt. We have evidence."

"If you already know my guilt and possess evidence of it, you do not need my admission."

Fra Tomaso's voice became taut, tensile, like an overdrawn bowstring.

"You are wasting my time. The instrument will be applied."

"I shall not give you any answer other than the one I have made."

"Pain will help you to change your mind."

Even now, after so many years, the recollection of what followed fills me with anguish; the memory of it grips my heart like an icy vice. As I write, I know that tears will soon come. A huge and heavy sadness covers me like a shroud, and I cannot shake it off; indeed, I do not want to – for every act of recall, every rearoused memory of what they did to her, merits the expiation of a fresh agony of the soul. A sword pierced and entered the fabric of my psyche that day, and it is there still, for I feel its blade, as sharp and as deadly as ever, move between the infinitesimal spaces where socket meets socket and joint meets joint.

The instrument was applied. The work was done by two hugely-built, silent men who concentrated on nothing but their own brute efficiency, as dispassionate and as objective as a fatal disease. Her head was held back, a long band of muslin was placed over her mouth which was forcibly prised open, and from a stone jar they poured in cold water. She moaned and writhed, choking and gasping. I saw the contours of her throat, suffused with blood, knotted with pulsating veins, throbbing in an agony of suffocation.

"Tell me the names of your fellow heretics," the Dominican said, removing the linen band.

"There – there are – none –"

It was reapplied. I could not look up. Even with my fingers in my ears, I could hear her pitiful retching.

"Tell me their names."

Silence.

"It is not my will that you should suffer. Tell me their names."

Again, the wracking gasps.

"Tell me their names, and this torment will cease."

Then they placed a metal circlet about her naked foot, to the inside of which was affixed needle-sharp points. It was tightened by means of a small, threaded handle.

"Tell me their names."

Her screams rang out in that terrible room, and I saw blood, fresh and hot, seeping down across her clenched toes. Still she did not speak.

"Again. Again. Tighter."

A pitiful, ophicleidic wail of agony.

Fra Tomaso sighed deeply, and I saw him motion to the torturers.

"This interrogation is suspended," he said wearily. "It will resume again when I so instruct." Then, to the monk at the desk: "Be certain that you write 'suspended.' It is not yet concluded."

The lady Laura was slumped in her chair motionless, her head on her chest.

"I have no further use for you, little cripple," he said to me. "You have not been accused. But I know someone who *might* be pleased to take you. Stand up."

I hauled myself to my feet, my eyes fixed on his sallow face, my heart overflowing with a vast and terrible loathing. I had not even loathed the woman who called herself my mother, as I loathed the Dominican.

He said:

"Take him outside."

As they bent back my arms and dragged me to the door, the lady Laura managed to glance at me surreptitiously; miraculously, the swollen lips shaped themselves to form a single unspoken word: *Master.* Master!

What did she mean? What Master? And where?

Master . . .

Then a chamber in my heart slammed shut as I looked back upon that sweet, sweetest, pain-darkened face.

Libera, Domine, animam servi tui

My life now took a completely new and unexpected turn; the 'someone' whom the Dominican Fra Tomaso della Croce thought might have a use for me was a sly, avaricious, unprincipled bastard (in both the literal and the figurative sense) by the name of Antonio Donato, who called himself 'Master Antonio' and claimed to be related to certain members of the Florentine nobility, but who in fact made his living by travelling around with a freak show and exhibiting his freaks in whatever town or city was prepared to accommodate him. I was now numbered among that select little group.

"Hmm," he said, looking me up and down doubtfully, his cadaverous features creased in a melancholy frown. "Not much of you, is there? Christ and his Holy Mother only knows how that pious shit-eater managed to get twenty ducats out of me for you."

"Twenty ducats?" I echoed.

"That's right. That's twice what I normally pay."

"Normally? I don't understand."

"I quite often have occasion to do business with our holy and self-righteous friend the inquisitor. Generally speaking, I take the remains of the poor cunts he's had cut up and knocked about. Why shove 'em in gaol and fork out good money to keep 'em alive, when he can get a reasonable price from me? You'd be surprised what you can do with a heretic whose tongue has been pulled out, or feet burned off. I once had someone I used to exhibit as the 'Human Pincushion'. God knows what they did to *him*. I didn't make inquiries, if you know what I mean. I never do. Still, at least with me you'll be fed and kept warm, and that can't be all bad. Just think: you could have gone to the stake."

"I hate him."

"Who?"

"Tomaso della Croce."

Master Antonio shook his greasy head.

"Look," he said, "you're mine now, I bought you, and you'll have no time for private vendettas. I warn you Shorty, you'll do as I say, or I'll have you thrashed – and I *mean* thrashed. Be a good boy, and you'll make out alright. Now sod off and get something to eat. Christ's bones, I don't know what we're going to make of you – I'll have to think about that. We'll see. Go on, go and meet your new friends. They're waiting."

"I hate him," I repeated quietly.

Master Antonio looked at me for a moment, his eyes deliberating, wondering. Then he said:

"Take my advice, Shorty: bury the pain. I don't know what it is, and I don't want to know. Bury it. Forget it. I've got no use for it. If you try to live with pain, you'll end up dying of it. Even an ugly-looking bastard like you must want to live."

"How do you know?"

"Sod off and come back later."

I did not bury the pain. I did not wish to bury the pain. I was incapable of burying the pain. I lived with it, but I did not die of it, as Master Antonio had predicted. It was always there, gnawing at my heart, sucking my blood, feeding on my innards. It filled my dreams, turning them into nightmares, and I cried out in my sleep, fending off dark chimeras; I did battle with chameleon-like foes who changed their shape the moment I grasped them; I was pursued by cowled monks with invisible faces, and strident, pitiless voices that shrieked *Heresy! Heresy!* in my head.

Above all, the inward vision of *her* lovely face marked me day and night, like a fresh cicatrice, and I frequently fell into fits of wracking, uncontrollable sobbing. The anguish of our separation tore me apart; worse still, my ignorance of her fate accused me like a festering guilt. She was ceaselessly by my side, yet brutally taken from me, and with every beat of my heart I silently whispered her name: *Laura, Laura, oh Laura!*

No, I did not die, but lived on. Perhaps I was kept alive by my hate for Fra Tomaso della Croce, I do not know; all I know is that the resilience of the human spirit is astonishing, and in the midst of unendurable pain, I managed to adapt myself to the new life that had been forced upon me. There were even moments – rare and tenuous, I admit – when I was actually able to displace my preoccupation with my own misery with other concerns; and for this, even though (perhaps *because*) such moments came as a relief, I cursed myself fervently.

We travelled from place to place in a sort of extended caravan of horses and carts, but our progress was tediously slow, since the horses were in the main tired, aged beasts, and we needed to stop constantly to rest and water them. Master Antonio was ever solicitous for their well-being; indeed, he thought more of the horses than he did of his wretched collection of freaks. We were housed in what I can only describe as covered wagons, two occupants to each; Master Antonio's precious 'equipment' followed up the rear: bundles of long wooden poles, bolts of hemp cloth, oil for the lamps, sacking, dried and salted fish and meat, water, various other kinds of preservable provisions, and the tatty, stained bills to announce our arrival in the town, which Master Antonio solemnly told us he had had handmade in Germany at great cost. We slept late in the morning, travelled in the afternoon, and 'performed' at night. Nobody ever tried to escape: some were physically incapable of attempting it, while others – guilty of some crime or other (usually thieving or heresy) – knew that they would be hunted down and killed as soon as they left the caravan. They were safer with Master Antonio.

My own situation seemed to confuse Nino, with whom I shared a wagon; Nino was advertised as 'The Barbary

Ape', because he was simian in appearance and extremely hairy. Artificial hair was added to his face and body, and he wore special gloves and leggings that were not only hairy, but ended in great, curved, horny talons. It was a ridiculous get-up, but it was enough to fool the gullible and to give the impression of a creature which was neither ape nor man, but something rather nasty in between. This, of course, provided the element of vaguely threatening mystery, so necessary to attract the customers.

"I do a bit of roaring and growling," he said, "enough to make them feel just a mite afraid, even though they know they're safe enough. It's the *thrill,* see?"

"Not really, no."

"Same as sex."

"A *frisson* of quite another kind," I said musingly.

"A what?"

"It doesn't matter."

"Where did you learn to talk fancy like that? I thought you told me you're from Trastevere –"

"So I am, but it's a long story. Don't tell Master Antonio, or I'll be in trouble."

"Don't worry, I won't. I wouldn't tell that fucker how many lumps of shit come out of me in the morning. But what I can't understand is why you're here in the first place."

"I'm a heretic." At any rate, I supposed that's what I was.

"And you got away from the Inquisition?"

"No. They let me go. Well, actually, they sold me to Master Antonio. To be perfectly precise, one man sold me to Master Antonio."

"You weren't accused, then?"

"No."

"Then what in the name of Christ Almighty is keeping you *here*?"

"I wish I knew, Nino. I have to find someone, but I don't know where to look."

"What someone?"

"He is called 'The Master'."

Nino shrugged his hairy shoulders.

"Never heard of him," he said. "You want to feel my prick? It's like a baby's arm."

"Yes, I know, but no thanks, if it's all the same to you."

"Well excuse me, won't you? A big fella like mine needs a lot of seeing to."

By 'seeing to his big fella,' Nino meant masturbating, which he proceeded to do, turning over onto his side on the pile of foetid sacking beneath us, and pulling down his grubby hose.

"Must be something to do with the bumping of the wagon," he murmured, then he fell silent save for the occasional low moan.

Nino appeared quite naked as 'The Barbary Ape', since an ape was an animal, and no-one could be prosecuted for exhibiting a naked animal; the customers, unsurprisingly, could never quite make up their minds, but when they saw that massive, misshapen chimera, you could almost *hear* them struggling with incredulity. Nino was paraded by one of Antonio's cronies on a long, golden chain, affixed to a gold collar studded with garish glass beads around his thick, rugose neck; the crony walked him up and down, patting him affectionately on the back, occasionally prodding him in the private parts with the toe of his boot.

"Don't come too close, ladies and gentlemen, don't come too close if you please! He's a quiet beast in my hands, but that's because I feed him, and I can't guarantee he'd be the same with you. Stay clear, little one! Look at those eyes, ladies and gentlemen, look at that savage gleam! Now don't you fret about him running loose and murdering you all in your beds, because that isn't likely to happen; no, we've got him well under lock and key here, ladies and gentlemen, I do assure you of that. Straight from the dark and steamy forests, this one came, torn from the arms of his stinking comrades – apes are none too particular about the company they keep, you understand."

71

A few people usually sniggered at this, taking it as a comment on the keeper himself – known to us as 'Arseface Arnoldo' – but the joke was beyond him. "Howled and moaned the whole night long, so they did. Took seven strong men to chain him up, just so you could have the privilege of seeing him here tonight!"

While this diatribe was being recited, Nino made little grabbing gestures, and occasionally managed to catch someone's robe – usually a woman's; there was always an outburst of frightened shrieking, and sometimes several of the men drew their swords in braggardly outrage. Nino growled, then he let the robe drop and made whimpering noises. The ladies applauded and the men who had drawn their swords strutted and preened. The men who had not drawn their swords looked sheepish.

The end of the show came when Nino started waggling his finger about in his mouth and Arseface Arnoldo announced:

"If you'll excuse us now, ladies and gentlemen, these here beasts from the wild get up to things that no decent Christian ever should –" and here he would wink conspiratorially at the men, "– eh, gents? And I don't think this is quite something the ladies would care to see."

As they were herded towards the exit however, he went on, in a lower tone of voice:

"Nevertheless, if any of you fine gentlemen here would care to pay an extra half-ducat, I think we could extend the show for private entertainment only."

Usually, about half a dozen men did remain, paying the extra, and the 'private entertainment' consisted of watching Nino apparently *eat* a live rat; actually, all he did was bite the head off, spit it out, and make chomping, slurping noises. Even so, this was sickening enough, and some of the strongest stomachs rebelled against the sight. They goggled as the head of the panic-stricken rodent disappeared into his mouth; they gasped as the dark, gelatinous blood oozed from between his lips. When he ejected it, which he did with great shrieks and cries which the ladies who had been sent outside were intended to hear, the entertainment was concluded.

"There we are, gentlemen, well worth half a ducat, as I'm sure you will agree. You've seen something no godfearing Christian ever will again, nor ought to. I bid you goodnight."

At that moment, Nino uttered a long, shuddering sigh of satisfaction, his caducous pleasure ended, and rolled over onto his back.

"That's better," he murmured.

I was suddenly struck by an inspired idea.

"Nino," I said, "you know that Master Antonio still doesn't know what to exhibit me as, don't you?"

"Yes, I did hear. You're a bit of a problem, I think."

"How about if I work with you?" I said.

"But I already work with Arseface Arnoldo."

"I know that, but I've got a better idea. Listen!"

Nino sat up, leaning on his elbows. The acrid smell of his sweaty feet in that enclosed space was overpowering.

"Arseface Arnoldo has you on that chain because he's the man and you're the ape, right?"

"I suppose."

"What if we were to reverse the order of things, and *you* were to hold the chain? Wouldn't that be something? Then, instead of a man exhibiting an ape, we could have an ape exhibiting a man!"

"But who would I exhibit?"

"Me!" I announced triumphantly.

"*You?*"

"But of course! What else? They'll not have seen the like before, I tell you! Why, an ape exhibiting a man? It's never been done. They'll flock in droves to see us, believe me."

Nino shook his head slowly, but a light was beginning to dawn in his black eyes.

"It doesn't sound right to me, Peppe," he said. "It might be against the Bible."

"Have you ever read the Bible?"

73

"Of course not, I can't read. Besides, that's what we've got the priests for."

"Well I *have,* and it doesn't say anything about an ape exhibiting a man being wrong."

"It could be heresy, though," he said. Then he added wistfully: "So many things are."

"What does that matter? We're all thieves or heretics here, anyway."

"But how could I exhibit you? I'm supposed to be an ape, I can't do any talking. That'd give the game away."

"Will you stop fribbling and listen to me, Nino? You told me a while ago that we have to *thrill* them, right?"

"Right."

"What bigger thrill could they have, than a complete reversal of the order of nature? It wouldn't just thrill, it would completely shock. Especially if we banned the younger ladies from the show – say, anyone under sixteen. That would bring everybody else flocking. And you needn't worry about the talking, I'll do that. I'll do it in a way that nobody else would be able to match – I'll paint pictures with words! I'll use words they've never heard of before, I'll spin gold and silver with words and leave their minds reeling! I'll take them to a strange and dangerous world with words, I'll make them *feel* the hot, malodorous forest nights, the harsh cries of weird and wonderful creatures, I'll make them see and touch and taste and smell the horror and the savagery, and the heat of an alien sun – all with words!"

"What about the private entertainment for gentlemen only, afterwards?"

"Do you *enjoy* biting the heads off live rats?"

"Of course I don't; it's disgusting."

"Then we'll scrap it, and I'll think of something else."

"What, exactly?"

"I don't know, but I'll come up with something, believe me."

"It's okay by me," Nino said. "All you've got to do now is convince that bastard Antonio."

"That's no problem. It won't take me long to convince *him*."

And as it transpired, it didn't.

"You think it'll bring in the crowds, eh?" he said, rubbing his unshaven chin.

"Bring them in? Why, I tell you, you'll have to employ half-a-dozen strong men to keep them out!"

"I can't afford to hire any more –"

"Poetic exaggeration," I said hastily. "You'll be knee-deep in half-ducats."

"Are you sure you can manage Arseface Arnoldo's patter? How did you come to be such a dab hand with fancy words?"

"You told me once that you never inquire into the backgrounds of your purchases. Don't inquire now. Just trust me. This will make you a wealthy man, I promise."

He looked me up and down.

"I *am* right," I said. "One hundred percent."

"Okay Shorty, you're on."

Nino and I were billed the following night as *"Man versus Ape: a Tragedy of Nature."*

We were, just as I predicted, an enormous success; in fact, Master Antonio had to put on an extra show to accommodate the huge numbers of people who came to see us. The big canvas tent in which we worked stank, and with the great crowd crushing in, the atmosphere was stifling. The oil-lamps flickered and spluttered in the gust of over two hundred simultaneous exhalations of astonishment as the sacking that concealed us was drawn back, creating an eerie, other-worldly dappling of light and shadow, a *chiaroscuro* of good and evil, the human and the bestial.

Nino held the golden chain that was attached to my collar, in one great gloved fist, the fake talons curled. I paced to and fro as I spoke, as far as the chain would allow me to. Then Nino yanked me back, uttering a low, throaty growl. The conclusion of my patter (which was quite magnificent, if I may be allowed to say so) was based upon an inspired reference to my own deformity.

"Let me tell you something further, my friends. Look at me, regard me well. What do you see? A pathetic, twisted, stunted form, a cripple, a crook-back! Who would wish for the prison of such a shape as this? Yet – yet once I was not so."

There were gasps. Nino jerked the chain a little, and drew me closer to himself. The people at the front of the crowd moved back hastily.

"Indeed I was not. Once I was tall and strong and straight, as tall and strong and straight as Adonis himself. Then what came to pass? What terrible affliction came upon me, you ask, to reduce me from a man to a midget? I will tell you now: it was the life-sucking humours and vile airs of that dark and sickly forest world into which I so foolishly ventured. Yes – alas! –"

I sobbed a little, and buried my face in my hands.

"They shrank me, and that is the literal truth. As washed skins drying in the sun will shrink, so I shrank. My body was drained of its vital fluids, my bones knitted together, my blood thickened, my flesh welded and hardened, growing knotty and coarse. I once was a man. I became – I became but half a man, a human gewgaw."

Nino lunged out at the crowd, and there were shrieks, but no drawn swords; they were still too much under the tale of horror I had woven, to be able to react.

"And now my friends, I must ask the ladies among you to depart. The beast requires me to perform an act upon him that is too depraved for feminine eyes. Those gentlemen who wish to witness the depths of my shame and the immensity of the tragedy which has fallen upon me, may pay their half-ducats now."

All the ladies and only one gentleman left. There were still over a hundred people in the tent when I stood between Nino's legs, and 'performed the act' upon him, the nature of which I leave to your own imaginations to guess at. And of course, there were over a hundred extra half-ducats in the collection sack at the end of the performance.

"I'm delighted, Shorty!" Master Antonio cried, baring his carious teeth in a broad grin. "Look at that! Why, there must be –"

"You will give Nino and myself one quarter each of the extra takings for the first performance of every evening. Just the first."

The grin faded immediately.

"Just the *what?*"

"You heard me. One quarter each of the extra takings. You keep the remaining half for the first performance, and the whole lot for the second and third."

"Why, you thieving, conniving little cunt! I'll thrash the life out of you, see if I don't! One quarter each? You'll get nothing from me, crook-back."

"Then you won't get any more performances like to-night, and you'll lose money."

"You can't bargain with me – you're mine, I bought you, remember? You filthy, witless little heretic –"

"Listen to me, Antonio: if you do not pay us what I ask, then we will not perform, and you cannot make us. That means you will be over fifty ducats down on every show, because the customers won't want to hear Arseface Arnoldo's diatribe after tonight. You'll have an empty tent. Give Nino and myself a quarter each, and you will be twenty-five ducats up on the first peformance, and fifty ducats on the other two. Three shows a night, that makes one hundred and twenty-five ducats a night. Six nights a week, that makes –"

"I know what it makes, you stinking bastard!" Antonio screamed, but he clearly saw the logic of my argument.

"Besides which," I said, "I do not consider twenty-five ducats too much for jerking off Nino three times a night. Take it or leave it."

He took it.

*

77

At the time of which I write, Italy was being torn apart by conflict and chaos. In 1498, two years after I had begun jerking off the Barbary Ape three times nightly, six years after Giovanni de' Medici had been elevated to the cardinalate, and four years after Alexander VI Borgia had ascended to the throne of Peter, Louis, Duke of Orleans, had succeeded Charles VIII to the throne of France, and he had at once claimed the title *King of France, Jerusalem and Sicily, and Duke of Milan*. The French invaded our shores for a second time, with the intention of taking Milan. One of the reasons why our grotesque caravan moved continually north was that Master Antonio, for all his limited acumen, realised that there might be too much trouble for us south, in the Kingdom of Naples and beyond, which was still licking its wounds after being raped by the French – Charles VIII had been crowned 'King of Sicily and Jerusalem' in the cathedral at Naples only three years earlier; the Republics of Perugia, Urbino and Siena offered us a more hopeful prospect. In fact, although the French forces of the first invasion had been quickly driven out after Charles' return to France, unrest and fear continued to haunt the countryside, and everyone knew that it would not be long before Louis, once Milan was taken, would turn his attention to Naples. What nobody could possibly know or anticipate was the fearsome havoc that Caesare Borgia, Pope Alexander's bastard son, would wreak on the whole of the Romagna in his lust for power; in this, he was assisted and encouraged by Louis, whose marriage Alexander had obligingly dissolved, leaving him free to wed Anne of Brittany. Caesare Borgia had followed in the wake of Louis to Milan, but the chaos he was soon to inflict waited as yet in the wings. The man who was to become Pope Leo X, who was to enter my life and change its course irreversibly, was at this time travelling around Europe, for the Medicis had been expelled from their beloved Florence in 1494, and would not be able to return until seventeen years had passed.

None of this greatly affected the day to day lives of us

freaks, except to caution prudence in the direction of our travels, and occasionally to create a vague atmosphere of forboding, which put Master Antonio in a pessimistic mood, and therefore also a vicious temper. Indeed, news of the political turmoil spread slowly, in frustratingly incomplete chunks: a little gossip picked up here, rumours abroad there, a declaration pasted up on the wall of some rural town, speculation and surmise and uncertainty. With myself and Nino, Master Antonio was unfailingly surly, reluctantly delighted with the money we were making him, and ungraciously frustrated that he had to give a minute fraction of it to us. Everybody in the caravan became moody, snappish, keeping themselves to themselves; this was a pity, because on the whole we tended to be a friendly lot among ourselves, for our wretched condition forged a common loyalty – speaking of which, I think now is the time for me to tell you of the other exhibits in our little company.

There was Luigi, who was billed as 'The Human Snake' because his skin, afflicted with some disease the likes of which I had never seen before, appeared serpentine in a half-light; they painted him of course, and made him wear some ridiculous garment on his lower body which covered his legs, so that he finished in a 'tail' instead of feet. Luigi told me he had raped a nun, and had escaped from prison by dressing as a woman, but this seemed unlikely to me. Then there was Beppo, 'The Two-Headed Man', who was nothing of the kind; however, there grew upon his neck a large excrescence of fleshy matter, out of which they created another little head, and by carefully flexing the muscles of his shoulders, Beppo could make this mannequin head 'move.' Beppo was a matricide. Don Giuseppe however (he insisted that he should retain his title), was a former priest who had preached heresy in the church of Santa Maria dei Monti in Rome, and had been found guilty not only of this, but also of blasphemy, and of abusing the sacrament of confession by physically molesting his women penitents. He was a bitter, self-pitying creature,

79

and I did not greatly care for him, yet the story he told was remarkable: unrepentant, he was condemned to the stake, but before the flames could devour him, an unexpected and unpredicted storm broke with surprising rapidity, and the torrent of rain unleashed by it extinguished them. Under cover of the smoke and in the general confusion, he managed to snap his bonds, half-consumed by the fire, and escape. He had met Master Antonio in a tavern and had been taken on and promised safety in return for his services; these services entailed appearing three times nightly as 'the Skull' – for his ordeal by fire, though ultimately and by disposition of providence not fatal, had burned away much of the skin on the lower half of his face, and now the bone beneath visibly gleamed. When he bared his teeth (he never smiled), the effect was truly horrific. And there was Antonella, a woman of fifty years or so, who was exhibited as nothing other than herself; she had murdered all five of her children in a fit of madness, and was presented as 'Satan's Daughter'. She sat on a chair in her tent, bound and gagged, and one of the hired hands stood beside her, attired as an executioner, a burning torch clutched in one fist. The real point of this tableau was to bring to life the patter that accompanied it, in which she was luridly described as an adulteress, a whore, a Jew-sucker, a miser who had killed her children for money (it was never explained exactly how their deaths could have been of financial benefit), and a devil-worshipper. Every night, three times a night, the poor woman was cursed, spat upon and abused. Her face was scarred where people had scratched at her in hatred. My heart sometimes wept for her. Incredibly, the fit of madness which had afflicted her and provoked her to her appalling crime had entirely vanished, and thus she endured this endlessly repeated horror as a perfectly sane woman. Being sane, she was also overwhelmed by the most dreadful guilt, and several times attempted to do away with herself. Once, she tried to claw her own breasts off. She spoke to no-one, and at night we could hear her crooning to herself in her wagon, crooning and sobbing and muttering. Master Antonio had purchased her from a corrupt magistrate and she had been with him for twelve years. My mind could not grasp it fully: twelve years of insults, spittle, blows and curses. I had made up my mind that before I abandoned Master Antonio and his caravan of freaks forever, I would bestow upon her the greatest mercy possible, and kill her as she slept – if she ever slept.

Il Mago Cieco was neither a magician nor blind, despite his billing; his name was Luca della Cordina, and he told fortunes by means of a special pack of cards and a mirror. The heaven-blessed destinies he dished out to his customers were utter drivel of course, but that didn't seem to matter. His costume, of which he was inordinately proud, was that of a Moorish potentate. There had only ever been one problem in his long career with Master Antonio, and that was when the same man came on two different nights, and was given two quite different predictions.

"How was I to know?" *Il Mago Cieco* complained. "On Monday I told him he was destined for priestly orders, and would become a rich and important bishop. On Tuesday night I said he'd have twelve children by a young and beautiful woman."

"Don't the two *usually* go together?" I said.

"The customer didn't seem to think so, the humourless bastard. He demanded his money back. I'm sure Master Antonio would have docked it out of my wages, if I hadn't protested."

"He doesn't pay us any wages."

"I know, but it's the thought that counts."

There were several other minor freaks – what we major freaks called 'tiddlers' – but none of these are really worth mentioning in detail. There were also half-a-dozen or so 'normal' and exceedingly brawny men (they were known to us, contemptuously, as *goyim*) who looked after the equipment and took care of troublemakers.

The thought of Laura and what might have happened to her was of course always tormenting me too, but I had begun to learn how to endure that particular pain without showing it; sometimes, at the end of the evening, I was too exhausted even to feel pain.

"Jerking you off is tiring work," I said to Nino one night, as we settled down to sleep in our wagon. When he took the clawed leggings off, the smell of his unwashed feet was almost unendurable.

"Yes, I reckon it is," he said, "with a monster like mine."

Then he did an extraordinary thing: he leaned over me, placed his rough lips against my cheek, and kissed me with an exquisite reverence and dignity.

"Still," he whispered, "I'm glad it's you."

I could not stop the tears flowing, and neither did I wish to. *I* was glad it was me, too – exceedingly so – for my thrice-nightly ministrations enabled me to truly live out the oath I had taken with the lady Laura; I had sworn not to indulge in sexual activity, or to do so only with the intention of scorning and abusing it. This is exactly what I did every time I masturbated Nino, with that leering crowd of hypocritical perverts gawping lasciviously. On one level, I was totally disgusted by something which I found repellent in the extreme, yet on another, deeper level, I rejoiced, for I was fulfilling the oath I had sworn to the 'one true God.' What I did with Nino expressed all my abiding scorn for the flesh in which we are imprisoned, for its loathsome and wicked purpose – which is to imprison yet more souls – and it became for me a private curse on the flesh. It became a curse and, I hope, a fervent benediction on the poor, mutilated, deformed wretches whom Master Antonio kept in servitude, and for every poor, mutilated and deformed wretch in the world.

Calling to mind my oath meant also calling to mind the inward vision of Laura, so that the curse, the benediction, the oath and the act together, constituted a single sweet pain, a commingling of horror and joy, and a transmutation of one into the other.

Florence was the big dream; Florence hung on the horizon

82

like a never-setting sun, all seduction, all glorious gold and crimson light, all sweet promise. Except we always seemed to be in a permanent state of nearly getting there but never actually doing so. Once, we went as far north as Genoa, passing by Florence altogether, as if Master Antonio had suddenly decided that Florence didn't matter so much after all. In fact, by the time we finally *did* get there, I had been one of Master Antonio's freaks for seven long years. It was 1503. In many ways it was a remarkable year. Caesare Borgia, after a rapaciously bloody campaign in the Romagna, was fully established in a power which, whilst in theory belonging to France, was absolutely his and his alone; as a matter of fact, he proved to be quite a good ruler, and replaced the anarchy which had hitherto prevailed (for the most part attributable to him) with an admirable degree of order. However, his father Pope Alexander died – as the result of ingesting some of his own fatal poison, it was said -and Caesare did not last long after that, succumbing to a mysterious illness, most probably poison-related, which is hardly surprising when one considers the predilection of the Borgias for that particular substance. The new pope, Pius III, was old and sickly, and managed to cover the chair of Peter with his bony backside for only twenty-six days. Giulio della Rovere was elected in October 1503, and took the name of Julius II.

Leo, still Cardinal Giovanni de' Medici, whose fate the hand of destiny had yet to entwine with mine, had returned to Rome three years earlier, and was no doubt hoping for better conditions in Florence, which would permit the Medicis to come back from exile. Leo's brother Pietro had also died in 1503, which meant that Leo was now head of the family, for his handsome brother Giuliano was younger than him.

And the freaks arrived in Florence. Personally, I did not care for that city, for I found it too self-conscious and haughty by far, too supremely aware of its own lustrous pedigree. Even so, even with the Medicis in exile, it was, I found, the spirit and soul of that superb family, who were

83

all as arrogant as Lucifer anyway, and that includes my beloved Leo. The shade of Lorenzo the Magnificent, Leo's father, was everywhere, and it was unmistakable.

It has been said (I forget by whom) that if Cosimo de' Medici, Leo's grandfather, was the father of Florence, then Lorenzo the Magnificent was its child; he grew up, indeed, in the city that Cosimo was really responsible for creating. Cosimo had almost singlehandedly directed the great artistic and literary revival that the city had enjoyed, and Lorenzo was able to cultivate the friendship of the artists, men of letters, poets and philosophers who had surrounded him since childhood. It was Lorenzo who encouraged a new reverence for the Tuscan tongue, which had been scorned by an earlier generation of humanists, and he composed a defence of Italian which, accompanied by some passably pretty lyrics, he sent to Federigo of Naples. Federigo's reaction to this youthful *largesse* is not recorded. In fact, Lorenzo was quite a dab hand at poetry:

> *Ah, quanto poco al mondo ogni ben dura!*
> *Ma il rimembrar sì tosto non si parte.*

Sentiments I wholeheartedly endorse.

Among Lorenzo's circle of *intimes* were to be found Marsilio Ficino and Pico della Mirandola, both of whom I have already mentioned – the former dominated, as an arch-priest dominates a liturgy, the Platonic Academy. There was Cristoforo Landino, who had written a commentary on our blessed father Dante; Poliziano, himself a poet of considerable talent, and a classical scholar to boot; the fey and shy Domenico Ghirlandaio, the obese and hugely gifted Sandro Botticelli, who held a cold chicken leg in one hand and his brush in the other, and – after Lorenzo had inherited his father's mantle of power – there was a rather tortured, dark-browed young man called Michelangiolo Buonarroti, who had been introduced to Lorenzo by the sculptor Bertoldo.

Lorenzo had been totally identified with Florence; he

was Florence, and Florence was Lorenzo. Florence was the Medicis. Alas, the serpent in this Eden was Lorenzo's inclination to tyranny, which the fiercely independent spirit of the Florentines abhorred; all the constitutional changes he effected were designed to have but one single purpose: to place more power in his own hands. Claiming to be a citizen like all other citizens, he was nothing of the kind; his marriage to Clarice Orsini alone made it quite impossible to regard him as an equal among equals. And if the Florentine soul had a passion for anything, it was above all else a passion for equality. Even before Lorenzo's death, there had been rumblings of disaffection, and those rumblings gathered into a mighty storm which broke over the hapless head of Piero, Lorenzo's son, known to all and sundry as 'Peabrain', who had inherited his father's position in 1492.

It was in this city that the Dominican reformer Girolamo Savonarola had ranted and raved at the crowds, exhorting them to abandon their lives of worldly luxury and embrace the cross; he established a sort of 'Italian campaign' for the period of a year, 1494-1495, during which he composed a document called *Rule and Government of the City of Florence*, guidelines to a moral reform of the city which amounted to a theocracy. Great bonfires were lit, and lewd books, the writings of the Greek philosophers, even luxurious clothes, were thrown by a spellbound populace into the hungry flames. None of this suited poxy old Alexander VI Borgia, who summoned Savonarola to Rome in 1495 to give an account of the prophecies he had uttered concerning the Church, the city of Florence, Lorenzo the Magnificent (this one proved to be fairly accurate), and himself; knowing well what such a summons meant, the God-obsessed demagogue refused to go. Alexander responded in the usual way by excommunicating him, to little effect. However, the Franciscans managed to incite dissent among the populace, already growing weary of piety, and doubtlessly regarding with regret their empty libraries and wardrobes; so Franciscan jealousy of the little Dominican's prestige finally succeeded where Alexander's rumblings had failed, and Savonarola, after a brief period of incarceration, was executed in the public market-place in 1498. They say that his body had been so badly twisted under torture, it had to be forcibly straightened before they could get him onto the gibbet. All this, I think, suggests that it is a perilous thing to rouse other people's passions; for when all passion has passed, the heat that it generated is likely, in the end, to ignite the faggots piled high around the stake. Besides, Savonarola – like most religious fanatics – had failed to learn the lesson that nothing palls quite so quickly as an enthusiasm for goodness; the Florentines were forced to choose between their fine clothes, their pornographic books, their meat meals, and a mania for God. They opted for the former.

Small wonder, in view of this luxurious history, and despite the fact that the Medicis were in exile, that I detected Lorenzo's shade still lingering in the city, like the echo of a distant voice, when I arrived there with the rest of the freaks.

On the afternoon before the first performance, Master Antonio gathered us together to give us what was meant to be an edifying peroration. There we stood, twisted and stunted, hairy and scarred, burned and deformed and covered in scales, and with his hands on his hips, he said to us:

"Now then *ladies* and *gentlemen,* just because we're in the big city, there's no need to get any ideas about painting the town red. I know what abnormalities like you get up to when you're let loose in the world of us normal folk; why, I once had a little squirt of a thing who got pissed, humped a woman and started a fight all at the same time. Keep away from all those big-boobed Florentine tarts, and you'll come to no harm. Christ and his Holy Mother, they'll be throwing themselves at you! How could they possibly resist the likes of you lot?"

Finding this hugely, uproariously funny, he guffawed uncontrollably, reminding me of the time my mother had wet herself laughing at me. Recovering his composure rather more successfully than she had managed to do, he went on:

"Tonight's the big night, so I want a blisteringly good show. Skull, grin a bit more than you usually do – scare the shit out of them. Tragedy of Nature (Nino and myself), I want a bit more – a bit more –"

"Filth?" I suggested.

"That's it exactly. *Filth*. Peppe, when you toss Nino off, make sure they can see what you're up to; roll your eyes a bit, pant, gasp, look really *sexy*."

He paused momentarily, looked me up and down, then said:

"Well, no, perhaps that's asking a bit too much. Mind you, I think it would help if you could manage to have a hard-on yourself. And Nino – when you shoot your load, do you *possibly* think you could manage to point it away from the front row? I don't want anyone's laundry bill."

And so on. He went through the entire company, making suggestions (most of them obscene), offering the illuminating sagacity of "twenty-two years in the business", and generally criticising the performances we had given thus far. As he turned away, he said irritably to 'Satan's Daughter':

"Can't you look a bit more evil than that, woman? *Scowl*, for the love of Jesus!"

She stared straight through him.

As it happens, I think most of us *did* give 'blisteringly good' performances, except for *Il Mago Cieco*, who turned up in a state of advanced inebriation; he was of course the only one of us who could walk about the streets without attracting unwelcome attention, and had presumably found a low-class tavern, where he could (and did) sit and get quietly drunk. Before Nino and I went on, we heard that he had predicted to a lady customer that she would conceive a kind of second Jesus Christ, whose elect would be exclusively limited to Florentines.

"And how will it be done?" the lady had apparently asked, bright-eyed with eagerness and anticipation. "Will I be overshadowed by the Holy Ghost?"

"Not exactly, my dear. *I* shall be the child's father."

"By spiritual commingling of some kind, then?"

"No, the normal way."

He had thrown his clothes off, standing before her sweaty and erect; she had fled the tent in terror.

'A Tragedy of Nature' drew the usual huge crowd, and after the first performance, so many ladies wished to remain with the gentlemen to witness the 'private entertainment', that I decided to let them do so; I reckoned that Master Antonio would not regret losing a little of the titillation of secrecy for so many extra half-ducats. Besides, I had begun to accumulate quite a nest-egg with my share of the takings, and I thought this would be an excellent opportunity to bring it a bit closer to hatching.

Late that night, an incident occurred which was to swiftly change the immediate course of events for me; *Il Mago Cieco* came hurriedly to our wagon to tell me that a *lady* wished to speak with me. Nino was asleep, snoring gently.

"What lady?"

"How do I know, my dear fellow? Just so long as it's a lady, why by God's holy truth are you bothered about her name? I'll talk to her, if you like –"

"You'll do no such thing."

"They never fail to succumb to my natural charm, you know. I say, if you want her warmed up a bit before you take the plunge –"

"You're completely disgusting. Get out of here."

"No need to be offensive, my dear fellow! I was only suggesting –"

"*Get out!*"

"That's the trouble with you dwarves," he muttered, withdrawing. "Utterly selfish. Tiny dicks, insatiable appetites."

When I saw her I recognized her at once; indeed, it

would have been difficult not to, for her fur-trimmed cape had slipped back to reveal two plump, wiggling hands sprouting straight from the shoulders. She had no arms.

"I've come for you Peppe," she said in a calm, controlled voice. "We must leave this place as soon as possible."

It was Barbara Monduzzi.

– 1503 onwards –

Discedant omnes insidiae latentis inimici
The Master . . .

As it turned out, the Master was none other than the father of my beloved Laura de' Collini; the Master was Andrea de' Collini himself, patrician of Rome. To say that Barbara had surprised me with this information would be an understatement; but then, surprise had succeeded surprise that night, tumbling one on top of the other like the waves of an incoming tide. In the end, *nothing* was a surprise anymore.

"Peppe, look – *Vicolo del Fornaio* – this is the street. His house must be here."

"Are you certain?"

"I remember exactly what I was told."

Looking back upon events as I do now, I must honestly say that the details of what *I* was told remain indistinct; however, I learned that like myself Barbara had received no news of the lady Laura, and had spent much of her time in the house of an aunt on the lonely wilderness of the Aventine, assuming the role of companion and nurse, living in constant anxiety. Finally a message from Andrea de' Collini urging her to come to Florence put an end to this intolerable state of affairs; he informed her that I was already in the city, asked her to seek me out, then instructed her to bring me to his house under cover of darkness. Much later, I began to see that the Master never *ordered* you to do anything – he always asked very politely, but you always did it.

"Tomaso della Croce is in the city," Barbara had told me. "He is on his way to Genoa to examine a woman called Caterina who talks with the suffering souls in purgatory, a woman they say is a saint. She flies in the air, she faints in ecstasy."

Suddenly her voice rang out much louder in the stillness of the night:

"There! There is the house!"

It was a large door in the side of what appeared to be a small *palazzo*; the stucco was grimed and crumbling, the high windows set with protective criss-cross iron grids almost black with age or dirt or both. I could see no light.

"Knock," Barbara commanded, and I began to hammer on the ancient wood with my bare fists.

"This is a waste of time – nobody's here – we'll only succeed in waking up the whole world with this noise!"

"Listen – listen! – someone's coming!"

And indeed there came a dull, thudding sound from somewhere in the depths of the old house. I stopped banging. Then I heard the shuffle of slippered feet, and finally the bolts being drawn back.

"Who's there? Who is it?" a voice demanded.

The door opened and a tall man holding a lamp stood before us, his face invisible in the flickering shadows. He was wearing a long, dark robe with a fur collar.

"What do you want?" he said. The voice was suspicious, but not unkind; indeed, it was a voice, I instinctively felt, that was familiar with words of kindness.

"My name is Barbara Monduzzi," Barbara said, taking me aback somewhat by her boldness. "You sent for me – for both of us, I mean."

"And I am Giuseppe Amadonelli."

The man seemed to sigh – a quick, shallow sigh of either relief or satisfaction.

"At last," he said, lifting the lamp high and stepping back. "I am Andrea de' Collini. You are welcome to my house."

Barbara and I stepped across the threshold, and in doing so we entered the dimensions of another universe.

"It's quite simple my dear Peppe – I *purchased* you."

"What?"

"I bought you from Master Antonio; and pray don't have the impoliteness to ask the price. Tomaso della Croce sells, and I buy. Antonio Donato either sells or buys, whichever he thinks will be the most profitable to him at the time. A great deal of careful planning lies behind your presence here in my house tonight. Did you imagine otherwise?"

We sat in Andrea de' Collini's private library, the book-lined room warmed and mellowed by the light of many candles; an ornate silver lamp burned in the centre of a large damask-covered table. He had given us goblets of hot, spiced wine, and we sipped gratefully.

"Neither is Tomaso della Croce the only inquisitor to operate a trade in wasted human lives; it isn't common, but I know of several of his colleagues who get up to the same tricks. The difference between them and him is that he probably doesn't keep the money – I should think he puts it straight into the poor-box. At any rate, it clearly causes our self-righteous friend no moral scruples. However, let us not worry about him tonight."

"We are in no danger then?" asked Barbara.

"I think not."

"How can you be sure?"

"I am given to understand that the inquisitor is no longer in Florence."

"But that's impossible!" Barbara cried. "You sent me the information yourself –"

"For some reason or other unknown to me the investigation into the case of Caterina Fieschi has been suspended. Her family has noble connections . . . perhaps pressure was applied. Tomaso della Croce has therefore no reason to proceed to Genoa, and certainly no reason to remain in Florence."

"He must be returning to Rome then," I said.

The Master lifted his hands in a little gesture of despair.

"Rome," he murmured. "Laura was still in Rome, according to the news I last received. She had been committed for trial, but I do not know whether that has yet taken place. She may be still in prison, waiting."

"And you, Master?" I asked, my voice trembling.

"I did not bring you both here for nothing. I have work to do – *we* have work to do. It is the work I first entrusted to my daughter, which I must now complete on her behalf."

"What – what is this work, Master?"

"Why, to make good Gnostics of you. What else? Therefore I shall stay here in Florence for the time being; indeed, if the inquisitor is returning to Rome, I *must* remain. He has known of me and my activities for some years now, and he has slowly become consumed by the desire to destroy me. I stand for everything he hates, and hatred is always a fatal sickness. He perceives me as an enemy of truth, and he has made it his life's work to rid the world of all enemies of truth."

"And *are* you an enemy of truth?"

"Truth can never be received raw," Andrea de' Collini said. "Rather, it is mediated through the prism of each man's mind, and coloured according to the nature of each man's temperament. I might say, 'Today the sky is blue and the sun is high', and you might say, 'Today there is no rain, but who knows how long that will last?'; both statements are true, are they not? Yet each expresses the nature of the one who uttered it. As I see it, some utterances are perhaps a little nearer the reality of the way things are, than others; I am convinced that what Fra Tomaso della Croce believes, and what his Church teaches, is frequently very far from the truth, in spite of the fact that this Church claims as its founder the Lord of Truth himself. But della Croce and his kind will tolerate no other perceptions or utterances than their own, and he strives to extirpate those who espouse gentler, more compassionate and wiser philosophies. They are afraid of the philosophy that I embrace and live by, because it threatens to undermine the power they have appropriated for themselves, and to expose it to those whom it enslaves, for what it really is. Oh, we are old enemies, the Dominican and I. Have I answered your question satisfactorily?"

"Yes," I said, "you have. And this – this philosophy of yours in which we are to be educated – the work your daughter began but which you must accomplish –"

"You were chosen for it, Peppe. All of you were. You have taken the Oath of Renunciation?"

I nodded.

"We *all* have," Barbara said.

"Then I see no reason why you should not lodge here with me and begin your education at once."

He rose.

"You will wish to sleep now," he said. "Give me but a brief while, and I shall have your rooms prepared."

Then he left us.

The new phase of our education began at once, taking the form not only of readings from the great Gnostic masters, but also of sermons from Andrea de' Collini and question-and-answer sessions between him and Barbara and myself. In his house there was a small private scriptorium where these sessions took place, and where he spent many hours copying or emending antique texts, poring over yellowing manuscripts by the candlelight from silver sconces which bore strange designs in niello; he would sit hunched at his writing desk, surrounded by tall piles of fascicles, like a prisoner in a parchment donjon, and whenever we entered he would look up, his eyes alight with some joyous inner glow, ready and eager to transmit the living truth of the philosophy he had made so entirely his own.

Barbara and I were, I think, able pupils; the lady Laura had in any case already honed my mind to a rich degree of receptivity, and had instilled in me both the capacity and the desire to think for myself. Barbara's intelligence was keen, even though at times, when she was perplexed by a particular point of doctrine, she would become something of a termagant, wiggling her fat little fingers, jabbing and prodding to emphasize her line of reasoning, uttering little grunts and squeals of approval or dissent. She was perhaps overly addicted to quillets, but in my experience this is endemic among the females of our species. The Master unfailingly displayed a well-nigh infinite patience with both of us.

It was this compassionate patience which, by degrees, brought Barbara and me to the point where we were finally able to cast aside all misgivings, all integuments of the mediocrity of convention, and admit that we were convinced Gnostics. This process can be likened to the sloughing off of an old skin, like that of a snake, to reveal bright, firm new flesh beneath, or to the metamorphosis of the caterpillar into a butterfly.

What, you may well ask, is the precise *nature* of Gnosticism? What exactly *is* it, and what is a Gnostic? As far as my beliefs are concerned I like to think of myself as a proselytizer but not, I hope, a prolix windbag; therefore I shall state our basic Gnostic conviction concisely: we hold that there are two equally-matched powers in the universe, one good and the other evil, and these are perpetually at war with one another. The good power created spirit, while the evil power created matter. Matter, material existence, corporeal form, the body, flesh, is evil. It imprisons and holds captive the spirit. In being born into the world of matter, we have fallen from our true spiritual state; the object of our existence is to return to it. The devil (or at least *a* devil) created this world, and it is hell. Now *that* is nutshell-Gnosticism, its quiddity in the palm of your hand. And can you wonder why I espouse it so eagerly, being cursed with a body like mine?

Think about it for a moment, I beg you: Could God have created anything which is subject to degeneration, decay and death? Could God have created anything which is designed to feel pain? To bleed, vomit, ooze ichor, shit, piss and drip pus? And even if he is capable of such an act of creation, would he *wish* to do so? Does it not seem to you that the maker of this world has well and truly fouled things up? Perhaps even deliberately so?

The great Gnostic masters were completely agreed on

these basic principles, but they set them down by incorporating them – embedding them – into various complex and recondite metaphysical systems of their own; very often these masters were inclined to euphuism, and sometimes it is – to be frank with you – a case of *ignotum per ignotius*. I will be the first to admit that sublime though his thought is, the texts of Valentinus himself – loaded with equivogues, archaisms, high-flown zeugmatic lyricism and just plain bile! – are frequently not easy to penetrate. I do not know why the Gnostics of old possessed this inclination to cultivate the *recherché*, but they did; their minds perhaps were oviparous instruments, hatching mental egglings heterogenously, and maybe this was inevitably so, in view of the fact that they were obliged to struggle against the torpor and darkness of a massive error that sprang into being almost before the Master of Truth had breathed his last on that gibbet on a windswept Palestinian hill. Perhaps they found themselves obliged to seek the gold amid the dross here and there – picking out a nugget of spiritual veracity from one philosophy, a second from another, and so on. Perhaps they were eclectics by default, I do not quite know.

I am sometimes moved to tears when, at the conclusion of Solemn Vespers in the Lateran, men's voices are raised in praise of the compassionate Virgin, and chant the words:

Ad te clamamus, exules filii Hevae, ad te suspiramus,
gemetes et flentes, in hac lacrymarum valle. . . . .

For it is certainly true that we are all 'groaning and weeping in this vale of tears;' the composition of the *Salve Regina* marked one of those rare occasions when Holy Mother Church actually got things one hundred percent correct.

Oh, I wish you could see what I look like! That would please me greatly; Master Rafael refused to paint me, as you know, and yet I long for some little gew-gaw of remembrance, some record of the appearance of the creature that I am! As a good Gnostic I shouldn't harbour such vain longings I know, but then – well, then the heart frequently nourishes hopes that the head dismisses as exiguous. It is said of that genius of unknown race from Alexandria, the blessed Plotinus, that when it was suggested he should have his portrait executed, he replied:

"What? Is it not enough that I have to carry the image? Would you have an image made of the image?"

As much as I stand stupefied before his stature, I do not – alas! – aspire to the spiritual integrity of Plotinus; and yes, I wish there was something, some way, some means, whereby you could behold the little minnikin that I am! My height is no height to speak of, as you must already know; I told you in the first chapter of these memoirs that my gaze, directed straight ahead, is roughly level with Master Rafael's arse (I suspect Leo envies me this), but that isn't any help to you if you don't know how tall *he* is. Well, he is fairly tall, I think. I don't have much of a neck – just a series of little corrugations, then my chest begins, and it sticks out horribly, as the chests of most dwarves do; this deformation gives the impression that I am constantly inhaling without any isochronous exhalation, which further gives the impression that I'm sparring up for a fight – or at the very least a verbal altercation. My hump is large, and is nervate with bony protruberances all the way down – these, of course, constitute what passes for a spine. It makes me look like a kind of irritable echinus. My arms are disproportionately long (which is no real surprise, since I am disproportionate altogether), and my legs grotesquely stunted; they are also turned in upon themselves. I have been told that I have a warm smile, but to be frank, I must say that this is something of a recent acquisition, since for most of my youth I wasn't even sure what a smile was, let alone have any cause to produce one. My eyebrows are thick and bushy, my teeth somewhat uneven. When I walk, I do so with a sort of osculatory inward swing, which means that my thighs rub together and frequently bleed, because the chafing is so bad.

97

For me, death will be nothing more than a process of unencumbering myself of this dwarf's carapace. In this sense, I have a head start on those of you who have been born strong, tall and beautiful: for those clean, straight limbs of yours will eventually grew knotty and withered, as mine are now; that face of Adonis will finally crease with pain and age, as my face is presently creased; and the organs of joy between your long legs that you are so proud of will, in the end, shrivel to half their size, just as mine have been shrivelled from birth. Time is a procrustean tyrant!

One afternoon, after a lunch of spiced vegetable stew (we had both given up eating meat by this time) the Master read to us an extract from a book which, I later learned, was a special favourite of his.

" 'For where there is envy and strife, there is a lack, but where there is unity, there is completion. Inasmuch as the lack came into being because the Father of truth was not known, from the moment that the Father is known, the lack will cease to exist. As with one man's ignorance of another – when one becomes acquainted, ignorance of the other passes away of its own accord; further, as with darkness, which passes away when light appears; so also does lack pass away in completion, and from that moment on – oh, blessed moment! – the domain of appearances is no longer manifest to seduce and beguile with the illusion of multiplicity, but rather will pass away in the sweet harmony of unity.

" 'For now we seem to be all dispersed and scattered, but when unity comes it will gather us into itself, and we shall be purified from our multiplicity into oneness, consuming matter within us, as by fire, and darkness by light, and death by eternal life. Let us then, be patiently and quietly, and with holiness, intent on unity.' "

At this point, Barbara interrupted to ask:

"Are *all* creatures included in this unity?"

"Indeed yes," said the Master gently. "How could it be otherwise?"

"Even those who persecute our kind?"

For less than the shadow of a second, a spasm of pain appeared on the Master's face, then it was gone.

"Yes," he said quietly. "Even those."

"Even Tomaso della Croce?" Barbara insisted.

"Even *him*. For if, Barbara, if but one single living being is excluded from such unity, it is unworthy of the name. The tragedy of men like della Croce is the magnitude of their nescience! The living, organic unity of the children of the true Father draws its infinitude from the Father's own being; eventually – God alone knows by means of how many lifetimes of ignorance, and the suffering which ignorance engenders – every child of the Father will turn away from the darkness of division and enter into the light of unity."

"Then nothing and no-one will ever be lost?"

"I have already told you – it cannot be."

"I do not speak of a living creature being excluded from the Father's unity," Barbara went on, her face reddening, the words coming more quickly now, "but rather of being – not lost, I mean, but –"

"Annihilated? Extinguished?"

"Yes! Extinguished."

"What is made cannot be unmade."

"Thank you," Barbara murmured in a tone of voice which I could not quite identify -was it resentment? Resignation? I don't know.

The Master closed the book and rested it on his knee.

"Is your love for the truth greater than your hatred for *him*, my dear?" he asked Barbara softly; her answer was disclosed in the silence which followed his question.

Then he turned to me and said:

"And now, Peppe, let me probe your understanding. Why is there evil and suffering in this world, and why does it far outweigh the good?"

"Because this world itself is evil."

"How can the world be evil, when scripture tells us it was created by God?"

"It was not created by God."

"Then by whom?"

"By a demi-god, a lesser god, a malign being who desired the absolute power of God and fumblingly aped God's divine creativity by fashioning the world of form and matter."

"And who rules this world, Peppe?"

"He does. Its creator. He demands all worship and adoration for himself."

"Who is this being? Where is his story to be found?"

"In the books of the Jews, where he is called Yahweh. Yaldabaoth is another name given him."

"What is the task of those who *know* – those who are called Gnostics?"

"To re-ascend to the heavenly Father."

"And how is this to be achieved?"

"Firstly through leading a good life, secondly through an ever increasing knowledge of the truth – that is, knowledge of the source and origin of men, their ultimate destination, and of their spiritual constitution."

"Of what principles does good living consist?"

"The repudiation of carnal acts –"

"Or?"

"Or engagement in carnal acts in order to scorn and abuse their intention and purpose. Abstention from flesh foods. Non-violence."

At last the Master leaned back in his chair and sighed very deeply. His whole body seemed to relax into a kind of stillness.

"You have done well, Peppe," he murmured. "Very well indeed. This shall be the first of many lessons. Soon you will be baptized, then you will begin your initiations."

"Yes, Master."

"Tell me, how do you feel?"

I thought for a moment, then I said:

"Almost faint with relief. I can't describe it. Happy and sad at the same time. I feel – some great weight has been lifted from me – I feel *free*."

"Free! Exactly so! Did not the holy Jesus himself tell us that the truth will set us free? Tell me, Peppe: why do you bear the pain and humiliation of a stunted, twisted, crookback body?"

I swallowed hard. I found it difficult to speak, I was filled with such an intensity of sweet, liberating emotion. Then I managed to say, haltingly and hardly audible:

"Because – I have this body because – *God did not create it*. God wishes only to free me from the prison it has been to me for so many years."

I began to sob uncontrollably, shaking and trembling. I put my hands up to my face and covered it. I was ashamed of my weakness.

"The world is awash on an ocean of human tears," the Master said softly, pensively.

I thought of poor Nino, subjected night after night to sexual humiliation, the cynosure of two hundred pairs of cruelly curious eyes; I thought of 'Satan's Daughter'; I thought of armless Barbara; of 'the Skull', half of his face burned away by the flames of the Inquisition; of all the cripples and freaks who had not managed to escape the gutters of the cities of this world, as I had done; of my drunken slut of a mother and her savage, pitiless laughter; of the dead, of those dying in agony, the bereaved, mad with grief; of Laura, wherever she might be now; I thought of every pain and every cry of human sorrow on the entire earth, and I wanted there and then to assuage them with my own tears. My tears became a prayer to the Father. For the first time in my life, I was praying in a silent act of lacrimation.

1520

I have been rather irritatingly interrupted in the writing of these memoirs; in any case, I only have time to work on them in the afternoons and evenings, in the privacy of my chamber. Giovanni Lazzaro, otherwise known as Serapica, came to tell me yesterday afternoon that His Holiness wished me to accompany him to the castle San Angelo, where we would watch the carnival parade pass by; Sera-pica (about whom you shall hear more) is a small, curious fellow, a papal chamberlain like myself, and I have been disconcerted of late to discover that I am rather jealous of him. Also, I could have done without the carnival parade, which I am obliged to watch from San Angelo every year. I sometimes think Leo is addicted to vulgar pleasure, in addition to books, buggery and humanist versifiers.

Two years have elapsed since I wrote the first sentence of these memoirs; I do not find that composition comes easily, and I sometimes sit for half an hour or more reworking a single sentence or a difficult phrase. Aeschylus had the same trouble, I believe; but then I can hardly compare myself to the great Greek tragedian, upon whom the gods bestowed such an abundance of talent that he was able to write the following sublime lines:

"He who would learn, must first suffer, and even in our sleep, the pain which will not forget, falls drop by drop upon the heart, and in our despair, against our own will, comes wisdom, by the awesome grace of God."

You will not be entirely surprised to know that I have made those words peculiarly my own. Ever since I first embraced Gnostic philosophy (you've heard a little of that already) – it seems so many years ago now! – suffering and wisdom have been inextricably entwined for me; so much so, I now find it difficult to say which is cause and which is effect. No matter – the meaning and the purpose is the same. I'd give my entire collection of rings to be able to pen sentiments like that.

It's been a funny sort of year so far, even though we're only a couple of months into it; Leo finally got around (with my encouragement) to issuing his oft-threatened bull, *Exsurge Domine,* against the heretic Luther, who is proving not so daft as we all at first supposed. As a matter of fact, he displays a real fox's cunning, that one. The bull didn't do a great deal of good as it turns out, and Luther apparently burnt it in the market-place, in front of a cheering mob. One in the eye for poor old Leo. To be pefectly frank, I don't think His Holiness has quite grasped the seriousness of the situation; I have a rather nasty feeling somewhere in the depths of my bowels that this affair isn't going to fizzle out like the usual two minute wonder that most anti-Roman rumblings turn out to be. *That* sort of thing is hardly even an inconvenience, and is quickly ended by a bull (papal variety, that is) and a burning – 'the two Bs,' as we call this procedure.* Furthermore, the support that is gaining disconcerting momentum in Germany for Luther is *not* merely a case of cheering on a local boy made good – far from it. The real truth of the matter is that the Germans are heartily sick and tired of cash flowing out to Rome through the sale of indulgences, quite apart from the dissent caused by corpulent bishops who sit on their fat arses in the Vatican all day reading erotica, and who can't even *spell* Germany, let alone visit their dioceses. I hope to God I'm wrong. Even though I love Leo and loathe the Church, I wouldn't want to see *Sancta Ecclesia Romana* split into two like a pig's backside. That would be the end of our civilization, I think. Time will tell.

Alfonsina Orsini (mother of Leo's nephew Lorenzo), in whom avarice and ambition contended for supremacy, died a short time ago, but that clearly didn't dampen Leo's enthusiasm for carnival week; he cried a little, then went back to watching the antics of the revellers from the ramparts of San Angelo. We had the lot: bull-fights in the streets (which I find particularly disgusting and Leo obviously considers hilarious), races and wrestling matches, plays and musical entertainments (some explicitly lascivious), and the ghastly pig-tumbling, which takes place at Monte Testaccio, and which, therefore, we were mercifully spared; it is a truly horrible event – cartloads of squealing pigs, shitting themselves with fear, are hauled up to the

* In the original manuscript Peppe calls this 'the two Fs' – *furia e fuoco,* 'fury and fire.'

summit of Monte Testaccio, then literally hurled down for the mob to scramble for at the bottom. Some of the weightier animals fall on people and severely injure or even kill them; by the time the ear-splitting screams of the pigs and the yelling of the populace has died away, at the base of the mount there is a tangled, bloody mess of human and animal bodies, and the air is foetid with the stench of evacuated bladders, both of man and pig. I really can't imagine why anyone should find this sort of thing entertaining.

Then we had that humiliating mock battle in front of the San Angelo castle, with the papal household specially rigged out in elaborate (and ruinously expensive) costumes of garishly fantastic design; the 'weapons' were oranges, which everybody hurled at each other with manic gusto. I absolutely *refused* to take part, even though Leo practically begged me.

"It's only fun, Peppe!" he cried. "Don't be such a killjoy!"

"Does your Holiness intend to participate? Perhaps dressed as Messalina, with an orange wedged up her arse?"

"That would be unseemly. I *command* you to join in."

"I respectfully refuse to obey Your Holiness's command."

"I'll have you flogged and thrown into prison, you arrogant whelp's cunny!" he screamed, stamping his foot and gasping in pain because in doing so, he jolted his inflamed backside (that hasn't improved very much in two years, but then neither have Leo's venereal antics).

"I'm sorry Holiness, but I won't do it."

"You'll damned well come and watch it, then," he said, storming off.

And I did. It didn't amuse me in the slightest, and several people were actually quite badly injured ('We shall pray for you," Leo announced pompously, blessing them as they were carried off on stretchers). He enjoyed it so much, he commanded a repeat performance the following evening.

The civic pageant was absolutely glittering, and adhered as closely as possible to the ancient style. I sat with Leo and most of the papal court on the ramparts of San Angelo, to watch it pass. As I have told you, I was interrupted in my writing of these memoirs by Serapica, precisely in order to do this. I think one or two of the snootier guests were rather shocked at Leo's unabashed delight in all these vulgar goings on, for I happened to come across a letter that Angelo Germanello was obviously in the process of writing to the Marquis of Mantua; Germanello had carelessly left it lying around in one of the reading rooms that adjoin the main library, and I did not feel at all ashamed in satisfying my curiosity at once. Actually, I have a propensity for reading other people's letters, as you may well come to perceive. I detected a slightly disapproving, self-righteous tone:

"El papa sennesta in castello tucto el dì ad vedere le mascare et omne sera se fa recitar comedie, et domane el Sr Camillo Ursino ad la presentia de la sua Sta deve contrahere li sponsalitii con una figliola de Johanpaulo Baglione. Hore è morta madonna Alphonsina cugnata del papa in Roma in la casa del papa quando era in minoribus . . ."

The juxtaposition of the death of Alfonsina Orsini with the description of the pope spending most of the day watching the general revelry was, I think, quite deliberate.

On the morning of *Giovedì grasso* the pageant started at the Capitol, made its tortuously slow way through the Via de' Bianchi to the castle of San Angelo (where we sat waiting for it and where it slowed down even further both as a courteous acknowledgement of Leo's presence, and so that we could get a longer look), then went on to St Peter's, and eventually wound up in the Piazza Navona at dusk.

This year there were thirteen floats in all, representing amongst other legendary or heroic figures: Italia, Isis (this was based on a statue in Leo's possession), Neptune, Hercules, Atlas, Æolus, Vulcan, the Tiber, the Capitoline She-Wolf, Alexander the Great (on horseback no less, if you please!); there were also two rather neurasthenic camels that some sycophantic potentate or other trying to curry favour had given Leo as a gift – I suppose he genuinely thought we would be gratified to have the malodorous beasts lumbering around the Vatican, dropping shit everywhere; and finally they had a gigantic globe of the world upon which, rather precariously, was perched an angel. This latter represented the triumph of religion. Fetching up the rear were about two hundred or so young men dressed in ancient Roman costume, representing the guilds of Rome, which carries its own brand of irony when you think about it, since the youth of Rome is known above all for doing no work at all, but rather idling on the street corners all day and causing mischief. Antiquity had, so to speak, laid its stamp upon everything; this is hardly surprising in view of Leo's passion for the culture of the ancient world. He was particularly gratified (I think he was genuinely moved) to spot a blue and purple banner, worked in gold thread and decorated with precious stones, depicting him as the Sun-god. Everywhere there were affectionate cries of *Viva Leone! Viva il Papa!* and these swelled to a massive roar, as if issued from a single throat, when the pageant passed beneath the ramparts of San Angelo; he waved enthusiastically, and I swear I saw him wipe a tear from his eye with the back of one fat hand. For a brief time, it was like the splendour and glory of the Republic born anew, now vested with the resurrection garments of antique learning, scholarship and art. The golden age of Pallas Athene indeed. The golden age of the Medici pope.

Inevitably, there were some unintentionally hilarious moments; a great many of the revellers were drunk, and had probably been drinking all week; they clambered onto the floats and swarmed in and out of the procession, until it was difficult to tell exactly who was officially taking part and who wasn't. Some of the male participants (those representing Neptune, Hercules and Atlas, for example), were required, in the interests of historical or mythical accuracy, to wear as little as possible, and even what modest covering they did wear soon came off. Wine-

106

sodden women screeched hilariously as they ripped away a hapless Atlas's fig-leaf, and threw it to the baying mob; and Neptune, rising from billows of artificial sea-foam, surrounded by fishy-looking female trident bearers, quickly had his scales removed, much to his horror. Shocked by this sudden and unanticipated display of male equipment, the angel representing religion nearly slithered off her globe. And this was just the beginning of the fun; God knows how rowdy things must have become by the time the procession reached the Piazza Navona at dusk. They do say that one third of all the infants born in Rome are conceived on the evening of *Giovedì grasso*. In the Piazza Navona, to be precise. I can well believe it.

During carnival week last year, Leo and I attended a most extraordinary banquet given by Lorenzo Strozzi, the banker, brother of Filippo Strozzi, who is well known in Rome (and perhaps beyond) for his epicurean inclinations; Leo came dressed as a cardinal, wearing a silly sort of eye-mask of black velvet. Nobody was supposed to know he was there, apparently, but as Cardinals Rossi, Cibo, Salviati and Ridolfi were also present, this absurd attempt at incognito was somewhat futile.

We were all led up a flight of steps to a door which had been painted black, through which we entered a large hall, entirely draped in black silk and velvet; in the middle of this hall stood a black table on which reposed two black glass flagons of wine and two human skulls, filled with the very choicest viands.

"Do you think the poor man is depressed?" Leo whispered to me.

"No. We're meant to be mystified, or a little frightened, or perhaps both."

After nibbling for a while, everyone was ushered into an adjoining hall, even larger, which was blindingly, brilliantly lit by innumerable candles and oil-lamps, some of the most exquisite execution, in gold and silver, adorned with precious stones. I caught Leo eyeing them enviously. We sat down at the huge table, and after some moments

107

were surprised – not to say shocked – by a deep rumbling beneath our chairs; one or two of the ladies swooned, and Cardinal Ridolfi, ridiculous old actress that he is, leapt to his feet with a squeal of horror and announced:

"The apocalypse has begun!"

In fact, it was the sound of a mechanical contrivance beneath the floor, which was so designed (cleverly, I concede, but all rather *de trop*) as to allow a great circular board to rise up from the room below, through the floor, until it was precisely level with the table at which we sat, and on it were heaped great dishes of victuals. Relieved more than anything else, several of the guests burst into applause. Lorenzo Strozzi allowed himself the faint trace of a smile, like a magician gratified at the success of his first trick, but knowing that there are even better ones to come. As indeed there were.

Servants placed a chased silver platter in front of each guest, who found, to his or her consternation, that what it contained was quite inedible. There were little cries of horror or delight or bewilderment; there was oddly forced laughter; some people began to look more than a little frightened.

"What have you got in yours?" I asked Leo.

He peered down at his plate and sniffed.

"It would appear to be half a pair of female undergarments," he answered. "Boiled."

"I've got a raw sausage."

"An empty eggshell!" a voice cried.

"A toad – oh Jesus – a *live* toad!" shrieked another, less enthusiastically.

"The heel of a shoe –"

"A kerchief, fried in batter . . ."

"Good God Almighty – a penis! No, no, wait a moment – ah! A blanched baby marrow, I think –"

Suddenly, the lights were extinguished. Quite how Strozzi managed it, I do not know; maybe there were servants hidden behind the drapes – in fact, now I come to think of it, this is the only way it *could* have been done. The great

108

hall immediately rang with the shrill screams and shrieks of all the ladies, and Cardinal Ridolfi. Then we heard the slow rumble and shudder of the mechanism again, which was clearly being lowered, freshly loaded, and sent up a second time. After this, the candles were re-lighted (which took some time), and – behold! – the great table at which we sat was laden. This time the applause was strenuous and prolonged.

For the first course we were served vegetable soup with *stracciatelli*, and *potage à la royne*, which were accompanied by enormous slices of bread fried in oil and garlic and piled high with finely minced and seasoned partridge and pheasant, decorated with *funghi porcini*, artichokes deep-fried in the Jewish manner (Strozzi was a banker, after all), and baby onions. There was also a *potage garni* accompanied by all manner of offal (which I heartily dislike, but in any case my Gnostic principles would not permit me to eat any of the meat.)

The second course consisted of venison broiled in stock, pies of every variety, pressed tongue, spiced sausages and salamis served with chopped melon and figs, and savoury egg flans. These delicacies were followed by huge roasts: more partridges and pheasants, larks (their tongues, basted in honey and orange with *basilico,* served separately) wood doves, pigeons, young chickens, and whole lambs. Then came a huge array of dishes made from butter, eggs and cheese – pies, flans, pastries, and so on; bowls of *melanzane* marinated in white wine and sprinkled lavishly with fragrant herbs, celery chopped with onions and peppers and drenched in oil, also put in an appearance. The wines flowed as freely as a drunkard's piss.

After several hours of continuous eating, I was feeling quite faint; indeed, I could not imagine how so many of the other guests were still happily cramming themselves. Leo, unsurprisingly, chomped his way through the lot; however, he had not as yet farted (although I expected a real stinker at any moment), which was some small blessing.

Lorenzo Strozzi, at the head of the table, finally rose to his feet a little unsteadily.

"Your Holiness – ah – Your Eminences, I meant to say, of course! – my dear and very *special* guests! I offer you now the climax, the apotheosis, the summit of this rather *unusual* evening."

He clapped his hands, and four servants entered the hall, bearing on their shoulders a massive silver dish, in which was heaped what looked like half the cream in Rome; it was decorated more richly than Leo's tiara, with bright red cherries, brown pine kernels, thin green strips of angelica, all kinds of nuts and berries, and was wound about with a great length of dried leaves that had been dipped in gold. The entire assembled company (including myself, I readily admit) drew in its breath.

Strozzi went on, clearly drunk:

"Ah, but all is not what it seems to be, my very dear and *special* friends! No indeed. What you see before you is but the phantasm of the thing itself – the accidents which occlude and conceal the substance, as our good Tomaso d'Aquino would have said. You see, Your Eminences? I am not entirely unversed in the queen of sciences. Excuse me, I digress. Yes, invisible to your eyes, most cherished guests, is a delight more subtle, more – what shall I say, what term to employ? – more *sensuous* (for that must surely be the word!) than the simple sweetness which mere appearances promise. And let me give you a small clue, a tiny hint, so to speak, of the secret which is shortly to be revealed: I provide no implements for this, my final and most exquisite offering; you must use *only your tongues.*"

And with that, he collapsed back in his chair.

The dish was placed somewhat awkwardly in the centre of the table; for some moments we all sat and stared at it. Then Cardinal Salviati stood up, leaned as far as he could across the table, stuck out a greenish, corrugated tongue, and dipped the tip of it into the great mound of cream. He closed his eyes for a moment, licked his lips, then opened his eyes again and nodded.

"Very delicious," he pronounced. "Very delicious indeed. Flavoured with *grappa* and wild honey, if I am not mistaken."

"Bravo, Eminence!" Lorenzo Strozzi cried drunkenly.

Embolded by Salviati's initiative, several of the gentlemen and two of the ladies did likewise; they giggled and nudged each other as they extended their tongues to taste their host's culinary 'apotheosis.' The technique, awkward though it was, was clearly catching on. It fell to Cardinal Ridolfi however, to finally expose the 'secret' of the extraordinary *dolce*; bending across the table and wiggling his tongue, he pushed it into the creamy mass only to withdraw it again with a piercing and womanly shriek.

"It moved!" he cried. "God's bones, I tell you it moved! Ah! –"

There was a general commotion as it was observed that the great mound of decorated slop was indeed moving; it shuddered and wiggled, as if suddenly endowed with an alien life all of its own. Clotted lumps of cream fell away, nuts and cherries flew off and showered onto the table. It seemed to be *growing*. Ridolfi by now was having an attack of the vapours, wiping his lips furiously with the back of his hand as though he had ingested poison; indeed, had this been a banquet given by Pope Alexander VI Borgia, whose memory still haunted curial slumbers, it might well have been.

Everybody was at the thing now, licking and scraping the cream off as fast as they could; people were stretched out across the table, plates were pushed aside or even fell to the floor; there was screeching and laughing and vulgar gestures. I do not think I have ever seen so many protruding tongues in my life, and it is a spectacle I care never to witness again; human beings look utterly ridiculous with their tongues sticking out. Leo should ban people doing it in all the papal states. As a matter of fact, I had entirely forgotten about Leo: he was slumped in his chair, spellbound by the goings on. His eyes bulged and watered.

There was a young woman buried under that grotesque

111

hillock of cream; furthermore, it quickly became obvious, as first a thigh was exposed, then a foot, a wetly glistening pink nipple, and finally a hairy pubic mound, that she was a very naked young woman. The cacophony of screaming and guffawing rapidly swelled in volume as people began to applaud. And still the tongues were at work, probing and wiggling and scraping lasciviously, lingeringly, across the smooth, pale flesh. Two men – one of them rather young for this sort of thing in my opinion – were licking at the same breast, contending for the stiff little nipple, occasionally looking into each other's eyes in a sly, knowing manner as they did so. Much to my surprise however, it was a lady (I use that term cautiously) whose face was buried deep between the shuddering thighs, sucking and slurping shamelessly, her long tongue darting rapidly in and out of the private opening hidden beneath the bush of black hair. I can well imagine what sort of cream she hoped to find down *there*. The young woman stretched herself out in the dish, still half-covered with rapidly liquifying slop; she writhed and groaned and fluttered her eyelids in a sexual ecstasy. The colloidal sludge oozed and squelched beneath her buttocks. Then she uttered a low moan:

"Ah . . . ah!"

The last two things I noticed were that the young man sharing a breast with a fellow diner had drawn out his quivering penis and was rubbing it surreptitiously up against a leg of the table, while the female devotee at the *other* end had pushed a cherry up into the hairy labial glory-hole which was so occupying her attention – presumably for the pleasure of sucking it out again.

"Your Holiness," I said to Leo, "it is time for us to take our leave."

"Yes, you are right, Peppe. Yes, yes."

As we passed through the door, I noticed Cardinal Ridolfi stretched out on the floor.

"He must have fainted," I said. "The sight of all that female flesh was too much for him, I dare say."

Leo glared at me.

As I said, that was *last* year; apart from the carnival, 1520 seems to have been rather quieter so far.

Tomorrow I must start work again on my memoirs.

1505

I received my Gnostic baptism on the twenty-third of May in the year 1505, exactly one week after Barbara. It took place in the small private chapel that the Master had constructed for himself at the back of the house. The air was fragrant with the sweet pungency of incense, the chapel illuminated only by a large oil-lamp suspended from the ceiling by a golden chain. On the walls were painted images of the sun and moon and stars. Behind the altar stood a tall alabaster jar containing fresh flowers, while on the altar itself, which consisted of a slab of smooth marble supported by two caryatids, was a large statue of a black Madonna, seated with great dignity, her divine Child in her lap. To the left of the altar, in the marble floor which was patterned with black and white squares, a deep bath had been sunk, lined in gold and filled with water scented with attar of roses.

The Master was dressed in a simple robe of white cambric, which came down to his ankles; on his head he wore a white velvet cap onto which had been stitched a representation of the sun, in gilded leather. He held a small silver pitcher in his right hand. I was entirely naked.

"Let the aspirant come forward," he said in a gentle but firm and clear voice.

I walked slowly to the edge of the sunken bath.

"What does the aspirant seek?" the Master intoned.

I answered, as I had been taught:

"Admittance to the sacred mysteries of our saviour the Lord Jesus Christ."

"Do you accept his true teaching and embrace the light?"

"I do."

113

"Do you reject Yahweh-Yaldabaoth and spurn the darkness?"

"I do."

"Shall you live your life according to the precepts of Jesus Christ and the Gnostic philosophy of truth?"

"I shall."

"Then enter the waters of life and claim the grace of our saviour Jesus Christ, and the mercy of our Father in heaven."

I lowered myself somewhat clumsily into the bath, steadying myself with my hands against the golden sides. When I was ready, I nodded to the Master. He bent, dipped the pitcher into the water, then straightened up again. Slowly, carefully, he poured the water over my head. At the same time, he began to intone the Gnostic liturgy in a beautiful, light voice, half-chanting, half-singing, every caesura a canticle of eloquent silence, and the pure, tender sound of it filled my heart to bursting. I knew I was about to be reborn.

Iesseus-Mazareus-Iessedekeus, the living river;
the mighty presidents, the great Jacobus and
Theopemptos, and Isauēl;
the entity that governs outflowing grace, Zepēael;
those that preside over the wellsprings of truth, Mikheus,
*   Mikhar, and Mnēsinous;*
the one that governs the baptism of the living,
the Purifier Psesemmen-Barpharagges;
those that govern the gates of the river of
life, Miseus and Mikhar;
those that govern ascent, Seldaō and Elainos;
the receivers of the holy race and incorruptible offspring,
mighty ones of the great Seth;
the servants of the four luminaries — great
Gamaliel, great Gabriel, great Samblo, and great
Abrasaks;
those entities that govern the sun's rising route,
Olsēs, Hymneus, and Heurymaious;

those that govern the sun's sinking down
unto the repose of life everlasting, Phritanis,
Mikhsanthēr, and Mikhanōr;
the protectors of chosen souls, Akraman and
Strempsoukhos;
the great power Telmakhaēl-Telmakhaēl-Eli-Eli-Mahar-
   Makhar-Seth;
the entity that is great, invisible, virgin and
unnameable in spirit and wordlessness;
the great luminary Harmozēl, where there is the
living, self-originate god in truth, with whom is
Adas the imperishable human being;
Oroiaēl, where there is the great Seth and Jesus of
life eternal, who came and crucified the enslaved subjects
of the law;
third, Daueithe, where the offspring of the great
Seth repose;
fourth, Ēlēlēth, where the souls of the offspring
repose;
fifth, Ioēl, who governs the name of the being
who will be ordained to baptize with the
holy, incorruptible baptism that is higher than
heaven.

Thus, through the agency of the numinous and incorruptible Poimaēl, for the sake of those worthy of baptisms of renunciation and the ineffable seals thereof, whichever individuals have acquired knowledge of their receivers, according as they have been instructed and prepared and have learned, shall not taste death.

O Iesseus!
Ioeouooua!
Solemnly, solemnly so!
O Iesseus-Mazareus-Iessedekeus!
O everliving fountain!
O child of the child!
O name of all glories!
Solemnly, solemnly so!

O eternal being!
IIII ĒĒĒĒ OOOO YYYY ŌŌŌŌ AAAA!
Solemnly, solemnly so!
EI AAAA ŌŌŌŌ!
O being, which beholds the aeons
Solemnly, solemnly so!

O existent for ever and ever
Solemnly, solemnly so!
IĒA AIŌ in the soul's depths!
O existent upsilon forever unto eternity!
You are what you are!
You are what you are!
And I shall truly declare your praise,
for I have comprehended you;
Yours, O Jesus! Behold, O eternally omega,
O eternally epsilon, O Jesus!
O eternity, O eternity!
O god of silence, we beg you utterly,
you are our realm of repose.
O Son, Ēs Ēs, the epsilon!

Raise up a human being by whom you will sanctify this baptized one into your life according to your ineffable and undying name! For this reason let the perfume of life be within this baptized one; for he has been mixed with the water of the rulers of life. In your company may he have life in the peace of your saints, O eternally existent in very truth!

Having finished the liturgy, the Master helped me to step out of the bath; he placed his mouth to mine and I received the benediction of his kiss of greeting and welcome. From a small table behind him, he took my new white baptismal robe, placed it over my head, and drew it down to cover my naked body.

"Welcome to the community of true believers, Peppe," he said softly; and with all the tenderness and solicitude of a mother (the mother, perhaps, I had never known), he held me to himself.

"Thank you, Master," I replied, overcome with the deepest of emotion.

Indeed, I *had* been re-born.

1520

I have been interrupted once again. Leo came bursting into my chamber, clutching a book in one pudgy hand, florid of face, his protuberant eyes bulging with wrath.

"Have you read what that German bastard is saying now?" he screamed, waving the book in the air furiously.

"Holiness, it is almost midnight –"

"By God's bones, I don't care what poxy hour it is! First he burns my bull in a public market-place, then he has the gall to send me, through a cringing emissary, a copy of his latest diatribe!"

"If your Holiness would calm himself –"

"Calm be buggered! Listen, Peppe, listen to this blasphemous horse-shit!"

He opened the book and began to read it aloud, waddling back and forth, sometimes almost choking with rage over the words.

"What has he entitled it?" I asked wearily.

"*An Den Christlichen Adel Deutscher Nation.* What a toad! An arse-licker! A ball-sucker! How dare he presume to address the German nobility over my head? Who does he think he is, another pope? But listen – listen, Peppe!

"'Although the canonization of saints may have been a good thing in former days, it is certainly not good practice now. Like many other things that were acceptable in times past, feast days, church property and ornaments, now are scandalous and offensive. For it is evident that through the canonization of saints, neither God's glory nor the spiritual benefit of Christians is sought, but only money and reputation.' (*God's blood!*) 'One church wants to have the edge over the other and would not like to see another church enjoy the advantages it has, in common. Spiritual treasures have even been misused to gain temporal goods in these wicked times so that everything, even God himself, has been forced into the service of Greed.' (*I'd have his bollocks flogged off if I thought he had any!*) 'Such an edge only encourages schisms, sects, and pride. A church that has advantages over others looks down on them and exalts itself. Yet divine treasures are common to all and serve all and ought to promote unity. But the pope likes things as they are.' (*Blasphemous, vindictive bastard!*) 'He would not like it if all Christians were equal and one with each other.

"'It is fitting to say here that all church licenses, bulls, and whatever else the pope has for sale in that skinning-house of his in Rome should be abolished, disregarded, or extended to all. But if he sells or gives special licenses, privileges, graces, advantages, and faculties to Halle, Venice, Wittenberg, and above all to his own city of Rome, why does he not give these things to all churches? Is it not his duty − ' [*the whelp's cunny has the temerity to tell me my duty!*] ' − to do everything in his power for all Christians, freely and for God's sake, even undergo martyrdom for them? Tell me, then, why does he give or sell to one church and not to another? Or must filthy lucre make so great a difference in the eyes of His Holiness among Christians, who all have the same baptism, word, faith, Christ, God, and all else? Do the Romanists want us to be so blind to all these things, though we have eyes to see, and be such fools, though we have a perfectly good reasoning power, that we worship such greed, skullduggery, and pretence? The pope is a shepherd, but only so long as you have plenty of cash, and no longer. And still the Romanists are not ashamed of his rascality of leading us hither and thither with their bulls. They are concerned only about cash, cash, cash, and nothing else!

"'My advice is this: If this foolishness cannot be abol-

118

ished, then every decent Christian should open his eyes and not permit himself to be led astray by the Romanist bulls and seals and all their glittering pomposities. Let him stay at home in his own parish and be content with the best: his baptism, the Gospel, his faith, his Christ, and his God, who is the same God everywhere. Let the pope remain a blind leader of the blind. Neither an angel nor a pope can give you as much as God gives you in your parish church. The fact is, the pope steers you away from the gifts of God, which are yours freely given, towards his gifts, for which you have to pay. He gives you lead for gold, pelt for meat, the string for the purse, earwax for honey, fancy words for goods, the letter for the spirit. You see all this before your very eyes, but you refuse to take notice. If you intend to ride to heaven on his unholy and cheap trinkets, this chariot will soon break down and you will fall into hell, and not in the name of the living God!' "

Leo stopped reading. He was panting, gasping for breath. His face had become alarmingly empurpled. I seriously thought he might be inducing a heart attack. He threw the book savagely to the floor.

"Holiness, please!" I said. "It's nothing more than a peasant's rhetoric."

"I'll see him burn, I swear it!"

"The language of the gutters. I heard it all the time, all around me, when I was a boy in Trastevere. Any wine-bibbing whore can do better than that."

I glanced regretfully at my memoirs lying on the table in front of me. A pity; I'd been getting on quite well, too.

"I'll see him roasted alive, Peppe," Leo breathed, calming a little now. "I'll see him burn in this life and relish the thought that he'll be burning eternally in the next. The man is a cancer, Peppe. He must be rooted out and destroyed."

"Yes, Holiness."

"What's that you're writing? That there, on the table."

"Nothing."

"You're writing nothing? Quite a literary achievement. Others have accomplished such a feat by accident –"

"Like Luther," I said.

"– but you have done it by design. How clever of you. May I see this masterpiece that consists of nothing?"

"I'd rather you didn't, Holiness. It's – well – it's rather private."

"How can *nothing* be private?"

"I spoke figuratively, as Your Holiness well knows."

"There shouldn't be anything private where the pope is concerned."

"Tell your Curia that, Holiness."

"Oh, I've tried, believe me . . ."

Leo stared at me curiously, with an introspective, vaguely dreamy look in his eyes, and I knew that he had suddenly abandoned all inquisitiveness as to the nature of my writing.

"Holiness?"

Then he smiled.

"Shall I tell you – no, rather, shall I *show* you – exactly what I think of this bastard of a German heretic?"

"As your Holiness pleases."

Leo unfastened and removed his *mozetta*, and laid it carefully over the back of a chair. He lifted up his alb and tucked it into his cincture. Then he pulled down his underdrawers, stood over Luther's book – which was still on the floor where he had tossed it – straddling it with his plump, pale, hairless legs. They quivered slightly. He grasped his penis in one hand, and pointed it downwards.

"Holiness! Not in *my* chamber!"

The protest was in vain. An enormous smile spread slowly across Leo's face as a glittering, steaming, golden stream of piss shot out from the tip of his prick and splattered all over *An Den Christlichen Adel Deutscher Nation*. Within seconds it was soaked. Leo grunted as he squeezed the last drop out; it fell with a tiny plopping, splashing sound onto the leather spine of the book.

"I only wish," he remarked, as he covered himself again

and reassumed the crimson *mozetta*, "that I could have done it over that German bastard's ugly face."

He slammed the door as he left.

1508

Barbara and I were finally professed into the community of believers in the spring of 1508; the ceremony took place in the Master's private chapel, as had our baptism. There were several guests present, including a lady, and they were attired in impressive liturgical robes of gold, worked with intricate designs in various colours. Barbara and I were in simple white. The Master stood in front of the black Madonna and Child that reposed on the altar; at his side there was a small table, draped in cloth-of-gold, and on it was a copy of the Gospel of John the Beloved, and a small clear glass bowl filled with pure water. There was also a napkin. The Master held in his hands his own preciously illuminated *Rituel de Lyons* of the *Catharistae*.

Looking in a kindly but solemn way at the both of us, he exclaimed:

"And so Peppe, and so Barbara, beloved children of the Father and of the Saviour Jesus Christ, you who have been baptized in his holy name: reject all idols and images and despise the most blasphemous idol of all, which is the fleshly body. Purify your hearts and cleanse them of all demons of impurity and error, that they may be visited by the Father and filled with the glory of his heavenly light! Know that you are eternal and immortal, and let death itself die in you!"

Then the Master read several prayers from the *Rituel de Lyons* which I am forbidden to give here. When he had finished reading, we came forward in turn and stood before him. He dipped a forefinger into the bowl of water and anointed us with it on the forehead, the palms of our hands, and on our bare feet, saying as he did so:

"Child of light, enter into the community of believers, now and forever. Jesus! Jesus! Jesus!"

Then he gave us the book of the Gospel of John to kiss.

Leading us by the elbow, he took Barbara to the woman participant, and myself to the men, and we exchanged the kiss of peace. Stooping to do so, each man carefully and tenderly placed his mouth against mine and held it there for a few moments. Then we embraced. I saw Barbara and the woman holding each other close. After this the company, led by the Master, burst into prolonged and warmly affectionate applause. This, I admit, moved me greatly.

The rite was concluded with another invocation from the *Rituel de Lyons,* which again I regret I am not permitted to reproduce here.

"Tonight," the Master said as we were quitting the chapel, "you and Barbara will be participants for the first time in our Rite of Renunciation. As fully professed members of this community of believers, you are not only entitled, but also *required* to attend."

I did not know it at that moment, but participating in the Rite of Renunciation was to rid me of any last vestige of the old life, and, furthermore, to render me almost invulnerable to emotional shock. You will see.

Of the women, I recognized only the one who had been present earlier in the day, at our solemn profession into the community of believers; there were four other women and six men, most of them rather young, and none of them (so it appeared) in any way deformed. I wondered how that was going to make Barbara and me feel. In a small antechamber adjoining the chapel, we disrobed (men and women together) and put on long, loose garments of silver, each bearing some kind of Gnostic sign or symbol in black on the breast; this was drawn in about the waist by a black leather belt with a silver buckle, the design of which was rather curious:

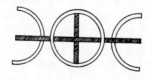

Later, I was told that the Perfect Ones of the *Catharistae* wore the selfsame belts, and that the belt of the Master was actually an original, having once belonged to Bertrand Marty, a Cathar bishop active in the Languedoc area of France two hundred years ago. My silver robe had obviously been specially made for me, since it was exactly the right length; either that, or it had been made for a child. We wore neither shoes nor sandals.

It was impossible not to be affected by the intensely spiritual atmosphere as we filed out, two abreast, into the chapel, which had been beautified by an artistically arranged assortment of pots and vases of fresh flowers; the black Madonna on the altar seemed *alive* somehow, moving within her own serene poise and stillness; there was the fragrance of some subtle, woody incense; the last golden light of the dying evening outside mingled and blended by some enchanted osmosis with the glow of candles, casting our faces in a rich amber, and the silver robes that we wore shimmered with an incandescent patina. The silence, deep, lovely and holy, enfolded us; it absorbed into itself all apprehensions and doubts (at any rate, *my* apprehensions and doubts), all unworded curiosity and hesitation, like a sponge absorbing water.

It was finally broken, as we stood in a semi-circle around the altar, by the mellifluous voice of the Master, our hierophant:

"Thus the blessed Apostle Thomas recorded: 'His disciples said: When will you be shown forth to us and when shall we behold you? Jesus said: When you strip naked without being ashamed, and take your garments and put them under your feet like little children and tread upon them, then you will see the child of the living. And you will not be afraid.'"

One by one (except for the Master) we unfastened our belts, pulled the silver robes over our heads so that we stood naked, and placed them carefully under our feet. I admit to feeling apprehensive as my turn to strip came, but I did it; I stepped onto my robe and tried to draw myself upright – a hairy, stunted, twisted little thing; yet no eyes lingered on me curiously, no lips curved in a pitying smile, and because of this I felt an equal among equals, possessing precisely the same degree of dignity as every other participant. I was more than a little moved. I could not help noticing that Barbara, who stood on the opposite side of the altar to myself, had a pair of fine, full breasts; in fact, she was really rather beautiful, and in other circumstances I might have thought it a pity that she lacked arms, but now it was impossible to feel anything but a deep and substantial pride in who we were and what we were doing. I cannot but also admit that the occasion was for me discreetly erotic; my commitment to what I had so far learned of our Gnostic philosophy was unreserved, and I entirely understood and approved of our renunciation of the purposes of the fleshly urge – yet it was impossible for me, as breasts rose and fell, as a dangling penis stirred here, a coppery bush of pubic hair caught the light and burst into radiant flame there, not to feel a more than mild current of arousal pass through my bowels and, rising to the surface, stipple my skin with delicious goose-flesh. This would, of course, have been quite impossible had I been made to feel in any way disgusting or ugly or physically revolting. The truth is, everyone's entirely unassuming acceptance of who and what I was, suffused me with a warmth that bespoke authentic *relationship* (I mean that we were a *part* of each other, united in a deep and abiding way), and where the warmth of such an emotional relationship is, the thought of *physical* relationship is not far away. *Ubi caritas et amor, Deus ibi est,* perhaps, but also the quiet savour of carefully controlled desire. *Erosque ibi est.*

"'The saviour said: The body of flesh is mutable, and what is mutable will perish and cease to be, and from that moment it has no hope of living. For the body of flesh is indeed an animal. Does it not result from sexual intercourse, like that of all animals? If the body of flesh, then, is from

124

sexual intercourse, how can it be anything different from the animal body? For this reason, you are children until you become mature.'"

When the Master had finished speaking (he was in fact quoting from *The Book of Thomas the Contender Writing to the Perfect*), we began to move slowly around the altar in a circle, and the discarded silver robes were twisted and creased beneath our naked feet.

Then the Master continued:

"'And the first governor said to the dominations dwelling with it, "Come, let us make a human being after the image of god and after our images so that the human being's image might serve as a light for us." And they carried out the act of creation by means of one another's power, according to the characteristics given to them. And each of the governors put into that being's psyche a characteristic corresponding to the representation of the image that they had seen. And they made an entity, after the image of the perfect first human being. And they said, 'Let us call him Adam, so that we might have his name as an incandescent power.' And the governors began:

> The first, kindness, made living bone.
> The second, forethought, made living
>   connective tissue.
> The third, divinity, made living flesh.
> The fourth, lordship, made living marrow.
> The fifth, kingship, made living blood.
> The sixth, zeal, made living skin.
> The seventh, intelligence, made living hair.'"

The Master, who until this point had continued to wear his silver robe, now removed it, and stepped upon it as we had done. I observed that he was lean and muscular, and that although the hair on his head was sprinkled with grey, between his legs it was fine, black and lustrous.

> " 'The first, Raphaō, began by making the crown of the head.' "

After every intonation, we paused and touched with a forefinger the bodily part named.

> " 'Arōna made the skull.
> Meniggesstrōeth made the brain.' "

(Here we touched the centre of our foreheads.)

" 'Asterekmē, the left eye.
Thaspomakha, the right eye.
Ierōnumos, the left ear.
Bissoumeemi the right ear.
Akiōreim, the nostrils.
Banēnephroum, the lips.
Amon-ffShata, the front teeth.
Ibikan, the back teeth.
Adabani, the nape of the neck.
Khaamani, the throat.
Tēbar, the left shoulder. (I experienced some difficulty here.)
Dēarkhō, the right shoulder. (Likewise.)
Abitriōon, the left hand.
Euanthēn, the right hand.
Astrōpsamini, the left nipple.
Barrōph, the right nipple.
Baoum, the left armpit.
Ararim, the right armpit.
Phthauē, the navel.
Gēsole, the stomach.
Aggromauma, the heart.
Mnashakka, the rectal orifice,
Eilō, the penis.
Sōrma, the testicles.
And Sōrma, the vagina.
Ormaōth, the left thigh.
Psērēem, the right thigh.

Akhiël, the left foot.
Phnēmē, the right foot.
Boozabel, the toes of the left foot.
Phiknipna, the toes of the right foot.' "

Then we slowly came to a standstill.

"What is the intention of Yaldaboath?" the Master cried.

"To imprison the light!" we sang back in unison.

"And what is our intention and purpose, we who bear the light?"

"To frustrate his will!"

At that moment, a rather beautiful young woman (nude, like the rest of us) came forward from the back of the chapel, bearing a richly decorated silver chalice on a crimson cushion of red silk; she approached the Master reverently, knelt at his feet, bowed her head.

"Then let it be frustrated," the Master said in a voice suddenly curiously subdued.

I was completely astonished when I realised what was about to take place, for I had never – not even in my most fertile imaginings – thought that within the Gnostic ambit, communal practice could be a corollary of collective belief. Indeed, the nature of the latter seemed to exclude the former; what had taken place between the lady Laura and myself had been a purely *private* lesson in the praxis of spiritual truth. At least that is what I had assumed. But now – now it seemed altogether an erroneous assumption. A horrid but delightful little shudder of shocked anticipation ran through me.

The woman had placed the cushion and chalice upon the altar, and was now once again kneeling in front of the Master. She reached up and took his penis in her hands, cradling it against her lips, and she began kissing it with great tenderness, as if it were a little living creature with a life all of its own – a bird perhaps, or a rosebud, a chrysalis. She worked her way slowly down the shaft, and the tip of her pink tongue left a glittering thread of moisture, like the track of a snail, along its length. The Master groaned softly – almost inaudibly! – and raised his eyes to the ceiling of the chapel, so that only the whites were showing. His penis was gradually becoming stiffer, nodding and bobbing into what would obviously be a rather impressive erection; the foreskin had slipped back to expose the head, already bloated, purplish. She massaged it with her finger-tips, rolled it between the palms of her hands; then she thrust it between her breasts and moved herself with an expertise that could (I imagined) only have been attained by repeated and devoted practice.

I was trembling, and I could not contain it, could not help myself; it had suddenly become very warm in the chapel – the effect, I am sure, of our combined excitation, the swell of involuntary desire, the heat and the power of Eros awakened – all moistness and laboured breathing – the odour of skin and sweat, the overwhelming fumes of a liturgically controlled animality. The eyes of the women were unfocussed and glassy, and their breasts rose and fell with each intake and exhalation of breath; the men stood with their legs spread wide, and some of them held their cocks in their hands, encouraging arousal with furtive, intimately rhythmic movements. What in the name of God were we to do? Or in the name of dark, manic Dionysus? I was caught, trapped, but I did not wish to be set free; I was struggling against some terrible and terrifying urge – an impulse to excess – and I was frightened by it, yet I knew that somehow, by some miraculous collective act of will, the power that we were unleashing was being restrained, was not our master but our servant. I felt as if I was drowning in a vast, sucking ocean which was neverthe-less subject to my command – paradoxical, impossible, exhilarating, phantasmagorical! But so. It was a bodily paean to sex that we were ritually enacting, but – I naturally assumed – it was one not of glory and praise, only insult and condemnation. Exactly how this condemna-tion was to be expressed, I had as yet conceived no idea.

Now the woman ministrant stood facing the Master,

and grasping his rigid penis in the fingers of one hand (it was thick and massive at the root, veined and darkly corrugated, straining upward, tapering to the swollen head), she drew it back and forth between her shuddering legs without actually inserting it, *stroking* herself with it – as they say the lascivious daughters of Egypt like to do with live serpents. Indeed, the Master's member did look rather serpentine: coiling and bending, flickering close to her damp private places, glistening richly in the mellow light, like the staff of Moses magically transformed into a cobra, the penis of a man, tractable to the sexual incantation we were silently weaving with the magic of our animal heat, now transmuted – a living, questing, snaking thing. It was a long, pliable rod of terrifying numinosity, and each time she drew it down across her belly, over the plump lips of her hairy cunny and then to the secret moistness beneath, she murmured something quietly to herself.

Her languorous, inebriated sigh was echoed by several of the women present.

At that moment I heard a small gasp come from across the other side of the chapel, followed immediately by a slick splattering sound; when I looked up, I saw that one of the men, presumably having lost control of himself, had ejaculated onto the floor. The Master's female ministrant began to moan deep down in her throat, her head rolling from side to side. It seemed to me that they must surely be but a hair's breadth away from actual intercourse – but was *that* the point of the ritual? I could not believe so. Then what? And how long could they keep up this astonishing foreplay without abandoning all restraint? I glanced around the chapel as unobtrusively as I could: I saw Barbara, her breasts heaving, and I observed that the wonderful little nipples were stiff; most of the men were now fully erect, rubbing themselves briskly, and some constantly shifted their weight from one foot to the other, like horses stamping impatiently on the ground, heady with anticipation. I myself, encased in my malformed little body, remained physically unaroused – but oh! – oh, my heart was thumping crazily, and my mouth was bone-dry – both sure and certain signs of sexual excitation.

At that moment the Master threw up his arms and screeched something incomprehensible (at least, it was incomprehensible to me, and I do not know whether or not the others knew what it signified), his voice high-pitched and strained. Immediately, the young woman went to the altar to retrieve the chalice; she held it to the Master's loins, and pressing down hard on his quivering penis with the palm of one hand, she manoeuvred it into the smooth, glittering silver concave of the bowl.

I saw the Master's whole body jerk convulsively – once, twice, three times – and then again, a fourth time – and a half-groan, half-sigh echoed around the chapel, a collective shudder of satisfaction and approval. The Master's eyes were now screwed tightly shut, and his handsome features were contorted in a spasm of sexual agony. *He was ejaculating into the chalice.* I was shocked, and I admit it. Why? Why in the chalice? There could surely be only one reason, and of that I didn't care to think in any great detail; when the probability that we would be called upon to *drink* from it in some grotesque parody of the Communion rite entered my mind as a relentless apprehension of the obvious, I immediately pushed it out again with a shiver of revulsion.

God alone knows how I would have reacted if the obvious had become actuality, but I was never to find out, for the rite was destined not to reach its conclusion: all at once, in what seemed to be a moment suspended forever in timelessness so that its horror was without end and thus able to seize and hold us in an inescapable embrace, the doors of the chapel burst open – oh, that shocking, ugly, clanging sound! – and we were precipitately plunged into the dark chaos of a nightmare.

Someone cried out:

"Finish it! We are discovered!"

I recognized him immediately: Fra Tomaso della Croce. A little older to be sure, a little greyer about the temples, but the dark eyes still gleamed with the familiar fire of merciless fanaticism. He was accompanied by six or seven armed men.

"Heretics!" he screamed, the corners of his mouth flecked with spittle. "Filthy, accursed heretics!"

The Master had fallen against the altar and the chalice clattered to the floor, spilling its incredible contents; we were all struggling to get back into our silver robes, but it was impossible to tell which robe had originally been whose. I grabbed the nearest and began frantically tugging it over my head. Some of the women had begun to wail.

"Make no resistance!" the Master shouted, raising one hand.

Then they struck. I saw poor Barbara, still naked, hanging on to one of Fra Tomaso's men, vainly attempting to ward off a blow, her little hands wiggling at the shoulders. Some of the males among us, despite the Master's call for non-resistance, were lashing out with their fists.

"A plenary indulgence for every heretic you dispatch from this world!" Tomaso della Croce cried, his arms folded across his chest, his face twisted in fury.

My hand flew to my mouth and I stifled a moan as I saw Barbara slip to the floor; her assailant stood over her, his arm raised high, the blade of his sword glittering in the yellow light; for a moment he paused, looking down at her with a self-satisfied smile on his lips. Then the arm swooped in a relentless parabola, and the sword entered Barbara's body, exactly between her two beautiful breasts. At once there was blood everywhere. She made no sound but slumped back, her tiny, ineffectual hands still moving, her eyes screwed tightly shut. The sword came out of her, then entered her again, this time through the stomach.

"Peppe!"

The Master picked me up in his strong arms as I saw someone else fall, pierced in the back of the neck.

"We can't do anything to help them!" he hissed to me. "We must escape!"

All this had happened in a matter of moments, as if a doorway in hell had suddenly opened and the underworld had emptied itself in the blink of an eye, vomiting out a myriad various nightmares simultaneously, and Tomaso della Croce had not had time to single out either the Master or me as objects of his murderous rage; indeed, whether he had ever intended to do so is doubtful – we were there, we were heretics, that was enough for him. Together we managed to reach the door to the antechamber of the chapel before I heard his outraged yell of frustration and hatred behind us. If it had not been for a young man who had thrown himself heroically onto the inquisitor's back, we would never have made it. God only knows what became of him. In the antechamber the Master put me down and bolted the door from the inside.

"Quick!" he said breathlessly. "I have horses. We must hurry!"

"Was it us he wanted?" I cried. "Is he slaughtering them on account of us?"

"I don't know – he wants all of us, Peppe! – oh, hurry!"

And I clung to his back, my arms crossed tightly about his neck, as moments later we were riding through the dark night, leaving behind us a night of horror and despair more impenetrable and deadly than the endless night of hell itself, to which Tomaso della Croce's furious curses had consigned us.

– 1509 onwards –

Commendo te omnipotenti Deo, carissima soror
In the house of Andrea de' Collini, there were three people seated down to supper on the night of April 23rd 1509: Andrea de' Collini himself, Peppe the Gnostic dwarf, whose memoirs you are now reading, and a young neophyte called Vittorino, who had received Gnostic baptism just days before Barbara and me. Vittorino had managed to escape from the Master's house in Florence with nothing worse than a broken arm, but he sobbed freely as he related the terrible details of the carnage that occurred in the private chapel of that house. Through his words we relived the horror we had witnessed, and came to learn of what had happened after our escape.

Five people had died, including poor Barbara, and six had been taken by the Inquisition. As far as he knew, only one other besides Vittorino and ourselves had got away.

"It was appalling," Vittorino said, drinking deeply from the wine we had given him, wiping away the tears with the back of his hand. "The women were hysterical; I saw one of them running around the chapel, senselessly, like a headless chicken, her right arm severed at the elbow. Oh God! Someone else – a young man, I think it might have been Lorenzo Caldi – threw himself onto the inquisitor's back, naked though he was, and tried to throttle him; he didn't stand a chance! They just pulled him off like a leech and cut him to bits."

"We saw him!" I cried.

"He saved us," the Master said quietly.

"Two of della Croce's men dragged an ashen-faced woman onto the altar – the sacred altar itself! – then one of them held her down and prised her buttocks apart with massive, bloodied hands, while the other penetrated her violently from behind. 'What's the matter, you heretic bitch?' he shouted when she began to scream and struggle, 'never been had by a real man before?' It was horrible, oh it was horrible. Another woman was spreadeagled on the floor, and I hope to sweet Jesus she was already dead, because one of the Inquisition's hired brutes had rammed his sword right up into her anus and was thrusting it about with sickening force, laughing, his eyes bright with pleasure – oh God, he was rubbing himself between his legs – he was stiff, rubbing it and laughing as he pushed the sword further in -"

"Vittorino – don't -"

"And they pulled Barbara's earrings off, ripping the flesh – but thank God she *was* dead by that time – the place was like an abattoir, everyone was slipping in their own blood, the floor was wet with blood and sperm, people were screaming and gouging and hammering with their fists – how in the name of God I got out of that slithering, bloody jumble of bodies I don't know – I just don't, can't – oh no, no -"

Master Andrea put one arm around the sobbing Vittorino's neck.

"No more now, no more," he said.

But Vittorino went on:

"He knew you were there, both of you – but it was too late -"

"I think we did not especially matter to him at that moment," the Master said. "Perhaps he did not even expect us. It was an heretical liturgy, that's all he cared about. He wanted victims, and he got them."

"But you'll matter very much to him *now*, won't you?" said Vittorino, twisting the stem of the smoked glass wine goblet in his trembling fingers.

"Yes," the Master said reflectively. A moment's pause followed, then: "I dare say we will."

"Certainly *I* will," I said. "After all, he had me once and let me go."

"He didn't let you go Peppe, he *sold* you."

134

"He sold me to Master Antonio because he didn't have any evidence against me. He has now – plenty of evidence."

"You must hide me!" Vittorino shrieked. "He'll come after me, too!"

"He'll come after us all, in good time," I said.

The Master shot me a curious glance, a look of something akin to surprise mingled with foreboding.

"Yes Peppe," he murmured, "you are undoubtedly right."

I have wondered ever since – and agonizingly so – whether I unwittingly planted the seed of madness in his soul with that single casual statement of mine; yet this wondering, this dark speculation, is itself an invitation to madness, and I dare not discuss it openly, not even with you my unknown reader. Analysis of this sort I leave to the sleepless hours between midnight and dawn.

The Master led Vittorino away to the chamber that had been prepared for him, with all the tender solicitude of a mother for her sick child; I was not to see Vittorino again, but I was later to hear of him from time to time, and to learn how Andrea de' Collini had provided for his comfort and security out of his own resources. I wished with all my heart I had not been obliged to receive the evil news Vittorino had brought, for the bloodsoaked images of violent death it conjured up remained with me – as I knew they would – for years to come; and yet I *had* to know. The Master and I both had to know, for quite apart from any purely practical considerations, the greatest tragedy according to our Gnostic philosophy (second only to being born into this world in the first place) is to live in ignorance, for ignorance is the weapon of Satan. Now ignorance is threefold – of God, of the world, of oneself; in this case, to shut out knowledge of what had taken place in that private chapel – however painful it might be – would be to suffer from all three varieties of ignorance. Firstly ignorance of God, since what happened to poor Barbara and the others revealed the direction of his holy will; secondly ignorance

135

of the world, because the perverted will of Tomaso della Croce was illuminated by his murderous acts; and thirdly of ourselves, for in bearing the terrible news brought to us by Vittorino, we measured the depths of our own courage. No, I did not want to hear it, but I knew I must.

Master Andrea and I had come back to Rome, driven like chaff before the wind, with no design or purpose other than that which our return itself suggested. We hoped, at least, to receive some news of the lady Laura; furthermore, it seemed to me that since hearing Vittorino's story, the Master was actually toying with the idea of forcing a confrontation between himself and the Dominican.

"He'll come after us in time," he said sombrely, and I shivered when I realised he was using my own words.

"Shouldn't we do whatever we can, now, for the lady Laura, then leave the city together?"

"No. If we are to help my daughter, we cannot be seen rushing about Rome with precisely that intention. We must be more circumspect than that. We shall initiate enquiries. I still have some people here who will assist us. We do not even know where she is being held; that's the first thing we must find out. Patience, Peppe, even in these adverse times."

I was angry and confused.

"Patience?" I cried. "Is that how little you care about her?"

"Never say that to me! Never!" he spat, his voice trembling with emotion. I was completely taken aback by his vehemence. "What have you ever known of a father's love? How could you possibly guess at the pain that wracks my heart, day and night, the nightmares that torment my sleep! I am ceaselessly on fire with the pain of her loss –"

I opened my mouth but could not speak.

"No, you must never say such a thing to *me*, Peppe. I know how you love her, believe me, but do not doubt for one moment that my love is any less. Indeed, it is infinitely greater."

"Master, I – I'm sorry –"

"You are forgiven Peppe," he said, calmer now. "I know that it was out of frustration, not anger, that you spoke. Neither of us is to blame. I promise you that soon enough we shall look for her."

He laid one hand on mine, and kissed me gently on the forehead.

"You have my word," he said.

So we came back to the house from which he had been absent for so long, and lived in daily expectation of Fra Tomaso della Croce's fist hammering on the doors.

"You *want* him to come, don't you?" I asked quietly.

"Yes, I do. This thing between us cannot go on forever. The sooner the final confrontation comes, the better it will be for all of us. I told you once before that there is something very personal in his hatred for me. So be it. One way or the other, I will end it."

And his words made me shiver once again.

The following evening I received a strange and by no means pleasant surprise; as a matter of fact, it was quite a shock. Passing the half-open door of Andrea de' Collini's private study, I heard his voice raised in earnest debate with that of another – and this other voice at once struck me as familiar.

"I asked you to carry out a commission," the Master said.

"And this I have done."

"Then the contract between us is concluded, my friend."

"No!" the other voice cried, and suddenly I knew who it was in there with the Master. It seemed impossible that it should be so – for what connection could there be between them? – and yet I *knew* it was.

I pushed the door fully open and walked into the study.

"Peppe –" the Master said, stepping forward as if to

prevent my entry, then realising it was too late. "I – I am with someone at present –"

"Yes," I answered coldly, "I can see that."

And I looked straight into the eyes of the man we freaks used to call the 'Skull.'

"Well, Peppe," he said in a tone of voice that I did not care for one little bit, "we meet again! Who would have thought it?"

"Don Giuseppe. Indeed, who would have thought it?"

"Perhaps each of us could be forgiven for thinking to have seen the last of the other."

Master Andrea was clearly feeling uncomfortable.

"Look, Peppe – I'll explain later – what you must understand –"

"Please, no explanations are necessary! It is not my right to know who your friends are, nor the manner of their coming and going. This is *your* house. I am a guest here."

"Peppe – don't be angry with me –"

"One thing however I *do* claim as a right, and that is to be fully informed about any business concerning the lady Laura. You shall not deny me this. It was *her* you were discussing, was it not?"

The Master sighed wearily and seated himself at his desk. The Skull, his patchwork face with its hideous travesty of a smile turned towards me, said:

"I suppose it must come as a bit of a surprise to discover that this noble gentleman and the likes of myself are acquainted. Oh, don't bother to deny it, Peppe! We eked out a miserable existence together in the same travelling hell for years –"

"Do you imagine I am likely to forget even one moment of those years? One second?"

Don Giuseppe shook his head.

"No," he replied softly, "I don't."

"You have abandoned Master Antonio, I take it?"

"Not exactly, little friend. He abandoned me, actually. I became hot property."

"Oh?"

"I talked too much and too loudly in a tavern one night – someone was listening, someone heard me – and information was passed on to the Inquisition. For a fair price, I've no doubt. I'm still a wanted man, remember."

"We all are."

"The Inquisition has a long memory and an even longer arm. Antonio Donato betrayed me. He sold me out."

"What?"

"The Inquisition took me – again."

I could hear the laboured breathing – more like a gentle sobbing – of Master Andrea as he sat slumped at his desk.

"They dumped me in the San Angelo."

"But how – I mean – how are you here? Did you escape?" I asked, astonished.

"Unless I'm in two places at once," he said with heavy sarcasm.

You *escaped* from that place?"

"Yes. But – but not before –"

"Giuseppe! No!" the Master cried, suddenly raising one arm.

Don Giuseppe shrugged his shoulders.

"What's the point?" he said in a tired voice. "He's got to know eventually."

"Know? Know what?" I shouted, unable to control my growing excitement.

"Besides, as he said himself, he's got a certain right."

The Master murmured:

"Oh, for the love of God."

"I saw *her* there," the Skull said.

Her! Laura! My heart was at once suspended between beats, each muscle of it stretched taut towards an excruciatingly painful infinity where each beat ran into the other and became a single ceaseless clamour.

"You saw Laura!" I cried agitatedly, "you saw her!"

"Yes. She was in a cell close to mine; I used to hear her weeping at night, weeping piteously –"

"In God's name stop!" Master Andrea yelled, "I cannot endure it!"

"Go on," I said, frozen in the icy calm not of consummate self-control, but raging fear and anger.

Don Giuseppe said:

"I knew who she was. She used to call on her father's name – and – and on *your* name, little friend."

"No –"

"Yes! You see, *I have known Andrea de' Collini for a long time*. When I heard that tormented creature cry out his name in the depths of the night – but who knows what is night and what is day in that place which is eternally night? – I understood. I understood who she was, and knowing who she was, could not help but understand the only possible reason for her incarceration."

Quite suddenly, with a swiftness of movement that shocked me, the Skull swung round on the balls of his feet, threw both hands high into the air, then brought them down hard upon the shoulders of Andrea de' Collini. He thrust his hideous face close to the Master's ear, and he hissed:

"Seems to be quite a habit of yours, doesn't it, Master? Getting your friends and family locked away by the Holy Inquisition!"

"Can't you see that I'm suffering enough –"

"Suffering? *You?* You don't know the meaning of the word! Was it you who had the flesh burned off his face to show the gleaming bone beneath? Was it you who was put on show night after night for people to jeer and spit at? Has it been you languishing in the stinking depths of the San Angelo? No! No, no, no! It has never been *you,* has it? It's me, me and that precious daughter of yours!"

The Master was sobbing uncontrollably now.

"Stop!" I cried, pulling Don Giuseppe's hands from Andrea de' Collini's shoulders. "How do you know each other? What do you mean by such an accusation?"

Don Giuseppe looked up at me wildly; his jaws were slack, his lips flecked with spittle, and I did indeed see the bone gleam in his half-destroyed face.

"I was once a disciple of the Master," he said, his voice

trembling. "Oh yes, I sat at his feet and absorbed his great and wonderful Gnostic teaching! So convinced was I that Andrea de' Collini possessed the truth, truth to ease the pain of the world and soak up the world's tears, like water being soaked up by a sponge, that I rushed out to declare it even in my own church. Oh, how gullible I must have been! They arrested me almost immediately and I was sentenced to die at the stake; however, as you know, Divine Providence spared me that ghastly fate – (here he touched what remained of his chin) – at a price, naturally. Oh, there's always a price, Master Andrea, isn't there?"

Andrea de' Collini raised his head. I saw that the backs of his hands were wet with tears.

"It is not truth's fault if you are punished for proclaiming it," he said softly. "It is the fault of ignorance."

"You couldn't help me though, could you? You let them take me and try to burn me."

"What could I have done, Giuseppe? I was powerless –"

"You should have at least *tried,* you bastard!"

The Master shook his head slowly. Then he became still.

"I heard you speaking about a commission, a contract," I said, shaken and distressed by these revelations, and fighting against a deep, dark despair that was trying to take hold of me; despair and hopelessness and fury that Don Giuseppe, the Skull – this *creature* - had seen my beloved Laura with his own eyes, while the vision of her loveliness, made unbearably poignant by her suffering, was denied to me.

"Then you will already know, little friend."

"No, Don Giuseppe, I do *not* know. What is that commission that you have apparently fulfilled?"

The Skull sighed.

"There *are* ways of getting out of that ghastly fortress," he said, "but they are few. Years ago, when I was first in there, I discovered one of those ways for myself, but it was too late to take advantage of it. The place hasn't changed, believe me – except perhaps that it's even filthier and damper. As you can see, my precious knowledge served me well this time."

"And?"

"I came here. Andrea de' Collini gave me money and charged me to return to the San Angelo with it, to give it to someone who would use it for *her*. To pay for some sort of comfort – fresh food, clean water. I can't say that I went back myself because I didn't – I don't have that much trust in my luck – but the individual I sent in my place is trustworthy and reliable – I guarantee it! – and whatever money can buy for her, she will get."

"Then the commission *is* fulfilled?"

"In a manner of speaking, yes. But in another way, no. I swore to Laura de' Collini that I would get her out of the San Angelo –"

"You actually *spoke* to her?" I cried.

"No, I sent a message to her through the agency of another. I did see her – twice – when they were taking her up for – for – interrogation."

"Oh, God!"

"Now he won't let me keep that promise. He's given me more money, money to make me forget the message I had sent to her –"

Quite suddenly, Andrea de' Collini rose to his feet; his cheeks were flushed, his eyes fixed in a concentrated state of resolution.

"It is not your place to decide my daughter's fate," he said in a voice which was all the more compelling for being so perfectly controlled and calm.

"But Master!" I cried.

"No, Peppe. No. If anything is to be done, I will do it. Perhaps there is nothing to be done, nothing at all. You must remember that there are many others – every member of our fraternity – whose safety depends upon our circumspection. I can never allow that safety to be threatened!"

"And so you will permit her suffering to go on? After so many years?"

"That is not my will. Yet neither is it my intention to endanger the lives of many for the sake of one."

"Even your own daughter?"

"What can be done, I will do, please believe me."

As I threw myself against the wall, pummelling it with my fists in an impotent rage, I heard the Master say quietly:

"Your being in my house serves no further purpose, Don Giuseppe. Please leave."

And the priest who had abused his lady penitents in the darkness of the confessional, the man who had publicly declared the teachings he once thought to be untarnished truth, the half-faced creature we freaks called 'the Skull', quitted the room silently.

Later, pacing the floor of his library, wringing his hands together in an agony of indecision and confusion, the Master said to me:

"I can't think why they put her in *there* of all places. Why, in the name of God?"

"Because of your status, presumably," I suggested.

"But that doesn't make sense, Peppe; if I'm a heretic, I have no status whatsoever, no rights, no property, nothing."

"But you *aren't* officially a heretic – not yet, anyway. You said yourself that Tomaso della Croce's vendetta against you is intensely personal in nature; might it not be that he has left no record of his dealings with you? That he wishes to save you for himself? Everything that needs to be documented can be done at the end, when he has you bound and chained, when he is in a position to gloat over his success and taunt you with his victory; but until then – why, it's between you and he. He wants to be absolutely *sure* that he has you where you have no chance of escape. Only then will he bring in the scribes and the other inquisitorial small fry. No-one in Rome knows what has been going on between you and della Croce – isn't it obvious? You come and go freely, your house is open, your friends still call."

"And Laura?"

"Laura doesn't interest him in the slightest, except as a cancer in the body of Holy Mother Church, to be rooted out and destroyed."

"He must surely be insane," Master Andrea said.

"He *is* insane. Insane in the name of God."

"He'll come for us, Peppe. I know it."

It grieves me, even now, to tell you that we did not have to wait for the coming of Fra Tomaso della Croce to be engulfed by the horror he had unleashed. The horror arrived the following evening, when we received the news that Laura Francesca Beatrice de' Collini had been found guilty of heresy on twelve counts, had refused to recant, had been sentenced by the court of the Inquisition, and handed over to the secular arm. She was to be burned alive in the Campo dei Fiori the following morning.

And the morning that I prayed would be swallowed up in endless night *did* come soon enough; it was a clear, bright, chilly morning – perfect weather for a burning. On windy days there was always a danger that the fire would get out of control – 'the Skull' had once told me that sparks from *his* fire, carried by the gusts, had destroyed several houses, even as the flames around the stake were consuming most of his face, before finally being put out by the unexpected downpour.

"They couldn't decide which burning amused them most, me or the houses. Callous bastards."

I begged, pleaded, threatened, screamed, wept and implored, but Master Andrea would not (or could not) listen to me; I know now that I failed to realise the intensity of the shock which paralysed him. At the time, he sounded so resigned, so passive, it filled me with total revulsion. I am also convinced that this shock was far more deeply-rooted than his reluctance to imperil the lives of others; the rationality of this reluctance was no more than a veneer with which his beleaguered psyche was attempting to cover the vast, seething irrational horror debilitating him from within. It was like trying to pour the ocean into a perfume flask. There was, too, another reason for his inertia which I was not to discover until the time − well − until much later. You will learn of it in due course.

"We must *try,* for the love of God!" I cried. My pathetic body twitched and jerked convulsively, making me look like a crazy marionette whose strings had become hopelessly entangled.

"No, nothing."

"For Christ's sake, we're talking about them burning Laura!"

"What could we do? We would be worse than useless."

"Andrea − please − don't keep saying that −"

"But it's true," he answered tonelessly.

It was quite hopeless. He sat slumped in a chair, staring morosely down at his hands, plucking and picking uselessly at the gold thread that edged his robe.

In one sense he was absolutely right: short of raising an army of courageous friends, there was nothing we could do to save Laura. She was as good as dead. On the other hand, I believed (and still believe, even though I now realise that shock had struck him more deeply than it *appeared* to have done) that the fatalistic despair into which he had fallen was far from helping *us.*

"I shall go to the Campo dei Fiori," I said, panting for breath after my terrible outburst. "They may let me see her for the last time − speak to her, even −"

"Do not expect me to come with you. I cannot. I will not. They will burn her, but they cannot force me to stand by and look."

"Then stay here. You shall not stop me," I said.

"Peppe − you would − would *watch* her burn? Have you ever seen a burning? It is too terrible for words."

"Then she *must* be rescued! Don Giuseppe will help us −"

"Peppe, no!"

"You heard what he said − he *knows!* He knows a way out of that place −"

"Too late, you stupid dreamer! Too late −"

Andrea de' Collini suddenly rose from his chair, his

145

handsome features contorted by some indescribable, demonic, agonising fury and loathing. His eyes bulged in his head, the veins at his temples and in his throat stood out like ropes. Briefly, he waved his arms wildly in the air, his fists clenching and unclenching with great rapidity.

And he screamed: a high-pitched, spine-tingling, hoarse scream of complete and total despair.

"Laura, oh Laura, Laura!"

Then no more. He was silent.

There was already a large crowd gathered in the Campo dei Fiori when I arrived, caitiffs and ruffians to a man – even among those who were unable to read the notices posted up by the authorities, news of a burning spread fast. It was just like a market day: many Trasteverini had crossed the river, gesticulating and cursing, stealing fruit from the stalls, looking for pockets to pick; a shudder passed through me as I watched them, like the miasma of an ancient sickness. Had I really once belonged to them? Was it possible that the woman who had called herself my mother was here too? It was just the sort of spectacle she would cross the river to enjoy. They were vile, these people – hardly people at all, little better than savages anticipating with gruesome relish someone else's suffering, instinctively and lasciviously rejoicing that it was not theirs. It was the feeling one gets when somebody slips and falls in the street, and the natural movement of pity is cut off at its source by the satisfaction of knowing it isn't oneself who has fallen – but magnified a thousand times, made garishly explicit, refined and honed by the subtle and pungent flavour of a dark eroticism. I felt their secret sex glands at work, pumping out fluid, stiffening or loosening, lubricating and arousing, and it rose up like a noxious cloud to choke me: excitement, satisfaction, anticipation, the stimulant of vicarious power over another human being, the reek of sadism – all these were compounded, mixed together like a highly spiced salmagundi. It was all I could do to keep myself from being physically sick.

146

I listened to passing snatches of conversation:

"– *deserves all that she gets, the patrician bitch!*"

"*No, I've never been to a burning before, this is my first. Will we be able to see from here?*"

"*– find ourselves a couple of juicy whores before things start to hot up – ha ha! – she'll find it too hot for her liking, you can be sure –*"

"*She fucked with dogs, I've heard tell.*"

"*Didn't she deny the power of the cross?*"

"*– you can smell it when the skin starts to burn –*"

"*That lily-white skin of hers, that'll burn alright!*"

"*– never done a day's work in her life, the little whore!*"

"*Not just with dogs – Christ, they say she's wide enough to take a fucking bull!*"

"*Who'll light the faggots?*"

"*Jesus, wait till you hear the white-skinned bitch start to scream . . .*"

They pushed by me, jostled me, too keyed-up for the big entertainment to take notice of a crook-back dwarf with tears streaming down his face.

The stake had been set up in the centre of the Campo dei Fiori, the ropes that would bind her to it hanging loose; the bundles of tinder-dry faggots had been piled high, to ensure that the flames would quickly burn away her feet then move up her body. There was scarcely a breeze. I did not know for sure, but I had been told by 'the Skull' that most victims were overcome by the smoke and rendered unconscious before the flames got to work; I prayed fervently that this would be so. I prayed for a good many things without much hope that my prayers would be answered: for a sudden downpour that would put out the fire as it had done for 'the Skull'; for a reprieve at the last moment; for dissent among the crowd, who might be moved to pity by the sight of her; for some sort of miracle which would prove the whole horror nothing more substantial than a nightmare. I even prayed for a mercifully swift death, but the histories told us that *La Pucelle* had screamed the name of Jesus for twenty minutes before yielding up her life to the flames.

147

I was not prepared to see the procession so soon; it entered the Campo in almost total silence, having presumably made its way from the San Angelo and along the river bank. At the head of it walked a Dominican friar, holding a crucifix aloft, and reading to himself from a book; I could not tell what it was that he read. Behind him came more friars, their white habits dazzling in the bright sunshine. Then the magistrate, an incongruously kindly-looking man dressed in a sumptuous samite overcloak trimmed with fur at the collar; and then – oh, then! – then came the cart in which Laura Francesca Beatrice de' Collini knelt, attired in the grotesque sanbenito, which victims of the Inquisition were required to wear as they went to the flames. That was a studied cruelty. Laura! Her head was bowed, her golden hair falling about her shoulders like a waterfall in spring sunshine. Her hands were tied behind her back. She held herself absolutely motionless. Behind the cart came acolytes, thurifers, a crucifer, and a raggle-taggle of minor ecclesiastical functionaries – all to enrich the lurid liturgy of her death-rites. Oh yes, why yes, if there's to be a show, make it a damned *good* one! Give the crowd something to really *gawp* at! Make sure the heretic bitch screams! Finally, at the rear, came the two fire-lighters carrying their flaming torches, their heads covered with black leather hoods so that only the small, glittering eyes were visible. The friars began to chant, and I covered my ears against that hateful sound; I, whose gasps of sexual delight had been her bridal hymn, was now forced to listen to the plangent threnody of her hour of death.

They led her from the cart and dragged her over the faggots; she seemed utterly limp and lifeless, her head hanging down, her legs like dead weights. They heaved her up to the stake, and as they began to bind her to it with the ropes, I saw that the fabric of her sanbenito had snagged and torn – her one perfect, milky breast tumbled out, and the pious caterwauling of the friars was drowned in a great roar of salacious approval from the *canaille;* the men applauded and raised their hands in the air to make lewd, ugly gestures. God only knows how they would have reacted if they had seen her deformity.

I tried to push my way to the front of the crowd; some mistook me for a child, and automatically moved out of my path. I saw the crucifer hold up his golden cross mounted on its long wooden pole, and position it so that it was directly in front of her eyes. The fire-lighters stood on either side of the pile of faggots. I was near enough now to see her face – the face of my *Laura* – and it was swollen, puffy with bruises; her lower lip had split, and there was dried blood in the corners of her mouth. Her eyes were closed. They had smeared something in cinnabar about her neck – some clerical curse that branded her a persistent recreant.

The crowd were very noisy by this time, and the friar who read the ecclesiastical conjuration – a bald, obese man with plump, trembling white hands – had to shout in order to be heard:

"Inasmuch as Laura Francesca Beatrice de' Collini has been adjudged guilty of heresy by the sacred tribunal of the Most Holy Inquisition; and inasmuch as the said Laura Francesca Beatrice de' Collini has persisted in her errors without recantation; and inasmuch as the said Laura Francesca Beatrice de' Collini has been handed over to the secular arm for punishment, all the while Holy Mother Church pleading with the secular arm for a merciful consideration of her errant daughter, let the secular arm now commit her body to the flames. And Holy Mother Church, the most compassionate and gentle of mothers, intercedes with her heavenly Spouse, Our Lord and Saviour Jesus Christ, begging him that her soul may be spared the eternal flames of the life to come. Yet notwithstanding, since the said Laura Francesca Beatrice de' Collini has stubbornly and wickedly persisted in her false teaching and pernicious error, let her, by the divine justice of the Most High, which renders to every creature its proper due, be consigned to the fire prepared by Our Lord and Saviour Jesus Christ for the devil and his fallen angels, from the beginning of time unto endless time and unending ages."

The magistrate read the sentence of the secular arm,

which was but a brief repetition of the hypocritical bilge intoned by the fat friar – that my beloved Laura should be burned alive.

The two hooded fire-lighters moved in; the golden cross hovered before Laura's closed eyes; a last check was made of the ropes; I was close enough now to almost reach out and touch the faggots, but I could not – dare not – cry out to her.

A single, full-throated yell from some bastard in the crowd:

"Burn the fucking bitch!"

And then, uproar as the torches were set to the faggots. They caught immediately and began to crackle into cruel, orange-red, flickering and hissing life.

The Master had once told me that the Perfect Ones of the *Catharistae* went to the stake singing, that the enactment of the *Rituel de Lyons* the night before had bestowed upon them some power to withstand the pain of the flames; I buried my head in my hands and silently prayed from that same *Rituel* – passages that I had learnt by heart. I desperately hoped, by some process of osmosis or psychic transfer, that any miraculous succour they might yield would pass from me to her. The words ran frantically through my mind, and I had to struggle to hold onto them, to concentrate (since the noise of the rabble was now deafening), until the prayers came to an end, and I could remember no more; I stood numb, helpless, abandoned, an exile in an alien land where every face, every voice, every cloud on the horizon, every speck of dust beneath my feet, was unremittingly hostile.

Oh! Oh, then I heard her scream! – and it was a scream of unmitigated agony. Immediately, a hush fell upon the spectators, and unable to help myself, I looked up.

The sanbenito was on fire; her hair spat and fizzled as it burned; the lower half of her body was a nigrescent blur, all sparks and charred fragments and wild, whipping tongues of flame, a living horror in black and red. People were moaning – low, throaty, animal-like moans of pleasure and dark, vile ecstasy. It was as if they were making love to the fire itself. Women clutched their breasts, their eyes wide with astonishment; the men moved their hands slyly, salaciously.

She was a human salamander, so that even in an unimaginable agony her beauty demanded veneration – from the flames themselves it seemed, for they flickered and darted and sucked around her like desire-maddened tongues, craving an appointment with private, vulnerable contours, spitting love-burns, their deadly caress all consuming seduction; then she was a goddess of some exotic pantheon, a numen whose devotees worshipped her with living images of death, the sun and the moon and the stars her garment, and she moved, smiling, in the heart of the fire; then a star itself, a distant orb glowing between tenebrous spaces in which stirred not the vast ethers of the heavens, but the sickening, convulsive appetite of an inhumanity that gorged itself, satiated, on her expended light. Then – and then again! – oh then, she was just a poor, dying girl tied to the Inquisition's stake.

"Laura!" I cried aloud, "Laura, Laura, Laura!"

She raised her head, bathed in an aureole of flame, and opened her eyes. They seemed simply to melt away in the heat, and she was immediately sightless.

"Laura!"

But she had *heard* me, for out of the fire came a hand! Luminous, incandescent, as if it held the core of the sun, the palm upturned, the fingers curved, and a shudder passed through the people – a kind of attenuated orgasmic 'aahhh' which rose then ebbed away like the rustle of dead leaves in a lonely, windswept alley.

A thumb and one finger came together at the tips, and formed the shape of a circle – the sign for perfection, for completion and infinity – and I knew beyond the shadow of a doubt that it was meant for me. Then the hand sank back and was gone. She had heard my voice, and she had responded.

The fire became an inferno, the roar of it like the rushing wings of the Angel of Death.

You may care to know that as I write these words, a full ten years after the burning of Laura Francesca Beatrice de' Collini, the page beneath my trembling hand is wet with tears.

INCIPIT SECUNDA PARS

My beloved Leo is dead.

No doubt you will wish to know all that happened in the years that followed the burning of Laura Francesca Beatrice de' Collini, and will require an explanation of how I came to enter Leo's service while he was still only Cardinal Giovanni de' Medici – and both knowledge and explanation will be provided; however, I feel that the passing from this world of such a man as Leo deserves the frank impact of an opening sentence, and this is what I have given it. Leo X, the Medici pope, is dead. He died at midnight, either at the last stroke of the 1st of December, or the first of the 2nd of December, depending on how chronologically meticulous you are. I am numb with sadness and grief, and have decided that the best way of dealing with both, is to plunge myself into the continuation of these memoirs; for where the variegated recollections of the past claim me, present melancholy cannot.

Therefore, I dip my nib in my ink and write:

– 1511 onwards –

Perduc eum, Domine, quaesumus, ad novae vitae

At the beginning of this year, a great celebration was held in the piazza in front of what was left of the old St Peter's and what had been begun of the new, to celebrate the victory, two years earlier, of the League of Cambrai over the Republic of Venice; actually, it was only in 1510 that Pope Julius had finally secured not only freedom of trade and navigation, but also confirmation of ecclesiastical rights in the Republic; papal troops had also regained Rimini and Faenza, and therefore some sort of spectacle to mark the occasion, however belated, was deemed appropriate. Whether it *was* appropriate or not is another matter, for Venice was now officially allied to the papacy along with Spain (England was soon to join) in the Holy League against France; Julius had already taken Modena from the Duke of Ferrara, who supported the French. The Holy League was backed (morally, anyway) by almost the entire aristocracy of Rome, since in a masterly display of diplomacy (the essence of which was, as always with Julius, *suaviter in modo, fortiter in re*), the pope had managed to unite the Orsini and Colonna families who, between them, carried a great deal of influence. The whole situation was thus somewhat complicated, not least of all by a series of unabashed tergiversations on the part of His Holiness. Still, the Romans have never really bothered terribly much about the *ultima ratio* of putting on a good entertainment, not since the days when the mob regularly pissed itself with excitement in the blood-drenched arena.

It was held on my last night in Rome before leaving the city – for I could not endure to remain, after Laura's horrific death; Master Andrea had dismissed his servants, locked up his house, and had given me a substantial amount of money.

"Go where you will, Peppe," he said with great weariness. "As for myself, I do not know; but we shall meet again before long, of that I am certain. God will arrange it when the time is right. May his benediction always rest upon you."

Oh, I understood his reasons – indeed, as I say, I did not wish to stay in Rome myself – but I was a little taken aback by his helpless, defeated resignation.

"I shall leave in the morning," I told him.

"Do you know where?"

I shook my head.

"Perhaps back to Florence, Master."

"Then I shall provide you with an introduction to

someone I know. He will be happy to offer you comfortable lodgings."

And that was that. I no more doubted than Andrea de' Collini did that fate and fortune would reunite us, but when that was to be, and in what manner it would take place, I could not begin to guess.

And so the victory celebration.

It seemed a savage irony to me, as I walked among the crowd, to know that many of them would have been in the Campo dei Fiori, glutting their stygian appetites on the sight of Laura being burned to death; now they had come to enjoy a spectacle of a different kind, but the same turbid yearning to be entertained and enthralled at any cost, marked the stupid faces of the draff with the sign of the Great Beast, the brand of Cain written large on every forehead. I hated them virulently. I wanted to lash out with my fists, striking wherever I could, hurting whomsover I pleased; I wanted them to suffer, as they had made me suffer. I ached to inflict *pain,* and I was vaguely, darkly aware that somehow the inner agony I was presently enduring was simply a protracted series of psychic callisthenics to prepare and properly equip me for the time (which would surely come!) when I *would* inflict it, violently and mercilessly.

The entertainment on offer was a remarkably clever *tableau vivant* depicting the movement of the planets; an enormous stage had been erected, bearing a great wooden *scena* covered in black velvet, and therefore impossible to actually see against the dark mass of the half-demolished, half-constructed basilica immediately behind it. What one *did* actually see was a series of openings, lit from behind by candles, in each of which sat a human representative of a particular planet or star; Venus, for example, was a stunningly beautiful young woman, bare-breasted, the lower half of her body swathed in shimmering silver; the sun was depicted by a young man painted all over in gold, carrying a glass orb in one hand and a sceptre in the other, and so

157

on. I have to admit that it was extremely impressive. All the more so when the 'planets' and 'stars' began to move! How they arranged it I do not know – I can only guess that a series of concentric rings, bearing their celestial personages, moved through the openings in the *scena*. Venus sank and disappeared, and the sun rose; various stars plunged through one opening and reappeared in another; and when the moon came into view on the extreme left of the tableau, the crowd applauded: a girl in blue and silver sat on a great white crescent, a circle of stars adorning her brow, a cascade of silver stardust falling from her lap.

Behind the *scena* the work must have been tough, cranking and winding the great cogs and wheels that obviously kept the whole thing moving; but the rumbling and grinding of the machinery was drowned out by the singing of the Sistine Choir, who performed a motet by Luigi Ferrari, in praise of the glory of God revealed in the firmament.

Pope Julius II watched from his window; I was just able to make out the frown-creased face and the long, luxuriant beard of the old man; his expression was one of tetchy impatience. As I made my way out of the crowded piazza, I heard someone say:

"It's all Leonardo's design, but he's not here."

"Why?"

"He can't bear to be in the same city as Master Michelangiolo."

That, I mused, was natural enough; Buonarroti and da Vinci both in Rome at the same time, would be like two queens in the one hive.

Early the next morning I left for Florence.

Fortune had meanwhile been smiling and frowning by turns upon the man who was soon to become the most important single influence in my life – Cardinal Giovanni de' Medici, the future Pope Leo X; on October 1st 1511, after I had been living for some time in Florence at a house belonging to the 'someone' to whom Master Andrea had recommended me (you shall learn his identity shortly),

158

Cardinal de' Medici had been appointed Legate to Bologna and the Romagna by Julius II. This was not only in order that the formation of the Holy League against France might be swiftly concluded, but also because Julius had his gimlet eye on the Florentine Republic, which supported the Council of schismatic cardinals at Pisa – as I have already told you, the Council was convened in order to curb Julius' power; for this reason alone, Julius favoured the exiled Medicis. However, the future Leo displayed a tardiness in setting about his new military duties which was not at all to the liking of hot-headed, fiery Julius, and after dillying and dallying for almost half a year, he was barely able to justify himself to the warrior-pope without being stripped of his dignity; further, the fickleness of fortune once again subjected him to humilation, and on April 11th 1512, the combined troops of Spain and the papacy suffered a severe defeat at Ravenna, at which Cardinal de' Medici was taken prisoner and carried off to Milan. Poor Leo! While he was there, Julius sent him powers to grant absolution from ecclesiastical censures to the men of the French forces who had captured him, and he therefore found himself in the paradoxical and doubtless bewildering position of bestowing spiritual succour upon his enemies. Why the hard-nosed French should have desired this grace in such droves I am at a loss to know, but they did.

The battle of Ravenna had taken place on Easter Sunday, April 11th, 1512, the two opposing forces having met on the banks of the Ronco about two miles from Ravenna itself; the French troops (who actually included Germans and Italians) under the command of Gaston de Foix, numbered about twenty-five thousand, and those of the Holy League, twenty thousand. The battle was initiated by the artillery, whose main strength was the guns of the Duke of Ferrara, a long-time supporter of the French. I quote from a letter written by Jacopo Guicciardini, to his brother Francesco, who was at that time the Florentine Envoy in Spain:

'It was truly ghastly to see how each shot blasted through the ranks of armed men, with helmets [and the heads inside them!] flying through the air together with arms and legs. When the Spaniards realised they were being blown to bits without a chance, they hurled themselves forward and initiated the hand-to-hand combat. The desperate fight lasted for many hours, and in the end only the brave Spanish foot soldiers held their ground, resisting stubbornly. In the end however, they were trampled underfoot by the cavalry.'

The battle raged from 8.00am until 4.00pm, and was finally decided by the steady endurance of the Germans fighting with the French forces; there were over ten thousand corpses on the field, including that of the French commander, the youthful Gaston de Foix. Generals Fabrizio Colonna and the Marquis of Pescara were taken prisoner along with plump, panting, shocked Cardinal Giovanni de' Medici. War was never his forte. Ravenna itself was hideously plundered, and there were rumours of strange, monstrous births: a woman was said to have borne a child with a giant carbuncle where its nose should be, another found herself the mother of triplets, joined together at the feet.

The news of defeat reached Pope Julius on April 14th, and the whole of Rome fell into a panic-stricken state; it was said that the spirit of Gaston de Foix would strike Julius dead and place a new pope upon the throne of Peter. Julius himself considered flight, but in the end the courage of his fierce warrior's temperament prevailed, and he railed at the quaking, clamouring crowds from his window, promising his tiara if he did not succeed in driving the French from Italy. He cursed the cowardice of the cardinals, and drove them through the Scylla and Charybdis of fear of the French and terror of his wrath. Giulio de' Medici, who had been dispatched to Rome under French safe-conduct by the prisoner Cardinal Giovanni de' Medici, reported to Leo that French losses had been enormous, that the new commander of the army, La Palice, was at loggerheads with the haughty Cardinal Sanseverino, and the French were in no position to march on Rome; that, indeed, Ravenna was but a Pyrrhic victory. Julius' determination to strike back was encouraged by the support he had miraculously managed to muster from the aristocracy of Rome, in particular from the Colonna and Orsini families.

The schismatic Council of Pisa, which had decamped to Milan, heartened by the victory of the French, now declared that Julius should be suspended from all spiritual and temporal administration, and deposed; but support for this gathering of disaffected nincompoops and self-seekers was gradually dwindling, and even the French King Louis XII admitted that it was nothing more than a spectre to intimidate Julius – which of course it failed to do even for one moment. Further, the schismatics were obliged to endure the humiliation of seeing many hundreds of the occupying forces throwing themselves on their knees before Cardinal de' Medici, imploring absolution from the censures they automatically incurred by waging war against the Supreme Pontiff. The Supreme Pontiff himself went ahead with the opening of the Fifth Lateran Council (partially convened as a counter-measure against Pisa), doing so with great and elaborate ceremonial pomp. This took place on May 3rd. England had by now joined the Holy League, and in the midst of presiding at the Lateran Council, Julius found time to send a precious 'cap of honour', adorned with gold and pearls, to Cardinal Schinner and his Swiss troops, all fiercely loyal to the honour of Holy Mother Church and the pope, and to promise them free passage through papal dominions, as well as a copious supply of provisions. At the same time that the Swiss army led by Cardinal Schinner poured into Italy, the Emperor Maximillian, now less eager to maintain his friendship with France, withdrew the German foot soldiers who had played such a decisive role in the battle of Ravenna.

The French were in a hopeless position; on June 14th Pavia surrendered to the Swiss troops, and under siege from the papal army commanded by the Duke of Urbino, from the Venetians and the Spanish, the Duchy of Milan rose up and rebelled against its French masters. The schismatic cardinals found their position intolerable and decamped to Asti; from there they moved to Lyons, where they were finally to peter out in a last gasp of foetid theological and political wind. Genoa repudiated her allegiance to the French and elected Giovanni Fregoso as Doge; Rimini, Cesena and Ravenna returned to the papal fold; finally, on June 20th, Ottaviano Sforza, Bishop of Lodi, entered Milian as Julius' lieutenant. Louis XII had lost everything, including the town of Asti, which belonged to his own family. A jubilant Cardinal Schinner wrote to Julius from Pavia, detailing the miraculous series of victories, and the whole of Rome exploded in a noisy effulgence of victory celebrations. The hysterical cry of *Julius! Julius!* rang throughout the Eternal City. The Venetian Envoy commented:

'Never was any emperor or victorious general so honoured on his entry into the eternal city as His Holiness has been this day. Now the Lord God leaves us nothing to ask for, and we have but to render him thanks for this triumph.'

Cardinal Giovanni de' Medici, whom the French had planned to take to France after abandoning Milan, managed to escape while crossing the river Po, and made a rather less than victorious flight to Bologna and to safety. Waddling no doubt, rather than running.

In the midst of all these goings-on, while Rome was making the rapid transition from panic to orgiastic celebration, I was living quietly and alone in the house of an absent stranger, attended by only two of his servants. In fact, the 'someone' whom Master Andrea said would be happy to provide me with lodgings was a man by the name of Giovanni Lazzaro de' Magistris, otherwise known by the soubriquet Serapica, on account of his small stature. He was a chamberlain in the household of Cardinal Giovanni de' Medici, and had shared his exile.

In my isolation, I did a great deal of ruminating; I wept for poor Laura; I yearned for the presence of Andrea de' Collini; I prayed for the departed psyche of Barbara Monduzzi. Furthermore, I reflected long and hard upon the nature of the Gnostic teaching that I now espoused; neither did I for one moment doubt that I *had* espoused it, fully and unreservedly, lock, stock and barrel, for as a working philosophy it provided me with everything I needed to confront life face to face. It *explained* things so well. Oh, I do not know whether the fantastic names and titles that we chanted in our dithyrambic liturgies actually referred to existent beings, or whether they were merely a poetic and convenient way of designating principalities and powers, knowledge of which was essentially *ultra vires*. Nevertheless, I do know that good and evil are precisely balanced in this material existence of ours, and that life on this planet, hallmarked as it is by suffering, pain and transience, is the handiwork of the latter. I know that he whom we call the 'one true Father' entirely transcends the realm of flesh in which we are imprisoned, and that he ceaselessly calls to us to re-ascend to his eternal bosom, from which we precipitately plunged.

I know that rejection of the allure of fleshly pleasure is our only safe way out of this hell; yes, the flesh *is* pleasurable, and its creator intended it to be so, in order that the hapless children of his ideation might endlessly perpetuate themselves. And as they thrash about in the mucus and the mire, Yaldaboath-Yahweh (or whatever his name is) stands above them, screeching: "Worship me! Bow before me! Adore only me, me, me!" He it was who gave me this crippled body, for it surely cannot be conceived that the one true Father would have wished such a burden on me. Therefore I *am* mindful of the exquisite raptures that the flesh can induce, and I *do* reject them, either by abstinence or abuse. I simply cannot forget that even as the sibilant darkness of the night is shrill with the moans and gasps of limbs locked in sexual systalsis, so each morning the tintinnabulation of countless death-rattles rises like an elegy to greet the new day; that lips pressed against thigh or breast in the heat of passion will, before too long, tremble like desiccated parchment in the final miasmal breath of extinction. Lovers may lose themselves in pleasure, but they will lose themselves again in the black, rectangular hole in the ground. I state the facts, and it is upon these facts that my adherence to Gnostic principles stands.

(Oh, I have just read what I have written! I am coming morbid in my old age!)

It was the supreme warlord Julius II who brought my lonely existence to an end, for he declared hostilities against the Republic of Florence, which had supported the French throughout their campaign against the papacy, and Cardinal Giovanni de' Medici was once again put at the head of papal troops assisted by the Spanish men at arms. Prato was cruelly plundered, and Cardinal de' Medici was unable to moderate the brutality of the Spaniards. Thoroughly frightened now, the Florentines yielded, and in September the Medicis once again set foot on their native soil – first came Giuliano, then the cardinal, but both were preceded by Serapica.

It was a terribly eerie sensation to be confronted by someone who was clearly not a dwarf, yet who came close enough to it to make me feel that had it not been for the fact that he was perfectly (indeed, rather beautifully) formed, he could well have been. He radiated a kind of fey delicacy which was extremely attractive; he wore his dark hair long, and this set off in a marvellous fashion the unblemished, nacreous skin, which was the colour of blanched steatite. He later told me that he bathed his face every morning in a compound of cream and boys' semen, but I was never able to imagine exactly how he might manage to obtain supplies of the latter, so I accorded it scant credence; it was, I think, one of those things which it amused Serapica to have people believe. The impression he gave was that of a rare stephanotic minikin, an exquisitely fragile bloom carefully nurtured in a hothouse ambience of elegance and refinement.

"So *you're* Peppe?" he asked rhetorically. "I hope you've been treating my house as you would your own, my dear! I've been away from it for so long, it must have been

164

pining for an inhabitant. The servants have looked after you well enough?"

"Very well indeed. I can't thank you adequately –"

"Oh, no need for thanks, my dear! Any friend of Andrea de' Collini is welcome here."

We sat at a round table of peach-coloured marble supported by three bronze legs whose intricate design was encrusted with verdigris; on the table had been placed a majolica pitcher of sweet wine, matching cups, and a bowl of almond dragées.

"I love them," he explained, popping one between his rosebud lips and sucking noisily. "This is what you might call my *private* residence, of course. I have other quarters with His Eminence."

"His Eminence?" I echoed. "Which Eminence, precisely?"

"My *dear,* Giovanni de' Medici, naturally! I've come ahead of him and Giuliano in order to make all the preparations. He's been away so long – can you believe it? Exiled from the city that his grandfather practically gave birth to. There's been the most *frantic* goings on, hasn't there?"

"Well, yes, the city has been unsettled," I said.

"Unsettled? My *dear,* the city fathers have been shitting themselves! Of course, nobody wanted His Eminence marching in and taking possession of the place, especially not at the head of those Spanish beasts – I hear rumours that at Prato they raped the *men* as well as the women – so they handed it to him on a plate. Quite right too; the Florentines have very short memories, you know. Anyway, I've got *heaps* to do before he and Giuliano arrive. You'll have to help, naturally. His Eminence relies on me *absolutely*, you see – quite a different kettle of fish to that old crustacean Sanseverino."

"Cardinal Sanseverino? The one who marched in through the Flaminia intending to depose Julius?"

"Him, yes. He promised me a career, and made me Master of the Hounds. Can you imagine? I just couldn't

165

manage the malodorous beasts – they were constantly pissing up my legs. And my *dear,* the noise! Making love to a woman (so I *imagine*) must be marginally less horrid. The satirists subjected me to constant ridicule, and in the end I simply made up my mind that I'd had enough; transferring from one Eminence to the other was quite easy, and I've never had cause to regret it. Giovanni is an absolute *darling,* and I just know you're going to get on. He'll be the real power here in Florence – Giuliano will be just a figurehead."

He giggled and clapped his manicured hands together.

"Everything is going to be such *fun* again!" he cried.

I sipped the sweet wine for a few moments, then I said:

"How do you come to know Andrea de' Collini?"

"Has he been accused of witchcraft?" Serapica asked, suddenly on edge. "I shouldn't be at all surprised. He gets up to all sorts of strange antics, I do know that much."

"He is my dear and cherished friend," I said quickly.

"Oh well, yes, of *course* my dear, I didn't imply anything untoward! It's just that – well –"

"They burned his daughter for heresy in Rome."

"Exactly. No smoke without fire, as they say. Oh my God, I didn't intend that pun! Still, I'm sure the Inquisition haven't got anything on Andrea, have they?"

"No."

"Besides, even if they did, he has far too many influential friends to have to fear the Inquisition."

"You haven't told me how you know him," I said.

Serapica fluttered his long, dark lashes.

"He lent me some money, once. Quite a deal of it, actually. You see, as well as working for His Eminence, I run a private business of my own – financial, I mean. Andrea de' Collini helped me to get started; he even recommended me to important clients. I owe him a number of favours. I haven't seen him for some years."

"He is grieving for his daughter."

"Yes, I can imagine."

Suddenly, he leapt up from his chair.

"But this is no time for gloom!" he trilled. "Let's celebrate! The Medicis are coming home to Florence!"

Serapica was a man of remarkably mansuetudinous disposition, which is perhaps why Cardinal de' Medici had taken him into his employment; as far as I could make out, his duties were general, but he also kept His Eminence's account books, and apparently possessed a truly astonishing gift for making the figures balance when all the evidence indicated that they would do precisely the contrary. His 'private financial work' consisted firstly in performing the same act of numerical thaumaturgy for other wealthy clients, and secondly in discreet money-lending. I did not feel inclined to make inquiries into either of these enterprises; indeed, why should I? It was none of my business. Besides, Serapica had accorded me, a total stranger, an immediate *empressement* for which I had every reason to be grateful to him; my status in his house was entirely usufructuary: I was free to come and go as I pleased, to avail myself of his goods and facilities, and it had become rapidly clear that he intended to draw me into his own social circle; I think this was a completely dispassionate act of human kindness – quite simply, he did not wish to see me lonely. He made no reference whatsoever, at any time, to my grotesque physical appearance; I am convinced that this was due to a natural consideration for others, and was not on any account an indication of sensitivity about his own small stature. It was not empathy. I am conscious of the irony of all this – for as you have already read, I grew to be shamefully jealous of him; neither did my jealousy have any foundation, for if anyone is to be accused of usurping Leo's affection, that man is me. However, you will be able to judge for yourself, in due course.

And if I did not interest myself in Serapica's monetary diversions, neither did he show the slightest curiosity about my relationship with Andrea de' Collini. I think he was telling the truth when he said that Master Andrea had once lent him money and had recommended his services to private clients; now I come to think about it, I don't recall Serapica ever uttering an untruth. Indeed, nothing about him was in any way equivocal, except perhaps the sexual innuendo in his malapert humour; he was, of course, a lover of men – not that this mattered to me in the slightest – and here was another reason, I suspect, why Cardinal de' Medici had taken him into his household.

One evening however, a rather curious incident occurred.

Almost the whole of the second floor on one side of the house was given over to Serapica's collection of antique statuary; there were sixteen or seventeen very fine and costly pieces, most of them Greek, and nearly all of them (being Greek) depicting the male nude in a variety of athletic or exotic poses. Now, I had made it my habit at the end of the day (having done nothing very much in particular during the course of it) to stroll along the gallery that ran the entire length of the room, since I found that the poised immutability and self-possession of the figures induced in me a stillness of soul which alleviated, to some degree at any rate, the emotional turbulence of recent memories. Sometimes I spoke to them, whispering all the secrets of my sad little heart into their marmoreal ears, believing that even if *they* couldn't hear me, someone, somewhere, could.

On this particular evening I wandered along the gallery a little later than usual, and the light in the room was beginning to fade; my silent, unmoving friends cast elongated shadows, their muscular limbs, frozen in a series of sporting actions which never were and never would be, tangled in a *chiaroscuro* of twilight and darkness.

Then, suddenly, as I stared down at them, I thought that out of the corner of my eye I detected a swift, sly movement; I dismissed it at once, knowing only too well what tricks a half-light can play. Then I saw it again, and this time I could not possibly doubt it: someone or *something* was stirring. I was of course alarmed; had a thief managed to break in? Or worse than a thief? Was an ill-intentioned stranger waiting to spring a trap for me? The possibility that it was an emissary from Tomaso della Croce even crossed my mind. I watched, fascinated and horrified (for the horrifying always fascinates) as an arm began to dip in a slow-motion parabola, a foot to raise itself languidly from the pedestal upon which, by rights, it should have been firmly fixed.

"Who's there? Who is it?" I cried out, trying not to sound afraid.

Immediately the reply floated back up:

"It's only me, my dear. Don't you think I look *divine?*"

Serapica stepped lightly off the pedestal and stood with his hands on his slim hips, looking up at me. He was stark naked, he had covered himself all over in some sort of white powder (ground steatite he later informed me, which accounted for the pearly pallor of his ·skin that I had noticed when I first saw him) and he wore a crown of bleached laurel on his shapely head.

"Don't mind me, my dear," he trilled. "Just my little fantasy. I regard them as my playmates."

"But what are you *doing?*" I called back.

"Doing? Why, nothing! I'm *being* rather than doing. I simply stand on my plinth for half an hour, feeling terribly Greek and frightfully athletic and in *such* nice company. Then when it starts to get chilly, the game is concluded."

Later, he elaborated on this *éclaircissement*.

"They actually belong to His Eminence – I couldn't possibly afford such exquisite pieces. His Holiness Julius II started his own collection at the Vatican some time ago, and His Eminence doesn't like to be outdone when it comes to devotion to antiquity – or, of course, to the male nude, although Julius wouldn't really be interested in that. Not unless it happened to be a male nude brandishing a sword, and even then he'd pay more attention to the tool of war than to the one between the legs.

"I don't know why I like doing it; I suppose, Peppe, for a short space of time it makes me feel like somebody else –

169

somebody spectacular, utterly admirable, impervious to the incursions of time. I'm egregiously envious of the *permanent*, you see; maybe that's why I like dealing with money, I don't know. Money is always there, isn't it? Everybody constantly uses it, needs it, hates being without it. Money changes hands, but it never changes, if you see what I mean."

"Yes, I think I do."

"Most of the time we are obliged to live with such a dreadful sense of impermanence; it makes one wonder whether anything at all is in any way durable. Republics rise and fall, demagogues come and go, heretics preach heresy and are burned, pacts and alliances and leagues are formed and dissolved with nauseating rapidity; even fashion is positively dehiscent with flux, and believe me my dear, I'm always careful to keep well abreast of fashion! Sometimes it quite makes my poor head spin.

"Ah well, cast away care! Tomorrow evening His Eminence comes here to dine, and I can promise you my little friend, it will be quite an evening!"

And the following morning, His Eminence Cardinal Giovanni de' Medici, accompanied by his brother Giuliano, entered the city in strangely muted triumph.

1521

I have just come back from poor Leo's funeral. What a penny-pinching, squalid, unworthy, shameful affair! And of course, the vitriol and the abuse began to pour in as soon as the news of his death had been announced; it makes me sick to the stomach when I think of those erstwhile flatterers and fawners and prick-suckers who bowed and scraped to him in the hopes of an extra ducat or two, now frantically scribbling their disgusting verses to distribute throughout the city. The encomiasts of yesterday are today's purveyors of scandal and lies. Every manner of accusation has been levelled against Leo; I wouldn't really care, but the things which *are* true – such as his penchant for being buggered by well-endowed young men – are hardly mentioned, while charges which have no foundation whatsoever – for example, that he was tight-fisted – are now as plentiful as orgasms in a brothel. Leo was about as tight-fisted as he was tight-arsed – which is to say not at all; he was, in fact, profligately generous.

One bilious pasquinade I chanced to read only this morning read:

"Intravit ut vulpes, vixit ut leo, mortuus est ut canis."

Antonio da Spello delivered the funeral panegyric, and one could not call it prolix – which it *should* have been, because they always *are* on such occasions; a tortuously long-winded periphrasis was what Leo deserved, but all he got was a curt acknowledgement of the indisputable fact that he was dead. At one point, I even detected a hint of *suggestio falsi:*

"Of course, His Holiness, as is well known, was prone to *caution* in foreign affairs, unlike his fiery predecessor," the old fox said. "A virtue in many circumstances, to be sure. The Book of Proverbs praises caution, and we are all aware that His Holiness was a man who loved and cherished the Holy Scriptures, if heartily disliking having to give prompt answers to questions of international import."

Well, it is certainly true that Leo was a *prudent* man, never rash in political decisions, but the implication that he was a chronic vacillator is entirely untrue.

The ubiquitous Paris de Grassis, papal Master of Ceremonies (doubtless as a dry-run for an entry into that *vademecum* of a diary of his) whispered to me:

"Ipse sermo fuit brevis, compendiosus et accomodatus, don't you think?"

"Oh, go away and leave me alone."

As for the burial – *parturient montes!* I know that poor Leo was a corpulent man, but surely six burly pallbearers could have managed between them to keep the bier level? At one point the rear of it tipped so far down towards the ground that Leo's body slithered a foot or two in the same direction; his mitre came off his head, and the papal vestments were dragged up almost around his thighs, revealing two plump, dimpled knees. I could have wept for him; in fact, I *did* weep, later. The great Medici pope, the inaugurator of the golden age of Pallas Athene, was accorded a very poor resting place – a simple tomb in St Peter's was all that covered his remains. Leo's final end was in striking and dramatic contrast to the brilliance of his reign. It is true of course that other popes have suffered worse indignities – Alexander VI Borgia for example, bloated and discoloured with poison and the stifling August heat, was thrown about the room and left to stink, while his chamberlains grabbed what loot they could – but what is that to me? Leo, who shone like the sun in life, should not have been allowed to flicker out like a guttering candle in death.

Where is the effulgent splendour that was Leo X? Where is the radiance of learning, the devotion to antiquity, to the arts and to culture, that was his greatness and glory? Passed away in a foetid breath, like one of his famous farts. Poor Leo.

Serapica was arrested this morning and is being held on charges of peculation; the silly little bastard obviously continued to exercise his genius for financial chicanery while working as Leo's privy treasurer – but I know nothing of this, since I kept my nose well and truly out of Serapica's fiscal services to Leo. I don't know where they are holding him, but a hothouse flower like Serapica is bound to wither and perish enclosed by four damp, dark walls. I might try and find out where he is, and send him a box of almond dragées, of which he is inordinately fond.

1512
On the morning that Cardinal Giovanni de' Medici entered Florence, I received a letter from Andrea de' Collini; it was undated, but had apparently been delivered from Rome. I was both surprised and disturbed; the burning of Laura had been a catastrophe and a horror of immense magnitude, yet it seemed to have struck the Master not with grief but confusion. I could not understand

this; neither could I reconcile the pathetic inertia that had come upon him with the courage and strength of character which I knew to be essentially his. I tore the ribbon from the letter and snapped the thick wax seal. This is what I read:

Peppe, my friend and disciple!
Greetings from his stricken Master and the blessing of the one true God.
I have made up my mind that he shall die. You know who I mean. I am beginning to discover ways – ways of justice – yes, justice, not vengeance! I shall come to and tell you all. So many things occupy my mind at present – sometimes I can hardly think. But in my soul I am strong. It can be done, it must be done, and it will be done!

Pray for me, Peppe.
A.

My heart was beating wildly; what were these 'ways' he spoke of? Ways to *dispose* of Tomaso della Croce? He wrote of justice, not vengeance, but unconvincingly so, for the voice that spoke to me in this letter was that of the fanatic, not the judge. I was loath to believe that inertia and confusion had been replaced by something far worse, but this was how things were beginning to look. It was with such dark speculations as these filling my mind that I met the man who was soon to become the most important person in my life.

When I first set eyes on His Eminence Cardinal Giovanni de' Medici, I was not impressed; *now there,* I thought, *is a truly fat man!* And of course, the adjective 'fat' also brought to mind other derogatory predications, such as self-indulgent, idle, greedy, stubborn; actually, he was none of these things. It is exactly the same when people see a dwarf like me, I suppose; being a dwarf *must* mean that you are also stupid, ignorant, wrathful, cunning and sexually deviant.

Serapica had put on what he called a 'Roman evening'; this meant that we reclined on a sort of *triclinium,* resting on one elbow and reaching across the table for the food, in

173

the ancient manner. I inevitably found this a little difficult, and so ate rather less than I would have liked. We were dressed, absurdly, in purple-bordered togas, and wore gold laurel wreaths on our heads. Mine kept slipping off. The servants were attired as slaves – which is to say, in practically nothing at all; one rather ungainly middle-aged female kept shooting Serapica murderous looks, clearly furious with him for subjecting her to an indignity unworthy of her domestic status.

His Eminence's protuberant eyes watered as he sipped his smoked glass goblet of Falernian wine; he smacked his ripe lips together sensuously and patted them dry with his napkin. Beneath the toga, his belly looked huge; it wobbled with a life all of its own whenever he moved himself into a position of greater comfort.

"Serapica tells me that you have been living in his house for some time," he said to me, clearly sizing me up (purely in the figurative sense) with a penetrating glance.

"Yes. I am grateful for his hospitality," I answered.

"Hmm. We have been away for some time, of course."

"Yes, Eminence. I rejoice that the feet of the Medici are now once again firmly planted upon their native soil."

"My *dear*," Serapica interrupted, "must you be so pompous?"

"The compliment is accepted," Cardinal de' Medici said. "What are we eating, Serapica? I can't quite see."

The room was lit only by a few oil-lamps in the shape of fish (in the interests of historical accuracy, of course) and a suspended cresset; besides which, Leo's sight was not terribly good.

"Red surmullet," Serapica answered, "in cherry sauce. Don't you like it?"

"It's very good. I just wondered what it was. Is this what our forebears ate?"

"They loved it, Eminence. Everything about this evening is quite authentic."

A smile crossed Leo's lips.

"Not quite," he said.

"Oh?"

"In ancient days, the slaves would have been completely naked."

Serapica pushed himself up on his elbow, his eyes wide.

"Really, Eminence?"

"Certainly. I do assure you."

For a few moments, a ghastly battle of wills silently raged between Serapica and the woman servant; clearly, even in the interests of historical accuracy, she considered that to be asked to remove her slave's garment – already scanty enough – would mean the termination of an employer-employee relationship which was even now under perilous strain. One could almost *hear* her challenging Serapica to issue the command, both of them knowing it would be his last.

Finally, Serapica shook his head.

"Well," he muttered, "I suppose one has to draw the line somewhere. More wine!"

It seemed to me that he was already rather drunk.

Cardinal de' Medici suddenly asked me:

"So, Peppe, what do you think of the pope's political ambitions?"

"Most of them seem to have been achieved," I answered non-committally.

"But what do you *think* of them? What is your opinion of His Holiness' foreign policy?"

"It seems to me," I said, "that the pope's ambitions belong to him as surely as does his beard, and both beard and ambitions are equally impressive. Without either, he would no longer be Julius. They are an enhancement of his person and his high office."

His Eminence clapped his fat hands together in delight.

"Bravo!" he cried. "A fine analogy! I like it, Peppe. I like *you*. Besides, I have every reason to be grateful to Julius, even though his attempt to transform me into a soldier like himself failed miserably."

"*That* attempt may have failed," I said, "but not the

175

purposes that he entrusted to your care. It is obvious that even though by nature you are not of a military turn of mind, you possess a considerable talent for the job. His Holiness and Your Eminence are two entirely different characters, each with unique skills and abilities, none of which the Church can survive without. Is an ancient manuscript of less significance than a cuirass? Not at all! It fulfils a different function and purpose, and must be precisely what it is, nothing other. To my mind moreover, the manuscript carries an infinitely greater interest, but that is a matter of personal taste."

Giovanni de' Medici gasped in astonishment and joy.

"You understand me entirely!" he cried, his flabby jowls quivering with emotion. "Oh, I wish I could have put it like that myself! I wish I could have said that to Julius. Peppe, I applaud you. I *thank* you."

I lowered my eyes modestly.

"Julius has worn himself out, of course," His Eminence went on. "Even a bull-hearted giant like him cannot maintain his physical strength forever. Besides, these political ambitions (and successes!) of his, which you, Peppe, quite rightly say are as impressive as his beard, cause him endless anxiety; the Spanish have been his strong right arm, even as the Swiss have been his clenched fist, but now I think His Holiness fears the power of Spain, and this induces him to maintain friendly relations with the emperor. In fact, the emperor's support is vital if the Lateran Council is to proceed smoothly and if France is to be isolated.

"I was present when the emperor's adviser made his entry into Rome –"

"Matthaeus Lang?" Serapica cooed; "they say he's absolutely *stunning*. Is he?"

"He certainly carries himself with a perceptible *hauteur*," the cardinal answered. "Quite a pompous fellow; he conducted himself as if he were an emperor himself."

"But my dear, what does he *look* like? Is he terribly handsome?"

"He has that austere, pallid northern handsomeness about him; his long hair is fair, his body well-formed –"

"Ah!" sighed Serapica.

"– and his features most pleasing. Julius was absolutely burning with eagerness to meet him, of course, since so much depended upon the establishment of cordial relations. Lang spent his first night in Rome in the Vatican. Julius and he chatted for hours; his entry into the city was triumphant! Their Eminences Bakócz and Grosso met him at the foot of Monte Mario (the other members of the Sacred College baulked at such a grandiose reception), and at the Ponte Molle, the Senator of Rome himself greeted this young beauty. The streets were thronged, I tell you!"

"They had come to gaze upon his face," Serapica said dreamily.

"Rubbish. They were arse-licking, at Julius' command. San Angelo shook to its foundations with the thunder of the guns. His Holiness was determined to conclude a close alliance with the Emperor Maximillian, which as we all know, he did. That is going to be the death blow for the schismatic Council – it's already dying on its feet."

"And what about Venice?" Serapica asked, slurping at his wine.

"Alas for Venice," said His Eminence. "Julius has promised to support Maximillian against the Republic with weapons both spiritual and temporal if she refuses to relinquish Verona and Vicenza and to pay tribute for the imperial fiefs. Lang was raised to the cardinalate – everyone expected it. Anyway, the Lateran Council is safe."

"Doesn't that go to show," I said, "that Julius is not merely a shrewd politician? That he is indeed concerned for the reform of the Church?"

"Nonsense!" Serapica cried. "The Lateran was only convened to counter Pisa, everybody knows that. Julius was so keen to gain the emperor's support because he fears the power of France. He *hates* France."

"I disagree," Cardinal de' Medici said. "Certainly, Julius

177

loathes the French, but then he has every reason to, as much as he loathed the Borgias; but the Lateran isn't merely an anti-Pisa ploy – no, the pope is anxious to be seen to be reform-minded. He won't be entirely happy until the schismatics have been utterly extirpated, but the Lateran is a Council in its own right. Don't forget that. Whether he will personally live to see the end of them, I can't say; he's been ailing for some time, and he seems to be particularly prone to fevers, which have considerably weakened even his iron constitution. Paris de Grassis informs me that the pope is not going to officiate at any further solemn functions."

"All the same," Serapica interposed, "he was present at the Good Friday procession, wasn't he?"

"Yes, and he's paid for it with a fresh attack of fever. He seems so restless these days, constantly moving from one residence to another, almost as if something is pursuing him. It certainly can't be the ghost of his own inadequacy or failure."

"Whoever comes after Julius," I said, "will have a hard time living up to his memory."

"Oh," His Eminence murmured, shuddering a little, "*don't*."

Serapica – not, I think, in the least jealous of Cardinal de' Medici's recent display of affection for me (he was probably bored with all this talk of the mighty Julius) – leapt up from the *triclinium* with a little cry.

"The entertainment!" he announced in a shrill, slurred voice. "I have arranged a rather *special* entertainment for us."

"What sort of entertainment?" His Eminence asked.

"Actually, my dears," Serapica went on, "this was something of a *trouvaille,* I must say. I've never seen anything quite like it before, and I know you're simply going to *adore* it. It's legend brought to life. It's scandalous and shocking, it's all the rage."

"But what is it?" Cardinal de' Medici demanded, his voice rising high with excitement.

178

"It's a sort of demonstration of a *freak of nature*," Serapica said, "a *tragedy of nature*."

At that moment, I was convinced that my heart had slipped between the bony bars of its cage and had sunk to the pit of my bowels, where it lurched and thumped sickeningly.

"Oh?"

"Yes, my dears."

He whispered to one of the servants, who immediately went out of the room.

"Don't worry," Serapica said, "I haven't made an obscene suggestion – he's just gone off to fetch them in. I discovered them travelling around with a kind of caravan full of freaks; apparently they've been giving shows up and down the length of Italy, and they're absolutely marvellous. I arranged things with the owner of the caravan, and he agreed to let them come here this evening and give a private performance. Now, my dears, settle back and be prepared for some real entertainment!"

I prayed and hoped and wished; I told myself that it wouldn't be, it *couldn't* be; I shut my eyes and pretended it wasn't. But oh – I knew with every ounce and fibre of my being that it *was*. And I was right.

Nino hadn't changed; he didn't even look a great deal older, but then under all that extra hair and in those grotesque taloned gloves and leggings, he was bound to look exactly as I remembered him. On the end of the golden chain that he clutched in one apish fist, was the gaudy collar, and inside the collar was a neck belonging to a man I had never seen before. The cardinal's watery eyes bulged in astonishment, the sensuous lips were parted, the folds of flesh shining with sweat, his several chins quivering.

Nino stopped growling when he saw me; it would have been exceedingly strange if he had not recognized me immediately, which he most certainly did. He was clearly dumbfounded.

"Begin! Begin!" cried Serapica.

All throughout the stooge's patter, Nino did not take his eyes off me; even when he reached out with one hairy arm to make a playful grab at Giovanni de' Medici (who pushed himself deeper into the recesses of the *triclinium* with a little squeal of horror), his glance did not falter. Actually, the patter was nowhere near as good as mine had been, even though both His Eminence and Serapica were enthralled by it; there was no *finesse* (that's always been a favourite word of mine), no polish, no style. He spoke in a subdued, reluctant voice, and I could not tell whether this was an attempt to highlight the tragedy of his predicament and thus part of the act, or whether he really was subdued and ashamed to find himself involved in such a performance. It came to its apotheosis.

"Yes, noble sirs, I am a slave to his every filthy desire. I am forced to do things to him that no God-fearing Christian would even dream of. Nasty things –"

Nasty? *Nasty?* Where was the thrill in this diatribe? Where was the *frisson* of it, the secret stirring of dark desire in the heaving bosom, between the sweat-drenched thighs? This idiot was ruining the act, and I could endure it no longer. I leapt up from the *triclinium,* unfastened the collar, and placed it around my own neck. I saw Nino beam with pure happiness; he began to growl and mutter and gesture in earnest. It was the old team, back in harness again!

"Oh yes, my good and noble gentlemen!" I cried; Cardinal de' Medici had collapsed into a great shuddering heap of total astonishment, his toga up about his waist, his watery eyes popping. Serapica was as high as a kite with excitement at this unexpected turn of events, and very much under the influence of wine.

"Yes, the tragedy is mine! Regard him well, this matted, stinking beast! for the outward appearance is but a manifestation of the inward corruption! Can you conceive of the lurid fantasies that pass through his fevered mind? The degradation of them, the shame, the depth of their perversity? No, you cannot! And the miracle is, gentlemen, the miracle is that he *has* a mind! He thinks and speculates and reasons just as we do, and there is the most shocking reversal of nature – most *unnatural,* one is obliged to say. Yes, the beast *knows!* He knows how to give rational form to the blind, mute cravings that rise up from his loins, penetrate his black heart, and so accumulate in that cunning, devious brain! He cannot speak, cannot utter words and the concepts which words signify, therefore he is unable to *tell* us the purpose and intention of his desires; but oh – he *knows* what they are! Therefore he is not possessed by them as brute beasts are, but rather, he manipulates them, intensifies their filthy sweetness, heightens the vile joy they bring, by articulating them to his own consciousness. They are the children now not only of his deviant nature, but also of his ideation. And I, wretch that I am, must serve those desires!

"Ah yes, gentlemen, I am the hapless slave of his craving for carnal pleasure, for the deepest and darkest of his turbid yearnings – and they are truly insatiable! Look into his eyes! Do you not see them? Can you not feel the heat of them oozing from every malodorous pore? Do not stricture me, but pity me! Do not apply your Christian standards of decency and your civilised moral outrage to my condition and state, for they *cannot* apply to one so smitten by unnatural tragedy as myself! No, gentlemen, have compassion, for I am sunk to vile depths indeed. Behold! Behold, the appetite of the beast stirs and rises, and again I am defiled, humiliated, degraded by the task I must perform!"

With superb instinctive timing, sensing that the moment was precisely right, Nino grabbed me by the shoulders and uttered an enormous roar; I heard Cardinal de' Medici scream, and saw his trembling hands fly up to his face. Serapica was slumped on the *triclinium,* gawping like one of the vulgar crowd that nightly used to pack our tent; in fact, where was the difference? Prurience is obviously one of life's great equalizers.

Nino spun me around to face him, and pushed my face into his crotch. This, I knew, was to be our finest performance, and closing my eyes, I went to work on him with a will. He clearly enjoyed every moment of it; he threw back his head and roared, he raised his hairy arms high in the air and gestured with his taloned fists. He gyrated his hips lasciviously.

"Pity me, pity me, gentlemen!" I cried.

All at once, Nino bent and hissed in my ear:

"Stand back old friend, I'm going to shoot my load – oh!"

He gave an almighty scream, his whole body jerked convulsively, and a jet of semen came out in a glittering arc, rose up, then descended to splatter upon the quivering bulk of His Eminence Cardinal Giovanni de' Medici.

"Well my *dear!* I never knew you had it in you," Serapica said, breathless. "How on earth? – I mean –"

"It was a stunning performance," Giovanni de' Medici said, clearly still not completely recovered from his excitement. "Not entirely suitable for mixed company though."

"Indeed no, Your Eminence," I said.

Nino had not for one moment given any indication that he knew me, and made it plain by glances and gestures that this was the way it had to be. When we each in turn took his hand to congratulate him on the entertainment, I held it a little longer than the others, and squeezed it gently. I know he understood. I also suggested that Serapica might like to make a small payment to both Nino and the stooge, over and above what he had arranged with Master Antonio – or 'the owner of the caravan', as I referred to him.

"Delighted to," Serapica answered generously, calling for one of the servants.

He gave them twenty ducats each.

"You will convey the gratitude of His Eminence and myself to your master," he said.

"Tell him," I added, "that His Eminence expects two such gifted performers as yourselves to be well cared for."

Then, completely to my surprise, Nino hissed in my ear:

"The tavern of Marco Saletti – tomorrow night, Peppe.

182

That precious Master of yours has *bought* us – the three of us! Remember, Marco's place. Be there!"

Then he was gone.

"It was all a matter of knowing what was to come," I said to Serapica afterwards, since he insisted on an explanation.

"Yes, but *how* did you know what was to come?"

I allowed the obvious answer to dawn on him, which it did rather rapidly.

"Oooh," he cried, "you little cheat! You trickster!"

"What, what?" Cardinal de' Medici said.

"Isn't it plain, Eminence? Peppe, like myself, has seen the show before –"

I put a finger to my lips.

"We all have our little secrets," I said.

That night His Eminence invited me to join his household as a junior chamberlain. I accepted without hesitation.

It was clear that Cardinal de' Medici was very fond of me; while Serapica was busy with the accounts and his own private enterprises, I followed His Eminence around like a kind of mascot, making him titter with my risqué jokes (which I think he marginally preferred to Serapica's frankly lewd, effeminate conversation), enhancing his prestige at glittering banquets, and otherwise rendering him a hundred and one little services which left him free to play the great statesman and prince of the Church. He came to regard my advice as invaluable, when in fact it consisted in the main of plain common-sense; not that His Eminence lacked this particular commodity – far from it! – but it meant that he was liberated from the inconvenience of having to work things out for himself.

It was while I was in the service of Cardinal Giovanni de' Medici that I met Leonardo da Vinci, who was paying the city a short visit, en route to France. I later learned that Leonardo only ever paid 'short visits' *anywhere,* so afraid was he that he would bump into Michelangiolo. He did have connections with Florence in any case, for his father had been a city notary, and as a youth he himself had studied with Andrea del Verrocchio for some years. Of late, the *Maestro* had become an itinerant; Milan, of course, was the city he best loved, but he had not lived there for any length of time since the French invaded in 1499.

I did not like Leonardo da Vinci one little bit. When I first saw him he was an old man approaching sixty, tall and stooped, with a mane of dirty white hair, and a long, unkempt beard that reeked of stale vomit. There seemed to be bits of half-masticated food encrusted all over his clothes; at least, that's what they looked like to me – I couldn't imagine what else they could be. In fact, quite apart from the vomit, he smelt very unpleasant altogether; I was not able to place it at the time, but Laura once told me that in the far east of India there grows a luscious-looking fruit called a *durian*, whose odour is so bad that one has to hold one's nose to eat it – something approaching a blend of human sweat and animal dung. On reflection, I conclude that this is precisely what Leonardo da Vinci smelt like, only he was *far* from luscious-looking. In fact, he had acquired this vile odour as a result of his 'experiments' with decaying cadavers.

His voice was curiously high-pitched and brittle; it seemed to me that it was the audial equivalent of a filament of rusty wire – an irritating, nervine, scranelling sound. He was also prone to elisions:

"I have 'cided to pass what 'mains of my poor life in France; the climate there is more agree'ble to my const'ution."

His Eminence was of course hoping to persuade the old man to undertake a commission, but Leonardo would have none of it.

"It is the time factor, Em'nence," he said. "I have other projects to occ'py my mind; as Your Em'nence is doubtless aware, I am first and foremost a *scientist*. I am an exper-'menter. I am working at the moment on a new version of my flying 'chine – oh, I am convinced that it *can* work! Man *can* im'tate the birds of the air! It is all a question of abs'lute accuracy in the calc'lations –"

"But *Maestro*," the cardinal wailed, "what of your *art?* What of that? Your 'Last Supper' in the convent refectory in Milan – an unparalleled masterpiece!"

"Your Em'nence is too kind. However, my flying 'chine . . ."

Leonardo did not show the same enthusiasm to discuss the machines of war that he had also invented; as to his 'experiments' – quite frankly, I considered that he was probably a diabolist. What a disagreeable, smelly old man!

Later, as we sat nibbling ratafia *biscottini*, Leonardo said to me in a sly sort of way:

"You must come and see what I am up to in my lodgings, Peppe; I think it will int'rest you."

"Oh?"

"Come tonight. Oh, don't 'fuse an old man such a small 'quest!"

"If you like," I said.

He crunched on his biscuit with stumpy, carious teeth, and smiled.

His lodgings stank even worse than he did – heaven knows how his landlady forced herself to put up with it; the room was gloomy, and a complete mess: manuscripts, books, little cups and bowls of strange liquids, a boiling-pan, discarded ends of candles, extremely peculiar-looking instruments which gave the impression that the only purpose for which they were designed was an unpleasant one, pots of ground pigment, writing implements, an unemptied night vessel still full of ordure – and so on. How could he possibly *live* in this mess? It was like one of the Stygian stables. And everywhere, scattered haphazardly *everywhere,* there were drawings – dozens and dozens of drawings.

"Would you care for a little 'freshment, Peppe?" he said.

"Thank you, no."

"Oh, but I 'sist!"

He excavated out of the rubble two small smoked glass goblets, and from a fictile gallipot that stood on the floor near his grubby mattress, he poured a translucent, gamboge-tinted liquid.

"What is it?" I asked.

"Try it, tell me if you like it."

"Yes, but what *is* it?"

"Something I learned how to make myself, while on my travels. It is very pop'lar in Arabia, so they tell me. Drink, Peppe!"

He handed me one of the goblets; I sniffed at it, then sipped cautiously. It was actually quite pleasant – rather like a liqueur distilled from some soft fruit such as – say – strawberries.

"It's good, yes?"

"Not bad," I said. "What precisely is it distilled from?"

"Aha! Shall we call that my little secret?"

"As you like," I said, shrugging. "I don't care what you call it. I understood, in any case, that the sons of the Prophet are forbidden intoxicating liquor – isn't there something against it in their scriptures?"

The old man smiled unpleasantly.

"The Bible forbids forn'cation," he said, "but that doesn't stop people doing it."

Quite suddenly, he thrust an osseous hand into the boiling-pan and pulled something out, holding it up between his thumb and forefinger. It was round, like a little ball.

"What is it?" I asked, intrigued.

"It is a human eye."

"What?"

"A human eye. I took it from a – a spec'min – that came my way. The boiling is ne'ssary if one wishes to examine the interior. Watch – like this –"

He picked up a thin, wickedly sharp-looking knife and, holding the eye on the palm of his left hand, sliced through it cleanly, neatly, exposing the indurated ichor within.

"See!" he hissed, an expression of total absorption on his wrinkled saurian features, "see the nerve filaments, the pigmented layers of the iris – ah, there it is! This nugatory little hazlenut of human tissue – nothing! – and yet a worker of miracles, an abs'lute enigma; for here in my hand I hold ev'thing that it is, and yet I do not know how it functions. I am like a child faced with a compl'cated mathematical form'la – every shred of ev'dence and every fact I need to solve it, yet I am unable to do so."

He had worked himself up into a little fever of enthusiasm; his gnarled hands shook so much, that the pressure of his fingertip grip on the boiled eye became too intense, and suddenly the two halves of it, still conjoined by a thread of tissue, shot up with a vile popping sound, and globules of jelly-like substance splattered across the front of his doublet, there to join the rest of the encrusted muck.

"Oops," he said.

I was quite sickened. He went on, his voice trembling:

"Oh, Peppe, exper'mentation is my true love! That human eye, for example: if a man could discover the 'cise nature of its workings and build a 'chine of some kind to im'tate it – why, what need would there be for daubers such as myself? Painters would become a dying breed – and portrait painters would be the first to go. For who would want their likeness rendered in oil and pigment when it could be done with pure light? Who would want to risk the poss'bility of a nose too large, a mouth too mean, a chin not quite right, when the perfect image is to be had? I *dream* of such a 'chine, Peppe – yes, I dream of it! Somehow, in some way that is presently 'yond our un'standing, it *must* be possible. A 'chine that paints pictures in light! I have even thought of a name for it: a $\theta\alpha o\varsigma\delta\epsilon\omega\nu$ – a *binder of light,* a miracle of 'vention that captures and uses light."

At the conclusion of this operose fantasy, he sighed a long, shuddering sigh.

"Oh yes, yes," he murmured quietly, "it *must* be possible."

"It is a dream," I replied. "Man cannot hope to imitate – to –"

Leonardo looked up at me sharply, suddenly alert. I had

187

almost said "Satan," since as a good Gnostic I believe it was Satan, the spirit of evil, who created material form; however, I caught myself just in time, and said:

"– to imitate the handiwork of his Maker."

"Peppe, I have a favour to ask of you."

I began to feel distinctly uncomfortable; I did not think it was beyond the bounds of possibility for him to say: "Can I have one of your eyes? I'm running short." He didn't actually ask that, but he did say something just as disturbing:

"I want your body, Peppe."

"Sexually, you mean?" I managed to choke out the words.

Leonardo grimaced.

"Of course not! For – well, for my own purposes."

"You mean for experimentation?"

"Yes, yes, for that. You have a most 'nusual body, of course –"

"I'm well aware of that."

"The poss'bilities int'rest me."

"What possibilities, precisely?"

He leaned forward, thrust his wrinkled old face close to mine, and with a rasp of vomit-laden breath, he said in a tone that was almost lascivious:

"Discov'ry! The poss'bilities of discov'ry! To find out what causes you to be the shape you are, what deform'ties lie hidden within, what obsidian fluids have crept their turgid course through your misshapen viscera –"

I was beginning to feel quite insulted now, as well as rather sick.

"– what alien pressure, and from what source, has twisted and squashed and lumpified –"

Lumpified?

"You might have rather a long wait," I interrupted quickly. "After all, you're an old man now –"

"Your kind never live long," he stated with unnerving frankness. "We can draw up a document, if you like – I'll pay you now, of course –"

"I don't need the money, thank you."

"– then when your time comes, I get your remains –"

"No, *Maestro*. That is an offer which does not tempt me."

"But the poss'bilities of exper'mentation!" he cried in an anguish which nauseated me because it was utterly genuine.

"Fuck your experimentation!" I shouted at him, angry now. "I'm not some giant eyeball that you can reduce to jelly in your boiling-pan!"

Leonardo leaned back in his chair, his hands raised in a little gesture of sad resignation.

"I had hoped you would be pleased," he said. "Clearly, you are not."

"No."

"It was merely an offer made *honoris causa,* in any case. As a scientific ideologue I have 'sured myself of other sources for my spec'mens."

"I am *not* a specimen, *Maestro* Leonardo."

"You *could* have been – and an excellent one. What does it matter to you what happens to your carcass after death?"

"I think," I said as even-temperedly as possible, "I would prefer to rest quietly beneath the earth rather than in your melting-pot."

"As you please, Peppe. But you have dis'ppointed me."

"I'm sorry if that is the case."

Then he suddenly became eager again, as if putting all his energy into one last attempt to persuade me:

"Well, couldn't I just have the really *grotesque* bits? Think, Peppe! Think what wonders could be 'scovered!"

"No. No, no, no. Besides, as you see, the *whole* of me is grotesque."

"Ah, well, there it is. You will take more liqueur?"

"I don't think so, *Maestro*. I ought to be returning. His Eminence will expect me to read to him tonight."

Leonardo turned away, picked up a little silver dish, and began cautiously sniffing the contents. He did not even bother to wish me goodnight. I could not understand, to be perfectly honest, how a man who was capable of producing such sensitive, accomplished and truly *great* works of art, could devote so much energy and passion to cutting up boiled eyeballs and asking people to donate him their bodies. In any case, I am thankful to say that this was not only my first acquaintance with Leonardo da Vinci, but also my last; shortly afterwards he left for Paris, no doubt collecting a variety of *spec'mins* on the way.

Meanwhile, Florence remained in a restless state even after the return of the Medicis, and there were constant rumours to the effect that one or another group of disaffected citizens would inspire a rebellion designed to lead to a second exile. In fact, His Eminence and Giuliano de' Medici were completely in control of the Signoria, but the days of Lorenzo the Magnificent had long gone, and the fervour of adulation had passed with them, being replaced by a muted toleration which sometimes made life a little uncomfortable. His Eminence once remarked to me that it was like living in a city full of ghosts.

Finally, definite news reached us concerning a plot to overthrow Giuliano and Giovanni, which was without a doubt connected to the fact that the Republic of Venice had raised both to the status of Venetian patricians. His Eminence was frantic.

"I can't bear it, Peppe! Not again!"

"Calm yourself Eminence," I counselled, but he ran around the palace looking for somewhere to hide, wailing pathetically; I was reminded of Claudius Caesar who, on hearing of the plot of his wife Messalina and her lover to depose him, dashed hither and thither through the imperial apartments, crying: "Am I still the emperor? *Am* I?" Of course he *was,* and Giovanni de' Medici was still a prince of the Church; I felt this was all a bit beneath his dignity.

"It's a terrible strain," he remarked to me, after the potential uprising had fizzled out and a few conspirators had been publicly de-gutted.

"What is, Eminence?"

190

"Never knowing from one day to the next."

"Never knowing what?"

"Well – I mean – whether I'm still in power."

"The Medicis will *always* be in power," I said.

"Oh, Peppe, do you really think so?"

"In power in one way or the other. I have linked my own fate to the fate of the Medici balls –"

"I beg your pardon?"

"I refer *only* to the insignia on your coat-of-arms, Eminence."

"Ah."

"For better or worse, my life is entwined with yours, as Your Eminence well knows."

At that moment, I *knew* that Giovanni de' Medici had become the most important person in my life: fat, voluptuous, spoilt, ulcer-ridden, childish, ridiculous and utterly fascinating, he was the lodestone of my days.

Finally, came another shock.

Giovanni was emerging from his bedroom, barely woken from a prolonged *siesta* when a messenger was shown in.

"What is it?" he screamed. "Is the city taken? Christ, what has become of Julius' promises now? Wait, wait – let me fetch my jewels –"

He dashed back into the bedroom and waddled out again after a few moments carrying fistfuls of glittering, gaudy baubles – chains, pendants, earrings, precious stones both cut and uncut, gold coins – and rings, scattering rings everywhere like an angel strewing stardust.

"What about *my* jewels?" I cried.

"Eminence, *please* – "

Clearly, this was all a shade too undignified for the messenger.

"I must take *something,* for God's sake! How will I survive?"

"You are quite safe, Eminence."

"You mean the city isn't taken? Then what? *What,* in Christ's name?"

"His Holiness Pope Julius is dead."

The infinitesimally small atom of stunned silence extended itself towards eternity.

Then Giovanni de' Medici whispered:

"What?"

And it was like the voice of God shattering the primal void.

"The pope is dead, Eminence. Your presence in Rome is required immediately."

"Say that again . . ."

"The pope is dead. Your presence –"

"No, no, stop! I understood you the first time –"

Then he slithered to the floor in a dead faint.

Serapica and I accompanied His Eminence to Rome as his conclavists. It has to be said that with the death of Julius, a great and mighty pontificate had come to an end, and the world must surely have wondered whether there was anyone even remotely capable of taking that old giant's place. Needless to say, there was no shortage of princes of the Church who *thought* they were ideally qualified in every way to do so.

At the time of Julius' death, the Sacred College consisted of thirty-one members, about twenty of whom were already present in Rome; five more arrived for the Conclave, so that twenty-five cardinals participated in the election, including that fierce-hearted old warrior Schinner, who had turned the tide of Julius' military fortunes almost single-handedly with his army of brave Swiss stalwarts. The haughty, supercilious Englishman, Cardinal Bainbridge, was also present. The schismatic cardinals who lingered on at Lyons with their dying Council petitioned Maximillian to intercede for them with the Sacred College, but in vain; Cardinal Carvajal in particular did his utmost to present their case in the best possible light. However, every prospect of their being allowed to participate in the election was blocked by the military precautions of Spain.

*

192

The period of the *sedia vacante* was peculiarly quiet; when we arrived in Rome, the whole atmosphere was one of a protracted *siesta*. I suspect that this was mainly due to the iron fist with which Pope Julius had ruled, but it was also, I am sure, at least partially a mark of respect for his passing, for Julius had been greatly loved by the people. Cardinal de' Medici was suffering from a painful attack of his 'fistula' (even in those days, this was what he preferred to call it), and we were obliged to hire men to carry him around in a sedan-chair.

"How *prophetic*," Serapica squealed.

"What do you mean? Ouch! – a pox on my arse!"

"Well, my *dear,* isn't it rather like the papal *sedia gestatoria*?"

"Oh shut up! The pain is excruciating."

Serapica shot him a totally unsympathetic look.

The Conclave was held on the second floor of the Vatican palace, the oath taken in the presence of the custodians in the chapel of Nicholas V, and the main business conducted in the Sistine Chapel; here, they had erected thirty-one (even the absent were catered for, but not the schismatic cardinals) tiny, dark rooms that looked for all the world like prison cells. Giovanni de' Medici groaned.

"Don't worry Eminence," Paris de Grassis said soothingly, "a rather more comfortable arrangement has been made for you, on account of your *problem.*"

Serapica giggled shamelessly.

Indeed, the room allotted to the cardinal was rather handsome, and included a specially soft bed; Cardinal Sisto Gara della Rovere was so ill he had to be carried into the Conclave. When he saw this, Cardinal Giovanni de' Medici sighed and said to me:

"I do not share his degree of sickness, but thank God I share the consideration they have shown. This room will suit me very well."

Serapica and I were housed near the Cantoria, quite close to Cardinal Soderini, who was to be indicted in the plot to poison Leo X.

Paris de Grassis and Blasius de Martinellis were the Masters of Ceremonies.

The Mass of the Holy Ghost was celebrated by Cardinal Bakócz before the Conclave officially opened, in the chapel of St Andrew; it was not possible to have it at the tomb of the Princes of the Apostles, owing to the reconstruction work in progress in St Peter's. The opening discourse was delivered by Bishop Petrus Flores, the Spaniard.

"I exhort you, most eminent Lords!" he cried in a querulous, fruity voice, "to see that the Holy Ghost guides you to elect as successor to Julius a man who will bring peace to Christendom – peace! Peace, which is enjoined by the Divine Master upon all his disciples! And who else but the Vicar of Christ on earth should be our example in the ways of peace?"

"I can't imagine that the shade of His late lamented Holiness is greatly enamoured of this bilge," Serapica whispered in my ear. "Julius didn't understand the meaning of the word. Peace? Piss!"

"Notwithstanding the imperative of the Lord to peace," Flores went on, "the successor of Julius must not relax the fight against the Turks! If the sons of the Prophet wield the sword of conquest, so too do we! Christendom must be protected at all costs against the infidels. Alas, that the holy places of the east so dear to our faith should be desecrated and despoiled by the barbarity of heathen contumely for Christ's holy Bride!"

And so on. On, in fact, for quite a time. One or two of the cardinals began to shift restlessly in their seats after half an hour, and I saw Cardinal de' Medici suddenly grow red in the face. His eyes bulged.

"He's trying to restrain a fart," Serapica said. "I've seen it before. He'll do himself a mischief one of these days; why doesn't he just let rip? It might shut that old fool Flores up."

In fact, Bishop Petrus Flores brought his periphrasis to a rambling conclusion in his own good time, and when he pronounced the final 'Amen' I heard not only a protracted sigh of relief from their assorted Eminences, but also a shrill, rapid pitter-patter of wind as Cardinal de' Medici finally allowed himself the relief of releasing the pent-up fart.

Then the Conclave began.

Their Eminences, with the memory of Julius' powerful and somewhat arbitrary will still fresh in their minds, commenced by drawing up a kind of election capitulation, to which they all swore on March 9th; this consisted of a great many articles, some of which were not to be made public, and included mention of the war against the Turks, the reform of the Curia, and the exemption of members of the Sacred College from taxation. It also stated that at least two-thirds of their number was required to agree to any punitive action taken against any cardinal. Among the articles to be kept secret was one relating to income – any cardinal who did not possess an income of at least six thousand ducats was to receive a monthly allowance of two hundred ducats. The new pope, it would seem, was to have his hands tied even before taking office. As it happened however, it was quickly realised that this capitulation was entirely uncanonical, and it was abandoned as summarily as it had been drawn up. What a farce.

Julius' bull against simony was read before voting began on March 10th.

On the first count, the Spaniard Serra received fourteen votes, but everyone knew that a countryman of Alexander VI Borgia had no hope of succeeding to the chair of Peter; the Chuch had had enough of popes who fucked, frolicked and made free with the arsenic. Grosso della Rovere received eight votes and went into a kind of spasm of pique. Accolti and Bakócz got seven each, and Raffaello Riario none at all.

"Someone voted for *me*," Leo said, slightly astonished.

And indeed, he had received a single vote.

"Are you sure it wasn't yourself?" Serapica whispered.

"Certainly not!"

Yet by the end of the day, it was obvious that Cardinal

de' Medici was going to be elected pope. Many clearly thought that ill-health and corpulence would make for a stop-gap reign, a succedaneum that would tide the Church over nicely until someone really worthy of high office could be found; you could say, in fact, that Giovanni de' Medici was elected on account of his 'fistula'. That night, he found sleep impossible.

"Do you think it really *will* be me?" he asked, like a child doubting the promise of a sweetmeat.

"But of *course,* my dear!" Serapica cried. "It's an inevitability, now."

"How? Why?"

"Don't ask *me!* I expect they all think you've got one foot in the grave instead of an ulcer up your arse. They're looking for a mild-mannered caretaker pope."

"Charming."

"Well for heaven's sake, don't be churlish! What does it matter *why* they make you pope, just so long as they do?"

The following morning, March 11th, the votes were once again taken in due order, and Cardinal Giovanni de' Medici was elected Vicar of Christ on earth. He took the name of Leo X.

Actually, it might be a little unfair to give all the credit for Leo's election to his arse, even though the fact that he was obliged to undergo an operation in the middle of voting seemed to indicate that his reign would be a brief one – at least, that's what it indicated to their Eminences; personally, I find the conviction that someone could be done to death by their own backside highly ridiculous. It would seem that the Sacred College was divided roughly into two halves, one representing the older cardinals, and the other the younger members. These latter had apparently wanted Leo from the beginning (since he shared their youth), but had kept their intentions secret, with the result that only tough old Cardinal Schinner had voted for him on the first count. I think the fact that Leo was a Medici also had some influence, as did his career under Julius. The younger cardinals were, I know, attracted by his gentle manner, his naturally courteous temperament, and his reputation for generosity.

The Hungarian Bakócz had entertained his own hopes, reckoning on the assistance of the Republic of Venice in promoting his candidature, but two factors weighed heavily against him: firstly he was not an Italian, and the Roman mob would rather have a dog's turd in office than a non-Italian; secondly he was extremely wealthy, which meant that Julius' bull against simony would suggest his election was bought, even if it wasn't.

Cardinal de' Medici's private secretary, Bernardo Bibbiena, who had accompanied us into the Conclave, had also (it later transpired) worked clandestinely to secure our master's election; I quite liked Bibbiena and got on well with him, but he and Serapica constantly seemed to be at loggerheads – indeed, some days they hardly spoke to each other, which irked the cardinal beyond measure, and he was ceaselessly trying to effect a reconciliation. Actually, I don't think reconciliation was ever really on the cards, since the acrimony between them amounted to no more than a clash of personalities.

Oddly enough, as senior Cardinal-deacon, it was Cardinal de' Medici's job to read out the voting papers, which he did very modestly, in a calm and unwavering voice. I was rather proud of him.

Thus, still not quite thirty-eight years of age, Cardinal Giovanni de' Medici became Pope Leo X. He was ordained priest on March 15th and consecrated bishop on the 17th; his coronation was fixed for Saturday the 19th, the Feast of St Joseph, in order that he should be properly pope before the great ceremonies of Holy Week began.

I simply *must* describe Leo's procession in state to take possession of the Lateran! It was an occasion never to be forgotten.

First of all, the most extravagant preparations for the

street decorations were made, and everything that was antique (and a lot that was just old) was trundled out and put on display to contribute to the greater glory of the Medici pope. The weather was absolutely wonderful – one of those perfect Roman days, a flawless azure sky and a warm but merciful sun; the Duke of Ferrara (whose ecclesiastical censures, applied by Julius, were removed by Leo so that he could participate in the procession) led the horse upon which Leo was mounted to the centre of the piazza of St Peter's, where he was relieved of this duty by the Duke of Urbino, Giovan' Maria da Varano, and Lorenzo de' Medici, the pope's nephew. The procession then began making its way to the Lateran.

It was headed by two hundred mounted lancers, followed by the members of the Sacred College of Cardinals and the papal household – this included Serapica and myself, as well as Bernardo Bibbiena; I must have looked a strange sight! – a crook-back dwarf garishly liveried in the papal colours of white, red and green, with the Medici badge fixed to my breast. Behind us were the standards of the papal cursori and the custodians of the university banner, which bore a brilliantly flame-coloured cherub that looked like a great splash of fresh blood in the midst of all the white and gold; the standard of Rome was carried by Giovan' Giorgio Cesarini, who walked together with the Procurator of the Teutonic Order of Knights – their emblem was a white banner surmounted by a simple black cross – the Prior of the Knights of St John, and the Captain-General.

Next marched the papal Marshall, accompanied by nine white stallions bearing an equipage of crimson and gold, followed by the chamberlains of honour, two of whom carried Leo's mitre which was, needless to say, a magnificent piece of work – the pearls and precious stones caught the sunlight and exploded into a fire of multi-coloured light, quite dazzling to look at. Two other chamberlains carried the papal tiara, equally richly set with exquisite and costly jewels. Behind the mitre and the tiara came one of the most spectacular groups of all – the aristocratic families of Rome and members of the Florentine nobility: the Colonna, the Orsini, Savelli, Conti, Santa Croce, Medici, Soderini and Strozzi. Oh, how magnificently arrayed these arrogant peacocks were! Marching like gods, their heads held so high that their necks were extended! I do not think I have ever seen so vast and superb a quantity of human pride gathered together in a single space; surely Lucifer must have plunged from heaven into the eternal darkness for less pride than that! Together with these families whose trademark was *hauteur,* came the diplomatic body: the envoys of the provinces and towns belonging to the papal states, the ambassadors from Florence, Venice, Spain and France.

The members of the papal court who followed behind the diplomats presented no less an impressive spectacle: the ostiarii, the apostolic sub-deacons (carrying a brilliant gold cross), the white palfreys bearing on their backs the tabernacle that housed the Blessed Sacrament, surrounded by twenty-five grooms with torches. Next, the papal choir, then two hundred and fifty abbots, bishops and archbishops, behind whom came the rest of the cardinals, each accompanied by eight chamberlains; between Cardinal Gonzaga and Cardinal Petrucci walked Alfonso of Ferrara, attired in his heavy ducal mantle embroidered in gold and set about with pearls. Finally, the Swiss Guard, their burnished armour glittering in the bright sun, declared the approach of the pope.

Under a richly worked canopy supported by Roman citizens, Leo X came riding on a Turkish steed; ironically enough, it was the same horse he had ridden when he was taken prisoner by the French at Ravenna. Weighed down by all the insignia of the papal office, Leo's corpulence somehow enhanced his dignity; sitting at a dinner table he would simply have been *fat,* but astride a steed at the rear of this fantastically elaborate procession, he was *majestic.* Leo was followed by the *maestro di camera* and several papal chamberlains who tossed gold and silver coins to the crowd; the whole entourage was concluded by four hundred cavaliers.

The streets were absolutely thronged, and the enthusiasm of the people was truly magnificent; *Palle! Palle!* they cried – for this is the name for the balls on the arms of the Medici (only those of a cynical disposition interpreted the yells of the mob in an alternative sense). Near the San Angelo bridge stood representatives of the Jewish community of Rome, and from these the pope received the scroll of the law, signifying his rejection of 'false' Jewish comprehension of it; at the end of the bridge was the first of a series of specially erected triumphal arches, which carried the inscription: 'To Leo X, promoter of ecclesiastical unity and peace among Christian nations.' The second arch stood at the entrance to the Via Giulia, and thereafter a series of others marked the route to the Lateran. The streets were decorated with silk and velvet hangings, garlands of brightly-coloured foliage and fresh flowers; the people leaned out of their windows, shouting and yelling, praising God for the dawn of a new age. *Leo! Leo! Palle!* rang out ceaselessly.

The most artistic and elaborate of the triumphal arches had been put up by the wealthy bankers; Agostino Chigi, for example, had one erected near his house on the Via del Banco di Santo Spirito, which was engraved with the words, 'To Leo X, felicitous restorer of peace!' and it was decorated with all kinds of pagan figures, some of them rather unseemly: Apollo, Mercury, Pallas, nymphs, undines, and so on. Between these figures was threaded a banner, embroidered with the verse:

> *'First Venus ruled; then came the god of war;*
> *now, great Minerva, it is thy day which dawns!'*

The first two references were to Alexander VI Borgia, and Julius II; poor old Cardinal Piccolomini, who reigned evanescently as Pius III, was entirely forgotten. The arch put up by Ferdinando Ponzetti, the clerical chamberlain, was adorned with representations of Perseus, Apollo,

200

Moses, Mercury and Diana; perched on the top of it was a living boy, who threw flowers down onto the people below. No-one seemed disturbed in the least by this curious and frank admixture of the Christian and the pagan; indeed, one particular bishop (later to become Cardinal Andrea della Valle), crowded the front of his house with nothing but antique statuary: Bacchus, Mercury, Hercules, and a rather salacious-looking Venus, her hand cupping one ripe breast in a gesture of uncoy invitation. All this, no doubt, was a reference to Leo's well known love for the arts, antique culture and learning; indeed, as the procession passed the house of the Genoese banker Sauli, a handsome child stepped out onto the balcony and declaimed some verses in Latin which lauded precisely this devotion. I think it was partially perceived as a sort of antidote to the military austerity which had characterised the reign of Julius, who had certainly been a patron of the arts, but was more than anything else a worshipper at the altar of Mars; from the very beginning, Leo was extolled as a lover of peace and a devotee of learning, and memories – still very fresh – of the harshness of Julius' character enchanced Leo's natural gentleness without any real effort on his part. The humanists in particular, of whom even as a cardinal the new pope had been a true patron, proclaimed frankly that the age of iron had given way to the age of gold. The golden age of Pallas Athene.

After the protracted ceremonies in the Lateran, the huge procession wound its way back to the Vatican palace; the streets were now illuminated by many thousands of candles and lamps, and the festivities were continued by the people well into the night. Sitting for the first time in one of the papal chairs, Leo kicked off his red shoes and let out a long, shuddering sigh of exhaustion. Serapica, Bibbiena and myself sat at his stockinged feet.

"Well," he said at last, "God has given us the papacy, so let us enjoy it."

Then:

"God's bones, I'm bursting for a pee."

Esto eis Domine, turris fortitudinis a facie inimici

"What was the name again?"

"Tomaso della Croce, Holiness."

Leo looked down thoughtfully at one gold-slippered foot.

"You say that this man is responsible for much suffering?"

"Yes."

"He *is* one of my inquisitors, after all," Leo sighed. Then he continued: "The Inquisition is a fairly autonomous body, you see. Besides, even I don't know everything that goes on. I'm not responsible for –"

"I am not suggesting that your Holiness is responsible. This is precisely my point: this man Tomaso della Croce is entirely responsible for the disruption of my life, and the cruel snuffing out of another."

"The girl was pronounced guilty in the usual way?"

"Yes, Holiness," I said.

"Then there seems to be little I can do, Peppe. Even for your sake."

"But you're the pope!" I cried, frustrated and annoyed with Leo's lack of sympathy. Frankly, it surprised me; I brought up the subject in the first place only because I had thought that it would be an easy matter to have Tomaso della Croce dealt with. I was determined, in any case, that *something* had to be done, even if only in order to pre-empt any foolhardy plan Andrea de' Collini might come up with. If Leo couldn't or wouldn't do anything for me now, I made up my mind to pressure him again and again on future occasions until he most definitely could and would.

"And the pope is weary of this discussion," he said

petulantly, very much aware that he had disappointed me. "Let us have no more of it."

Actually, in the first few years of his reign, there were a great many matters that Leo would have liked to 'have no more of,' but political exigence obliged him to give them a considerable amount of attention. He learned early on the need for circumspection, which as you know, some later interpreted as vacillation. In the very beginning however, before the schemes of nations and the ambitions of kingdoms compelled him to learn the art of subterfuge and strategy in the service of Holy Mother Church, family matters were uppermost on his mind.

We Italians are a people naturally disposed to love home and family (which is one reason why my childhood was so miserable, since both, for me, were utterly unlovable), but in Leo this was a veritable obsession. His brother Giuliano and his cousin Giulio both came to Rome immediately after the Conclave elected Leo pope, as did Lorenzo his nephew, son of his brother Piero. Leo immediately bestowed upon them the Roman patriciate, doing so with immense and spectacular pomp, in the Capitol. Giuliano had actually been intended by his father Lorenzo the Magnificent for a career in the secular state, but his health was not good (neither were his abilities, for that matter), and Leo had him remain in Rome, giving him the title 'General of the Church,' which was purely an honorific. It was Lorenzo to whom the task fell of governing the Republic of Florence, even though he was only twenty-one years old, and to Florence he returned on August 10th 1513, the first year of Leo's pontificate; naturally, he buzzed back and forth like a blue-arsed fly, picking up what goodies he could whenever he returned to the Eternal City.

The Republic of Florence was governed at this time in much the same way that it had been under Lorenzo the Magnificent; two councils legislated for everything, one consisting of seventy members elected for life, the other of a hundred who were changed every six months. However, disciples, adherents, sycophants and toadies of the Medici were in a majority on both councils, which meant that whatever Lorenzo wanted, Lorenzo got; he resided in a beautiful palace in the Via Larga, dispensing largesse and bestowing favours for all the world like a monarch – or a pope, it might be said. Thus, the independence of the Republic was a mere form, for the house of Medici ruled supreme. In September 1513, the feast of saints Cosmos and Damien, patron saints of the Medici, was accorded the status of a public holiday in Florence.

Lorenzo seemed to possess all those qualities which should have equipped him to be a worthy nephew of the Medici pope, and on top of this he was urged to be ambitious for power by his mother Alfonsina Orsini. She dreamed up the most lofty plans for him, including that of gaining the principality of Piombo; she burned to see a crown on her son's head, and it didn't much matter what kind of crown it was. With surprising integrity, Leo himself strenuously resisted this idea; I think that in some way, by means of an intuition which he did not fully understand but which he nevertheless trusted, Leo saw in Lorenzo the future decline of the Medici.

And now to His Eminence Cardinal Giulio de' Medici! Giulio had in fact lived rather quietly in Lombardy as an inmate of the Capuan Priory of St John, but Leo's elevation to the throne of Peter precipitately ended this obscurity; on May 9th 1513, he was made Archbishop of Florence, and after the question of his legitimacy had been swiftly dealt with (his 'father' had been murdered by the Pazzi), he was raised to the cardinalate on September 23rd 1513. I have never liked Giulio; even before I heard him and Lorenzo muttering against Leo in that corridor, I could not take to him. I don't trust him, and I think Leo is a fool to do so – but then, as I said in the beginning of these memoirs, Leo is blind when it comes to his family. People tell me that they find Giulio a gentle and kindly man, and rather weak in temperament, but I cannot agree with this estimation; he is prone to melancholy it is true, but this in itself does not indicate a gentle nature, and I am convinced that it is a melancholy born of reflection upon what he covets, and what he has actually been able to attain. I believe his introspection (and he *does* give the impression of introspection) is in fact nothing other than a continual meditation upon his ambitions. He's always hatching up schemes, particularly with the pope's nephew Lorenzo, whom he has introduced to secret vice. Whenever Lorenzo comes to Rome, Giulio makes sure he has a thoroughly wicked time. Lorenzo's mother Alfonsina warned him about Giulio's influence, but Lorenzo merely replied tartly:

"Io mi voglio dare piacere hora ch'io sono giovane et ch'io posso per haver un papa . . ."

Alfonsina is said to have kicked him in the balls.

Bernardo Dovizi, known as Bibbiena after the town of his birth, was also made a cardinal in the first year of Leo's pontificate. As I believe I have already mentioned, I quite liked Bibbiena, but he and Serapica were constantly at loggerheads, which sometimes made the atmosphere in the papal household a little chilly, to say the least. Bibbiena had been closely connected with the Medici for many years; in Florence it was he who had supervised the studies of the young Giovanni, before becoming his private secretary. He had also shared the exile of the Medicis, and had stoutly defended Leo's interests to Pope Julius; finally, as you know, Bibbiena worked secretly but tirelessly for Leo's cause during the Conclave – as indeed did Serapica, even though the two hardly said a single word to each other. In the first years of Leo's reign, Bibbiena's star was very much in the ascendant, and he had virtually free access to the pope at any time, night or day; to be fair, so did Serapica and I, but Bibbiena was now dignified with the rank of Cardinal, which galled Serapica no end.

Under Innocent VIII, the *capo* of the pope's private secretaries was the *segretario intimo*, through whom all business passed, and to whom all papal secrets were confided; inevitably, this extraordinary office became the

205

object of hysterical envy among the other secretaries, and was greatly abused. Bibbiena persuaded Leo to reorganise the system, and the post of *segretario intimo* was much reduced in importance; in fact, Bibbiena placed *himself* between the pope and the *segretario intimo* of the time, Pietro Ardinghello. Later, Bibbiena was replaced by Giulio de' Medici. Many people (besides Serapica) were intensely jealous of the power and influence Bibbiena had appropriated for himself, especially after his elevation to the cardinalate: state secrets were often confided to him alone, and Giulio stormed around the palace mouthing vulgar curses, complaining that Bibbiena was 'a power-crazed ball-sucker' and 'a treacherous sodomite'. In fact, he was neither of these things – Bibbiena adored beautiful women, and his conducting of liaisons and affairs became a scandal even in the papal court, which was generally inured to such goings-on. Certainly, he was a worldly man, devoted to literary and artistic enjoyments (but then, so was Leo), but neither did he despise diversions of a grosser character. As an organizer of festivities that included more than a nuance of the vulgar, Bibbiena had no equal, and Leo loved him for that. Even after his influence had begun to wane and Giulo's to wax, people still called him the *alter ego* of the pope. A visiting Venetian dignitary declared, somewhat crustily, "Bibbiena is all and everything."

Leo, Bibbiena, Serapica and I often dined together in the private papal apartments; Leo was essentially a man of peace, and he longed to reconcile Bibbiena and Serapica, but as I said before, since this actually amounted to a personality clash, there was very little he could do about it. He persisted in his efforts however, and these intimate *soirées a quatre* were very frequently excruciating.

"And how went the day?" Leo would ask rather stiffly, like a talentless actor in a third-rate historical drama.

"You'd better ask Bibbiena, Holiness; after all, *he* organised it."

"I meant *your* day, Serapica."

"So did I."

"Is this fish fresh?"

"You'd better ask Bibbiena, Holiness – he hired the cook."

"Oh shut up, for Christ's sake!" Bibbiena would eventually say.

"And what would you know about Christ?"

"I *forbid* you to talk like that at my – at *Our* table!"

"Hadn't you better consult Bibbiena before issuing a command, Holiness?"

Then a glacial silence would descend, broken only by the occasional fart from Leo; on one occasion, after Leo had let rip with a rich, juicy expulsion of gas, Serapica looked across the table at Bibbiena, smiled angelically and said:

"Did you say something, my dear?"

As for me, I had certain other diversions to protect me against depression in the face of all this bickering and bitchery, and also to distract me from the constant comings and goings of Giulio, Lorenzo, and other minor members of the Medici clan who were always on the lookout for an opportunity to advance their own interests – particularly the financial ones. I had an apartment in the Vatican, as did Serapica, but both he and Bibbiena maintained private houses elsewhere – Bibbiena had his own place in the Belvedere, where he could escape the cut-and-thrust of Serapica's acerbic tongue; it was therefore very necessary for me to have access to another, less claustrophobic world, and this was that of the Gnostic Brotherhood.

I had of course kept my appointment with Nino, Beppo and the Skull in the tavern of Marco Saletti, and there Nino had confirmed the news he had briefly hissed to me – that Andrea de' Collini had *purchased* the services of the three of them from Master Antonio; to my mind this was astonishing, especially since I had received no further word from the Master himself. Then, one morning while Leo was away hunting, Serapica sidled up to me and whispered:

"He's back in Rome, my dear!"

"Who?"

"Your friend – Andrea de' Collini."

"Don't you mean *our* friend?" I said, somewhat irritated.

"Well yes, of course! It's just that – well – you know we can't afford to –"

"Thank you for the information," I said, as coldly as I could.

He tiptoed off.

I did not have any idea what the Master might or might not have been planning during the time that had passed since I last saw him; my feelings for him were in any case going through a phase of ambiguity – I continued to love him for all that he had given me (had he not opened my heart and mind to truth?), as well as for the fact that he was Laura's father, but – to be perfectly honest – at the papal court I was beginning to some degree to achieve a sense of *permanence* (to use a favourite term of Serapica's) and I did not wish this rare and painfully acquired commodity to be eroded in any way. Was this a selfish attitude? Reflecting upon the matter I came to believe that it was, but despite this there was little I could do about my feelings. My feelings I had to live with.

I found the Master a greatly changed man when I finally saw him again. He was by this time completely *obsessed* with Tomaso della Croce, and seemed unable to give his attention to any other subject; furthermore, the knowledge that he had Nino, Beppo and the Skull at his disposal, intensified the apprehension that his obsession caused in me. Even so, he did not lack for sincere and committed disciples, and I for one cannot be surprised at this: he taught, after all, that if this world is hell there is no need to live in fear and trembling of a theological hell of fire and brimstone in the world to come; that if this world is hell, it is neither one of unmitigated torment, nor of eternal duration. It is a hell in which the human person may be obliged to endure the depths of degradation and pain, yet where at the same time the fragrance of the purple clematis is blown inland by the gentlest of sea breezes on cloudless summer days; a hell in which squalor, poverty and decay are omnipresent, yet where the cherry-blossom carpets the earth in late spring like a wedding-gown. In short: a hell which offers a surfeit of suffering and a plenitude of beauty. If this life marks the utmost limit of our separation from God – beyond which we cannot go – and if it is the beginning of a long journey back to him through realms increasingly more light, more pain-free, more bearable, then the Gnostic philosophy which teaches these truths is above all a supremely optimistic one. Perhaps this is why the light it sheds in our darkness was beginning to attract a steady flow of devotees who desired admittance to the Gnostic Brotherhood. Andrea de' Collini was still living in his own house, conducting regular meetings for philosophical discussion and worship, and he maintained a small group of students who would finally be admitted to Gnostic baptism; the campaign of hatred waged by Fra Tomaso della Croce appeared to all intents and purposes to have fallen into an inexplicable – and doubtless temporary – lull. I know – because my informants told me – that the Dominican was often in Rome, but Andrea de' Collini was left unmolested. I do not think for one moment that this was because he believed Laura's burning to have been punishment enough – della Croce would not rest until Andrea himself had been dispatched in a similar manner; rather, I suspect that the attention of the inquisition was too much taken up with Luther and the events in Germany to spare the time for relative small-fry like the Gnostic Brotherhood. On a purely personal level Tomaso della Croce *despised* Andrea de' Collini – I have never been more sure of anything than that – and he would have despised him even had the Master been a model of Catholic orthodoxy, but the inquisitor had too much of the fanatic's integrity to act simply from personal motives.

I once again attended weekly meetings at the house of Andrea de' Collini, but not for any new teaching he had to offer; rather, I was more intent upon discovering his intentions towards Tomaso della Croce. And I always had to exercise a prudent caution, since I was by this time fairly well known as an intimate of the pope; indeed, looking the way I do, and being present at most public papal functions, how could I fail to be known? Leo noticed my regular absences but said nothing; perhaps he imagined that I was keeping a mistress somewhere? Only once did I have the unpleasant and rather sinister feeling that Bibbiena was keeping a watchful eye on me; if this was the case, it would only be because I favoured Serapica rather than himself, not on account of any real curiosity about my extracurricular pursuits.

No, Andrea de' Collini himself was not the man I once knew; before he had been all authority, all fire and zeal, whereas now he slumped when he walked, he frequently muttered to himself, he forgot the words of the liturgy that he had once known by heart. Furthermore, he had become obsessed with what he called the 'science of numbers', and this seemed to have something to do with his desire to force a final confrontation between himself and Tomaso della Croce; personally, I could not fathom the abstruse and tenuous speculations he tried to interest me in, for they seemed to me the wildest fancies, concocted with the most obscure and unrelated of principles, serving only to heat his brain to fever-point, and cloud his once crystal-clear intellect.

This was all terribly sad. I suspected that the day would soon come when I would be asked to take over as Master of our Brotherhood; I had no idea how Andrea de' Collini would be likely to act in the case of this eventuality coming to pass, but I was prepared to assume command for the sake of preserving not only our Brotherhood, but the Gnostic creed itself.

The Master managed not to answer any of my questions concerning his 'purchase' of the three freaks; neither did he seem the slightest jot embarrassed by the fact that I had discovered the transaction made with Master Antonio, or that it was obvious I *knew* he was evading my questions.

"You see Peppe," he said to me one evening after the group had dispersed, "it is an *exact* science; there is no possibility of error, no possibility of illusion or failure. When one has grasped the numerical series and set the cause and effect which they indicate into motion, the final result is assured. Guaranteed!

"Look: the name of Tomaso della Croce gives a combined total of 8. This – oh! – this is the supreme number of disaster! It is ruled by Saturn, by dark and unpredictable Saturn, bringer of chaos, misfortune and adversity! Della Croce is fated to a bleak end, believe me, Peppe. In the final confrontation, which I shall engineer, his numerological matrix will bring forth destruction. The die is cast."

"How on earth do you arrive at the number 8?"

"Here, here, let me show you!"

His face burned bright with an inner fever, his eyes glittered with the mania of a hopeless obsession as he wrote down the following calculation for my elucidation:

```
T O M A S O    D E L L A    C R O C E
4 7 4 1 3 7    4 5 3 3 1    3 2 7 3 5
```

"You see it? There! You see, you understand? The name 'Tomaso' yields a total of 26, which we reduce to 8 – Saturn's number! Already we are being given an indication of what is to come. 'Della' and 'Croce' add up to 16 and 20 respectively, which we reduce to 7 and 2; then, 8, 7 and 2 combine to produce 17, which comes back once again to 8. To 8, Peppe! Oh, I could not have wished for a more perfect reduction!

"The number 7 indicates travel; it gives us the image of a man who is restless, forever on the move, an individual governed by the tides of Neptune, whose ebb and flow is endless. The tide is never still, Peppe, and neither is our friend Tomaso della Croce. Some inner lust for movement and motion drives him on; we know, in any case, that he does indeed spend his days travelling from one place to another – usually in pursuit of some poor wretch whom he has determined to torture and destroy. Our first indication then, is lack of fixity, fluidity, an inability to settle; this, we know from experience, is to be interpreted as a lifestyle involving perpetual journeying. Thus, the numbers tell me I must overcome this factor if I am to bring him to me, face to face.

"The number 2 reveals the soul of a man under the spell of a romantic ideal; 2 is governed by the Moon – the planet of dreams, of night-fire, of spells, enchantment and idealism! And indeed, della Croce is spellbound by his dream and ideal of pure orthodox truth, in defence of which he would, I am sure, expend even his life. He is guided by no other light than that of the moon of his dream of perfect and inviolate doctrine. Yet 2 is not only the number of the dreamer and the poet, it is also that of the fanatic; it is 2 which has inspired him to inflict physical pain upon countless poor creatures who happened to disagree with his notion of truth. It is 2 which fuels the fire, which piles high the faggots, 2 which drives him to extremes of cruelty in the service of his faith.

"Then, 'Croce' yields once again the number 8. Saturn! Oh, Peppe, what a happy marriage of name and number! For the cross indeed is darkness, suffering and death, and all three shall be *his*. The sum total of 'Tomaso della Croce', as if to confirm the truth of the indications we have been given, produces the ubiquitous 8."

"But what does it all *mean?*"

He stared at me as though I were an imbecile.

"Can't you see it at all?"

"Not really."

"Look: these hints and allusions and indications give me the *means* whereby I may bring him to myself; and having brought him to myself, they further assure me that the outcome of our last struggle will be victory for me. Victory, Peppe!"

He was breathing hard and fast, and his eyes seemed almost sightless, fixed on some inner vision to which I had no access. This vision clearly enthralled him.

212

"First," he said, "I must put an end to his wandering and bring him here to this city; I must do so by appealing to his fanatical devotion to what he considers to be religious truth."

"How?"

"Simple! *Roma* gives the number 14, which we reduce to 5; hence, I must contact him in some way which exposes him to the number five – an anonymous letter, perhaps, informing him that the fifth member of an infamous group of heretics has recently arrived in Rome, or a name which carries the numerical total of 5 – and he will be unable to resist coming here. The rest of the procedure will be easy."

It all sounded like a lot of magical mumbo-jumbo to me, but I refrained from saying so. When I left him, he was still hunched over his writing-desk, his face contorted in a spasm of intense concentration. I grieved silently over the loss of the man I had known and loved: the transformation of a noble soul into a fool obsessed with numbers, runes and mystical mutterings.

Meanwhile, when Leo was not under the spell of his own obsession with the Medici clan, he began to find himself thrust into the centre of the stage of endless political dramatics.

Louis XII of France, having been reconciled with Rome, had begun to make frank overtures of friendship to King Ferdinand of Spain; as the price of an alliance, he offered the hand of his daughter Renée (a thoroughly spoilt bitch, by all accounts) to either of Ferdinand's grandsons (whichever of them would be happiest married to a bitch, I suppose), together with Milan and Genoa, and the renunciation of all his claims to Naples. Ferdinand apparently did not regard this offer as an attractive one and it was not taken up, but a year's truce was concluded between Spain and France on March 13th 1514. Poor Leo was utterly taken aback and completely shocked by this turn of events; he wished, at all costs, to keep Spain and France apart, and dreaded the supremacy of either power in Italy. As an Italian, he loathed the thought of a significant foreign presence in the Italian peninsula, and as the pope he was pledged to guard the spiritual and temporal independence of the Holy See; he therefore began immediately to direct his efforts against any step which would lead to Naples and Milan being brought together under the same sovereign. He was also dismayed that he had, in one swoop, lost all the advantages which the enmity between France and Spain had hitherto yielded.

He sent urgent epistles here, there and everywhere, condemning the proposed marriage between Renée and one of the royal Spanish grandsons – as I say, the proposal would never become an actuality in any case, but Leo was not to know this at the time. The Florentine ambassador, Roberto Acciaiuoli, was sent to France in an attempt to influence Louis; in fact, because he feared the potential supremacy of Spain more than that of France, Leo managed a stunning *volte-face* and suddenly appeared all smiles and welcomes to the representative of Louis in Rome, whom he had until this point treated with the utmost disdain. None of this helped the protracted negotiations between Cardinal Lang, the representative of Maximillian, and the Republic of Venice, who had for a long time been attempting to reach a reconciliation; Lang, whom I have already described to you, was a supercilious, avaricious man with delusions of grandeur, and in the middle of these delicate and thus far unfruitful negotiations, suddenly demanded for himself the post of permanent Legate in Germany. Leo had no intention of granting this, but did not wish to refuse personally, as Maximillian had sent a persuasive letter supporting Lang's demand; therefore, with great cunning, he told the Consistory of cardinals held on May 10th exactly what the granting of this favour would mean for them (considerable loss of curial revenues for a start), and left it to their Eminences to reject it, which they did. Lang eventually took leave of Leo in a farewell audience, during the course of which he spoke lengthily and haughtily of his own abilities and skills (now, of course, lost to the papacy, as he considered), and left in a huff on May 11th for Loreto, where Bibbiena happened to be at the time, licking the wounds inflicted by Serapica's rapier-like tongue.

The whole situation was absurdly complicated. There were treaties and anti-treaties and alliances and broken alliances flying about all over the place, and rumours, gossip and reports from spies filled the papal apartments with the stink of treachery and duplicity as much as Leo's farts filled them with the stink of expelled gas. Sometimes all this activity reached absolute fever-pitch, and Leo was obliged, for the sake of his sanity, to give himself over for a few days solely to the pursuit of pleasure, which most often required the services of young studs from the gutters of Rome. As time went on and the various international crises deepened, it was rumoured in the city that His Holiness was so consumed with anxiety that he passed many nights without sleep; I can confirm that he did indeed go sleepless night after night, but it had nothing to do with anxiety.

Matters were eventually given a new and unpredictable twist by the death of Louis XII and the accession of Francis I to the throne of France. Francis was young, gifted and ambitious, and much under the influence of his mother, Louisa of Savoy, who was a power-hungry old hag; even during the reign of Louis, Louisa's sister Filiberta had been proposed as a bride for Giuliano, the pope's brother. This was laughably obvious as a political manoeuvre, because Filiberta was as ugly as sin, and far too old for Giuliano; however, Giuliano and Filiberta were in fact married on June 25th, 1515. Leo's basic problem was this: should he publicly and officially ally himself with France, or with Spain? In between these two extremes of the spectrum were a dozen or so principalities, powers, thrones and dominations clamouring for him to come down once and for all on one side or the other. Giuliano, now the husband of the aunt of Francis I, naturally urged Leo to favour France; but Bibbiena had drafted terms for a coalition between the papacy, Maximillian, the King of Spain, Milan, Genoa and the Swiss, which was intended to check both the power and ambition of the French king. Leo entered into a protracted period which some called 'vacillation' but which I prefer to acknowledge as consummately skilful and prudent procrastination. In fact, he declared the terms of the League ratified, but continued to carry on negotiations with Francis.

It looked very much like war. Leo tried twice to get Francis to give up his claims on Naples, once through Ludovico di Canossa (a gifted and highly astute diplomat) and once through the French ambassador, Montmaur; both attempts failed. Leo decided to make military preparations. The terms of the League consisting of the pope, the emperor, Spain, Milan, and the Swiss (but not Genoa, which had defected to the French cause), conceived by Bibbiena, were finally fully ratified, although Leo delayed the issuing of a public proclamation; it was only the striking of the first military blow by the young and inexperienced Duke of Guise, which eventually brought this about. Still no-one quite believed it, after Leo's procrastination; I heard Bibbiena say to the Venetian ambassador:

"Ch'el Papa havia dato la bolla de la liga fata agli oratori yspani."

And that was about the closest anyone got to knowing precisely and definitely quite *what* Leo had actually done.

"What *have* you actually done, precisely and definitely?" I asked one evening.

"Oh don't *you* start!" Leo groaned, scratching his stomach. "I've got a rash coming on. Do you think it could be something I've eaten?"

"Or something you've picked up," I said.

"Pig. As always, totally unsympathetic. Why don't you amuse me? You never provide any entertaining antics, these days."

"Your Holiness seems to be providing enough of those yourself," I remarked.

Leo glared at me, his eyes watery and wobbling.

"I *must* do things in my own way!" he cried defensively. "What am I supposed to do, leap into the first alliance that happens to come along? One needs to exercise great caution in these matters – but what would you know of that? Everybody accuses me of dithering and changing my mind –"

"I'm not accusing you of any such thing," I interrupted. "At least *I* know that what appears to be vacillation is, as you say, the exercise of caution. I'm just wondering why you left the public declaration for so long . . ."

"I always held out the hope that Francis could be persuaded to change his mind," Leo said. "Even at the last minute."

"Well, Holiness, the last minute has come and gone."

Leo exhaled deeply and pushed himself further back in his chair.

At last, he murmured:

"I think I may have a private assignment for you, Peppe."

"Any particular preference?" I asked.

"Well-built, of course . . ."

"Well-built, or well-*endowed?*"

"Both, naturally."

And the rest I'm sure you know by now.

Francis had an army of thirty-five thousand men concentrated at Lyons, sixty cannons and one hundred culverins; among the generals were Trivulzio, Trémouille and Robert de la Marck. It was this army which crossed the Alps through the Col d'Argentière, blasting rocks and throwing bridges across chasms as it advanced, and took the Milanese cavalry led by Prospero Colonna totally by surprise. Before long, the French possessed the western part of the Duchy of Milan, and had thrown the Swiss troops into utter confusion. The papal army under Lorenzo de' Medici thrust and parried half-heartedly, but did not even bother to cross the Po river.

Leo immediately began to babble of flight.

"I shall go to Gaeta," he pronounced.

"You *can't,* Holiness!"

"Why not? Alright then, Ischia; it'll be nice in Ischia this time of the year."

"For heaven's sake!"

"Ah, I can see the French occupying Rome already!"

Serapica began to cry shamelessly.

"They'll utterly ruin my collection of statuary and steal all my antiques," he sobbed. "You know what the French are like – barbarians! That bloody bitch Filiberta will be positively *gloating* – oh –"

Then Leo started to cry too.

In fact, he had been astonished at the French victory, for he had thought that the watch kept by the Swiss on the Alpine passes, combined with the military skill of Prospero Colonna, should have been more than enough to keep the French advance at bay. Bibbiena, for whom I had begun to feel more than a little sorry, pissed in his underdrawers with shock – after all the League had been his idea. He wasn't really a politician or a diplomat in any case, and found the effort of trying to reconcile his dependence upon the Medici and his commitment to Church interests, with hard political facts, both wearisome and difficult.

"It's all his fault!" Serapica screamed, pointing a trembling finger at a florid and indignant Bibbiena.

"You witless bastard! How dare you!"

"Shut up, for the love of God!" Leo yelled, dancing between the two of them, until all three were dancing around each other in a little *allemande* of supreme outrage. It was so absurd, I began to laugh. Ah, if the eyes of princes and kings and prelates could see what I saw! They'd never believe me.

Then Cardinal Giulio de' Medici, whom Leo had appointed Legate with the papal troops headed by Lorenzo, came in for trouble; Leo had specifically ordered Giulio to keep a check on the cities of Modena and Reggio, which the avaricious Duke of Ferrara was longing to possess, and

218

Bibbiena had to argue on Giulio's behalf against the imposition of this further burden. Leo was not sympathetic.

"I should never have made him Legate," he said. "Every day I get letters of complaint from him, grumbling about dangers and difficulties – Christ's precious blood, does he imagine I'm sitting on my arse in supreme comfort and confidence? I still blame Giulio and Lorenzo for the disgraceful performance of my army. I will not listen to any defence of him!"

Now *that* was a hard thing for Leo to say in view of his blind and obsessive love for his relatives; nevertheless, he said it. In fact, to be fair, Giulio was perfectly well aware that even as all this was going on, Leo was still secretly and shamelessly negotiating with Francis; such knowledge was hardly conducive to zeal on the field of battle. There was one curious event, however: for some time King Henry VIII of England had been asking Leo to raise Thomas Wolsey to the cardinalate, but thus far he had refused; now, in order to provide himself with at least *some* support in case everyone else turned against him, he did proceed with Wolsey's nomination in the consistory held on September 10th 1515. Everyone was rather surprised at this.

The army of Francis I had meanwhile approached the neighbourhood of the capital of Lombardy, and had pitched camp at Marignano; the redoubtable and ferocious old Cardinal Schinner, who always seemed to be fighting somebody somewhere, did all he could to stir up the Swiss troops, and in fact succeeded in driving the French back, but the battle ceased with nightfall. It was reported to Leo that Francis himself slept on a gun-carriage.

"More likely had a whore on a gun-carriage," Leo remarked acidly.

The following day, the Swiss were defeated by the French, who had been joined by a troop of Venetian horsemen. Actually, the news was somewhat slow in filtering through, which caused considerable embarrassment; first we received the intelligence from Lorenzo that Schinner had driven the French back, and everyone but Leo went mad with joy. Bibbiena toured the city in a carriage, deliberately running down as many Venetian and French citizens as he could find, and screaming obscenities at them. Then came word that the Swiss had been soundly thrashed, despite their heroism, and everyone was plunged into mourning. The Venetian ambassador, Marino Giorgi (he was always up to something or other, poking his nose into other people's affairs and generally making a nuisance of himself), came at once to the Vatican at some unearthly hour of the morning, attired in full ceremonial robes of state. Luckily, it was Serapica who met him first.

"I must speak with His Holiness," Giorgi said.

"His Holiness is still in bed, sleeping."

In fact, His Holiness *was* in bed, but whether he was sleeping or not was anyone's guess, since his bed was presently being shared by a young man procured on his behalf by me the night before.

"You must rouse His Holiness!" Giorgi insisted.

"Certainly not," Serapica said in his most queenly, disdainful manner.

"I insist on speaking to His Holiness!"

Eventually, after I had entered Leo's chamber to find Zeus and Ganymede *both* asleep, and had dragged the bewildered, naked youth out of the papal bed into a closet, Giorgi was finally admitted into the presence of the pope. Serapica and I lingered, to see what the ambassador would say. That he would gloat, we had no doubt.

"What do you want?" Leo hissed, pulling the bedcovers up around several of his chins.

"Holy Father, after the example of Christ, I will return you good for evil. Yesterday your Holiness gave me bad and at the same time false news; today I bring in exchange good news which is also true: the Swiss have been defeated."

"We have also received this news," Leo replied courageously, "but the defeat has been inconsiderable."

"Your Holiness can see the truth by this dispatch," Giorgi said unctuously, handing the pope his own official letter, together with that of the Venetian representative to the French king.

Leo was very badly shaken, but tried hard not to let Giorgi see it. His sloppy mouth opened and closed like that of a fish gasping for water, but he turned it into a prolonged yawn. It was, if I say so myself, exceedingly manfully done.

"With Your Holiness's permission," the ambassador said, "I shall withdraw, so that Your Holiness may attend to his toilet."

Withdraw he did, but only so that he could rush off to inform Bibbiena and the other cardinals of the news. Giorgi kept away from the Vatican for a few days, since the Swiss Guard was so enraged, they threatened to tear his balls off and fry them in a pan for supper, if they caught sight of him. He did in fact attend an audience some time later, during the course of which Leo – humbled and depressed – said to him:

"We will throw ourselves into the arms of the most Christian king and beg his mercy."

"Most Holy Father," Giorgi replied, "if you do so, it will be neither to your detriment nor to that of the Holy See. The king is a true son of the Church."

Leo immediately began to make arrangements for a reconciliation with Francis. I had never seen the poor old dear looking so downcast as then. Bibbiena was all for a renewal of the fight, with the combined forces of the Holy See, the emperor, Spain and the Swiss, since he was desperate to shore up the crumbling League at all costs, but Leo would have none of it. Even Alfonsina Orsini put in her two ducats' worth, writing to Lorenzo that "Bibbiena will by his doings ruin us for the second time . . ."

The peace negotiations were rather protracted, but Francis proved himself surprisingly generous; this was probably because he feared that a coalition between the Maximillian and Henry VIII of England (who was a firm friend of Leo's now that Thomas Wolsey had been raised to the cardinalate) might rob him of the fruits of victory before the pope had a chance to confirm them. The Venetians more than everyone else were alarmed, since the terms of the treaty when they were made known, seemed to ignore Venetian interests completely; I for one, was delighted at this, since I had long felt that the haughty, imperious, treacherous and conniving Republic needed to be taught a thorough lesson. Marino Giorgi was practically in a state of apoplexy, I heard tell, although – sadly – I was not able to see this for myself.

The hardest term of the treaty was the renunciation of all papal claims to Parma and Piacenza; this was a bitter potion for Leo to swallow, but swallow it he did – besides, he harboured hopes that through the purchase of Modena, that territory would once again be united to the states of the Church. In fact, this is precisely what happened.

Francis I entered the capital of Lombardy in great triumph on October 11th 1515; Leo retired to Viterbo under the pretext of taking an autumn holiday, and both Serapica and I accompanied him. While we were there however, amusing ourselves in our own various ways, news reached us that Francis himself wished to come to Rome for a personal audience with the pope. This astonished us, I can tell you! However, Leo wanted to keep Francis out of Rome at all costs, and proposed that they should meet at Bologna, and Francis agreed to this. So we packed our bags and headed north, intending to journey to Bologna via Leo's native city of Florence.

The city did us proud. Leo grumbled a great deal on the way, since his ulcerated arse was giving him a great deal of trouble, but even he managed to smile when he saw the welcome that had been carefully designed for us. Artists of the stature of Jacopo Sansovino, Andrea del Sarto and Pontorno positively vied with each other in contriving decorations which were a felicitous combination of architecture, sculpture and painting; twelve triumphal arches had been erected and adorned not only with reproductions of the most famous specimens of the architecture of ancient Rome, but also with inscriptions which sang eloquent praises of the first Florentine pope. On the smooth facade of the Duomo, Andrea del Sarto had painted a truly marvellous picture in *chiaroscuro*.

We were greeted with music as we entered the city by the Roman gate, and several times Leo commanded our procession to halt, so that he could enjoy the decorations and works of art which had been put on the walls, some portions of which they had even levelled to accommodate them. The exact order and detail of the state entry had been painstakingly arranged by Paris de Grassis, who was an expert in that sort of thing. Eighteen cardinals took part in the procession, as well as Lorenzo de' Medici and the Florentine municipality; in fact, one would have thought that it was Francis capitulating to Leo, and not the other way round. Cardinal Giulio de' Medici said Mass in the Duomo, and afterwards Leo gave his customary blessing and indulgence. After that, it was time for business.

Leo consulted with Paris de Grassis concerning the ceremonies with which Francis would be greeted in Bologna; he was anxious to have the French king receive a truly magnificent gift, and de Grassis suggested a jewelled pax, but Leo rejected this idea. In the end, he decided on a cross of pure gold set with precious stones, which had once belonged to Cardinal Ascanio Sforza; this came from the treasury of Julius II, which was very ironic when one considers how the French hated Julius for the humiliations he had inflicted on them. Poor old Julius would have been turning in his grave if he had known. Having concluded business with de Grassis, Leo said Mass in San Lorenzo with much emotion, and afterwards knelt in tears before the porphyry sarcophagus which contained the body of his father, Lorenzo the Magnificent; he also paid a visit to his brother Giuliano, who was lying in bed in the Medici palace, seriously ill.

On December 7th we arrived in Bologna, where there was no welcome at all, to speak of; Leo had favoured Bologna's enemies far too often for the city to feel any warmth for the Medici pope. The Bentivogli positively loathed him, and as we passed through the streets the cry of *Sega! Sega!* could be heard – for the Bentivogli bore a saw on their coat-of-arms. The cardinals who accompanied us were absolutely incensed by the Bolognese animosity, and demanded that Leo halt his entry in order to express his displeasure, but Leo refused, preferring to advance with a rictus of a smile on his face as if noticing nothing untoward.

Francis I entered Bologna on December 11th with great pomp and ceremony, and all the bells of the churches pealed out in his praise; nineteen cardinals waited to receive him at the Porta San Felice. Cardinal Riario made a short speech of welcome, during which the rest of the cardinals uncovered their heads; Francis replied in French, also with his head uncovered. As a matter of fact, the entourage that Francis had assembled disappointed the thousands of people who had turned out to see it, for it bore no arms, and its hallmark was simplicity. Leo watched it from a window of the Palazzo Pubblico.

The actual meeting of pope and king was so long-winded that it became tedious; there were also some moments of pure absurdity. The great hall on the second floor of the Palazzo Pubblico was so crowded, thronged with cardinals, lesser prelates, members of the nobility and assorted spectators of various ranks and status, that the floor began to creak and groan alarmingly, and there was a genuine fear that it might actually give way. I suspect that Leo secretly hoped it *would*. Leo looked magnificent, I must say; he wore a jewelled tiara and a cloak embroidered with gold and pearls, and on each slipper was affixed a huge ruby. Francis experienced a little difficulty in approaching the papal throne because the throng packed into the hall was so dense; there were unseemly scuffles as the Master of Ceremonies tried to clear a path, and at one point, the tip of his sword ripped the multicoloured hose of some effeminate old dandy who was trying to get closer to the king for a better look.

"Look what you've done, you clumsy bitch!" he

screamed, and that section of the hall rang with ribald ochlocratic braying. Francis pretended not to notice. As he drew nearer to Leo, I heard the dandy's voice murmur petulantly:

"Orlando bought them for me . . ."

Francis made the three customary genuflections before Leo's throne, and knelt; Leo raised him up with his own white-gloved hands and embraced him warmly. They greeted each other briefly, Francis in French and Leo in Latin; then the Chancellor, the aptly-named du Prat, commenced a ridiculously extravagant eulogy of the wisdom, prudence, skill, compassion, bravery and glory of the Medici family, and of Leo in particular, to whom, he fanfaronaded:

". . . God has entrusted the sacred barque of Peter, to steer it through perilous shoals into the haven of safety."

He then went on to praise the kings of France, who:

". . . from of old have surpassed all other Christian princes in their devotion to the Holy See. Treading in their footsteps, His Majesty Francis I, in spite of the disdain of advisers who were of a different mind to himself, has hastened over mountains and valleys, forests and rivers, and has run the gauntlet of the Swiss, in order to do homage to the pope, as an eldest son to his father, and the Vicar of Christ, and lay all he possesses at his feet."

All this, of course, was pure shit. Thousands of men dead, mutilated and wounded on the battlefield, strewn across the north of Italy, and all so that the king could, by giving the pope a hug, present his territorial avarice as an exercise in pious hypothecation. In the course of a single, rambling prolegomena, everyone had forgotten the treacheries and machinations, the curses and imprecations, the rivalries and ambitions, and above all, the ghastly and unforgiveable waste of human life. It was, to my mind, utterly incredible; but then, I'm only a simple old Gnostic dwarf.

Francis and Leo met again twice the next day, but what transpired between them remains a secret even now, since everyone save the interpreters were excluded. On December 13th, Leo celebrated High Mass in the church of San Petronio, and although Francis displayed every courteous attention to the pope – even to the extent of offering to carry his train – he would not receive Holy Communion from his hands. During the Mass, a French nobleman, overcome perhaps by an excess of piety, suddenly leapt up and cried out that he wished the pope to hear his confession, accusing himself of having fought against Julius II with great bitterness, and of disregarding the ban of excommunication; Francis immediately accused himself of the same thing, and begged Leo to absolve him. Leo magnanimously did so, his fat hands trembling as he raised them at the words of absolution. Then, unexpectedly, Francis said in an emotional voice:

"Your Holiness must not be surprised that we hated Julius so much, for he was our greatest enemy. In all our wars we have had no enemy so terrible or fierce as he, for Julius was a superb general, and far better suited to be such, than to be pope."

Francis then led the entire French suite in kissing Leo's slippered foot; so many kisses in fact did it receive, that the gold thread on it was partially worn away. One elderly dignitary even tried to bite off the ruby decorating the toe, but this action, it was generally felt, was not due to a surfeit of piety. That evening, Francis dined privately with Leo, and Cardinal Giulio de' Medici, Bibbiena, Serapica and myself were also present. I do not wish to say anything about this dinner, except to remark that it was of course sumptuous, an edacious dyspeptic's nightmare; in spite of myself, I was overcome with great emotion, for I could not drive the thought out of my head that it is indeed a strange turn of events when a cripple from the Trastevere gutters ends up dining with the King of France. Is it not?

On December 15th Leo granted Francis a farewell audience, and the king departed, leaving Duke Charles of Bourbon behind as his representative in Lombardy.

"Let's get ourselves out of this inhospitable privy of a

city," Leo said to me, and on December 18th we left for Rome, sojourning in Florence for some weeks, so that Leo could see his brother Giuliano, who was by now close to death. On February 28th, 1516, we arrived back in Rome amidst general rejoicing, which was, however, expressed only in ecclesiastical solemnity, since it was Lent. On March 17th of that same year, Leo's brother Giuliano finally expired, and the ugly, bad-tempered Filiberta returned to her sister Louisa, mother of Francis I.

Now I must tell you of the plot against Leo's life which I mentioned in the first chapter of my memoirs. It was devised, organised and led by Cardinal Alfonso Petrucci, one of those entirely worldly princes of the Church who have no other aim in life than that of accumulating power and wealth, and generally enjoying both. Petrucci had a special reason to hate Leo, since in March 1516, shortly after our return from Bologna via Florence, Borghese Petrucci, brother of the cardinal, had been banished from the government of Siena with Leo's consent; after this, Alfonso Petrucci occupied himself with dark thoughts of vengeance. Consumed by an insane hatred, he considered an attack on Leo while the pope was out hunting, intending to murder him with his own hand; it was the dangers and difficulties attached to this scheme which finally made him abandon it, rather than the horror it would have caused throughout Christendom. Petrucci had in fact become a crazy old man whilst still a youth.

In the end, he decided on poison, and bribed Battista da Vercelli to assist him in his plan; Vercelli was a doctor of some considerable repute who had come to Rome from Florence in the hope of being invited to treat Leo's arse, and it was during one of the administrations of such treatment that he was supposed to introduce the poison into Leo's corpulent body. It's quite amusing really: most poison is ingested orally – trust Leo to almost take it via his arse. He frequently complained that it would be the death of him. Battista da Vercelli let it be known that he had discovered a remedy for Leo's posterior trouble which was guaranteed to be efficacious and offered to apply it to the petrine rump personally; had Leo accepted this offer, that would have been the end (excuse the pun) of him, but for some reason he refused.

("It was an intuition, a pure hunch," he said to me later.)

Cardinal Petrucci was furious. He ranted and raved and succumbed to a sepsis of bile, declaring that he would be the liberator of the despised and enslaved college of cardinals, which had become Leo's piss-pot. Without taking leave of the pope, Petrucci fled to an estate in Latium belonging to the Colonna, where he quite openly plotted with his brother who was living in Naples. Leo himself wrote to him, warning him of his folly, but Petrucci, with perilous arrogance, continued to machinate with all and sundry, carrying on a particular correspondence with his secretary, Marc Antonio Nino, who had stayed behind in Rome. It was through Nino that Petrucci suggested that Battista da Vercelli should once again offer to treat the pope's arse, and whilst doing so, pump it full of poison. Petrucci's folly in this open correspondence is hardly to be credited; every word he wrote assured his doom. He even suggested that Serapica could be persuaded to become involved.

"My dear, can you *imagine?*" Serapica screamed, outraged. "I wouldn't approach Leo's arse with a tent-pole, let alone a phial of poison!"

Marc Antonio Nino was arrested and put to the torture; more specifically, they burned his foreskin off with red-hot pincers, which had the effect of persuading him to make copious and damning admissions. Screaming like a hyena in labour, he admitted everything they wanted him to, and more. He even admitted to having had intercourse with a cow, which they didn't ask for, and were rather surprised to receive; this was dismissed as an irrelevancy, however. Cardinal Petrucci was promised the restoration of his rights in Siena on condition that he came to Rome in person, but he hesitated to do this, even though he knew nothing of

Nino's confessions, which had not been made public; however, Leo coaxed him with the promise of a safe-conduct, and so on May 18th he returned to Rome. On the following day he arrived at the Vatican in the company of Cardinal Sauli, an intimate friend, and both were promptly arrested. A consistory was called at once, and Leo informed the cardinals of the proceedings against Petrucci and Sauli; at the same time, papal briefs were sent to the more noteworthy princes and princelings, giving them the news.

The wildest rumours began to fly about the city, and these increased when it was seen that the Vatican was now closely guarded and that troops had been brought in; some of the cardinals objected to the fact that Petrucci and Sauli had been incarcerated in the lowest and foulest dungeon of San Angelo, known as the Marocco, but Leo refused to have them moved. Battista da Vercelli was arrested and tortured, as were certain other individuals suspected of complicity, including a servant of Petrucci's, named Pocointesta. A second consistory was called on May 29th, and as they were assembling in the Vatican, Leo sent for Cardinal Accolti; they spoke for some time in Leo's private chambers, where there was a military guard present. Presently, Cardinals Riario and Farnese appeared, and entered the room, apparently cheerful and relaxed; I was waiting outside. As soon as Riario and Farnese were inside, Leo made a hurried exit, and hissed to me:

"Close the door, Peppe! Quick! Pull the door shut!"

I did so, and Leo then told Paris de Grassis to dismiss the consistory; Leo was trembling and seemed to be in some confusion. His face was flushed and sweaty. Riario was arrested. It later transpired that Petrucci and Sauli had named him as a fellow conspirator. On June 4th, he was transferred to the San Angelo castle – in fact, he was so overcome by a veritable paralysis of fear, that he had to be carried there on a litter, and once entombed in the Marocco, he soon made a full confession of his guilt.

In a third consistory on June 8th, Leo informed the agitated assembled Eminences that a further two of their number were involved in the abortive poison plot, and he urged them one by one to whisper their loyalty into his ear; as Cardinal Soderini did so, Leo accused him in a loud voice of being one of those two. Soderini threw himself at the pope's feet, begging for mercy, as also did Cardinal Castellesi, the second co-conspirator. Leo granted this at once, but the consistory imposed a fine of twelve thousand, five hundred ducats on each, and commanded them to maintain their silence concerning the entire proceedings. Leo then received the ambassadors of Germany, France, England, Spain, Portugal and Venice, and informed them that the cardinals involved in the plot had all been pardoned, with the exception of Petrucci, Sauli and Riario; Soderini later fled to Palestrina and lodged himself with the Colonna, while Castellesi hurried in disguise to Naples, by way of Tivoli. They say he got himself up as a woman selling oranges, but I cannot confirm this; they also say that he was raped by a brawny farmer's son, who took him for what he appeared to be, but I cannot confirm this either, more's the pity.

The trial of Petrucci, Sauli and Riario went ahead, and they were duly declared guilty; the sentence was that they should be stripped of the dignity of the cardinalate and handed over to the secular arm – this latter was the sentence that my beloved Laura received, and as you now know, it is but a euphemism for execution. In a final consistory held on June 22nd, which was by all accounts long and stormy (I was not present of course), Leo rejected suggestions by some of the cardinals that the sentence was too harsh. On June 27th, Battista da Vercelli and Marc Antonio Nino were hanged, drawn and quartered most bloodily and very messily, having been severely tortured on the way to execution. The sentence of death was carried out on Petrucci, as I related in the first chapter of these memoirs, and the fiery-tempered, manic braggart was reduced to a whimpering coward by the ultimate experience of life, which brings life itself to an end, and to which we shall all finally be required to submit.

Urgent appeals were issued from various quarters on behalf of Sauli and Riario: Cardinal Cibo and the city of Genoa pleaded the cause of the former, as did the French king, most eloquently and movingly; among others, the Venetian ambassador (him again) interceded for Riario, whose relatives even wrote to King Henry VIII of England. In the end, strict conditions were laid down for pardon in both cases: Riario was to acknowledge that he had been lawfully deposed, and owed his restoration solely to the mercy of the pope; he had to promise in public that henceforward he would be the pope's loyal and devoted servant, and have no dealings with any prince or cardinal except on purely personal matters; he was to pay the enormous fine of one hundred and fifty thousand ducats in instalments, security being advanced by friendly bankers or curial officials, and by the ambassadors of Germany, England, France, Spain, Portugal and Venice; he was never to leave his domicile except with the express permission of the pope, and the cardinals who had agreed to his deposition were appointed to ensure that these promises were kept. Sauli was restored a few days after Riario, and was required to pay a fine of twenty-five thousand ducats; further, he was never to leave the Vatican for the remainder of his life, and although reinvested with the dignity of the cardinalate, his voting rights were removed.

Sauli appeared before Leo clad as a simple priest, humbly acknowledging his crime and asking for pardon; he promised in the future, as Riario did, to prove himself a loyal and faithful servant of the pontiff. Very irritably (for he did not care much for Sauli, whom he suspected of recidivist tendencies), Leo replied:

"Let us hope your deeds correspond to your words, although it is my belief that no-one will be surprised when you fall back into your sinful ways once more."

In fact, Sauli died in March of the following year, a broken and depressed man. To his credit, Leo had him buried with full honours in the church of Santa Sabina.

As for Soderini, who had gone from Palestrina to Forli,

he was not to return to Rome again until after Leo's death. Castellesi, who had made his way to Naples in disguise, eventually found a refuge in Venice; he might have passed his days there unmolested, were it not for the fact that Cardinal Wolsey of England coveted his benefices, and did all he could to pressure Leo into bringing Castellesi to justice. Leo did in fact summon him to Rome, but he refused to come, and on July 5th 1518 he was stripped of all his dignities and accused of complicity in Petrucci's plot. I might add that this unfortunate man lived on in Venice quietly, devoting himself to prayer and study, occupying an apartment in the palace of his friend Giacomo da Pesaro; after Leo's death, he was obliged to return to Rome for the Conclave, but he seems to have disappeared somewhere along the way, and at the time of writing these words, it is still assumed that he was murdered by a treacherous servant.

Sic transit gloria hominorum.

I perceive that I have now come full circle, so to speak: I have reached the year 1518, which was when these memoirs were first begun. When I started on my task, I was of course writing in the present – now I am *looking back* on all the events which have occurred up to the time of Leo's death; they are in the past, like the shadows of dreams, like the fallen and desiccated petals which are all that are left of a once glorious blossom. They come back to me like snatches of strangely alien music, half-remembered, half-forgotten, weaving tales of people and places that I *thought* I used to be familiar with. Some of these events are in fact still close to me in time, yet how far away they all seem now! So many things seem far away since Leo died. *Everything* was bound up with him; Leo was the horizon towards which the landscape of my life stretched – endlessly as I once thought! I loved him deeply. I miss him painfully. And yet . . . yet . . . but no, this is not the moment to weave the final thread into the tapestry of my tale; for that, you will have to wait a little longer.

Well now, since I have indeed reached full circle, it would seem to be appropriate to begin my narrative again with the character who figured prominently in its opening: I refer to Martin Luther. Before I do so however, there is another incident I must relate to you, for it is one which was succeeded by the most dire and calamitous events; indeed, it stands in relation to these events as cause stands to effect, as fire to heat. I knew, deep down in the depths of me, that *something* would come – some climactic, dark apotheosis which could be forestalled for a brief span and no longer – but the precise nature of it I never imagined, nor the manner in which it was at last to be revealed. This is perhaps the way of all climaxes save the sexual climax, which is of course unfailing and wearisomely predictable.

Precisely what happened was this: I received news that Andrea de' Collini had held a 'trial' of Tomaso della Croce *in absentia*, and that the inquisitor had been found guilty; the Master had passed the death sentence. It was all madness, needless to say, but what could I do? Andrea de' Collini was beyond my reach, at least for the present. A tenuous, fragile flame of hope *did* flicker somewhere deep down in the darkness – a hope that at some time, for a space howsoever brief, the light of unoccluded reason would return to him and that he would once again be receptive to the love I continued to bear him – and I protected and nourished it as best I could. It was this love I cared about; the ultimate fate of Tomaso della Croce did not preoccupy my speculations, but that Andrea de' Collini should not make the final descent into insanity was a prayer ceaselessly resonating in my heart.

– 1518 onwards –

Ut Ecclesiam tuam sanctam regere et conservare digneris, te rogamus

It was the indulgences which started it all. According to custom, Leo revoked all indulgences granted by his predecessor, as soon as he had ascended the throne of Peter – with the exception of those granted by Julius II for the furtherance of the erection of the new St Peter's basilica. Oh, what a costly mistake *that* proved to be! The Germans had always been particularly grouchy about the ceaseless flow of cash to Rome, but when on December 22nd 1514 Leo extended the St Peter's Indulgence to the ecclesiastical provinces of Cologne, Treves, Salzburg, Bremen, Besançon and Upsaala – *and* the possessions of Albert, Archbishop of Mayence and Magdeburg (who actually wanted to be Archbishop of Everywhere, if the truth be known), he was really asking for *trouble*. As I told you in the first chapter of these memoirs, the said Albert, having been elected as Archbishop of Mayence, wanted to stay Archbishop of Magdeburg and Halberstadt, which he already was; in the normal way of things, he should have relinquished these two bishoprics upon his elevation to Mayence – this shows you what a greedy old bastard he was. He did in fact achieve this ambition, but at a very high price: for his confirmation in all three sees, he had to pay the staggering sum of fourteen thousand ducats, plus an extraordinary tax of ten thousand, the combined total being advanced by the banking house of Fugger, presided over by the shrewd and clever Jacob Fugger. In order to pay his debt, Albert of Everywhere was entrusted with the proclamation of the St Peter's Indulgence in the ecclesiastical provinces of Mayence and Magdeburg, including the diocese of Halberstadt, and throughout the territory of the house of Brandenburg.

Half the proceeds went to the pope (ostensibly for funding the building of the new basilica), and he kept half for himself, out of which he made his repayments to Fugger; by this rather neat arrangement, it was intended that all parties should be kept equally contented.

However, a great number of people were deeply discontented, and had always been uneasy about the sale of indulgences – and this is what it was, *a sale,* despite the theological niceties which surrounded the exchange of money. The idea was quite simple: the sinner paid his cash, acquired his indulgence, and his sins were remitted – or more precisely, the punishment due on his sins was remitted. Various sins, earning various punishments, commanded various prices, naturally; if, for example, you had murdered your mother in a fit of pique because the soup was cold or too salty, you were due for a pretty severe punishment – if not meted out now, in this life, then in the next; remission of this punishment required a hefty payment. On the other hand, if you'd merely been having it off with the baker's wife while your own spouse was out sweating in the fields, relieving yourself of this spiritual burden wouldn't cost quite so much. More than this: if your charming old uncle Heinrich had indulged his appetite for fair-skinned girls right up to the day he died, you could be sure he was languishing in purgatory's fire, the wizened old cock that had been his undoing now licked not by girls' tongues but by cruel flames; now, if out of love for the shameless renegade you wanted to release him from his suffering in the next world, you simply paid your money, applied the indulgence to him, and *pronto!* (as we Italians say) – Uncle Heinrich's soul, miraculously shimmering white and stain-free, winged its way upwards to the realm of the blessed. Some cunningly far-sighted individuals even purchased indulgences for sins which they had not actually committed, but which they certainly intended to; it was an easy enough thing to pop a coin in the collector's box before going off to spend the night at the local whore-house (not that many would have considered *that* particularly sinful – the local clergy were at it all the time, after all).

It was this grotesquely blasphemous set-up that Martin Luther had intended to criticise when he nailed his ninety-five theses to the door of the castle church of Wittenberg, and *not* the Dominican Tetzel, who preached the St Peter's Indulgence most powerfully and persuasively; against Tetzel, I do not think Luther had any personal grievance. In any case, although Tetzel was without a doubt an eloquent preacher, his powers were overestimated by friend and enemy alike; furthermore, I am inclined to believe that the charges of gross immorality levelled against him by supporters of Luther (they say he had buggered over a thousand adolescent boys) had no foundation whatsoever. It was not Tetzel who was the villain of the piece – as I have said, it was the system. Mind you, it *was* Tetzel who, declaring that indulgences could be applied to the dead, came up with the now infamous verse:

> *"As soon as money in the coffer rings,*
> *the soul from purgatory's fire springs."*

In fact, after Luther had begun his series of attacks, Tetzel mustered enough fire and brimstone to reply, then retired to the Dominican convent at Leipzig at the end of 1518, since the preaching of indulgences became virtually impossible, so hostile was the reception it received.

At the beginning of the year, Archbishop Albert of Everywhere sent Leo a letter informing him of the extent of the 'new doctrines' which Luther was apparently preaching; on February 3rd, Leo commanded Gabriele della Volta, the Vicar-General of the Augustinians, to remonstrate with the troublesome friar, either by letter or through an envoy. Luther stoutly resisted all efforts to bring him to heel, however. I have already recorded in the earlier part of these memoirs exactly how furious this resistance made Leo. The ever-watchful Dominicans, faithful brethren of Tetzel, had in fact drawn the attention of the Curia to the danger of what was going on, but nobody had taken much notice of them; still, I strongly suspect that one of the reasons why Andrea de' Collini remained unmolested was that the Inquisition was too interested in the events taking place in Germany to spare any time for him. The acrid odour of fire and burning flesh was in Dominican nostrils, and when they get a whiff of that, they are considerably worse than mad dogs who scent blood.

At the beginning of July 1518, Luther was summoned to Rome to give an account of his 'heretical' doctrines and of his obvious contempt for the pope and the papal court; Luther replied with a broadside attacking his opponents as Italians and Thomists – the former designation caused more fury than the latter of course, since both were used in a derogatory sense. He acknowledged the supremacy and infallibility of the canonical books of scripture alone, and maintained that both councils and popes are subject to error. Curiously enough however, he also said that the Roman Church has always held the true faith, and that it is necessary for all Christians to be in unity with Rome.

"If that is meant to be a plea for mercy," Leo remarked, "I spit on it."

"Why waste spit?" Serapica said. "Piss on it, my dear."

"Why waste piss?" I said. "Shit on it."

Luther also wrote to Maximillian, advising him that he should have a care for the honour of his University of Wittenberg, but Maximillian was not inclined to be drawn into the affair. Leo sent off a letter to Frederick, the Elector of Saxony, demanding that he assist in having Luther handed over to Cardinal Cajetan (another Dominican), who had been appointed Legate to the Diet of Augsburg, but Frederick refused to comply, expressing the desire that Luther's case be heard in Germany. As a matter of fact, Frederick was not entirely convinced that Luther's doctrines were heretical, and wished to investigate for himself. As a compromise, he suggested that Luther and Cajetan should meet at Augsburg, which they did.

Cardinal Cajetan's career stood as a testimony to the truth that it is not only money which can ensure a rapid advance – a golden tongue helps too, and this is what

Cajetan most certainly possessed; he had once engaged in friendly debate with Pico della Mirandola, and had defeated the so-called 'philosopher' Pomponazzi, who denied the immortality of the soul. Cajetan (in Latin, his name means 'the man from Gaeta') was a thoroughgoing Thomist however, and shared the views of Aquinas on papal supremacy; he more than once remarked that if there was a bad pope in office, everyone must simply grin and bear it, since the authority of the pope, be he good or bad, is absolute. I think it is fair to say that Cajetan also laboured under a misapprehension regarding the true *zeitgeist* of the German people, whom he regarded as aggrieved, but essentially pious and loyal to Rome.

Cajetan made his appearance in lavish style, entering Augsburg on a white palfrey caparisoned in purple; he requested that the rooms set aside for his use be lined with purple satin, and that a curtain of purple silk be used to screen off his dining table from curious and vulgar eyes. The vile Ulrich von Hutten apparently made much of this, putting it about that Cajetan complained that German meat was tough, German wine sour, and German bread coarse; none of this helped poor Cajetan's cause at all. It was quite true that the cardinal did not like Germany – he was a small, scholarly man who longed for the Mediterranean sun, and half froze to death in the less kindly northern climate.

Cajetan and Luther met three times, but nothing really came of it; Cajetan was by all accounts fatherly and kindly, and Luther surprisingly humble. However, although many superficial promises were made on both sides, Luther refused to retract those theses which denied that the merits of Christ and of the saints constituted the 'treasury' of the Church, and also the sentence in his *Resolutions* which claimed that the beneficial effect of the sacraments depended upon the faith of the recipient. It was, I suppose, a case of nothing ventured, nothing gained, but in the event, nothing was gained. Luther sensed the futility of the meetings, and fled back to Wittenberg. Frederick,

Elector of Saxony, refused Cajetan's request that Luther be ejected from his territory and forcibly sent to Rome.

Cajetan some time later came back to Rome to report to Leo in person, and attended a private dinner at which Serapica and I were present.

"He's a peasant of course," Cajetan remarked, chewing on a tough morsel of veal for a few moments, then finally removing it from his mouth with his fingers.

"That isn't news," Serapica said. "My dear, we *all* know he's a peasant."

"With a peasant's cunning," the cardinal went on. "Never forget that. He knows *exactly* what he's doing, believe me. When I first saw him, I was surprised, I admit – I had expected someone more bombastic, more self-confident; in fact, he's rather a shy man. He moves very heavily, slowly, as if weighing up every physical motion, calculating exactly how to place one foot in front of the other when he walks. I honestly don't think he's terribly bright. He was dressed quite simply, in black, he wore wooden clogs, and there were holes in the heels of his stockings. And do you know what? He *reeked* of stale urine. A big, bluff, slow peasant's son, stinking of piss."

"Your Eminence," I said, "tell me one thing: is he honest?"

Cajetan reflected for some moments. Then he said:

"Unfortunately yes. Completely and totally honest – about his convictions, anyway. Oh, he's capable of duplicity, as we all are, but he is disastrously sincere in what he believes. He isn't aiming to become pope himself, if that's what you mean. He has no ulterior motives. He thinks what he preaches is gospel truth. The trouble is, professor or no professor, he isn't a scholar, and not being a scholar is a hindrance when it comes to perceiving truth. This is precisely why the masses need to be *told* what the truth is. Luther can't see that of course, or doesn't want to. He's also got quite a problem with his father."

"Oh?"

"At least, I think he has. At one point during our second

meeting he kept repeating: 'You can't please God by what you do. Nothing you are capable of by yourself can please him. You can't earn God's love, it's a gratuity.' Then, suddenly, he made a slip, and said: 'You can't please *father*.' He immediately tried to cover it up by continuing: 'The Father's love and mercy is freely bestowed on whom he pleases', but I wasn't fooled. He was referring to his own father."

"My dear," Serapica murmured, "do you really mean to tell me that this whole scandalous affair is the result of Luther's inability to please his father?"

Cajetan shrugged.

"I don't know about that," he replied, "but I certainly think that it lies behind his condemnation of good works. After all, it isn't too unreasonable to assume that if Luther can't please his own father by doing good, he must feel that he can't please God by doing good either. I did try to get him to open up a little on the subject of the old man, but every time we started to discuss him, Luther had to dash off to the privy. 'I think my bowels are going to open', he would say. Disgusting. Apparently he has trouble with constipation."

"Figs," Serapica said. "They always do the trick – so I'm told."

"Figs don't grow in Germany," Leo put in. "At least, not properly – *so* I'm told."

"Isn't it amazing?" I said. "His Holiness *does* have something in common with the mad monk after all."

"Oh?" Leo muttered threateningly. "And what might that be, pray?"

"Arse trouble."

Cardinal Cajetan coughed discreetly into the palm of his hand, and Leo refused to speak to me throughout the rest of the meal.

"I tried to be reasonable," His Eminence went on, "but like all fanatics, Luther is incapable of listening to reason; and he *is* a fanatic, there can be no doubt of that. Why, you only have to look at his gaunt head, the deep-set eyes,

240

the haunted expression! He cared absolutely nothing for my learning, nor the logic of my arguments; to tell the truth, I felt rather humiliated at having to dispute with such a blockhead. 'Recant!' I demanded, 'Recant! Do not let me see you again unless it is to recant!' Yet all he could do was stand there reeking of stale urine, with holes in his stockings, and tell me – *me!* – that whatever couldn't be found in scripture couldn't be believed. 'Are mushrooms to be found in scripture?' I cried, stunned by the absurdity of his thinking, 'or honey-basted almonds? And if not, must we then disbelieve in mushrooms and almonds?'

"I urged Staupitz to press recantation upon Luther, since it seemed to me that Staupitz was a man of some sense at least, but he evaded the issue, neither replying that he would, nor that he wouldn't; he even claimed that Luther's intellect was superior to his own (which was clearly nonsense), but that he himself submitted humbly in all matters to the judgement of the Church. Rather incongruously in view of his avowal of submission, he actually had the gall to suggest that I was 'out for Luther's innocent blood.' I tell you, this monk has some hold over them all! Some strange, magical influence; they worship the ground he walks on. I have no doubt that there is witchcraft involved, as well as heresy."

"The sooner we burn him, the better," Serapica said.

"Ah! But the wretch is so *elusive!* One never knows where he is from one moment to the next."

Luther had the gall to send a letter to the pope, which was manifestly insincere; at one point, he claimed that although he had called Leo the Antichrist, he couldn't quite make up his mind whether he was the Antichrist or merely his emissary.

"A scrivener's fart!" Leo fumed.

"A paronomasia!" I cried.

"A *what?*" said Serapica.

Leo mimed the action of wiping his arse with the fractious missive.

And so, tediously and with much vituperation on both

sides, the affair dragged on. Luther had his famous disputa-
tion with Johannes Eck at Leipzig in June and July 1519,
and Eck some time afterwards came to Rome, where he
assised in the drafting of the papal bull, *Exsurge Domine*.
Luther, meanwhile, apparently accepting that his complete
secession from the Church of Rome was now inevitable,
allied himself with the revolutionary-minded humanist element in Germany, most notably with Ulrich von Hutten,
who was an evil, bloodthirsty guttersnipe. A debate which,
however acrimonious, had hitherto been purely theological,
now assumed explicit and sinister political characteristics.
Under Hutten's influence, Luther took up nationalistic and
revolutionary ideas, issuing pamphlets and preaching revolu-
tion to the people, not only in theological but also political
matters. The common herd screeched its approval: *Father-
land! Liberty! Gospel!* was the incongruous mixture of sentiments heard across the land. It was this new and highly
inflammatory material which led directly to the writing
and publication of Luther's *An den Christlichen Adel Deutscher Nation von des Christlichen Standes Besserung;* Leo pissed
on that, with great fury and immense relish.

On June 1st 1520, *Exsurge Domine* was read out in the
consistory, and approximately two weeks later, was published; in August, Eck arrived in Germany with the bull to
find that through the treachery of a Roman official, its
contents were already known. At Leipzig poor Eck was
threatened and manhandled by the students from Wittenberg, and the copy of the bull he had posted up was
smeared with ordure and torn down; the same thing
happened at Torgau and Döbeln. The Rector of the University of Wittenberg, Peter Burkhard, refused to accept the
bull, as did the University of Erfurt; the University of
Vienna accepted it only after the emperor had obliged
them to, and the University of Ingolstadt did so with great
reluctance. Even the bishops hesitated before publishing it
– some through lack of loyalty to Rome, some through
fear.

The supremely haughty Cardinal Mattaeus Lang, Archbishop of Salzburg, had never from the beginning uttered any word against Luther, and now in the publishing of the bull, he displayed an arrogantly supine behaviour; the Duke of Bavaria likewise hesitated, and encouraged the bishops of the Duchy to adopt a similar attitude. It was, I think, symptomatic of the general lack of awareness of the gravity of the situation that staunchly Catholic Bavaria should have behaved in this fashion. Nobody, even at this stage, really thought that the mad monk would actually divide Christendom in half; such a thing was unthinkable, however vexing and troublesome he had become. Rome was getting a sound kick up the arse, that was all, and it had long deserved that. Eventually, the bull of excommunication against Luther, *Decet Romanum Pontificem* was issued on January 3rd 1521, definitely excluding Luther and his followers from the communion of the Church, and that was that: the disease had at last been fully diagnosed, and there was no remedy. It was a sickness unto death. I give thanks to the true God, the Father in heaven, that Leo did not live to see the gaping wound which cut his Church and the whole of Europe into two gasping, writhing, pain-wracked halves. Shortly after the issuing of the bull of excommunication, the evil Hutten sent a copy of one of his revolutionary pamphlets to Rome, but Leo was too ill to read it. I *did* read it however, and this was what it said:

> *"Den Aberglauben tilgen wir,*
> *Die Wahrheit wiederbringen hier,*
> *Und d'weil das nit mag sein in gut,*
> *So mutz es kosten aber Blut."*

Isn't German an ugly language? I've always thought so.

Meanwhile, in the midst of the beginning of the end of Christianity as it had been known for nearly two thousand years, I was preoccupying myself more and more with the intentions of Andrea de' Collini and the whereabouts of the Dominican Tomaso della Croce. That was another sickness unto death, and I was determined that the death should not be that of Andrea de' Collini. Every time I saw the Master I found him still poring over manuals of magic and numerology, still obsessed with the numbers 7, 2, 5, and above all the sinister 8; he made endless, incomprehensible calculations, murmuring and muttering in either delight or despair, according to the mood of the moment. There were occasions when he seemed to have entirely forgotten that the farce of della Croce's trial had ever taken place, and at other times he could prattle of nothing else; at one moment he would look at me with something approaching love in his eyes, and at the next he would round on me, spitting and cursing. For myself however, I did not doubt for one moment Nino's conviction that the Master was 'out for the kill.' It was merely a matter of how and when; *that* was what troubled me so. It had become sadly obvious that his leadership and care of the Brotherhood had now taken second place to his mania for revenge – indeed, that the tending of the fragile flame of Gnostic truth carried little or no importance for him beside the primary task he had set himself, that of forcing a confrontation with Tomaso della Croce. What was left to me was to hope and pray that *something* could be done about the Dominican before such a confrontation came to pass, to free the Master of the dark daemon which had infected his soul, and give him the opportunity to return to his former senses; in fact, as you already know, I made up my mind that I would have to get to the inquisitor before the Master did. With Tomaso della Croce gone, I reasoned, the Master would have no further need for numbers or murderous plots. *It was up to me to do something.*

I thought about things long and hard; I brooded late into the night, collating all the facts, gathering every scrap of knowledge I possessed about the mind of Andrea de' Collini and the character of Tomaso della Croce, shaping them into a clear, compact and intelligible picture. Upon this picture I meditated, sifting alternatives and possibilities, probing opportunities, weighing up one option against another and gauging them against the probabilities of success or failure. In the end, I finally came up with a plan which I thought – *desperately hoped!* – had a reasonable chance of working. I knew that time was not on my side however, and having once decided on my plan of action, I lost not a moment in implementing the first step. Accordingly, I arranged an audience for myself with Cardinal Cajetan, who was still in Rome – pondering, no doubt, on the fruitlessness of his meetings with Martin Luther.

"Tomaso della Croce is a highly gifted priest and a skilled inquisitor," the cardinal said, offering me a goblet of his best Sicilian wine. "Try one of these sweetmeats – they're called 'Nipples of Adonis'. They're very good."

"Thank you, Eminence," I said, biting into the creamy, sickly-sweet confection.

"You have some cause to be angry with this man?"

"I simply wish to know where he is," I said.

"On a private mission; it is purely Inquisition business. Besides, you have the pope's ear; why not ask *him?*"

"His Holiness prefers not to discuss the subject," I answered cautiously. "Besides, as he explained to me, he can't be expected to know everything that goes on in his own Church."

Cajetan sucked noisily on his sweetmeat.

"Well," he said slowly and thoughtfully, "it might help if I knew why you need this information."

"I don't *need* it, Eminence; but I do *want* it. Besides, I can always wait until Tomaso della Croce is back in Rome."

"That may not be for some time."

I shrugged.

"I'm not an impatient person," I said.

"Have some more wine; I hope you find it good."

"Very good, Eminence."

"Listen, little fellow, I have a proposition."

"Oh?"

"Yes. You will come back to me in three days' time, after I have consulted with – with certain people – concerning the nature of your request. If, when we next meet, you are willing to provide me with a particular service – do not ask me at this moment what that service is! – I will be happy to give you the information you desire. How does that sound?"

"Enigmatic," I said. "Rather mysterious."

Cajetan laughed gently.

"Perhaps I am a mysterious person," he murmured.

And that was the conclusion of the audience.

"Peppe," Leo said, "Do you think I ended the Lateran Council too soon?"

The Lateran Council of course, had been convened by Julius, partly to counter the schismatic Council of Pisa, and partly because he genuinely recognized the need for reform. Leo had concluded the final session of the Lateran, with great pomp, on March 16th 1517. Most of the reforms it had published were already a dead letter.

"Why ask me, Holiness?" I said. "I'm not a theologian. Why, I'm not even a priest."

"Your life here with me is as privileged as any cardinal's, and well you know it!" Leo snapped. "Answer my question: did I bring the Council to a premature end?"

"The Council was Julius's idea, Holiness."

"Yes, and Julius died, and I was left to finish the work he had started. By Christ, it was like being asked to complete one of Michelangiolo's statues – impossible!"

"Well," I began cautiously, "bearing in mind this Luther business –"

"Must we drag *him* into every discussion?"

"I was about to say, Holiness, that if the reforms promulgated by the Council had in any way been a genuine effort to meet the obvious *need* for substantial reform in the Church, Luther might not be kicking up the stink he is now."

"You're right, Peppe," Leo said sulkily. "You're not a theologian."

To be fair, I think the Lateran Council had done what it actually could in the way of practical reform, even though this amounted to little; its task, to begin with, was Herculean. After all, how effectively can you preach chastity to a woman who has been a professional whore all her life? Most of the enactments of the Council were, in any case, merely old regulations more stringently formulated. These formulations were dispatched far and wide, but apart from Italy, they were only really put into effect in Spain and Portugal; most of them were totally ignored. For example, in spite of the conciliar decrees, the grotesque practice of bestowing ecclesiastical benefices and dignities upon children continued unabated; this was too lucrative a source of income for the Curia for it to be abandoned. Why, only three years ago, little Alfonso, the Infant of Portugal, was declared capable of holding a bishopric or an archbishopric at the age of fifteen! And this was in express contravention of the Council's enactments. Can you imagine it? Some little brat of a boy, waddling around the palaces of Portugal with a jewelled mitre perched precariously on his tiny head? As a matter of fact, Leo himself repeatedly disregarded the enactments of the Council; most of the bishops, many of whom had not even attended the Council sessions, simply carried on in the same old way. Much as I hate to say it, Cardinal Giulio de' Medici was one of the rare exceptions; he did actually go to the trouble of convening a provincial Council in Florence in order to give practical effect to the decrees of the Lateran, but that didn't amount to very much. When you come to think about it, it may have been that Martin Luther *did* have a valid point or two after all – but I dared not say that to Leo.

"Well?" Leo said. "Did I, or didn't I?"

"Did you or didn't you what?"

"Close the Council too soon."

I sighed.

"No," I said in the sincerest tone of voice I could muster, "of course you didn't."

Leo beamed happily, as under my breath I whispered:

"The real problem is that it was opened too late."

★

I returned to Cardinal Cajetan three days later, as he requested me to. This time, I found him in an expansive, warm mood; he spoke to me almost as an equal, and not as he had done the first time we met, like a household pet.

"You will be happy to know that I am now in a position to provide you with the information you require," he said, smiling.

"Where is he? Where is Tomaso della Croce?"

"He is here, in Rome."

So much for all the Master's mumbo-jumbo computations with the number 5!

"What? In Rome?" I said, dumbfounded.

"Yes."

"But surely – I mean, then why –"

"Fra Tomaso is not presently at liberty."

"At liberty to what?"

"You misunderstand me, Peppe. He's not actually at liberty to do anything; what I meant was that he is not a *free* man."

"He's a prisoner?"

The Cardinal sighed indulgently.

"Do you see any alternative to freedom other than imprisonment?" he said gently.

"But I don't understand!"

"Why should you? Tomaso della Croce has been held in custody for these past three weeks."

I could scarcely believe what I was hearing.

"Why is he in prison?" I asked, my eyes wide with astonishment. I could hardly even blink.

"There have been certain – well, to be frank with you Peppe – certain *accusations* made against him."

"By whom?"

"No-one of significance."

"What are these accusations, exactly?"

"Abuse of inquisitorial powers. It has been said that he – *disposed* - of certain individuals not actually pronounced guilty by the tribunal, in an unorthodox manner."

Master Antonio!

I tried to control the emotion in my voice as I asked Cajetan:

"Would the name of his accuser by any chance be Antonio Donato?"

Now it was Cajetan's turn to be surprised.

"How do you know that?" he asked sharply.

"Would it shock you to learn that *I* was one of those whom Tomaso della Croce disposed of in this 'unorthodox' fashion?"

"It would, very much."

"It's true – oh, don't ask me to tell you about it, because it would make too long a story! But it *is* true."

Cardinal Cajetan leaned back in his chair and placed his fingertips to his eyelids, as though suddenly overcome by a great weariness.

"We cannot afford a scandal," he said. "Not at this time. Not in *my* Order! This is precisely why we have had to hold Tomaso della Croce in custody, until the accusations are proved to be false. We cannot permit the least sign of laxity, not with the way things are in Germany at the moment. It would only serve to provide more fuel for that raving peasant's fire. Already the fire is rapidly becoming a conflagration."

"And what do you think *I* could possibly do about it?" I said.

"I want you to see this man Antonio, and persuade him to drop the charges. This was what I was going to ask you to do in any case; now that I know you are acquainted with him, the task would appear to be so much easier."

"Antonio Donato *bought* me from Tomaso della Croce." I said.

"You are still bitter about this?"

"No, no, not any more."

"Then you will do as I ask?"

I was silent for a few moments, then I said:

"Yes. It will suit my own purposes."

"And what purposes are they, Peppe?"

"To save the soul and the sanity of a man I love.'

249

"Then I entrust you with this mission – I willingly do so."

"Where is Tomaso della Croce being held?"

"In the church of the Minerva. But first you must speak to the man who calls himself 'Master Antonio'."

"And where will I find him?"

"In a cheap lodging house. I will write down the address for you."

"You will," I said, "also issue me with your personal, written permission to visit and speak to Tomaso della Croce."

Cardinal Cajetan held out his right hand, the fingers spread, in front of his face and looked at it silently for some while. Then he drew off his ring – a large amethyst surrounded by tiny pearls. He gave it to me.

"Here," he said in a soft voice, "this will help. They will recognize it. I shall also give you the written warrant."

"Thank you, Eminence."

Cajetan regarded me for a moment or two with glittering, pensive eyes. Then he said:

"I hope that your purpose and mine are directed towards a mutually sympathetic end."

And I took my leave.

Master Antonio was staying with a fat, malodorous widow in her cheap two-roomed apartment on the edge of the Jewish quarter; I suspect that he did not only pay her in cold cash for this luxury, for as she served us warm, sourish white wine, she cast him unsubtle glances of nauseating affection, and her great bosom heaved yearningly when she leaned over his shoulder to put the wine on the table.

"Alright, you can get out," he said to her irritably.

She looked at him as a faithful dog might look at the master who beats it continually, but whom it continues to adore.

Jerking his head in the direction of the door through which she had disappeared, Antonio remarked to me:

"The silly cow can't do enough for me. A man doesn't want to be smothered, does he?"

"No, I suppose not."

His eyes became dreamy.

"Mind you," he said, "she's got a ripe pair of thighs. All meat. It beats half a ducat a week in rent."

He poured himself some wine, slurped at it thirstily, and looked me up and down.

"Well, my stunted little friend, you seem to have done well for yourself, don't you?"

"Meaning?"

"Meaning I never saw you dressed up like a bishop's bumboy when you worked for me, eh?"

"My lifestyle has changed somewhat, I agree."

"Hobnobbing with the high and mighty now, I hear tell."

"Is that so?" I said.

"Yes, it *is* so."

"Who says?"

"Nobody says, Peppe, but everybody knows. You've become quite the little princeling, running in and out of His Holiness's skirts, with rings on your fingers and bells on your toes –"

"So he may have music, wherever he goes."

"Well, it's true, isn't it?"

"Yes, it's true."

"So what are you doing talking to the likes of me? If you've come here to tell me you're going to have the Swiss Guard tear my balls off with their bare teeth – if you've come here to gloat –"

"No, it isn't that, much pleasure though it would give me to do so."

"What, then?"

I drew in my breath deeply.

"I have come to ask you to drop your charges against Tomaso della Croce."

Antonio whistled through his carious teeth.

"Well now," he said, leaning back in his chair, "there's a

turn up for the book! Fancy you wanting to see that bastard go free! I wouldn't have thought you have much cause to love *him*."

"I don't love him," I answered. "But I do want the charges dropped."

"You, or somebody else? Somebody higher up the ladder of power?"

"Perhaps."

He guffawed.

"For all your fancified ways, you're just a fucking messenger boy!"

"Not in the least. It is true that the request I put to you comes from another, but I have my own reasons for advancing it, or I should never have agreed to undertake this mission."

He looked slyly at my right hand.

"Where did you get that ring?" he asked in a low voice. "It must be worth a small fortune."

"It belongs to Cardinal Cajetan."

Antonio raised his eyebrows in surprise.

"*That* high up, eh?"

"Do you like the ring?" I asked.

"Course I like it! Who wouldn't?"

"You can have it, if you drop the charges."

"How much, exactly, are you authorized to offer me?"

"I'm not authorized to offer you anything," I replied. "But I have powers of discretion, which I may use freely. Well?"

"I could never sell a ring like that, could I? They'd want to know how I came by it. What's that sign engraved on it?"

"It is His Eminence's coat-of-arms."

"That settles it then. I won't take the ring."

We both helped ourselves to more wine – how much it reminded me of the gut-rot my mother used to sell! A thousand and one bitter memories came beating at the doors of my mind with every sip of that even more bitter brew, but I kept them locked out.

"Why did you bring the charges in the first place?" I asked.

"He cheated me, the money-grabbing bastard!"

"How did he cheat you?"

"He sold me some snotty-nosed kid for five ducats, just the sort to draw sympathy from the punters, he said, just what I needed to pull the crowds. What he didn't tell me was they'd beaten the poor bastard up so badly, he couldn't survive long. He died after three days. Five ducats for three lousy days! No-one cheats Master Antonio, I can tell you. Besides, he's had it coming for a long time; I swore I'd get even with him, and now I have."

Some intuition deep at the back of my mind – which, frustratingly, would not come to the fore – told me that Master Antonio was lying; or at least, that he was not telling me the whole truth. But what *was* the whole truth?

"There has been no process against him as yet," I said.

"I'm a patient man. The process will come – it's got to. Charges just don't go away, do they? I'm doing a nice bit of business just outside the city right now –"

"The show is back in Rome?"

"That's right. Want to come and see it? I'll let you in free, gratis and for nothing, seeing as how you're an old friend."

He cackled uproariously, wine dribbling out of the corner of his mouth, sweat beading his florid features. I despised him.

"It is an invitation I must regretfully decline," I said.

"Oh, my! It's an invitation he must *regretfully* decline!" he echoed in a high-pitched, epicene voice.

"Why did you allow Andrea de' Collini to purchase the services of Nino, Beppo and the Skull?" I asked. My voice was calm, but inwardly I trembled.

"He *part*-purchased them, Shorty. And it's none of your business."

"I have made it my business."

"So much the worse for you. It's a private arrangement, see? Who am I to turn down five hundred ducats? It was a

253

bargain; I get to keep them, he uses them when he needs them."

"What need of such creatures would he have?"

"Why not ask the venerable gentleman yourself, Shorty?"

I did not reply.

"Well," he said, "is this the end of our delightful little *tête-à-tête?* If so, I've got to get back to the caravan. There's a show to put on tonight."

"There's something you aren't telling me, isn't there?"

He leaned back in his chair, smirking.

"Oh?" he said slowly, luxuriating in the knowledge that he presently had the upper hand. "And what might that be?"

"I don't know – there's something, but I can't quite grasp it –"

"Something, Shorty?"

"Yes. There's more to this than just being cheated by Tomaso della Croce, isn't there? If he cheated you at all, that is, which I am inclined to doubt. There *has* to be! He's been useful to you in the past ... you wouldn't suddenly turn on him like this. You know what power he wields."

I struggled, trying to clear my mind, to think straight, to grasp the oh-so-obvious but oh-so-elusive *fact* that must surely be staring me in the face -

"I'm not afraid of that pious bastard," Master Antonio said.

"You know he can send you to the stake."

"On what charge? You forget, *I'm* the one bringing the charges around here –"

Of course! Charge – trial – verdict and sentence – oh, of course! The rusty clockwork of my brain was suddenly flooded with the oil of comprehension.

"Andrea de' Collini paid you to bring this accusation against Tomaso della Croce, didn't he?"

Master Antonio's face told me at once that I had struck home.

"Is that what you think?" he said, guarded now and on the defensive.

"It's what I *know!* I was a fool not to see it before! Listen to me, Antonio Donato – you will withdraw the charge, and you will withdraw it *immediately* – "

"And if I refuse?"

"I will have your 'show' closed for good."

"No you won't – you haven't got the authority. If the show was going to be closed down, someone higher up than you would have done it long before now. They daren't. They know what a stink I'd kick up, then their precious inquisitor's name would never be cleared."

"If you keep them waiting too long, you'll end up in an alley somewhere with a knife in your guts."

"I can look after myself, Shorty."

"Drop the charge," I said.

"Why should I?"

"For money."

He hesitated before asking:

"How much?"

"For more than Andrea de' Collini paid you to bring it. How about five hundred ducats? That's a great deal of money, for you."

"But not for you, eh, Shorty?"

He poured more wine into his glass and sipped at it; he was slightly drunk by now.

"Tell me something before I give you my answer," he said.

"What is it you want to know?"

"Did *you* kill 'Satan's Daughter'?"

"Yes."

I was not prepared for what he did next. He stood up unsteadily, threw his wine full into my face, and screamed furiously:

"You murdering bastard! Woman-killer! You thieving assassin!"

I gasped for breath, the wine running down my face and soaking my otter's fur collar, but I remained seated and tried to give the impression of exercising an iron self-control.

"Why? Why, in Christ's name, why?" he wailed, slumping down again in his chair.

"I had my own private reasons."

"Private reasons, for the love of God? *Private reasons?* What harm had she ever done you?"

"None at all."

"Then why did you kill her?"

"Is there any chance of your understanding what I mean, if I tell you that it was an act of compassion?"

"No, there isn't. No, no, no, no! You're a murdering bastard."

"Will you take the five hundred ducats and drop the charge?"

"Tell me why you killed her."

"Look," I said, "is it going to make any difference?"

"It might. Tell me how you killed her, Shorty. I want to know."

I allowed my thoughts to wander back to that night; I remembered that the fires were still burning and I could smell the roasted meat that had served as a communal supper. There was laughter somewhere at the back of the supply wagons – no doubt one of the *goyim* was taking his pleasure with a whore from the city. No-one saw me, and I saw no-one.

"It was the night I left the caravan," I said. "Someone had come to take me away, but I made them wait while I went in search of her. I found her in the wagon, but she wasn't asleep. There was a stink of urine and sweat. I could hear her breathing.

"'Don't be frightened,' I whispered. 'You needn't be frightened any more.'

"She rolled over onto her back, and lifting her head slightly, looked at me with those sad, dark eyes.

"'Do you know who I am?' I asked her. 'I'm the dwarf. I've watched you, watched you for so long. I've come to keep a promise that I made years ago, when I first saw

256

what they make you do. Do you understand what I'm saying?'

"My heart began to race as I saw the slightest, tiniest of nods – barely a movement at all, gone in the blink of an eye! – and I knew she *did* understand. Carefully, I put my hands around her grubby neck and I began to squeeze. I squeezed as hard as I could, but even though she didn't make the slightest attempt to resist, it was a terrible strain for me. Her eyes bulged; she shut them tight, then opened them again. Her lips parted and bubbles of saliva appeared. Deep, deep in her throat she groaned. She turned her head to the left.

"'Keep still!' I cried, 'keep still or it will never be over with!'

"I felt my fingers sink into her flesh; it was like kneading dough. My knees were pressed into the side of her stomach, and I heard a rumbling, broken fart. I inhaled deeply and exerted more pressure. A little blood oozed out of the corner of her mouth, and her face began to change colour. Oh, there was a pounding, pumping noise in my ears, as if the sea itself was inside my head, the furious swells rising and crashing against the breakers of my skull!

"Then she turned her bulging eyes towards me and the eyelids flickered. After this she became motionless, the tip of her tongue showing between the foam of spittle and blood on her lips. They were bluish. I wasn't trying to hurt her, I didn't want her to suffer – I just wanted her dead, so she would never have to suffer again. The veins in her neck were as thick as ropes, I swear it. Suffused with blood. I kept squeezing and squeezing, panting with the effort. A long, rasping breath came out of her, like the sound of water hissing into steam on hot bricks. Then, at last, silence. She was dead."

Antonio Donato was utterly still. He seemed transfixed.

"Well?" I said, my voice trembling a little with the emotion aroused by the memory of that night. "Have you nothing to say to me?"

Finally, in a sneering voice, he murmured:

"You're no better than the rest of us, are you, Shorty? Whatever fancy way you like to dress the story up, you're a cold-blooded killer."

I made no reply.

"Alright, I'll take your shitty blood-money."

"You will be required to sign a witnessed statement. Or make your mark."

He lifted his head and looked at me balefully, his eyes red-rimmed and watery.

"I'm perfectly capable of signing my own fucking name, Shorty."

"Good. The statement will be prepared for you and the money will be paid as soon as it is signed."

"Oh, for Christ's sake clear off and leave me alone, will you?"

As soon as I was out of that sweaty, stinking room, I leaned up against the wall and vomited.

"He has agreed to sign the statement," I told Cardinal Cajetan.

"Excellent! I couldn't be more delighted! It can be publicly issued and Tomaso della Croce released."

"No."

"I beg your pardon?"

"I said, no."

"But I don't understand, Peppe. The whole success of this enterprise –"

"It *has* been successful," I interrupted. "The statement will be issued, Master Antonio will be paid his five hundred ducats, and you will never hear from him again."

"And Tomaso della Croce –"

"He must die."

Cajetan looked at me as though I were completely mad.

"I do not think I heard you correctly," he managed to say.

"Yes, yes you did. Tomaso della Croce must die. You will leave the arrangements to me."

"But this is absurd!"

"Why so? At least he can die an innocent man, although he is far from being that. The whole idea is to clear his name, isn't it? To prevent scandal? This will have been achieved as soon as Antonio has signed the statement and received his money. There is nothing scandalous about a man's death; men die every day."

"I cannot believe you are saying this –"

"But I *am* saying it, Your Eminence."

"And was this – this ghastly idea – was *this* the private purpose you spoke of? To engineer his death?"

"Yes."

Cajetan, in a state of some anxiety, got up from his gilt chair and began pacing to and fro across the room.

"What you ask is too much, Peppe. Tomaso della Croce is a priest – a member of the Dominican Order – he is – you are requesting murder!"

"Yes."

"I cannot countenance it. Never."

"Then Antonio Donato will not sign the statement."

"Antonio Donato be damned to hell! I shall have him –"

"Killed, Eminence? And what difference is there between the murder of a freak-show owner and that of a Dominican priest?"

Cajetan came back and sat in his chair again. His face was pale.

"How?" he hissed in a low whisper. "How would this thing be done?"

"I still have your ring. They will admit me into the Minerva."

"*You* will kill him?"

"No, Your Eminence. *You* will."

For a full minute Cardinal Cajetan could not speak; his face was contorted now, the muscles working furiously to fight off some fearful explosion of outrage and horror. Then he said in a trembling voice:

"You dare to suggest it? You dare?"

"To be more precise, a document issued by you will

259

kill him. Or even more precisely still, he will kill himself."

"I – I don't understand –"

"Monster though he is, Tomaso della Croce is fanatically honest according to his own principles; he would move heaven and earth to track down and burn someone he believes to be a recalcitrant heretic, but he would go to precisely the same lengths to protect someone who he thought was not. He is a consistent monster – that is his tragedy. If I could prove to him that he destroyed one who was not a heretic but a faithful child of Holy Mother Church, the horror would be too much for him to endure. He would be impelled to expiate his guilt with his own life."

"And send his immortal soul to hell?" Cajetan whispered.

"I know nothing about that; I know only his mania and his mind."

"How can you be sure he would do it?"

"I have no infallible guarantees, but I *am* sure. I have thought about this for some considerable time, believe me."

"Suicide . . . but it could not be declared such."

"Of course not. You could blame his death on his accuser – an innocent man subjected to false accusations, intolerable anguish of mind, derangement, whatever you like. Bury him with as much honour and ceremony and pomp as you care to. But bury him, then forget him. Forget the whole terrible business."

"And the document?"

"It must state that the lady Laura Francesca Beatrice de' Collini, burned as a heretic, was innocent of all charges brought against her."

"Impossible! If the tribunal pronounced her guilty –"

"You will sign the document personally. No-one else need see it except myself and Tomaso della Croce. Indeed, I myself shall take it to him. Afterwards it can be destroyed."

"It is an audacious plan," Cajetan said, but I could see

that he had already accepted it. Indeed, I knew he would. He had no real choice.

"It will succeed."

"And if Tomaso della Croce does not kill himself?" he asked.

I shrugged.

"I do not envisage that eventuality, Eminence. Make out the document and let me have it. Now. I will do the rest."

Cajetan rose and looked down on me with sad, thoughtful eyes.

"I am more wary of you than ever I was of Martin Luther," he said quietly.

"Give me the document, Eminence."

He went to his writing table.

He looked the same: the burning glances, the haughty mien, the nervous, tensile movements, the cap of close-cropped hair, now greyer than ever I remembered it. His prison 'cell' was in fact a large, well-furnished room; there were books, writing materials, a prie-dieu, a statue of the Virgin, thick rush matting on the stone floor.

"I never thought we would meet again, little man," he said in that icy-cold monotone of his; hearing it, I shuddered.

"I told you once, a long time ago, that we would do so."

"Did you? I can't remember. Why are you here?"

"I have something to deliver to you."

"Oh?"

"From His Eminence Cardinal Cajetan."

Momentarily his eyes widened, and he made a movement in his chair, as if to rise.

"The charges!" he said. "The charges against me have been dropped!"

"As to that, I do not know. I do not believe that they have."

His self-control was masterly.

"Then what?" he asked.

"It is a document. It states that you destroyed an innocent person."

Tomaso della Croce laughed a soft, joyless laugh.

"That can never be," he said. "I bring to justice only the guilty, never the innocent. My whole life has been about precisely that."

"Laura de' Collini was innocent."

"Her?"

"Yes, *her*."

He said in a soft, reflective voice, as if reluctantly musing on some hitherto forgotten and entirely insignificant past:

"I recall the name. A friend of yours, I believe." He sneered unpleasantly as he pronounced the word 'friend', making it sound like a euphemism for something disgusting.

"I loved her," I said. "You destroyed her."

"The burning of heretics is not an act of destruction, little man, but one of healing. It is to remove a cancer afflicting the Body of Christ, the Church. Personal sentiments do not enter into the matter."

"I loved her."

"So you said."

Then he leaned forward across the table, thrusting his face close to mine, and it was suddenly contorted, transfixed by a rictus of malevolence and obsession. I could smell the garlic on his breath.

"Has it ever occurred to you that I have rendered you an inestimable service in ridding the world of that impious slut? Have you for one moment considered how otherwise she would have dragged your soul down to hell with her own? To hell! Where there is a fire that *never* grows cold, where the torment goes on eternally – and such a fire would make the flames of the stake seem like a cool bath by comparison! *There* is where your pretty little heretic now writhes and screams and curses! If I could have saved her from that, I would have done so; if I thought that pain would have brought her to her senses, I would not have hesitated to inflict pain of the most hideous kind upon her for the rest of her natural life. What is bodily pain compared to an eternal agony of the soul?

"Do not imagine that I hated her – I did not; what I hated and despised with all my strength was the filthy error and corruption of faith that had seized her mind and heart. It is the heresy I pursue, never the heretic. If I can save but one single human soul from the awful price of heresy, then I will continue to torture and burn a hundred thousand human bodies, knowing that God himself urges me on.

"Laura de' Collini refused to recant; she persisted in her error and so was subjected to the ultimate penalty. But let me tell you this: if I for one moment thought that it would have brought her back to the truth of Holy Mother Church, I would have willingly stepped into the flames myself. Can *you* say as much, you who claim to love her? Indeed, by loving her, you encouraged her in her error; I, on the other hand, by pursuing her with Christ's law, sought only to save her soul from eternal torment. Now tell me, which of us proves the authentic lover?"

My mind was barely capable of assimilating the horror of his words.

"Laura Francesca Beatrice de' Collini was innocent of heresy," I said.

"That cannot be."

"Why not? Can't you admit that you might have been mistaken?"

"No! It would be the Church who was mistaken in such a case, and this is impossible, since she is guided by the Holy Spirit. To make such an admission would be to introduce chaos into order – then what certainty could we ever have, what guarantee, what safety?"

"Life consists entirely of uncertainties," I said.

"No, my friend, it does not; who could survive if it did? Besides, do you think I failed to make adequate investigations? I *know* that Laura de' Collini was a heretic. I *know* of

263

the meetings she held, the philosophy she taught, the obscene rites that her father conducted. Do you take me for a simpleton?"

"And yet you have not pursued Andrea de' Collini . . ."

Tomaso della Croce lowered his eyes, almost slyly, guarding some deep secret of his own.

"That is my affair. I have not forgotten him, believe me."

"Neither has he forgotten you."

"I do not doubt it, little man."

"And despite the perversity of your logic, I have come, Tomaso della Croce, to introduce chaos into the order which you seem to think must be preserved at such high cost."

He looked up at me guardedly.

"What do you mean?" he asked.

"I have come to rob you of the certainty, the guarantee, the safety you so greatly prize."

"Satan's work!"

"No! Your own work – for *you* are the one who is in error."

"You must be insane," he said.

"That is exactly what I have always thought about you."

"You consider me insane because I ally myself with the cause of truth? Heresy is insidious because it refuses to ally itself with anything but its own inflated, pernicious half-truths, opinions and lies; but truth is objective, it has been revealed by God, it is guarded and taught by Holy Mother Church, and not one iota, not one jot of it may be altered for the sake of personal opinion. What kind of anarchy would reign if each man taught his own interpretation of truth?"

"Perhaps," I said, "what is true for one man may not be so for another."

"That has never been my experience. Neither am I deceived by your heretic's rhetoric. They say that Satan has a golden tongue."

"And they say that Satan infects the ranks of the Church you love —"

"Is this all you have come here for, to attack the Church of Christ?"

"Laura Francesca Beatrice de' Collini was *innocent.*"

"You lie! The witch deserved to burn! Did I not see her own father presiding over that obscene coven he called a liturgy? I should have killed them all. You were one of them, you should know."

"Yes, I was one of them. Yes, I know. But *she* did not. She was entirely unaware of her father's activities."

"Impossible. You met weekly at her house —"

"At her father's house, you mean. We were *his* guests, not hers."

"I — don't believe you — it can't be —"

I threw the document down on the table in front of him.

"Read it for yourself," I said. "It is signed by the cardinal."

He took it in trembling hands and began to read, slowly, forming the words with his thin, bloodless lips, like a woman at prayer. Then it fell, fluttering, from his fingertips.

"You tortured and destroyed an innocent human being," I said softly. "How does it feel to have done that? You extinguished a pure and blameless life. You condemned her to a hideous and fiery death, and she was not guilty of the crime of which she was accused. Because of you, Holy Mother Church has lost one of her children. What is God saying to you now, Tomaso della Croce?"

He made no reply. His eyes, sightless, were staring at the document which lay on the table.

"You will doubtless wish to be left alone to contemplate your guilt," I said.

But he was now deaf as well as blind.

I closed the door quietly behind me.

The following morning I waited in a feverish ague of

apprehension and excitement to hear the news of Fra Tomaso della Croce's death. It did not come. What I heard instead was utterly astonishing: the inquisitor had been snatched away from his place of confinement by an intelligently planned use of bribery, misinformation and force; four men had been involved in the abduction, three of whom were described as 'half men, half beasts'. A young monk who had been given the task of attending to della Croce's needs had been brutally slain.

Andrea de' Collini. The Master. How devilishly patient he had been, brooding over his plan, honing and refining the details, exulting in his own cleverness, thrilled by the dark mantle of secrecy in which he had wrapped his true intentions . . . the madness then, had well and truly risen to the surface; now I plainly saw what had been hatching and festering in his crazed brain, as clearly as I saw my own tardiness.

Once and for all, this *had* to be ended.

Ecce, in culpa natus sum, et in peccato concepit me mater mea

It seemed, at the beginning of 1520, that I was entirely alone in my personal world – a world which combined the unreality of high farce with the very real presence of blood and death. Leo was left to me – but not for long. Serapica had grown strangely old quite suddenly, no longer prancing and mincing hilariously through high affairs of state, but now given to much brooding and introspection. Bibbiena's star had long since waned, and it was Cardinal Giulio de' Medici who currently held sway, conducting himself like a second pope, granting 'audiences' to all and sundry, and amassing a considerable private fortune in the process.

There is also a significant death of which I must speak: that of Master Rafael. His last real creation was the truly inspired depiction of Christ's Transfiguration; this had been commissioned by Cardinal Giulio de' Medici for his cathedral church at Narbonne. I suppose it must be rather difficult to convey the impression of a human body being lifted into the air, without making it appear wraith-like or plain silly; now, I am no artist, nor am I familiar with the various complicated techniques of design and application, but it does seem to me that Master Rafael achieved a veritable triumph. Christ himself radiates an impossible admixture of majesty and humility, activity and passivity, glory and gentleness; it really is quite remarkable, and all the more so because it is totally *credible*. Being a Gnostic, I am also something of a mystic, and I can tell you that this painting of Rafael's is a *work of mysticism*. One does not simply stand before it and look at it – one is invited into the world it portrays, so that observer becomes participant. One is *drawn* in, if you like, for the power of spiritual attraction which it manifests is irresistible. It was also particularly suitable for the times, since it is essentially a magnificent statement of faith in Christ (such as I have, even if the Church would appear not to), and it did much to intensify Christian outrage at the encroachments made by the infidel Turks. As a matter of fact, Pope Callixtus III, after the defeat of the Turks at Belgrade in 1456, had declared that the festival of the Transfiguration should be kept annually on August 6th throughout Christendom, and this event was still fresh in the recollection, if not the memory, of many people. Master Rafael finished only the upper half of the painting (which is in any case its essence and heart), for in the last week of March 1520, he fell ill with one of our perilous but all too prevalent Roman fevers, and this weakened his vital forces terribly – for they were already much depleted by work. He died on Good Friday, April 6th. The unfinished masterpiece was placed at the head of his bier. He was thirty-seven years old.

It behoves me to say at this point, that *I* knew a darker side to Master Rafael – a more shadowy, demonic Rafael than the pallid, fey and beautiful genius that I have described; I caught a glimpse of it thanks to a pretty but rather fat girl who worked as a cook's assistant down in the kitchens of the papal palace. Her name was Filiberta. She had obviously overheard, somehow, a snatch of conversation between Serapica and myself in which we had discussed the attributes of Master Rafael, both physical and spiritual. I do not quite know how this might have come about, but Serapica and I were, in any case, always bumping into each other in corridors and ante-rooms, exchanging titbits of gossip; Serapica was an incorrigible *gobe-mouche*. Leo's unrequited passion for Rafael was frequently a topic of discussion between us – especially on those evenings when he had been invited to dine with us.

The girl called Filiberta sidled up to me one afternoon and whispered:

"His Holiness might pine from afar, but I don't have to."

"What?"

"You heard what I said. Ten ducats says I'll have him tomorrow night. You can watch if you like, just to be sure."

I hesitated for a fraction of a second, then I said:

"How dare you suggest such a thing."

Totally unabashed, she replied:

"Don't go getting on your high horse! I'm only saying that Your Grace might care for a little wager."

"I am *not* 'Your Grace'."

"What are you, then?"

"You might well ask."

"Ten ducats says I'll have that great paintbrush between Rafael's legs inside me by tomorrow night."

"You're disgusting," I said. "Where?"

"Anywhere you like; he's sleeping here this week, isn't he? In his private apartment, then. I'll have him there."

"You wouldn't *dare*," I hissed.

"Ten ducats?"

"You're on. You know I could have you flogged for this, don't you?"

"Yes. But you won't. You're one of us."

"What's that supposed to mean?"

She looked me up and down critically, then she said:

"Not one of *them*."

The following evening, while Master Rafael was in audience with His Holiness, I hid myself in his apartment, behind a small card-table; I waited for almost an hour before I heard them come in.

"I can't imagine what a noble gentleman would want with a poor kitchen-maid like me," I heard Filiberta say with a nauseatingly affected coyness.

"Why did you offer yourself, then?"

There was a cold, relentless hardness and fixity in Master Rafael's voice that I had hitherto never heard.

"Shall I get undressed here?"

"Yes."

"You'll have to promise never to tell! This could cost me my job."

"It could also cost me my health, I don't doubt."

"What? Are you suggesting that I've got something no decent girl should have?"

"Precisely that. Disrobe yourself."

"I love that fancy talk."

"Just get undressed!"

His voice was now not only hard, but urgent, imperious.

They lay together naked on the floor, their limbs entwined, rubescent in the vermeil-gold light of the subsiding fire; his lean, muscular body – the opalescent buttocks, downy with dark hair, slyly and secretly moving – sank into her *embonpoint,* the plump, spread thighs and the pendulous melon-ripe breasts, into a tessellated embrace of inchoative desire.

But passion stirred soon enough! An effluxion of urgent longing, an *émeute* of explicit wanting, lusting. Among all lovers, I had heard that he was *facile princeps*, but it seemed to me as I crouched low behind the little card-table, hidden in the flickering shadows, that it was *she* who led, who inspired with her hortative little groans, she who offered the sexual febrifuge, while he, almost passive, languished in the heats of bodily hunger. They were kissing now, guttling with lips and tongues, licking and sucking noisily. He encircled her nipples – visibly stiff, erect, like twin nut-brown girandoles – with the tips of his fingers, and she moved beneath him, moaning voluptuously.

"My lovely boy . . . oh, my lovely darling!"

He raised himself up on his elbows, and I saw the incredibly long, thick rod of his penis, red and glistening at the tip, quiver against the plump expanse of her belly; she stared down at it with avaricious eyes.

"Oh, look! There it is! My monster, my Goliath, my king of cocks, – oh, oh –"

Passion was reducing her to absurdity; for a brief instant, the question flashed through my mind: *What are you doing here, watching this fat, vulgar cow being humped?* But I dismissed it, since curiosity as to Master Rafael's performance was stronger than my sense of the ridiculous — at that moment, anyway.

She slipped a grubby, dimpled hand down between her legs, running her fingers through her own bush of glaucous hair, panting a little as she did so, turning her rather large head from one side to the other. Then she grasped the rugose pouch of his scrotum and let it rest on the palm of her hand.

"Feel the weight of it," she breathed horsily.

"I do," Rafael said, "every day."

And he sank down onto her — or rather, I should say *into* her, and in two senses: firstly, he was embowered in the generous landscape of her body, a little portion of muscle-and-bone *terra firma* enisled by the ocean of her syllabub-like flesh; and secondly his cock found entrance between the pearly thighs and slipped home, silkily, smoothly, buried up to the root.

"Oh God, oh God!" she moaned, and it was at that moment I noticed there was a small ferruginous wen on her left hip, like the devil's tell-tale insignia. Did she, I mused, cast spells in Satan's name, crooning by candlelight, and suckle a familiar? I thought it perfectly possible. There *had* been rumours down in the kitchens . . .

"Plough my furrow!" she screamed. "Scour my donga! Paint my canvas!"

Then, obviously stuck for any further metaphorical imperatives, she uttered a high-pitched eldritch shriek and headed for the home stretch towards the *ne plus ultra* of passion.

What happened next was spectacular. As you know, my Gnostic proclivities mean that I am no *fidus Achates* of Priapus, but even I was impressed; for after the apotheosis of thrusting and panting had been reached and La Filiberta subsided into a silly fit of satiated crooning, Master Rafael drew himself out of her and off her, and straddled her procumbent body, one foot on either side of her, *and he was still erect*. She opened her eyes and looked up at him incredulously.

271

"Get up," he commanded gruffly.

She did so, her flesh wobbling like a jelly, her thighs glistening with raindrops of inspissated lubricating fluid, steadying herself by placing a fat hand on each hip.

"My lovely boy –" she began, but he pushed her roughly against the wall, squeezing her breasts with his fingers, and entered her again, thrusting frenetically, slipping in and out of her, unsatiated, still tumescent, craving a satisfaction which the contortion of bewilderment on her flabby face suggested she would not be able to meet.

"Oh, oh *Maestro* – "

He had her once more on the floor, then twice standing in the middle of the room, and still he had clearly not achieved a climax. Her exhausted gasps were an objurgation that he totally ignored. He took her for a fifth time, and now a note of panic was beginning to creep into her voice.

"Look here," she squealed, "I don't think –"

"Open your legs, you damned bitch!"

I reminded myself to make a mental obelus against that text of Tacitus which informs us that Messalina, prostitute-wife of the Emperor Claudius Casear, rose up from her nights of whoring unsatisfied; for if Filiberta was a latter-day Messalina, she was certainly no match for this sexual energumen.

"Oh Rafael – oh please –"

But he forced her to the floor and they had intercourse yet again. Now she was utterly passive, absorbing his apparently insatiable lust insouciantly, as a sponge absorbs water, her eyes screwed tightly shut, her sloppy mouth slack, her great legs quivering from time to time – whether with pleasure or pain I could not tell – as he plunged into her repeatedly. He grasped the nipple of her left breast between his teeth and she moaned.

Finally, he reached his climax, fervently and noisily, and – I watched this with great curiosity – as he did so, he raised himself on the palm of one hand, and with the other hand slapped her sharply across the face. Then again, harder this time.

"Oh no, God —" she said.

"Oh yes, yes, yes," he murmured.

A fillip to signal the end of the performance; although I for one would not have been surprised had it been but an *entr' acte*.

Later, Filiberta came to collect her winnings.

"I said I'd have him," she sneered.

"On the contrary," I replied, "he had *you*. Repeatedly."

"I took it though, didn't I?"

"Yes," I said, shoving the money into her hand, "just about."

And this was the sublime genius who painted the *Transfiguration;* was there some essential connection between the two Rafaels? Something I was not quite grasping? What was passing through his mind as he humped away on top of Filiberta, and did it bear any relation to what passed through his mind as he created with brushstroke and pigment the numinous, airborne figure of the Lord? It is, I suppose, all a matter of vital energy, and how such energy is utilized; but considering the extremes which must have pulled the psyche of that marvellous creature apart, I think if anyone was a born Gnostic, Master Rafael was. Not that he would ever have known this, and I certainly had no intention of informing him of the fact. When I saw him again the following day, he was once more all lightness, all easy grace and gentle amiability; one would never have thought that the dark storm of solipsistic lust had ever shaken his soul.

"Do you think he was poisoned?" Serapica asked me in a hushed voice, with more than a nuance of vulgar eagerness.

"No, of course I don't. Who on earth would want to poison him?"

"My *dear,* half the husbands in Rome, of course!"

"And half the kitchen-girls in Rome would stop them," I said.

"What?"

I told him the story.

"You *watched* them at it?" he cried, outraged.

"Of course; I told you, it was a wager."

"Then perhaps this Filiberta poisoned him? You say she has the devil's mark on her body?"

"A wen on her hip, to be precise; and no, she didn't poison him. God's blood, why must poison always be suspected every time someone of reputation or high office goes to meet the Lord?"

"My dear," Serapica replied, "haven't you learned by now that *no-one* of reputation or high office dies of natural causes in this city?"

These words of his, as you will eventually hear, came to constitute a most exquisite irony, and subsequently I often had cause to call them to mind.

"What I have told you," I said to Serapica, "must remain our little secret."

"It won't remain a secret for long in His Holiness's kitchens, I can tell you that."

"Nevertheless."

"Nevertheless what?"

I shrugged.

"Just nevertheless," I answered.

"I wonder if Leo ever guessed at his beloved's goings-on? And in the papal palace, too!"

"I don't suppose it would have bothered him in any case, do you?"

"Perhaps not; Leo may be lustful, but he's not possessive."

"He's a pure voluptuary," I said.

"Anyway, as far as Master Rafael was concerned, I'm sure that even Filiberta was preferable to the mushy petrine posterior."

"Precisely. Is there anything quite so sad as unrequited love?"

Serapica sniffed haughtily.

"My *dear,*" he said, "why ask me? I've never experienced it."

"Never experienced love?"

"Never experienced *unrequited* love. All my little infatuations have been entirely mutual, I'm very glad to say."

"Except in the case of Master Rafael," I said.

"I'm not going to rise to *that* bait my dear; you know that I did not pant after that *rara avis*, not in the slightest. Oh, I adored him, of course I did, just as we all did, but I was *never* enamoured, if you know what I mean. I knew he kept a ravishing hetaera somewhere in the city; his versatility was, I fear, limited to his brush."

"Things won't be the same without him," I said, anxious to end the conversation now, since I was beginning to feel like a scandalmongering fishwife in an *estaminet,* addled on wine and tittle-tattle.

"I shall miss him greatly," Serapica said. "I shall take to my room for days on end and beat my breast, like Niobe."

And he fluttered off, a papilionaceous nectar-drinker, in search of the next blossom of gossip.

The grief of the papal court – and of Leo in particular (to say nothing of three-quarters of the ladies of Rome) – was both deep and sincere. In his own way, Leo had loved Rafael; I think he really *had* loved him, quite apart from lusting after a certain (and legendary) part of his anatomy. Most of the well-known poets (Bembo, Ariosto, Tebaldeo *et alia*) vied with each other in celebrating Rafael's fame in verse. There was a widespread opinion throughout the city that had he lived, he would have achieved the greatness of Michelangiolo Buonarroti, but I think this is unfair; he *did* achieve the greatness of Michelangiolo, but the expression and manifestation of his genius took a different form. After all, who would think of asking whether a ruby is greater than an emerald, or a hyacinth greater than a rose? It is absurd! One is not greater than the other – they are *different*. Michelangiolo is all massively-muscled thighs, the serenely perfect faces of young men, the semi-divine grandeur of the human body; on the other hand, Rafael is transluscence, fluidity, spirituality, peace. The two cannot be compared, for they are what they are. At least, that's the way I see it. Master Rafael was buried in the Pantheon (at his own stipulation) and he had entrusted his good friend Lorenzetto with the execution of a statue of the Virgin, which was executed finely and set in place.

"I'm getting old, Peppe," Leo said to me sadly. "All my friends are dying or dead."

"Funny you should say that, Holiness – I feel exactly the same way. Still, we've got each other, haven't we?"

Leo looked at me curiously. Then, with a little sigh, he said:

"Hmm. Yes, I suppose we have. That will have to do."

Charming.

Actually, like Serapica, he *was* looking old; he was fatter than ever now, and had adopted the ridiculous habit of alternating rigid fasts with the consumption of gargantuan meals. This must have played havoc with his innards. He sweated profusely nearly all the time, and was obliged to walk everywhere between two attendants – taking slow, measured paces – just in case he needed assistance. At least the waddle used to be funny; the *lentissimo* walk was plain sad. He had also given up his young men from the streets, since his backside was by now in a dreadful state, and not even rare herbs or virgin's piss could do anything for it.

"Do you think I am being punished for my sins, Peppe?"

"Far be it from me to judge *that*, Holiness."

"But *do* you?"

"Well, since you ask –"

"If you say 'yes', I'll have *your* backside reduced to an ulcerated pulp by means of a horsewhip!"

"Ah."

No, I didn't think he was being punished for his *sins* (you know my views on sexual morality in any case), but he *was* paying the price for not looking after himself.

The new basilica of St Peter's was still only one-third finished; for all Rafael's genius, he really hadn't progressed much on it at all. This affirms my belief, stated earlier in these memoirs, that you can't automatically expect a great painter to be a great architect too. Poor Rafael had been directing the project for six years, and in all that time was constantly plagued by lack of funds; Leo had originally assigned an annual donation of sixty thousand ducats, raised from the sale – sorry, I mean 'preaching' – of indulgences, but there was very strong popular hostility displayed against this. I think people everywhere, not simply in Germany, were beginning to catch on to the fact that indulgences were just a thoroughly crooked business. Even Cardinal Ximenes of Spain (most of the time more Catholic than the pope) protested against the St Peter's Indulgence. Leo's personal extravagance didn't help matters much, either; he quite often spent money that was supposed to go towards the building work, on rare books and manuscripts, and – of course – rings. Some of these he didn't even wear. I think he just liked looking at them. There was at one time a rather nasty rumour to the effect that the pope had given half the receipts from the sales of the St Peter's Indulgence to his sister Maddalena; however, I can assure you that this is entirely untrue. Not *half* anyway – more like one quarter.

The new basilica became something of a joke; I happened to see a copy of a letter (don't ask me how, because I've no intention of telling you) that the Ferrarese envoy wrote, which contained the sentence:

'The Master has often been very strange since he took Bramante's place . . . '

Now, I wonder what he meant by 'strange'? It is certainly true that Rafael had been having what one can only describe as 'fits of introspection', but I consider that these were entirely due to the frustrations and difficulties imposed by his task. What I mean is this: the 'strangeness' didn't cause the lack of progress, the lack of progress caused the 'strangeness' – whatever its precise nature. Actually, I just think he was depressed. Some people say he became so sick and tired of not getting anywhere with St Peter's, he just upped and died, since this was the only way he could rid himself of it. I'm inclined to believe this. Be that as it may, when Rafael died, a little part of Leo died too.

As for myself – a great deal of my time was spent in a desperate attempt to discover where they were holding Tomaso della Croce; whatever they planned to do with him – or rather, whatever Andrea de' Collini planned to do with him – would, I knew, be sure to end in tragedy for all of us. It was as if he had quite disappeared from the face of the earth. I lived in an almost permanent state of apprehension.

The political situation was absurdly complicated; poor Leo was once again reduced to sitting on an uncomfortable fence from which he *knew* he would sooner or later have to leap down to one side or the other, and this was a serious strain on his health. It also put him in a very bad mood most of the time. The choice lay between France and the emperor (it nearly always *was* between France and the emperor, or France and Spain); pious, somewhat simple-minded, honest, arrogant Maximillian had died, and Leo had been forced to support the election of Charles V to the imperial throne. However, after Charles had become emperor, Leo feared his ascendancy more than ever; the Hohenstaufen had always been avaricious, had always been drawn to the idea of supremacy, like iron to a lodestone. More than ever, Leo was aware that if the independence of the Holy See and the liberty of Italy (such as it was) was to be preserved, he himself needed to maintain a delicate and sometimes impossible balance between Charles V and Francis I, both of whom contended for his favours.

A secret treaty had already been signed between Leo and the French ambassador, Saint-Marceau, in which the pope pledged to defend the interests of France with weapons both spiritual and temporal, and to refuse Charles the crown of Naples in conjunction with that of the empire. This document had been signed on October 22nd 1519, and Charles knew nothing about it. However, Charles V sent a new ambassador to Rome, who arrived in the city in lavish style on April 11th 1520, and Leo received him with effusive warmth; Cardinal Giulio de' Medici invited him to stay in his palace in the Cancelleria, where many a night was spent in revelling, they say – well, Serapica said, anyway, and I believe him. The ambassador, a supercilious Castilian called Juan Manuel, brought with him the draft of a treaty which Charles wanted Leo to sign, but without altering a single word – *"sin mudar palabra,"* Juan said in his resonant, pompous (but rather attractive) voice.

Poor Leo – having signed a treaty with Francis which nobody knew about, he was now being asked to sign one with the emperor; small wonder he delayed giving a decision. In the end he *did* sign it, but only because he believed that it might help matters in Germany, and Charles V had issued his edict against Luther in compliance with the pope's wishes. Francis began to be a nuisance at the beginning of 1520 by pretensions to the guardianship of Catherine de' Medici – a matter which Bibbiena managed to smooth over, but the concord was not to last long; after demanding that Cardinal Gouffier de Boissy's office as Legate in France should be extended for five years, he then forbade the proclamation of the anti-Lutheran bull of Maundy Thursday in France, with the curious warning that anyone who did attempt to proclaim it, should be drowned. With astonishing arrogance, Francis then asked Leo to make his relative, Jean d'Orléans, Archbishop of Toulouse, a cardinal, and he objected vociferously to the same dignity being bestowed on the Bishop of Liège, which the emperor had specifically requested. When, after tormenting himself with worry over this matter for weeks, Leo eventually acceded to Francis's demand, raising d'Orléans to the cardinalate, but *not* the Bishop of Liège, imagine his surprise and outrage when it was Francis himself who objected to this!

"It's almost as though he's actually *trying* to pick a quarrel with me!" Leo wailed.

"It would seem so, Holiness," I said.

"My dear," put in Serapica, "the French are as unbearable as allies as they are formidable as enemies."

(Later, Leo was to repeat this remark, and it was assumed to be his own, much to Serapica's chagrin.)

"I will not tolerate that arrogant little ball-sucker telling me what to say and what not to say in my own consistory!" Leo shouted, angry now.

"A basso i Francesi!"

Serapica and I had now assumed the role of a kind of Greek chorus, always commenting on Leo's thoughts, words and deeds; together, we were like three old curmudgeons tottering about centrestage in some prolix, high-minded and totally irrelevant domestic tragedy, while all around us – before our very eyes, so to speak – the audience, far from paying any attention to what was going on, was in a state of riot. It was all rather farcical and sad and somewhat unnerving.

I think it was about this time that Leo turned his back on the French once and for all; even Bibbiena gave up the increasingly difficult task of advancing their cause and promoting their interests. Besides, the absolute necessity of the emperor's help in quelling the Lutheran revolt in Germany became more and more apparent to Leo with each day that passed; the news from that country was by now truly disquieting. The emperor's ambassador, Juan Manuel, had actually advised Charles not to show any mark of favour whatsoever to "a certain monk known as Brother Martin", or to Frederick, Elector of Saxony; the shrewd Manuel knew well enough that imperial disapproval of Luther *and* the astonishing behaviour of Francis, could not fail to drive Leo into the arms of Charles. In fact, this is exactly what happened. Charles himself meanwhile, had loyally carried out the anti-Lutheran bull in the Netherlands, and at his coronation at Aix on October 23rd, he swore to "defend the Holy Catholic Faith as delivered to the Apostles, and to show all due submission and fidelity to the lord pope and the Holy Roman See". Somewhat pompously, but with kind intentions, Leo wrote Charles a latter which included these words:

'As there are twin bodies in heaven, the sun and the moon — whose brilliance outshines all other stars — so there are two great dignitaries on earth, the pope and the emperor, to whom all lesser princes are subject and owe obedience.'

Charles V was a young man; his skin was smooth and very pale, and his chin was absolutely enormous, looking for all the world as though God had stuck it on his face as an afterthought, with a lot of *prima materia* he had left over. His eyes were heavily lidded and sleepy, and to be honest, when he held his head in a certain way, he gave every appearance of being a cretin. I think, though, it was just the Hohenstaufen 'look'. They say that when he read the words of Leo quoted above, a thin trickle of saliva dribbled out of the corner of his mouth and down that vast, unhillocked, flat landscape of a chin — a dribble of pure pleasure.

On January 3rd 1521, the bull of excommunication against Luther, *Decet Romanum Pontificem,* was issued, and the pope requested the emperor that a general edict be issued for its execution throughout Germany. The question of an alliance with Charles, which had hitherto hinged on political considerations, was now entirely a matter of what he could do about and against Martin Luther. Leo was beginning to awake from his dream of the eternal and unchanging durability of papal authority, to the reality of a Christendom divided by the blood and the sword of a heresy struggling (rather successfully, it appeared) to become the new orthodoxy. How strange that sleep should produce the comforting dream, and waking, the terrifying nightmare.

In the end, afraid of what consequences the Lutheran revolt in Germany might lead to (and which in fact that *did* ultimately lead to), and goaded beyond endurance by Francis, Leo signed an offensive (as opposed to purely defensive, I mean) alliance with Charles on May 8th 1521.

By this alliance, "the two real heads of Christendom unite to purify it from all error, in establishing universal peace, in fighting the infidel, and in introducing a better state of affairs throughout." Such high ideals.

Oddly enough, Charles actually offended Leo in his very efforts to please him; for the emperor had summoned Luther to the Diet of Worms, which Leo thought should have been a prerogative reserved for himself. Luther was also allowed the opportunity for religious debate, which Leo was completely against; after all, why give a condemned and excommunicated heretic the chance to air his heretical teachings? In the event, Charles did show himself entirely on the side of Catholic orthodoxy, and proved to Leo's satisfaction that he had no intention whatsoever of using events in Germany for his own advantage; on April 18th, after Luther's first examination, Charles actually sent Raffaello de' Medici to Rome to submit to the pope the draft of the treaty of alliance. Leo could not praise Charles highly enough, and after the treaty had finally been concluded, war with France became a matter of inevitability.

In order to frustrate a plan by Girolamo Morone, the Vice-Chancellor of Maximillian Sforza, to gather an army of Milanese who had been driven out of Milan by the French, the brother of the Governor, Lautrec, invaded the territory of the Holy See by marching into Reggio and demanding that the Milanese 'army' be handed over to him. This invasion gave Leo the opportunity he was waiting for to declare himself openly against the French. The alliance with Charles, hitherto secret, was now made public, and Leo began preparations for raising a papal army. Francis, suddenly aware of the storm that was threatening him, tried to win back the pope's favour, but to no avail; they say he foamed at the mouth with rage, rolling on the floor of his palace naked, thrashing and screaming like a whipped dog; by all accounts he cried out in fury: "Before long I myself shall enter Rome and impose my own law on the pope!" I don't know whether these rumours are actually true or not, but I suspect they might well be;

remember – this little cripple from the Trastevere gutters once dined with Francis I, King of France, and I *know* what he is capable of, what demon of pride lies beneath the veneer of haughty, pallid, glacial piety.

After a great deal of threatening and cursing, Leo finally informed Francis that unless he handed over Parma and Piacenza to the Holy See, he would excommunicate him and his generals, and place France under an interdict. Now on paper, an interdict doesn't seem too much for anyone to worry about, but in practice it is a truly dreadful thing: no Masses celebrated, all churches closed, bodies are left to rot and stink because they can't be buried, infants die unbaptized, the dying are left without the consolation of Extreme Unction. *Nobody* can put up with such a state of affairs for very long.

The struggle to retake Parma and Piacenza did not go terribly well for the papal army and its allies, even though they had been joined by about six thousand German *landsknechte*; moreover, Charles began to suspect that once they *were* taken, Leo would not wish to prolong hostilities further. However, the impetuous and warlike Cardinal Schinner succeeded in getting together a large army of Swiss mercenaries, who allied themselves to the papal forces when Prospero Colonna crossed the river Po at Casalmaggiore to ensure that this is exactly what happened. They advanced from Chiavenna into the territory of Bergamo, and thence onto Reggio, where the intention was to re-take Parma and Piacenza for the pope; in fact, although the Swiss had pledged themselves only to fight in *defence* and not in offence, Schinner persuaded them to join Gambara and the combined forces of the papacy and Spain and to make a descent upon Milan.

Imagine it: Cardinal Schinner and Cardinal de' Medici rode at the head of this force! There they were, with their gold pectoral and legatine crosses flying, their beringed hands red with blood, plundering and looting and blaspheming with the best of them. To Schinner of course, this had become a way of life, but for Giulio de' Medici – I can only say that it confirms what I've always thought about him. On the field of battle, his 'mildness of manner', I am sure, is nowhere in evidence.

The union of Swiss, Spanish and papal troops gave the allies a clear superiority; in particular, a number of Swiss mercenaries who had been fighting in the French army grew weary of Lautrec's high-handed manner, and when it became obvious that there was no money to pay them, they deserted in droves. Also, they had never been entirely happy about fighting their fellow-countrymen. Late in the afternoon of November 19th – a cold and rainy afternoon – the allied forces appeared before the walls of Milan; Cardinals de' Medici and Schinner decided that certain suburbs should be attacked first, so Pescara made for the Porta Romana with his Spanish marksmen, Prospero Colonna for the Porta Ticinese with the Spanish mercenaries and the German *landsknechte*, and in a very short time the gates of the city were forced open. Lautrec at once retreated, and during the night Maximillian Sforza was declared Duke of Milan to an overjoyed, French-hating populace. The fall of Milan decided the fate of the whole of Lombardy: Piacenza, Pavia, Novara, Tortona, Alessandria, Asti, Cremona and Lodi all willingly threw open their gates to the allies. Then, on November 24th, the English Chancellor concluded a defensive *and* offensive alliance with Leo and Charles against Francis – better late then never, I suppose. Francis had finally lost everything.

The English had always seemed to be on the periphery of things; what an enigmatic, pale-faced, disdainful, secretive and oh-so-correct race the English are! I've never known quite what to make of them. I suppose it is something to do with the northern climate; I have heard that in England when it isn't snowing it's raining, and when it isn't raining it's foggy. England? *Fa sempre la grigia!* as we Italians say. Yet give me an aloof Englishman to a treacherous Frenchman any day.

Leo had been delighted by the stand taken by England's King Henry VIII against the mad monk Luther; on May 12th 1521, in St Paul's Churchyard, in the presence of a vast multitude, the solemn publication of the papal brief against Luther had taken place, together with the burning of his writings. Leo was informed by the English envoy, a man called Clerk, that on this occasion Thomas Wolsey had conducted himself as if the papal tiara (which he had long coveted) were already on his head; Leo didn't like *that* one little bit, even though he was delighted to hear of the publication of the brief and the burning of Luther's rambling diatribes.

On the same day, the dispatch to Rome of King Henry's book against Luther, *A Defence of the Seven Sacraments Against Luther* (which was apparently nearly all his own work), was announced. This was received on September 14th, and presented to Leo by Clerk. Leo read the first five pages or so, peering through his little gold-handled magnifying glass, and positively squealed with delight.

"A prodigy! A marvel! A gift from heaven!" he cried.

"The book, Holiness, or the king?" Clerk asked in his dry English way.

"Both, of course," he replied a little testily, displeased I think, to have his rhapsody interrupted.

"I shall convey Your Holiness's pleasure to His Majesty."

"Look! Look at that!" Leo cried. "Have you seen the dedication? *England's King Henry sends Leo X this work as a sign of faith and friendship.* God bless England's king!"

Leo begged Clerk for five or six copies of the book, which he wanted to give to the cardinals, and invited him to address a secret consistory, which he did on October 2nd. Leo further issued a bull on October 26th, bestowing upon Henry the title of 'Defender of the Faith'. Cardinal Wolsey, who had dreamed up the whole thing, rose like a flaming star in the firmament, earning the heartfelt gratitude of his royal master.

Then we all forgot about England. Well, for one thing, it was terribly far away.

I, however, had by no means forgotten the abduction of Tomaso della Croce. Leo's troubles with France had come to me as a welcome relief, since for a time they enabled me to concentrate my mind on something other than Andrea de' Collini's treacherous and cunning acts of mania; after the defeat of Francis however, the horror returned with a vengeance.

As a matter of fact my position was pretty hopeless, since there was nothing I could do without first discovering where the inquisitor was being held, and this proved an impossible task. I met with Cardinal Cajetan several times at his private residence, but the necessity for circumspection prevented me from acquiring any useful information – always assuming of course, that there was any to be acquired. I doubted it.

Cajetan was still in a fury, and his attitude to me was one of exasperation mingled with suspicion; in the cardinal's eyes, if I was not a gross incompetent then I was a traitor, and it was clear that he by no means dismissed the possibility that I was both.

"I ought never to have allowed myself to be persuaded!" he hissed through clenched and carious teeth. "Never! Look at the results of your grotesque scheme! Where is Tomaso della Croce now? Can you tell me that?"

"No Eminence, I cannot."

"Then who took him?"

"I cannot tell you that either."

"I cannot have my inquisitors simply disappearing. Who worked with you on this plot of yours? Names, Peppe, I want names!"

I shook my head firmly.

"Eminence, there was no other. I alone am responsible for –"

"For what? For his abduction? Is that what you mean?"

"No Eminence, I swear it! I have no idea whatsoever who might have done this thing! It was never part of my purpose. I *explained* the plan I had devised."

"Yes – that Tomaso della Croce would kill himself and be forgotten, and that everyone else would be happier as a consequence. But he *didn't* kill himself, did he? You were so *sure* of it!"

"Precisely, Eminence. Does not that very certainty prove my innocence?"

Cajetan pursed his lips. This thought, at least, seemed to strike him as reasonable.

"Perhaps," he said quietly. "Perhaps after all you had not expected this."

"Of course I hadn't expected it!"

"And you cannot tell me his present whereabouts?"

"No, Eminence. You have my word on that. In fact, I was rather hoping *you* might be able to suggest —"

"Tchah!"

I did not bother to finish the sentence.

"You will excuse me," the cardinal said, "if I do not offer you any refreshment. I have a great many other tasks to undertake besides looking for a missing inquisitor."

"Eminence."

"You will of course inform me the moment you come by any information."

It was not a request, it was a command.

"Certainly, Eminence."

And I took my leave.

Oh yes, yes, I found them in the end — found them that is, only to lose them again! Indeed, I should have guessed what they would do with him, where the one place was they could be sure he would never be discovered; after all, Tomaso della Croce was, by all normal standards of human decency, a freak — and where best to hide a freak? Where best to hide a tree but in a forest? Where best to hide a freak but in a caravan of freaks? Andrea de' Collini had doubtlessly paid Antonio Donato handsomely; but then, one Master had the money and the other 'Master' was always in need of it, so what better arrangement could there be? I had been a fool in so many ways.

My primary intention had been to speak to Antonio Donato, thinking that I might persuade him to end his dealings with the Master – by pleading, by force of common-sense, by threats, by any means I could – and let the inquisitor go. But I had not reasoned things out fully enough; how could they *ever* let him go, having once taken him? What would happen if they set him free? The stake – the stake is what would happen. Inevitably and inexorably. They had gone too far to turn back, and della Croce was now like a venomous serpent, a scorpion they had cooped up in an airless box; once released, his rage would know no bounds – he would bite and sting whatever moved. He would clamp his fangs around the hand that opened the box to liberate him. I *knew* that this whole ghastly *incubus* could have but one ending now; I knew, I saw, I could not doubt, and yet I continued, absurdly, to hope. Yes, I had been a fool.

As it happens, I did not get the opportunity to speak to Master Antonio, nor even to catch sight of him; when I arrived at the caravan site, the second show of the evening was already in progress. I wandered aimlessly from tent to tent, saddened and depressed by the lascivious appetite of the vulgar crowd crammed into each, a microcosm of the beastliness of the whole world. I noticed that Master Antonio had acquired one or two new acts – two frightened-looking little girls (I saw the horror and bewilderment in their large brown eyes and my heart was squeezed by an invisible hand) joined at the hip and exhibited entirely naked, to my great disgust; a miserable wretch whose testicles were so swollen he could actually sit on them; an immensely fat woman who was little more than a tired version of the traditional 'Bearded Lady' -except that in this case, the lady's whiskers were manifestly false. Master Antonio was truly scraping the barrel.

It was in the fourth tent that I found him.

There he was, gagged and bound, his wrists and his ankles purple-blue where the ropes cut into the flesh, wriggling and writhing helplessly, and billed as *The Man Possessed by a Hundred Demons*. I do not know which sensation was the more powerful in me – shock, fear or hilarity. For it was a shock of the most nerve-jarring intensity suddenly to come upon him like that, without warning or premonition of any kind – like looking into a mirror and *not* seeing your reflection, the shock of the utterly unexpected; it was also a moment of heart-stopping fear, because if one of those ropes had broken – or if the gag had slipped out of his mouth – oh, Christ, the fury he would unleash! And finally it was a spectacle of complete and total ridiculousness – this semi-naked, blue-in-the-face *functus officio* of the Holy Roman Church, a man who had spent most of his life hunting down the demons in others, now being gawped at by the scum of Rome's suburbs who had each paid half a ducat to see a man possessed by a *hundred* demons. The world had turned topsy-turvy.

They had yanked him up against a long, stout pole (meant to resemble a stake, no doubt) and had secured him with more rope; a furtive-looking 'priest' stood nearby, intoning some mumbo-jumbo from a tattered book. Every so often he rang a little cow-bell that was attached to his wrist.

"Begone, in the name of the Most High! Take flight! Depart, lewd and lascivious sprites, from the soul of this Christian creature!"

Then, turning to the crowd, he announced:

"He has the marks of the devil all over his wretched body – even in his most secret places have the lips of Lucifer lingered in an unchaste kiss! See! Wherever the devil's mark is, the man possessed by a hundred demons feels no pain –"

At that moment a retarded-looking brute shuffled on stage and pulled up the filthy, knee-length smock that they had put on the inquisitor; he had not even been accorded the dignity of underdrawers, and several of the women (I do not say 'ladies') in the crowd guffawed. I watched, open-mouthed, as the pale bulge of his belly rose and fell violently. The brute ran his fingers through the inquisitor's pubic hair for a few moments, smirking witlessly to himself, then with absolute indifference – boredom, even –

drew a bodkin from his sleeve and thrust it – *pushed it* – into Tomaso della Croce's stomach.

Cry out! Scream aloud! I silently exhorted him (to relieve not his agony, but mine), but no sound issued from his mouth because of the gag. Someone at the back of the crowd did scream as the bodkin went in a little further. When the torturer withdrew it, it was bright with blood: a trickle no thicker than the breadth of a human hair marked the inquisitor's flesh, like a crimson fissure in smooth marble.

"Begone, denizens of hell!" cried the idiot dressed as a priest, and the hulk of a *goyim* turned Tomaso della Croce round so that his back was to the crowd. Then they pushed his head down, so that he was bent over, creased at the waist. The smock was lifted and again the bodkin went in, this time into the right buttock. I saw the muscles clench in a pitiful spasm. The bodkin was not large, true, and whoever had devised the act (surely Andrea de' Collini) had clearly indicated exactly where it was to be plunged in so as to inflict no real damage – but even so, the pain – oh, the pain must have been excruciating.

The crowd had fallen silent now, both enthralled and appalled, but rooted to the spot. What dark and secret magnetism held them there, what disgusting and lascivious urges sustained their total submission to the enactment of this monstrous spectacle? Such is the tragedy of the human person: that each is an amphibian, moving now in the ethers of heaven, now in the miasmal mire of earth, suspended between paradise and the inferno, an angel and a devil; the more we try to pull ourselves up to the kingdom of the stars, the more we slip and slither in the beastly sperm, mucus, mould and excrement below, and the hand upraised in prayer is the same hand that strikes a defenceless child. Oh, to be free of contradiction!

The 'priest' now tapped the inquisitor's backside with his book of incantations.

"Where?" he whispered in a voice charged with sexual emotion. "Where are the devil's marks? Ah, Satan is cunning, and hides the traces of his obscene kisses well! Here? Or perhaps here?"

He moved the book down under Tomaso della Croce's exposed arse, where there was dampness and darkness and tender, private swelling.

The bodkin followed the path that the book traced, and *en route,* so to speak, to its final destination – wherever that might be – book and bodkin made several unscheduled stops; each time the pages of the book fluttered against pale skin, the bodkin glittered and the crowd inhaled on a single breath. They *wanted* to see it go in, for Christ's sweet sake.

"Here?"– around and about the scrotum, up within the cleft of the buttocks and into the small of the back (I saw the thighs quivering) -

"Or maybe – ah! – maybe here?"– along the knobbly ridge of the ribs and deep into the bushy armpit -

Aaahhhh! sighed the people, *yes, oh yes, yes, let it be there!*

"Again, might we find the mark of Satan here?"– oh God, into the right ear!

And so the cruel tracery went on, butterflying patterns of eight across the wretched inquisitor's back, caressing his arse, the leaves of the book whispering intimations of the love that is death, leaving an invisible trail like the gleaming trail of a slug, a tell-tale track where the yearning for pain had passed on its way. Then at last the book was withdrawn and the bodkin hovered and then – now! -

"There!" screamed the judge, and "There!" cried the executioner.

Then the bodkin went in deep, deep into the fleshy padding of the left shoulder, and once again I saw the buttocks clench while the inquisitor's silence sang a blood-rich, heart-full paean of praise to pain.

A single, lust-coarsened voice rang out from the crowd:

"His balls! Stick it into his balls!"

They were not spectators, these animals with human faces, they were participants. They shared both the torturer's casual delight and the victim's soundless agony.

291

They were Cain and Abel. Whatever it was that had awakened in them this vile approbation of the infliction of pain I do not know, and neither did I share it; when Tomaso della Croce was pulled around to face them again and the bodkin approached his nipples, I turned and fled. That Andrea de' Collini should have devised this! That in him, the operation of reason had become distorted by an obsession with revenge – even to the point where he had violated every principle of the faith that his daughter had suffered and died in the flames for – that any of this should be so, I could hardly believe. It was a judgement to be sure, but the wrong judge; deep in my heart I did not care that Tomaso della Croce was enduring a prolonged agony, but I could not bear to think that the Master was the instrument of its application.

I caught Nino just as he was pulling off his absurd 'talons' and struggling to get out of his leggings.

"So then," I cried, "everything is as plain as a pikestaff now, my friend! And to think I was blind, groping about in the dark, imagining that things were just 'happening', no more than opportunities being seized by a madman and the three stooges he'd bought and paid for! But he'd planned things from the very beginning, hadn't he? I ought to have known from the moment we had news of Laura's sentence – that apathy, the inability to respond, to act – oh yes, yes, I see it all now. The purchase of you and your friends, the gathering of evidence, the accusations, the trial, the sentence, the abduction, and now – now *this,* Nino – the torture! Purchase one, evidence two, accusations three, trial four, sentence five, abduction six, torture seven – and what remains but the eight, the execution? Eight! That number he's so crazy about! Eight, eight, eight – a tragedy in eight acts! Well Nino, am I right? Am I?"

"I don't know about any numbers –"

"Don't try to make an even bigger fool of me than I've already been, Nino. You don't have to pretend anymore, I know it all. I can see it clearly. Just tell me: the final act *is* the execution, isn't it?"

292

"Yes! Yes, the execution!"

I was panting, panting and gasping, and my mis-shapen chest shook like a pair of old bellows.

"Tell me where it is to be," I said as calmly as I could.

Nino opened his mouth to speak, but at that moment there was a yell of fury and alarm somewhere behind us. I turned to see Master Antonio with several of the *goyim* running towards us; Master Antonio was pointing, waving his arm and gesticulating. The *goyim* were armed with heavy sticks; one of them seemed to be carrying a knife – I saw the blade glitter in the yellow light of the torches that were suspended outside the tents.

"There he is! The dwarf! That's the one, boys!"

"For God's sake, Peppe – get out of here! Go! Run!"

"I must know, Nino – I must –"

But Nino was already loping away across the field.

"Tomorrow!" I heard him shout. "Tomorrow night! Tomorrow!"

And his voice trailed away behind me as I forced my twisted little legs into their own unique *pastiche* of a sprint.

The following night found me in a state of feverish apprehension bordering on hysteria; I paced my chamber again and again, wringing my hands, lighting then extinguishing then relighting the candle. Fortunately for me, Leo was entertaining a dealer from England who specialized in discreetly erotic works of art, and so I was free to indulge my fraught nerves alone. It was intolerable to know *when* the final act of the tragedy was to be played out, but not *where*. In the end I decided I simply had to get out into the city, and it was this impulsion which led me to the discovery which hours of running frenetically around Rome chasing rumours, false trails, gossip and plain mischief could not.

It was at the tavern of Marco Saletti. Why I chose to go wandering in that particular district at that particular hour I do not know, but I did; perhaps some integument of a hope that had been all but vanquished remained in my weary soul, or perhaps there were other forces at work – fate, destiny, *dharma* as the eastern devil-worshippers call it, some inexorable and fathomless Will – dragging my twisted little legs in a direction of which I was barely conscious until I suddenly looked up and saw an ugly, graceless brute of an inebriate come stumbling out of a doorway, and I knew then where I was.

"Watch where you're going!" I cried, moving out of his way before he came tumbling down on top of me.

He leered at me in the foetid gloom.

"Oh," he said, "it's you again. The dwarf."

"Do I know you?"

"Maybe, maybe not. But I know *you,* little runtikins. You were in here once before, you and your cunt-faced friends. Christ Almighty, I've never seen so much fucking ugliness all in one place. There ought to be a law."

"You *know* them?" I asked, feeling the excitement rising, as sudden and as irresistible as sexual arousal.

"Once seen, never forgotten. Mother of God, who could forget faces like that? I'm well enough acquainted with old Nino, runtikins. Me and him, we usually have a bottle or two together whenever he's passing through. I can't say I've had the pleasure of the bastard they had with them, though. If you've come here looking for them tonight, mind, you're too late."

"Too late? I don't understand –"

"Your hobgoblin chums went off about an hour ago."

"What!" I cried, hardly able to choke the words out, "you mean they were *here* in this place? Tonight?"

"That's what I said, didn't I?"

"And there was another man with them – someone you didn't recognize?"

"Sure there was. Didn't look none too happy, either. Mind you, I couldn't see his face on account of the way they had him done up."

"For God's sake man, where are they now?"

"And what are *you* so keen to know that for, runtikins?"

As calmly as I could I said:

"They are in danger, all of them. Terrible danger."

"Nino didn't say nothing about danger. I never heard him say anything about that."

"Nevertheless, what I tell you is so."

"Old Nino in trouble?"

"I *must* know where they went!"

He rubbed his hands together, smiled a black-stumped smile, then chuckled to himself.

"Then it's your lucky night, you short-arsed poetaster!" he said. "Old Nino got into some kind of squabble with the monster what's only got half a face, and they started shouting the odds, see? So I caught a bit of what they were saying, here and there."

"And? For God's sake!" I screamed, barely able to contain myself.

"And old Nino said something about the Colosseum."

"What?"

"That's right, the Colosseum. Skull-face tried to shut him up, but not before yours truly had heard it. I've got pretty sharp ears, and it didn't take much savvy to know that they were up to something as what they oughtn't to be. Get my drift? Ha!"

"You're quite sure it was the Colosseum?"

"Sure as I've got the pox."

"And – and the other man –"

"They had him trussed up good and proper, like a fucking goose! They'd gagged his mouth so he couldn't speak. Who was he, anyway?"

I hesitated. Then I said:

"Just a bad piece of work. Nobody important."

"Important enough to them, though. And to *you* by the sound of it."

"Didn't anyone try to stop them? Challenge them?"

"In this shit-hole? Do me a favour! Why do you think they came here in the first place? Marco is blind to everything. Good God in heaven, you could walk in with a stone-dead fuck-naked tart over your shoulder and no-one would bat an eyelid."

I took a coin from my money-belt and pressed it into his greasy hand.

"You have my thanks," I said.

"Mark you, I never said a word, see?"

He staggered off down the filthy alley.

The Colosseum has been a great heap of ruination for centuries. Plundered by the Church for its marble and bronze studs, it fell into a state of ravaged decay which could not possibly have been envisaged by those who designed and erected it; for this vast theatre has never died but has merely lingered on into an infinitely prolonged decreptitude of old age. Grass grew everywhere, in every crack and cranny, widening the perilous gaps between the great building-bricks and forcing them over the years, inch by inch, degree by degree, to yield their hold and come tumbling down. By day, cows grazed within its shattered circular enclosure; by night, it became a refuge and shelter for inebriates, vagabonds, thieves, cutpurses and worse, and for illicit love-makers – the dregs of human society taking their nocturnal pleasure – and where once its walls rang with the screams of the martyrs as they perished by fire or by beast, now were heard only the echoes of sexual pleasure, the strident voices of beggars squabbling over stolen scraps, the low and helpless sobs of those lost in their own nameless despair.

It was an entirely appropriate setting for the horror which was shortly to come, for here the followers of Christ had been dipped in pitch and ignited; twelve-year-old virgins had been deflowered by squawking hyenas; so much human life had been violently expended for the delectation of a savage mob insatiable for novelty, that the stink of every bodily fluid imaginable could be detected even in the imperial apartments on the Palatine hill.

Breathless, terrified of what I would find, I scrambled over the great chunks of fallen masonry; I could hardly see where I was going. Once I called Nino's name aloud, but the only answer that came was the cackle of distant and obscene laughter. I stumbled across a pair of lovers, catching one of them in the side with my foot.

"Watch where you're going, you bloody little monster!"

"Pervert!"

I held back the tears, pulling myself painfully over rocks and stones almost as tall as myself.

Then I saw them.

Nino, Beppo and the Skull were huddled together; Andrea de' Collini stood slightly apart, motionless, brooding. And there – there on the ground lay Tomaso della Croce, face down; they had stripped him of his clothes and bound his wrists and ankles with rope.

"Peppe!" Nino cried, catching sight of me. "What the hell are you doing here?"

"I've come to ask you the same question," I said. "Have you entirely taken leave of your senses? Beppo! Don Giuseppe! What the hell made you agree to this – this – lunacy?"

Then the Master turned his face towards me.

"They are here at my command," he said softly. "You are not. Why have you come?"

"To talk some sense into all of you!" I growled.

"I had thought to spare you this, Peppe."

"Spare me what? What are you going to *do* with him?"

"You will see."

"Look," I began, "it isn't too late – there's still time to let him go –"

"You fool!" the Master hissed, and the vehemence in his voice made my blood run cold. "Do you still not understand? This is the final confrontation, our own private Armageddon! Do you really imagine that you – or anyone else! – can stop me now? After all that I have planned? No, no, no! Remain here with us if you will my friend, but do not attempt to interfere with what has been ordained."

Stretched out naked in moonlight, Fra Tomaso looked almost beautiful; his marble-smooth flesh, seemingly translu-

297

cent, gleamed with all the enigmatic, dreamlike seductiveness of the moon's world – a world of signs and symbols, of silver shadows, of stillness, magic, illusion and midnight yearnings. It was the world of Yesod according to the ancient kabbalists: of those irrational stirrings too deep for the waking mind to comprehend or define, of anxiety fluttering in the pit of the stomach, the bowels turning in apprehension, and of whispered revelations from phantasms, ghosts, earthbound shades of the long dead. Here, enclosed by the crumbling circular walls of the Roman theatre, like a talisman in the centre of a *temenos,* della Croce seemed both reality and illusion at the same moment. And this moment contained within itself an infinite variety of alternatives and possibilities: he could be loved, made love to, adored ... he could be ravaged ... he could be worshipped as a shy sylvan god ... he could be bloodily murdered. The terror and the bliss of all these things – and of anything – could be worked upon him, for he was held – as we all were – transfixed and motionless, in the palm of a dreamworld's hand.

When Andrea de' Collini spoke, it was not to break the spell that held us all in thrall, but to prolong it. His voice was low, soft, icily controlled, yet I swear it could be heard all around the theatre. Shapes and forms moved in the moon-rich darkness – a muffled cry of pain or sexual ecstasy, the rumble of broken snoring, a despairing sigh. These constituted the psalmody which accompanied our rites of madness.

"Do you know what day of the month this is?" the Master asked.

"It is the eighth day," Tomaso della Croce answered, his face pressed against the grassy soil. He seemed, unbelievably, to be completely composed.

"The eighth. The eighth day! And do you know what hour it is since sunset?"

"It is the eighth hour after the setting of the sun," the inquisitor replied.

"Again, Tomaso della Croce, you are right. The eighth

day, the eighth hour. The number of Saturn. The planet of darkness, of catastrophe and death. *Your* planet!"

"This is the devil's work! You shall rot in hell, Andrea de' Collini, along with your heretic whore of a daughter!"

The Master raised his head, as if scrutinising the occluded heavens. Then he let loose a long, crooning wail, like a dog howling at the moon. Of fury? Of grief? Pure and simple madness? I could not tell. That he *was* now mad however, I could no longer doubt.

"Brave words, inquisitor!" he cried. "Oh, we shall see how brave you can be soon enough, believe me."

"Devil-spawn!"

The Master began to undress; he did so with an almost mathematical care, paying great attention to the way in which he rolled up his clothes, placing them neatly in a pile. Then, naked, the Master straddled the motionless body of Tomaso della Croce, placing one foot beside each white thigh.

"Now tell me, inquisitor, what is the first and most essential tenet of our Gnostic faith?"

"I know nothing of heresy."

"Answer me."

"Your so-called 'faith' is so riddled with filth and corruption that I would not know where to begin, Andrea de' Collini."

"Then allow me to assist you. Matter. Matter and Spirit. The first and most essential tenet of our faith is that material existence is evil and was created by Satan."

"Heresy!" screamed della Croce, spitting dirt from his mouth.

"It is the truth. The body is a vile, stinking thing, for all flesh is the handiwork of the Evil One. It is a prison in which the soul is incarcerated. *Say it.* Say that flesh is of Satan."

"Never. The universe was made by God our Father, the Father of our Lord Jesus Christ, and everything he has made is good."

"Flesh is good?" the Master asked slowly.

"Yes, flesh is good, and hell shall be your eternal home for saying otherwise."

"Very well, inquisitor. We shall see how good *your* flesh is."

It was at this point I noticed that the Master was now fully erect. My heart began to beat wildly. I knew that there were some tormented souls who could be aroused to sexual desire only by pain or by contemplation of the infliction of pain; this I could not understand, but I knew that it was so. But the Master? Surely it could not be. I *knew* that it could not be, but the horrid madness of his now quite obvious intention left no alternative conclusion – or, rather, left no reasonable, logical conclusion that was in any way tractable to comprehension. But then, perhaps I was forgetting that the impulsions of madness cannot be comprehended.

"We shall see how sweet your flesh is, Tomaso della Croce. Oh yes, yes, we shall learn together, by a journey of such exquisite agony, you and I. Ah, what wonders shall my loving lesson inflict! Oh, Tomaso, Tomaso, let the learning begin . . ."

The Master, his long penis quivering, sank to his knees. He inserted his fingers between della Croce's pale buttocks and tenderly prised them apart.

A single, terrified shriek:

"In the name of God, no!"

I watched, horrified, as he let himself fall onto della Croce and plunged his rigid member deep, deep into the inquisitor's anus; then he began to thrust. Still he crooned, whispering into his victim's ear, his lips flecked with spittle, panting, ramming again and again with merciless ferocity.

"Yes, yes, yes, did I not tell you? Did I not warn you, my sweet and beloved enemy? Oh, oh, oh, is the flesh good now? Is the pain a cause of joy? Has your God invented *this* for your delectation? Tell me that I am right, Tomaso della Croce – oh! – tell me that my philosophy is true. Have I, then, a wretched heretic, a deeper insight into

300

truth than you, a faithful, devoted and murderously bloody son of Holy Mother Church?"

"You – oh Jesus, Jesus, deliver me! – you are damned –"

"And *you* - my hell on earth – you were damned the day you were born . . ."

We watched this ritualized act of brutal rape open-mouthed, almost entranced; but does such a horror entrance or bewitch? The Master was going at it with a furious energy – fuelled, doubtlessly, by a lethal blend of hatred and despair – so furious that I thought he must be quite deliberately intending to tear della Croce's bowels to shreds.

Then, frantically, as his climax came upon him:

"Oh Tomaso, Tomaso . . . how . . . how I *despise* you!"

He slumped and was still for some moments, and the bodies of the two naked men, marinated in moonlight, seemed to me like a single and astonishing unity of form, figures of statuary long fallen from their pedestal; a per-petual oneness at the heart of immobility, a rich eloquence captured, timelessly, in the unblinking eye of silence.

This was insane.

When the Master finally pulled himself out and tottered to his knees again, I saw that his penis was slick with blood; it glittered sumptuously, the integument of both triumph and tragedy. Semen dripped from the bloated tip; semen and blood – the meaning of life and the meaning of death.

"Tell me now, inquisitor," he murmured, "is the flesh still good?"

Della Croce made no reply.

Then, seized afresh by his mad strength, he ordered:

"Peppe! You others! Nino! Here – turn him over onto his back!"

We did so reluctantly, unwilling to look at him; we untied the ropes that bound his wrists and ankles, and pulled him into a sitting position. Incredibly, in spite of the pain in his eyes, he was composed; indeed, a faint smile played about his thin, dry lips. The tender fold of flesh in his hairless belly moved me, suddenly and unexpectedly, to an exquisite and unbearable compassion. I do not know why. Sometimes this happens: a child's tear, shadows and sunlight on an old woman's face, the curl of dark hair in the nape of a stranger's neck, and one's heart lurches. At times, the frailty of the entire universe seems to be contained in the callouses of a farmboy's hand; a beggar's downcast gaze can move one's soul with unutterable poignancy.

In a quiet, controlled voice, he said:

"You can never let me go now. If you do, I shall have all of you arrested and burned. More than this: I myself shall put the torch to the faggots."

"It is not my intention to let you go," the Master said.

"Look, this is crazy," the Skull interjected. "For Christ's sake, let's get out of here!"

"No! I have purchased you, remember? You belong to me, and you will do exactly as you are told," Andrea de' Collini said. "Or *I* shall have you arrested and burned, and I will step into the fire after you. Understand?"

We said nothing.

"Get up, Tomaso della Croce."

As the inquisitor raised himself unsteadily to his feet, I saw that the backs of his legs were speckled with blood.

"Nino – you have your blade?"

"I've got it, yes. You asked me to bring it."

"Good. Now listen, all of you. One of us – either him or me – is going to die. We shall fight, here and now, and it shall be to the death. No weapons, no instruments, no trickery, just two men, two naked bodies, no more and no less. Like *animals*. Ha! I like that. It is highly appropriate. That is, in the end, what each of us is reduced to in this fleshly existence. When the fight is done and one of us lies dead, *you,* Nino – you will kill the victor with your blade."

Nino shook his head fiercely.

"Nope," he said firmly. "Not me."

The Master glared at us, his eyes wide, his nostrils dilated.

302

"You *must* do it!" he hissed. "If I emerge from the fight triumphant you will kill me; if you do not, I promise you I shall deliver all of us into the hands of the inquisition. If Tomaso della Croce wins, then you will use your blade on him; if you do not, the result will be the same, for he will never allow you to escape the stake. Believe me, I have planned this very carefully; your only hope of liberty is to destroy the victor. Before the night is over, both I and the inquisitor will be dead. Now, do you understand me?"

Yes, yes, we understood. It was not our comprehension but our credulity which the Master had taxed. But what could we do? What choice did we have?

I said softly to Nino:

"He's right. Let them get on with it, for Christ's sake."

At last, Tomaso della Croce spoke:

"I refuse to fight you, Andrea de' Collini," he said. "I refuse –"

The Master's reply took everyone by surprise: his clenched fist shot out with incredible force and swiftness, and struck della Croce full in the face. The inquisitor reeled back, blood pouring from his nose and mouth, his eyes wide with astonishment and shock; and in the moment that followed the blow, the Master was on him, tearing with his bare hands, biting and gouging and flailing. The two men, now locked together, tumbled away from us and fell heavily to the ground where they rolled over and over, like dogs fighting for possession of a scrap of meat, like – yes – like *animals*. This was vile and savage murder, yet it could have been the frenzy of vile and savage love. It is often said that the distinction between the passion of love and the passion of hate is not a chasm but a hairline crack; now I knew this was true, for I could see it for myself. It seemed to me that it would take no more than a breath of some magic charm, the lightest whisper of an incantation, for their brutal blows instantly to become sighing caresses of mutual desire. They made no noise apart from the sharp intake of breath and the occasional growl of pain, and this in itself was so very strange. It was like watching the tortured unfolding of a grotesque nightmare, except that any nightmare would have been preferable to this. Nino, Beppo, the Skull and I stood helplessly by, trussed up like chickens in the mesh of fear, knowing that whichever of them was finally killed, a further death would have to follow if we were to claim liberty.

Everything passed in a flash, a blur, a swift flurry of arms, legs, backsides, contorted, hate-ravaged faces; it was impossible to see clearly what was happening, except for those moments when, here and there, a single horrid image presented itself before being swallowed again up in the formless chaos: the inquisitor's hand yanking at the Master's testicles, scrabbling in the hairy darkness of his groin; the Master's teeth tearing della Croce's breast, ripping away bloody skin, clamping around a nipple that was stiff and swollen with the chill of the night and with excitation; a toe gouging at a terrified eye, an ear attached only by a thin filament of pink and red flesh; fingers thrust into a splitting nostril; Andrea de' Collini's fist pummelling relentlessly into Tomaso della Croce's ribs. Oh, when would the horror come to an end? When would the madness cease? I could not endure it any longer.

Behind me, I heard the Skull whisper:

"They're crazy, both of them."

I could not discern which of them presently had the upper hand, for their frenzied flailing made it impossible to tell which arm or leg belonged to one and which to the other; but then, suddenly, I saw the inquisitor break free and struggle to his knees. He slipped and slithered for a moment, but managed to pull himself to his feet. The Master rolled over onto his back, his stomach heaving, his head twisting from side to side.

"Is this your victory?" della Croce cried hoarsely. "Your revenge? Oh, Andrea de' Collini, the truth of the gospel has triumphed!"

"And what is the truth of the gospel?" the Master breathed.

"This!"

And raising one foot, he brought it down with sickening force onto Andrea de' Collini's face. Even as he did so, the Master reached out for his ankle, pulled on it hard, and the inquisitor went down again with a yell of fury. The *cauchemar* began anew. They hugged each other close, chest to chest, their legs were entwined; like this, they fought with their mouths, biting and snapping and ripping.

"Oh God come to my aid!" screamed della Croce, pulling a hand free and ramming it down between the Master's thighs. I heard a sharp intake of breath, followed by a low moan of agony.

They rolled apart momentarily then came together again; immediately the Master twisted his whole body around and shoved the heel of one foot between the inquisitor's buttocks, pummelling his rectum mercilessly, pounding the place which had already been torn and smashed by the rape. Tomaso della Croce cried out; he cried out and he snatched up the Master's leg, gnawing into the calf with his teeth.

I saw a sight at that moment which I never want to see again; it is imprinted upon my brain, my memory and my psyche, a single terrible image, vivid and clear, which even to this day haunts my daydreams and frequently comes unbidden to prevent sleep at night. It is the face of Tomaso della Croce, his eyes popping from their sockets, wild with horror and dismay, the eyes of some wretched beast about to be slaughtered; and in his mouth a chunk of ragged flesh, dripping blood; and the moonlight full on that face, like a translucent silver shroud, making it a reflection of the face of death itself; the face of a human being become a mad, slobbering blood-crazed beast.

Despite the fact that none of us who stood watching felt able to endure it for a moment longer, it was Nino who broke; with a great cry he sprang forward, his face wet with tears, and I saw that he held a large chunk of stone in one hand.

"Stop it, stop it, oh stop it!" he screamed.

"Nino!" I cried out, "no! No!"

But it was too late; he had reached the rolling, kicking figures, and now stood over them, peering down, seeking his target, his arm raised high. They were unaware of him.

"I told you to stop!" he yelled, and the arm came swinging down, smashing into a head and sending up a great spray of bloodied bone and brain.

But whose head was it?

It seemed that a universe had passed away in storm-clouds the colour of blood, and that another had sprung up in its place; it seemed that now the night was eternal, that eternity itself had been compressed into every passing moment of that night. Then a voice spoke in the darkness, the stillness.

"Peppe will do it," said Andrea de' Collini.

He rose up from where he had been sitting on the ground, still naked, and came towards us. His face was ravaged: one eye had been torn out, his nose was broken and bloody, his lower lip bitten through, his body covered in scratches, weals, blackly slick and gaping wounds where here and there the bone showed through. That he could still stand upright was little short of a miracle.

"Nino brought our little contest to an untimely end," he murmured, his voice thick and hoarse. "I regret that, but what is done is done. Now you, Peppe, you must do your part. Take Nino's blade. Push it in here –" he raised one hand slowly, and touched his throat with a finger – "and push it in deep. Swift as you can. Then go. I want them to find us together, Tomaso della Croce and I."

"Why?" I cried, lifting my head as high as I could and looking up into the vast expanse of the night sky, where innumerable stars, thousands upon thousands of them, glittered like tiny brilliants.

Softly, tenderly, Andrea de' Collini said:

"Why, Peppe? *For love*."

I lowered my head and gazed into his eyes. Then he said again:

"Do it for love of me."

Then, an extraordinary gesture:

Bending down, that mutilated face close to mine, the Master pressed his swollen lips upon my lips, and kissed me with the sweetest, most ravishing kiss – so sweet and so wonderful, it was exactly as I remembered the kiss of Laura! – and my psyche fell into a kind of swoon. For a moment I lost all consciousness of the *incubus* that gripped us, all awareness of my pathetic, stunted body, all sense of the world, of time, and I was suspended in an insensible moment of eternity. All longing, all restless urgency and yearning, all desire of mind, heart and genitals were assuaged in that extraordinary kiss: the arms of a father, the loins of a lover, the loyalty of a cherished friend, the first cry of birth and the last silence of death were brought together, made one, and released in a single movement of *extasis*. Oh Andrea, Andrea!

He drew away. In his eyes shone an exquisite tenderness.

He said:

"I love you, Peppe. In the heart of madness, the indestructability of love. Love me in return, and do this thing."

I held out my hand and after a few moments I felt Nino put the blade onto the palm. My fingers closed tightly around the handle.

"One blow, hard and fast," the Master said, "so that you open the vein. Don't be afraid. I will bend toward you so that you can reach. Here – let me help you –"

He took my fist in his fingers – they were sticky with blood – and drew the blade up to the side of his throat.

"That is the place," he said. "Now, strike."

"Master – in the name of God –"

"For Christ's sake do as he says, Peppe!" Nino cried. "Do you want us all to burn?"

"Do it, Peppe! Do it now!"

I did three things simultaneously, as I recall: I closed my eyes tight, I let loose a long wail of despair, and I pushed the knife into the Master's throat as hard as I could. At once, I felt a hot, thick fluid spurt out and gush down over my hand and arm. Then I pulled the blade out and dropped it to the ground.

"You've *done* it, Peppe!"

It was Nino who had spoken. Then, incredibly, the faint voice of the Master:

"Yes, you have done it, little disciple. Or should I call you the *Master* now? I am content that my plan has been accomplished – at least in part. He and I will plague your life no longer. I have but a little time left – listen to me, Peppe! Listen to what I say! Oh, the shocks are not yet over for you, my friend. There is another to come. In the name of the one true God, I ask you to remember me with kindness."

Then a sudden silence.

When I opened my eyes again, I saw him walking unsteadily towards the body of Tomaso della Croce; when he had reached it, he fell awkwardly to the ground and positioned himself so that they were lying side by side. The expanse of his chest was crimson. I saw blood still pumping from his throat. Then he placed his hands across his muti-lated private parts to cover them, and was still.

"Master?" I managed to whisper. "Master?"

"He's dead," said Nino. "At least, he will be in a few more moments."

"Now," the Skull hissed, "let's get out of here!"

As we ran from that theatre of blood and dreams – nightmares! – the Master's last words echoed in my brain: *The shocks are not yet over for you, Peppe.* What could he have meant? Had his wretched plan not yet achieved its final conclusion? How much more horror was yet to come? In fact, I might tell you now that the last 'shock' of all came upon me like the radiance of a sunrise after the tenebrous deeps of an extended night; a shock, yes, but oh – then again, but *no* – you shall hear for yourselves very soon, I promise.

I did not see in which direction Nino and the others fled, and neither have I set eyes on any of them since; I do not think I particularly want to. I shall always miss Nino, it is true, and will doubtless wonder from time to time where he is and how he fares, since he occupies a place of his own in my heart; on the other hand, to be preoccupied with Nino would mean living under the shadow of Tomaso della Croce, and *that* I have promised myself I will never do.

I had succeeded Andrea de' Collini as Master of the Gnostic Brotherhood some time before his final disappearance, and it was in this office that I dutifully informed the brethren – with the unreserved honesty that persecuted minorities always demand of their own kind – that whatever they might hear to the contrary, the Master was dead and had died faithful to the light of our Gnostic truth. It was a light that continued to shine in my own life – that and the oblique light of Giovanni de' Medici, Pope Leo X; the tragedy was that one light could never be reconciled to the other, and they had at all costs to be kept apart. Like the sun and the moon, I suppose – both give light, but cannot shine together.

It was this tragic exigence which finally led me to contemplate and execute the deed which – of all the deeds for which I am responsible! – caused me the greatest anguish of mind and heart that I have ever known.

I killed Leo.

I had to. I had no choice. My dear, dearest, my beloved, wonderful, generous, good and kind Leo – I killed him. He had given me so much! He was everything I had. When he died, my heart – which had already been divided in two by Laura's passing – was dismembered once and for all into tiny, useless portions. The miracle was that, sundered and ravaged, it continued to beat. Now I have no heart at all, but merely a mind which recognizes, grasps and obliges me to live by the truth as I have come to know it. And above all things – all love, all relationship, all peace and security, and even above life itself – that truth takes precedence.

The beginning of the thing was the discovery of Tomaso

della Croce's body; reduced to a worm-eaten pulp slickly clinging to broken bones, there nevertheless remained enough of the face of him to be recognized and brought to Cardinal Cajetan, the highest prelate of the Dominican Order. What happened to the body of Andrea de' Collini I do not know; perhaps it was consumed by the wild dogs which roam the ruins of the Colosseum by night, or – even more horrible! – by the wretched scum of humanity eking out a wondrously vile existence there, eating and excreting and copulating in the ancient filth they have made their home.

Unsurprisingly, His Eminence fell into a fresh fury of outrage and suspicion.

"I could hardly bring myself to look at him!" he roared, "so appalling were his injuries! What do you know of this, Giuseppe Amadonelli?"

"Nothing, Eminence."

"Nothing, nothing, nothing! Was it nothing which snatched away Tomaso della Croce from the Minerva? Was it nothing which brutally murdered him and left his body to rot in that ghastly place?"

"Do not ask me where the guilt lies, Eminence, for I cannot tell you."

"Cannot, or *will* not?"

"I cannot, Eminence."

"And you expect me to believe this?"

"If it pleases your Eminence, yes."

"But it does *not* please me! Not in the least!"

The cardinal slumped in his chair, holding his chin in the palm of one hand. His eyes, smouldering, were fixed on me.

"Let me tell you something, Peppe."

"As your Eminence wishes."

"Certain information has come my way . . . information concerning the activities of a – what shall I say? – a *confraternity* of heretics here in Rome. I do not know the precise nature of their theological errors, but I have reason to believe that it is some kind of Gnosticism. Dear God, truly there is nothing new under the sun, as Quoheleth states! Gnosticism! It did not die with Basiledes or the Albigensians, then."

He was watching carefully for the slightest reaction on my part, I could see that.

"I know little about such heresy," I said. "And I know nothing at all about the Albigensians."

"They were exterminated, praise be to God and our holy father Dominic," he answered. "But apparently not their satanic teaching. It is born anew here in Rome, and it thrives. I will not tolerate it!"

He paused momentarily, then, in a softer voice, he said:

"The burning of that witch – Laura de' Collini – was a matter of some importance to you, was it not?"

I made no reply. He went on:

"Important enough to be an element in your ridiculous and bungled attempt to rid the world of my inquisitor?"

"As you say, Eminence."

"The coven of heretics presently flourishing in Rome has some connection with the girl, does it not?"

"I really do not know, Eminence."

"I tell you it does!" he cried, suddenly angry again. "And when I discover the precise nature of that connection – when I – my fury – my fury will come down upon them like fire from heaven, be sure of that! Are they linked to the inquisitor's disappearance and death?"

"I do not know."

"Are you lying to me, Peppe?"

"No, Eminence."

"Where is the girl's father, the patrician Andrea de' Collini?"

"I have no idea."

At least that much is true, I thought.

"And what link is there between him and the heretical confraternity?"

"Again Eminence, I have no idea."

Now the cardinal's voice was even, measured, perfectly controlled, and absolutely terrifying in its menace.

"I shall pursue my own inquiries, Peppe. If I find – by God – if I find that you are in any way mixed up in any of this –"

"I assure you, Eminence –"

"If that is what I find, I shall make you cry out for death. I shall make you curse the day you were born."

I've been doing that for years, I thought.

"You are under my suspicion, Peppe. I regret it, but it is so. Furthermore, until I have conclusive proof that you are entirely innocent of any involvement with either the death of my inquisitor or the coven of heretics, you and I are not friends. Do you understand that?"

"Unhappily Eminence, I do."

The following day, during an audience with Leo at which I was present, Cajetan told His Holiness about the information he had come by; fortunately for me, Leo was in a distracted mood and not really able to keep his mind on what Cajetan was saying. I knew that the squabble with France was greatly preoccupying him.

"A *Gnostic* sect, you say? Heretics?"

"Gnostics can hardly be otherwise, Holiness."

Leo pulled himself up off his chair with a huge effort.

"I will *not* tolerate such a thing in my city! I will *not!* With Germany in the turmoil it presently is, I cannot afford heretics on my own doorstep. *Gnostics,* you say?"

"Yes, Holiness. So I am reliably told."

"What error do they perpetrate?"

Leo said this with little or no interest; indeed, I think he hoped that Cajetan would not bother to reply, since all heresies are regarded by Rome as much of a muchness.

"Well, Holiness, the first principle of Gnostic philosophy –"

"See that the inquisitor is decently buried, will you? What's left of him, anyway. In the Minerva, I think; that strikes me as suitable. With full honours, of course."

"Of course, Holiness. As I was saying –"

"Where precisely did you say he was found?"

"The Colosseum, Holiness."

312

Leo shivered.

"What a ghastly thing! Were these Gnostics responsible? Here in Rome? Absolute impudence! Why don't they bugger off and join the mad monk? I suppose he's just a bit too much, even for heretics."

"The basic tenet of Gnostic belief, Holiness –"

"Oh, for the love of Mary, don't tell me, I don't want to know!"

"It is said that in the course of their – their blasphemous – liturgies, they perform unspeakable acts upon each other."

Leo suddenly became interested.

"Oh? What sort of acts, Cajetan?"

"Well, I – I *have* heard – women with women –"

"And men with men?" Leo asked with a little too much eagerness.

"Yes, Holiness, men with men. Disgusting."

"Well yes, of course. Utterly repellent! But what do they actually –"

"Your Holiness must act quickly to destroy this cancer."

"Certainly, certainly. I am at this time, however, rather preoccupied with matters of state. The war with France –"

"Your Holiness may leave it to me. But I will require a written commission."

"You shall have it, Cajetan!"

And the darkness covered me.

What could I do? If Cajetan went ahead and rooted us out, what would be left of truth in this world of error and deception? Moreover, my friends would be sure to lose their lives in the same way that Laura had – horribly, painfully, disgracefully. No! No, I could not permit that disaster to happen. Leo had to die before the Cajetan's authority could be issued.

Later, Leo asked me:

"What do you know about Gnostic philosophy, Peppe?"

"Very little," I lied.

"I know next to nothing. I thought the Gnostics had

313

perished long ago. Isn't it a heresy from the early centuries of the Faith?"

"So I believe, Holiness. But why be precipitate? Perhaps they aren't quite as bad as His Eminence makes them out to be."

Leo shook his head vigorously.

"No, Peppe, I can't have it. Not here in my city. Can you imagine what that bastard Luther would say if he knew? It would make matters a thousand times worse than they are already. I've made up my mind. If they do exist, they have to go."

And so I was forced to make up *my* mind also: Leo had to go. Leo must step into the darkness which had already received Andrea de' Collini and Tomaso della Croce.

I did it with poison, of course – no, *not* up his arse, but in his wine. It was easy enough to obtain – I told you before that Rome is a veritable city of poisoners; it's a buyer's market, to be quite frank. I purchased a powder which the old hag who sold it to me assured me was guaranteed to work, being a compound as it was of the the innards of a toad mixed with hair from a malformed abortus, and certain weeds which grew on the banks of the Nile.

"Cut out the sales patter," I told her. "Will it do the job?"

"You have my word, sir."

"And how much does that amount to?"

"If it doesn't work, bring it back to me and I'll drink it myself."

I couldn't quite grasp the logic of this offer, but I paid my five ducats anyway. She told me that in its effects, it closely resembled malarial fever, or the ague of a bad chill, which suited my purposes perfectly.

On the afternoon of November 24th 1521, we received the news that the capital of Lombardy had been taken; Leo, Serapica, Giberti (the Bishop of Verona) and myself had retired to Magliana, and here it was that Cardinal de'

314

Medici's secretary informed us of the glad tidings. Leo was in the middle of Lauds; he was just reciting the words, "..and being delivered from the hands of our enemies . . ." from the Benedictus, when the secretary came bursting in. Leo's excitement and delight was truly intense – in fact, it almost debilitated him, and he had to be carried on a litter to his private chamber, where he sat panting and gasping, his eyes popping, his mouth slack. Messengers were immediately dispatched to Rome to command that the victory celebrations commence, and that the cannon of the San Angelo castle be sounded. At Magliana itself, fireworks were set off throughout the night to the accompaniment of music and volleys of guns. It is said that hundreds of children were conceived in Magliana and Rome simultaneously that night.

Leo watched the cavortings from an open window of his room, even though the air was chilly; Serapica had rushed off to see the fireworks at close hand, and Leo and I sat together at a small table by the window. His face was sweating, his hands trembling, so overcome was he with an excess of emotion.

"Perhaps some wine, Holiness? The whole town is celebrating; why not us?"

"Yes, yes, let us drink wine."

And into his glass I put the poison. I don't know what kind of taste it had, but Leo didn't notice anything; however, this was hardly surprising, given his agitated state. He slurped the contents of the glass back at once, then refilled it.

It was as simple as that. Later, I cried myself to sleep. Poor, fat, excited Leo. It was so dreadfully, horribly sad. I looked at him before going to my room as he sat there at the open window, and I thought: *He's just like a big baby*. And so he was. And at that moment I loved him more than ever – loved him, needed him, wanted to protect him, to put my little arms around him, hold him, reassure him. Instead, I gave him poison. Is there any treachery blacker than the treachery of a lover?

315

On the afternoon of November 25th we returned to Rome. It was one of those glorious winter days which are perhaps possible only here in this ancient, alluring, seductive, raddled, painted whore of a city: a clear blue sky and a blazing sun, but fresh, sharp, clean air. Leo walked on foot and continually shivered. Serapica said to me out of the corner of his mouth:

"He should never have sat by that open window all night. Do you think he's caught a chill?"

The immense crowd were ecstatic. Everywhere there were cries of *Leo! Leo! Salve!* and the salvos of cannon were deafening. The cardinals embraced him, some even falling down to kiss his feet. Leo beamed – he beamed and waved and squealed in delight, and *shivered*.

That evening he dined well and slept soundly, but the next morning, during an audience with Cardinal Trivulzio, he was seized by a terrifying shivering fit, and had to take to his bed. Everyone assumed it was a fever, the result of passing the night at Magliana in front of an open window; the physicians administered remedies and took it for granted that by the end of the week he would have recovered – but the innards of a toad and hair from a malformed abortus (to say nothing of weeds from the banks of the Nile) are not so easily dissuaded from doing their deadly work.

"I feel a little better today, Peppe," he said to me on the Saturday of that week.

I simply couldn't bear it; I started to cry.

"What? Oh, Peppe, what is it?"

He put a pudgy hand on my knotty hump with tender concern.

"I'm happy that Your Holiness is recovering," I said, barely able to choke out the words.

Indeed, he was well enough to enjoy some music, but he took the precaution of making a general confession to his pious Benedictine confessor. In the night however he became very ill indeed, and the next morning, as he lay shivering in bed, he said to me:

"Peppe, I'm burning up! It's like a fire inside me . . .
then ice and snow . . . I'm so hot and so cold!"

I sat by his bed and held his hand in mine.

As the day wore on he seemed to rally, and those few
persons who had been admitted to the papal sickroom
were dismissed: the physician, Cardinal Pucci, Bishop
Ponzetti, the pope's nephews Salviati and Ridolfi, and his
sister-in-law Lucrezia. Ironic, isn't it, that there should
have been *another* Lucrezia present at a case of poisoning?
At eleven o' clock that night however, he was once again
attacked by the 'fever' and taken with a fierce fit of
shivering which was so powerful, the bed itself shook.

"Peppe . . . I'm going to die . . ."

"No, no, Holiness! Don't say it!" I cried, clutching his
hand, my eyes filled with tears. I am convinced that at that
moment I believed my own words. It was almost as if the
Peppe who loved Leo and wanted him to love forever, and
the Peppe who was responsible for his pitiful state, were
two different people. Perhaps this is how we deal with
those things we do which we cannot bear to admit having
done – split ourselves in two.

"Yes, Peppe, I know it. I can feel it – oh! – I'm burning!
Hold my hand, Peppe . . ."

I bathed his brow with rosewater.

"Have I been a good pope? I used to feel so inadequate
. . . I still do. Peppe, forgive me for all the wrongs I have
done you –"

"Wrongs, Holiness? You have given me everything I
have! You have shown me nothing but kindness and love.
You have been the greatest and most noble of popes –"

"Help me, Peppe – help me to be brave! I am afraid of
death."

"Holiness, please – do not distress yourself –"

He turned, shuddering, onto his side. A last spasm of
despair took hold of him:

"Where is my tiara? Where the triple crown? Who has
it? Oh, Christ have mercy on me, a sinner! Where is the
power of the Medici pope now? No, throne, no pomp, no

317

authority over kings and princes – nothing but the burning glance of the Everlasting Judge – oh Jesus, Jesus, mercy!"

I called for the Benedictine confessor to come quickly and administer Extreme Unction; because of his great weakness it was impossible for him to receive the Viaticum. I took the cross from around his neck and placed it against his lips; he kissed it, and again he kissed it, three or four times. After this, he looked at me with his protuberant, watery eyes, and tried to smile. I smiled back. His hand slipped from mine.

Then he turned his gaze up towards the ceiling and said softly, piteously:

"Jesus, Jesus, Jesus."

And he was gone.

– EPILOGUE –

Et iam non sum in mundo

Poison was never substantially suspected; indeed, there was no reason for it to be, since by the time of his death, everyone knew that he had passed a whole night exposed to chilly air, and the Magliana area is in any case notorious for its malarial vapours. The body became rapidly discoloured and swollen, which Paris de Grassis *thought* might indicate foul play, but Leo's corpulence made it difficult to actually tell which bits of him were unnaturally bloated and which weren't. The physician Severio was present at the post-mortem examination and declared that there was not a single jot of evidence to support Paris de Grassis' suggestion. As a kind of precautionary measure, Bernabò Malaspina, the pope's cup-bearer (who belonged to the French party and was therefore disliked) was arrested and put to the torture, but no confession was elicited because I alone was responsible for snuffing out one of the great lights of this dark world. The English envoy Clerk, in a letter to Thomas Wolsey (he actually showed me its contents, but I would have read it anyway) declared that the idea of poison was completely absurd; he said that anyone who knew Leo's constitution, his corpulence, his bloated countenance and almost chronic catarrh – quite apart from his manner of living, with frequent fasts and heavy meals – would be surprised that he had lived so long.

And this opinion generally held sway. All talk of poison was forgotten.

Now I have to decide what to do with *myself*. Although, truth to tell, I have already decided. I have resigned the Mastership of our Gnostic Brotherhood, and Ludovico Francesi, a young man of keen intellect and intense devotion to our cause, will take up my duties after our liturgy in two day's time, which will be my last.

I have instructed my bankers in Florence to put my financial affairs in order and to donate the bulk of my capital to various worthy causes which I myself intend to designate by letter; I shall give away my collection of rings (I'll send one to poor Serapica, still languishing in prison on charges of embezzlement) with the exception of two or three, already selected. The proceeds from the sale of these will enable me to rent a little two-roomed apartment in the Trastevere area, and to set myself up in business as a seller of cheap gut-rot wine – which I will occasionally mix with a little Frascati, as my *quondam* mother used to do.

Yes, I am returning to my roots.

Does this seem strange to you? If it does, consider this: I *must* in some way atone for Leo's death; I must expiate my guilt. Going back to the misery and horror of the life I once knew – like a dog returning to its vomit – strikes me as an ideal way of doing this. I began as a pathetic little cripple, and I shall end as a pathetic little cripple. Now that Leo is dead, everything that happened in between seems like a dream, anyway. Less than that – like the nebulous shadow of the memory of a dream. Perhaps that was all it ever was. I shall live out what days remain to me in the tenebrous alembic of my origin, hawking my wine from door to door (I shall hire a boy – perhaps a dwarf like myself – to push the cart), until the time comes for me to stretch out the wings of my soul, extend them towards God's heaven, and pass from this world's darkness into the radiant light of eternity.

But . . .

Oh, but there will be a difference! And what a difference it will be!

For Peppe the crippled wine-seller of Trastevere will now be Peppe the crippled *Gnostic* wine-seller of Trastevere; he will know and understand and wrestle with the misery of life, whereas before he merely endured it like a

320

dumb beast. He will *know* that even within the most cruel and vile of human beings, there shines – however occluded – the effulgence of an immortal soul which has fallen from the bosom of the true Father in heaven, and upon which one can have nothing but compassion until it ascends once again to its true source and origin. He will *know* that the face of inhumanity is but a mask stuck fast upon the face of divinity. And in whatever way he can, howsoever inadequate, he will work to dislodge that mask.

And in his braver moments, when the darkness is deep and his strength is failing, he will look around at all the pain, all the suffering, the tears and the tragedies and the sheer meaninglessness; he will look around and shake his fist at the deluded, deranged Ego which vomited up this world, and he will cry out: *Non serviam!* 'I will not serve you, because you are not God.'

Indeed, this would be my advice to all of you: having once perceived and embraced the most fundamental tenet – that a God of love could not have created this material universe – contrive then to spend the remainder of your days disseminating it in whatever way you can. No effort is ever wasted, however feeble or inadequate it may be; after all, it is perfectly possible to turn a valley into an ocean *drop by drop*, if one has patience. If you are a king (or a pope for that matter), serve the light as you walk among other kings; if you are a poet or an artist, serve the light through the medium of your works; if you are a beggar, serve the light by your rags and your outstretched palm. This is exactly what I intend to do; and believe me, if there are enough of us scattered throughout the world, serving the light and spreading the truth in whatever way we can, then the world will begin to change. The world *needs* a secret army of Gnostics to bring it to its senses and make it aware – and all those who dwell therein – that it is nothing other than hell.

I feel very strange tonight! A few hours ago I sat in my chamber (it will not be mine for very much longer) and composed a song. I hardly need tell you that the sentiments refer to *her*. My Laura.

This is what I composed:

Canzone di' Peppe

Nel mio cuo - re mi' sen-to tan-ta pe -
na sì tan-ta pe - na: soff-ren-za del' a-mor.
Nel mio cuo - re mi' sen-to
tan-ta gio - ia sì tan-ta gio - ia: com -
pen - so del a-mor.
Il tu-o vi' - so il mi-o Pa-ra-di' - so
Le tu-e labb - ra la mi'-a sol spe -
ran - za. L'a - ni'-ma mi' - a in te in te per -
du - ta in te per-du - ta.
In te per-du - ta:
in te per-du - ta.

There will also be another difference – an immensely significant one – of which I must now speak to you; it is something which came as the most incredible surprise to me (not to say shock), and even now I am not sure that I believe it. Yet I *must* believe it, for the evidence is before my eyes; indeed, it will be before my eyes for the rest of my life!

Late the other night, when I was alone in my private chamber sorting out, musing over, and packing away my personal effects, there came a gentle tapping at the door.

"Come in!" I cried irritably, assuming that an official of the household had arrived to urge me to make speed and be gone.

The tapping was repeated.

"Come *in,* will you!"

The door opened slowly, and I turned to see a young girl standing in the half-light: a beautiful girl with golden-bronze hair framing a pale, oval face. Something deep within me stirred, like the memory of music not heard for a very long time, and the stirring of it unsettled me. I suddenly felt sad, apparently for no obvious reason.

"You are Giuseppe Amadonelli," she said. It was a statement of fact, not a question.

"And you? I – why – I seem, somehow to recognize you –"

"You have seen me on certain occasions."

"Oh?"

"In the house of Andrea de' Collini."

Then I recalled that indeed I *had* seen her before; she had been present at several of our liturgies, and had sat with other neophytes at the Master's feet to learn the principles of our Gnostic philosophy. However, I did not remember ever taking any particular notice of her. I had never spoken to her. She had been one among many.

"My name is Cristina," she said. Her voice was gentle, musical. "May I come in?"

"You are welcome to do so," I replied, "but as you can see, I am preparing to make my departure."

"Your life at the papal court is over, then?"

"Of course. My sun has ceased to shine."

"But a new sun will arise at dawn," she said quietly, and it seemed to me that there was a deeper, more significant meaning to her words than the one which was obvious; she was referring to something other than the election of another pope, but I had no idea what.

"There will never be a sun to shine as mine did," I said sadly. "There will never be another quite like Leo. And alas, when the sun has gone, all those lesser stars and planets which orbit by its radiance must wane also, and finally expire. Every light dies when the fire of the great sun is extinguished. Leo was my great sun."

"Yes, I know."

"You knew him?" I asked, surprised.

"Not exactly; doesn't everyone know the pope?"

"Everyone knows *of* him," I said, "but that is quite a different matter. I knew and loved the man himself."

Unself-consciously, she crossed the room and sat in the chair by my writing table; the very chair at which I always sat when engaged in the writing of these memoirs.

"What is it you want?" I asked.

The more I looked at her, the more that *something* within me stirred and flickered with a disturbing, unsettling life of its own; but what? What was there in her spun-gold hair, the pale, flawless features, the rise and fall of her soft voice, that at once both attracted and frightened me? Yes, to be honest, I *was* frightened, just a little. Why?

"I do not know how you will receive what I have to tell you," she said. "It has been hidden from you for so long. Oh, believe me, it was not all my doing! *He* insisted!"

"He?"

"Master Andrea. Andrea de' Collini. He thought it best. He said we must wait. But now – now that the Master is dead – I have nowhere ... no-one ... what's the point in keeping it a secret any longer?"

"Keeping *what* a secret?" I asked, bemused, and still curiously afraid.

"Can't you guess?"

"No, I can't, and I don't have time for riddles," I said.

"What do you intend to do?"

"To do?"

"With yourself, I mean. Your life. Where will you go?"

"Why should you be interested in me?"

"Oh, but I am, believe me! I have every right to be."

"What rights have you over me?"

She regarded me for some moments with her large, beautiful eyes, and in them there was a great melancholy.

Then she said softly:

"The right to protection, to sustenance, the right to companionship, to support."

I shook my head.

"I don't understand," I said.

After a moment of richly eloquent silence during which I heard the thump-thump of my own heart beating out its bewilderment like a drum, she said:

"The rights which any daughter may claim from her father."

Oh no, no – not this –

She went on:

"I am your daughter, Giuseppe Amadonelli."

That hair, that face, that voice – they were Laura's! The moment of recognition struck me like – sweet Jesu, what words are there to describe it? – like sudden recovery striking one who is old and ailing, like unexpected wealth falling into the lap of a pauper, like the noise of the entire world assailing a deaf man whose ears are precipitately unstopped. The shock of it was at once both thrilling and horrifying. For some moments I could not speak; I looked at her in stunned silence, and again in her lovely eyes, I encountered the gaze of my beloved Laura. But how? In the name of God, how?

"The Master was the only one who knew," the girl called Cristina said. "When I was old enough, he told me who I was – who *you* are – and he told me what had happened to my mother. I do not know why he did not

325

wish you also to know, but I was bound to respect his will. I – I owed everything to him. He took care of me, looked after me, sheltered and protected me."

"You lived with him?"

"After I had been released from prison, yes."

"And he never wanted me to know?"

"No."

"But – but it's impossible! Why, look at me Cristina! Look at me, then look at yourself – I cannot believe –"

She became suddenly urgent, eager.

"Oh, but you *must* believe!" she cried. "You must!"

"Must?" I echoed.

"You – you are all that is left to me –"

"Then you are poor indeed, my dear," I said.

"No! I have no-one now but you; where shall I go, what shall I do without you? You cannot refuse me – cannot turn me away –"

"But I am a stranger to you, Cristina!"

She shook her head slowly and smiled a little smile.

"Not at all," she said. "I know everything about you. The Master told me. He told me what my mother had told him."

"I cannot be your father. You must be mistaken."

"Do you not remember the night I was conceived?" she said softly.

I began to feel hot, hot and discomforted and nervous.

She went on:

"It was in the Master's house, was it not? *My grandfather's house!* It was my mother's way of passing on to you the knowledge you had to acquire in order to reject it. Was this not her teaching? The Master has told me that it was. She herself was your teacher, she herself bestowed this knowledge upon you. You made love to her, my mother Laura."

"It was the one and only time," I said, tears in my eyes now.

"And yet it was enough. That night, I was conceived in her womb."

"We never intended it – we never thought to make a child. Never. The whole point of my acquiring knowledge of fleshly delight was, as you yourself have pointed out, solely in order to subsequently reject it – either by abstinence or frustration of its purpose. How, then, could we have intended a child?"

"I do not know what your intentions were," Cristina said. "I know only two things: I know in the first place that you loved my mother –"

"More than I have ever loved anyone or anything in this hell of a world!" I cried.

"– and that she loved you. And I know in the second place that my birth was a great and profound joy to her. The Master often spoke to me of this joy."

"But it cannot be –"

"And yet it is. I was born while my mother was in prison. Have you never wondered, Giuseppe Amadonelli, why they delayed for so long before sending her to her death?"

"I never thought –"

"Then think now. Think! While she was carrying me, and all the while I depended on her to survive, her life was spared. They do not burn pregnant women or those with dependent children. I lived with her in that squalid cell. She reared me as best she could – oh, my poor mother! – and then when I had been judged to have attained the age of reason, they burnt her and released me. My grandfather took me back with him, and thereafter I lived in his own house. The inquisition would have preferred to lodge me with an order of nuns whose apostolate is to rear and care for the children of condemned heretics – good and holy women, I know – but grandfather managed to bribe the head of the commission which deals with cases like mine; this man, Bertrand Souzaine, was French, and I am sure my grandfather knew that way back in his family there had been Cathar sympathisers. At any rate, he let the Master take me. The nuns, I have no doubt, would have tried to make me one of themselves."

327

"All those years – I never knew –"

"You saw me often enough at our meetings, our liturgies –"

"Yes. I never knew."

"Why should you? I have told you, the Master did not wish you to learn my identity."

"I cannot understand that," I said.

"Nor I. But my duty was not to understand, it was to obey. He was not only the Master, he was also my grandfather, and I owed my life to him. Now he is gone, and I am alone. At least – if you turn me away, I shall be utterly and completely alone."

That something within me finally broke and burst, like a soap-bubble in sunlight, rose to the surface of my psyche, and flooded my mind and heart. I fell onto my knees, sobbing, and buried my head in her sweet lap. The smell of her, the touch of her, the warmth of her soft young body – all of it was Laura resurrected, Laura come back to me, Laura re-born.

"I shall not turn you away, my dearest," I cried. "Never that."

She took my head in her pale, slim hands and turned my face up toward her own. She too was weeping.

"Oh, how I have prayed to hear you speak those words," she said. "How I have tormented myself night after night with the thought that you might *not* speak them."

"Torment yourself no more, for I *have* spoken them. I will never let you go now. Never. We shall be together, you and I. We shall take care of each other, look after each other . . . we shall love each other . . ."

"As a father and a daughter should," she said.

Father and daughter. The words were like a prayer. They *were* a prayer – the kind of prayer which works miracles, which makes the impossible a dream, and the dream a glorious, astonishing reality. I at once knew what the Hebrew psalmist meant when he sang: *And my cup is filled to overflowing.*

I lifted my head from her lap and sat crouched at her feet.

Then, at that moment, I understood something else – a lacuna in my comprehension and a stain on the purity of my love for Andrea de' Collini suddenly vanished forever. Of course: she, my daughter, was the reason why he was so reluctant to attempt to rescue Laura from the St Angelo fortress – he *knew* that Laura was not in that cell alone, that Cristina was with her. Knowing this, how he must have feared for the child's life! If Laura had been snatched away from the stake, what would have become of his grandchild? Might they have burned *her* in her mother's place? He also knew that whatever happened to Laura, Cristina would be eventually released. How could he possibly take such a risk as Don Giuseppe and I were urging? The Master knew – such a tragic and unbearable knowledge – that the death of the mother meant the release of the child.

And in my mind I heard the words silently shape themselves:

Andrea, Andrea, how greatly I have wronged you.

In the deepest chamber of my heart I still believed that madness did finally overtake that noble soul, but even in madness he looked to the safety of his daughter's daughter; and in that chamber I made my own private prayer of penitence.

Then I spoke once again to Cristina.

"But you must know," I said, wiping my eyes on the back of my hand, "that I have decided to go back to the place from which I came. It is a hard, cruel place, and the lives which are lived there are equally hard and cruel."

She sighed.

"That is of no account to me," she replied. "What matters is that we shall be together."

"Yes, together."

"Indeed, nothing else in the world matters as much as that."

I paused before I went on to say:

"I have decided to go back, because it is the darkest kind

329

of existence I can think of; it needs the light – desperately needs the light! – of our Gnostic truth. From within that darkness I believe I can sow the seeds of truth; I can be, as it were, a flame of the true light which will by degrees illumine the tenebrous corners and angles where filth and misery breed. To shine and to irradiate – that is the task I have set myself."

"I understand all that you say, father."

When she spoke that word, 'father', an indescribable thrill of pride and wonder shot through me.

Even so, I said:

"Oh, my dearest child, how can you possibly understand?"

And to my overwhelming joy, she replied:

"I understand because I have long since embraced the same principles which guide your own life. My poor mother was my first teacher, even in the depths of that prison darkness; then, later, after my release, the Master himself took over my spiritual education. I received Gnostic baptism from him several years ago. I, too, am a child of the light."

"And you think you can endure such an existence? Share such a task?"

She paused momentarily before answering in a firm, resolute voice:

"I *know* I can. It is my wish to do so."

"Oh, Cristina!"

"Father."

"We shall not be poor – I have enough money for both of us –"

"Poverty is an affliction of the heart, not an empty purse."

"Nevertheless, we shall want for nothing. Our work from now on will be a work of the spirit. It will be hard, Cristina –"

"I do not doubt it. But we shall have each other."

"I thought – I mean, in time – I intend to form a fresh Brotherhood. Think of it! There must be others like me –

keen minds and questing psyches, souls burning up with a thousand and one questions, yet trapped in the ignorance of wretched and poor circumstances. Why should there not be other Giuseppe Amadonellis waiting to be rescued from the Trastevere gutters, as I once waited, and as I was once rescued . . . by your mother?"

"The work will be wonderful!" she cried, clapping her hands together.

"And perhaps, my dear, perhaps – when it all becomes too much for us, and our spirits require rest and refreshment, we will go away together, you and I, to a little villa in the hills that I shall purchase precisely for such a purpose. No-one shall ever know of it except we two; there, together, far from the squalor and the misery of Trastevere, we shall sit in the evenings and read from the great masters of truth . . ."

"We shall sing songs –"

"Recite poetry . . ."

"Oh, yes, we shall sing songs together!"

We clasped each other tightly, our cheeks wet with tears, half laughing, half crying, hardly knowing how to contain the great emotions which were welling up in both of us.

Then, slowly, I drew back and looked at her. I said:

"Can it really be? Can it really and truly be?"

She nodded, smiling.

"Yes," she replied in a most gentle and tender voice. "It can, and it is. I am your daughter, Giuseppe Amadonelli."

"And I am your father, Cristina."

"Yes."

"Oh, but look at you! Look at you, child – how beautiful you are. You are so very much like your mother. It is a miracle that the seed of such a broken, twisted creature as myself could have produced such a bloom, such a fruit . . ."

She said laughingly:

"It takes two to make a third, father."

"Indeed. Although the great doctor Tomaso d'Aquino

states that a female child is nothing more than an accident – a male gone wrong – due, perhaps, to the influence of a humid wind from the south. He declares that the woman adds nothing to the man's seed, but merely provides a receptacle in which it can grow and develop. If a girl is born, something must have gone wrong with that development. Thus says the Angelic Doctor."

"Do you believe that?"

"No more than I believe the moon is made of cream cheese!"

"No more than one might believe the stars to be diamonds!"

"And yet – oh, Cristina – and yet it *is* so hard to believe that such a perfect creature as yourself was born of a monster like me."

"You are *not* a monster. You are my father . . . and . . . and I love you."

When she spoke those words, the emotions aroused in me were so powerful, I could not say anything for a few moments. I struggled to contain them.

She bent her head, and kissed me tenderly on the side of my face, pressing her soft, full little lips to my rough skin.

"And I," I replied at last, my voice wavering, "I love you too, Cristina. I love you, and I shall never let you go."

"Then what else matters?"

"Nothing. Nothing at all!"

And once more, we embraced.

After some moments she pulled herself away from me, gently but firmly, and rose gracefully to her feet.

"There is no doubt remaining in your mind?" she asked.

I shook my head.

"No, none whatsoever."

"Then our new life together can begin."

Once again, I was unable to prevent the tears flowing.

It is time, now, for me to take my leave of you – whoever you may be. Before I do so however, I would like to bequeath you a testament of my Gnostic beliefs, which you

332

are of course free to consider, embrace or reject as you feel inclined. It is important for me to set this down, since at present I am understandably experiencing a sense of flux and impermanence; unlike poor Serapica, presently languishing in prison, I am unable to relieve it by getting myself done up as a Greek statue. Of course, now I have my daughter Cristina as the new lodestone of my life, and she will be for me the representation of all that is objectively true: truth, beauty, love, loyalty; yet even so, in order to preserve an inward sense of my own substance and reality (for so much that has happened in my life has been like a dream!), I need to see something real, tangible, black-and-white in front of me, that I can look at and say: *Yes! This is the essence of me – this is what my life means.* Or, as the mad monk himself once said with great bravery and considerable foolishness: *On this I take my stand. I can do no other.*

CREDO

I believe in one, true God, the Father, the Almighty, who dwells in heaven, in the realm of glorious light, and who is himself the Unoriginate Originator of that realm in which he dwells. From his loving bosom we have all fallen, and we have fallen onto this earth and into this world, which the Father did not make. For this earth and this world is a nothingness, full of the misery and suffering of nothingness. As the Beloved Disciple testifies in his Gospel:

Omnia per ipsum facta sunt; et sine ipse factum est nihil, quod factum est.

The Gnostic translation and interpretation of these words differs from that of tradition; the Church understands them as: *Nothing was made without him.* On the other hand, we teach: *Nothing was made, and it was made without him.* Every translation is an interpretation – how could it be otherwise? Now, the nothingness which is the hell of our world was made without the divine Word; yet it is not 'our' world

333

because we are aliens to it and exiles in it. Our origin and true home is the Father's realm of light. For this world was made by the enemy of the Father, the Devil, and all material form, all fleshly life and urges, all corporeal growth and decay is his doing.

I believe in this divine Word, Jesus the Nazarene who is the Christ, sent by the Father to teach us the nature of the world in which we are exiled. For our sake he descended from the Father's realm of light into the dark corruption of flesh; and as the great Valentinus states, he became patient in the schoolrooms of truth. Yet the thrall of the flesh never held him, and even as his body expired on the cross, his essence abided with the Father. In him, death was done to death, and flesh overcome. His teaching is the word of Truth, for it is the word of the Father, not the god of the Jews; the god of the Jews is Yahweh-Yaldabaoth, the creator of this world (by his own admission!) and the Devil. For this, the Jews hated the Christ and nailed him to a tree. But he is the Ever-Living One, whose glory is with the Father, and shall be so eternally.

I believe in the corruption of all things in this world, which is hell. I believe in the corruption of powers and principalities, of states and kingdoms, of nations. I believe in the corruption of the Holy Roman Church, for she has denied the word of Truth of the Saviour Jesus and has perverted his doctrine. Jesus has said: *You shall know a tree by its fruits.* The fruits of the Holy Roman Church are rotten.

In the scriptures we read that Satan offered Jesus all the kingdoms of this world if he would but bow down and worship him; does this not suggest that they belong to Satan in the first place? Else how can he offer them? You cannot give away that which does not belong to you.

I believe in the return of men to the bosom of the Father. From where we have fallen, to there shall we re-ascend, and this shall be achieved through knowledge – *Gnosis* – through an understanding of the spiritual truths bequeathed to us by Jesus the Saviour, and through a

334

practical application of those truths. I believe that in the final summation, all darkness will be overcome and vanquished forever, and that the light shall triumph unto ages eternal and forever.

As it is written by the Beloved Disciple:

Et lux tenebris lucet, et tenebrae eam non comprehenderunt.

The light has ever shone in the darkness, and the darkness has neither understood it nor overcome it. And so it shall be: the light will continue to shine – sometimes in the most surprising and unexpected of places.

I leave you with one final question: Take a long, hard look around yourself. Look critically, honestly, without prejudice, at this world. See the suffering, the misery, all the evil that this world holds, and ask yourself: *Did God really make this?*

You may well find that you too, are a Gnostic.

Now there is no more that I can write. The Chair of Peter will soon have a new occupant (let us hope one burdened with a less troublesome arse than poor Leo), and I cannot afford to be seen around the place when he takes possession. I've got quite a bit of packing to do. It's sad to see so many reminders of Leo still about: his papal slippers, jewels, his little gold-handled magnifying glass, even the odd phial of virgin's piss and rare herbs; when a pontiff dies, the chamberlains of the papal household usually run riot, grabbing what they can while there's still time, stuffing their pockets, filling sacks with stolen booty – fortunately Giulio de' Medici ensured that it did not happen *this* time. Everyone kept what was rightfully theirs, and *basta*. Leo deserved that dignity. I know that Leo and I will meet again somewhere, some time, in some place nearer to the effulgent bosom of the Father in heaven than this stinking cesspit of a world; and when we do, I shall kneel before him and offer two things: my gratitude, and my apologies. Until that time comes, how *much* I shall miss him!

One day, I shall tell my daughter Cristina all about Leo; I shall tell her everything, and she will understand. She will understand, and she will comfort me in my sorrow. How could it be otherwise, since I killed the man I loved in order that the philosophy both she and I live by, should be preserved?

We Italians like to say: *Arrivederci!* which, I think, is so much nicer and far less painful than a blunt, cold 'Goodbye.' Shall we ever encounter one another again in the dark and uncertain future? Perhaps the most that one can say, is:
Who knows?

The Vatican, Rome,
December 28th 1521

FINIS